TABLE 47

By Rolaine Hochstein

(*novels*)
TABLE 47
STEPPING OUT

(*nonfiction*)
(*with Daniel A. Sugarman, Ph.D.*)
THE SEVENTEEN GUIDE TO YOU AND OTHER PEOPLE
THE SEVENTEEN GUIDE TO KNOWING YOURSELF
SEVEN STORIES FOR GROWTH

TABLE 47

Rolaine Hochstein

DOUBLEDAY & COMPANY, INC.
GARDEN CITY, NEW YORK
1983

"I'll get by as long as I have you.
Tho there be rain and darkness too,
I'll not complain, I'll see it through . . ."

Words by Roy Turk; Music by Fred E. Ahlert
TRO © Copyright 1928 and renewed 1956 Cromwell Music, Inc.,
New York, Fred Ahlert Music Corp., Los Angeles, and Pencil
Mark Music, Inc., Scarsdale, N.Y.

Used by permission

Library of Congress Cataloging in Publication Data

Hochstein, Rolaine.
Table 47.

I. Title. II. Title: Table forty-seven.
PS3558.O3418T3 1983 813'.54
ISBN 0-385-18242-2
Library of Congress Catalog Card Number 82–45570

This book is dedicated to my father,
Martin R. ("Monte") Abrahams,
whose amazing vitality, resourcefulness,
generosity and zest for living
inspire all of us around him.

I want to thank my friends who helped with advice, insights, technical correction and encouragement:

Marcia Blackman Tager, Donald Kmetz, Gail Kessler, Joseph R. Cummins, Pamela Sommers, Dorin Klibanow, Beatrice Buckler, Joyce Jack, Martin Friedman, Martin Berck, Roger Zissu and Rabbi Baruch Frydmann-Kohl, my literary agent, Emilie Jacobson, three colleagues who were there when I needed them, and my husband, Morton Hochstein, who was always there.

Parts of this book were written at the MacDowell Colony and at Yaddo, to both of which establishments I am grateful.

TABLE 47

INTRO

THE BROADWAY KNIGHTS'
TWENTY-FIFTH ANNUAL AWARD DINNER

honoring

BERNARD J. BOSCULUS

Grand Ballroom   Dinner at 8 o'clock

Waldorf-Astoria Hotel   Cocktails at 7:30

CONTRIBUTION: $125 per person
$1,250 per table of ten

Of course, we didn't pay. We were guests of the honoree.
Two tickets arrived with a typewritten letter on engraved
bond paper. *National Broadcasting System. Bernard J. Bosculus, President.* We were still getting used to the idea that
Bibby was working steady, let alone president of NBS, let
alone mouth-droppingly successful at it. The columns said
that he had saved television from following vaudeville into
entertainment heaven. Now he was to be the guest of honor,
the toastee, the roastee, this year's recipient of the coveted
Golden Cock (or Coq d'Or, if you like French better).

He called the next day, out of the blue, like old times.
"I've . . . uh . . . taken a table for a few of my friends." In
his deepest telephone voice. "I hope you and Paul will be
able to be there."

"That's very nice of you, Bibby."

"I'll be on the dais, I guess. But . . . ah . . . Jennifer's
going to be at a table, at the table with . . . uh . . . some of
the company executives."

Jennifer is his new wife, younger even than Karen, his old one. Karen and her husband would be at our table, he said. *Great*, I thought. Karen was always a pain in the ass. "I'll be there for sure," I said and thanked him again for asking us. I wasn't sure about Paul, though, with his crazy new schedule.

"Let my secretary know," Bibby said, ". . . uh, when you find out."

Paul gave in after I stood on my head. "For the drama!" I kept telling him. "For a free meal, at least." But all he could think of was the pain of squeezing into his tuxedo. Good thing he didn't know Obe Morley would be there. I'd never have got him out.

"Remember," I said on the big night. "*I'm* taking *you*. Bernard J. Bosculus is *my* friend."

"Welcome to him," Paul said. But he looked pretty terrific in his old tuxedo that still fits. My gown was last year's gown so many years ago that it's beginning to come around again.

We pulled out the Toyota and set off for New York in hope and wonder.

It could have been the Americana or the Hilton but the Waldorf is best because it used to be so classy. Even now, with its "new element" of package tourists and suburban weekenders, there's still the mirrored walls and statues and the knock-your-eye-out lobby. Old oriental carpets remind you. The ballroom is still grand, too, though what's left of Society goes elsewhere for what's left of its cotillions. Today's occasions are Fashion Group luncheons, gigantic sales conventions, testimonial dinners, and dances for workaday charities that take money happily from anybody who has it to give.

This is April 23 and a cold, post-snowy one. *The better to wear your furs, my dear*. And that's what the dears are doing for this all-out affair. Out front on Park Avenue the taxis, not

TABLE 47   5

to mention limos, deposit men in tuxedoes and topcoats. While the men lean in to pay the driver, the women—in evening gowns and furs—are handed out by the Grand Doorman, to step on a red carpet, clear of sidewalk slush and under the great green awning that protects them from a snow-laden wind blowing across from Rockefeller Center, deco companion piece two blocks west. Celebrants are arriving in couples and groups, heading up the short flight of marble stairs to the lobby past other furred and gowned women, other tuxedoed and topcoated men with other plans for the evening, moving down the stairs and out to the waiting taxis. But you can tell the Broadway Knights: they glitter more— their clothes with the sheen of Fifth Avenue shop windows, their eyes with the shine of self-satisfaction. They move purposefully down the deep lobby on the oriental carpets between plush circles of poufs, under the chrome and mirror glass, along the aisle between rows of boutiques to the ballroom elevators in back. It's almost eight o'clock. Those who like group drinking have arrived early for the cocktail hour.

Here I am, Cindy Storey, bare head aswivel among tiaras and chandelearrings, Elizabeth Arden faces and the clash of strong perfumes. I hope it's Paul's arm I've got hold of in this packed elevator. "TV was in irons," a man is saying with kingly authority. "People were going back to the movies, reading books." I can't see through the crush. "No doubt about it," the king continues. "Bosculus turned it around." I squeeze the arm I think is Paul's.

Checkrooms are lined up like stables. It's still a man's world here. The men check in, topcoats and furs handed over the counter while women, shoulders bared, make decorative groupings in preparation for a big entrance. When I see the Grand Ballroom, I get the idea. It's wintry outside but the G.B. is seasonless. Timeless, too. Three stories high, it's like an open courtyard with permanent sunlight pouring down through permanent temperate weather on the colored hair and tightened faces of the permanently young and permanently smiling.

Some two hundred and fifty round tables have been set with sparkling china, crystal and silver. At each perfect place lies a souvenir menu, a souvenir program, a hand-printed place card. On the seat of each "lady's" chair lies a gold-lettered, flower-printed plastic shopping bag of souvenir gifts— which, I later discover, include a rain bonnet, a writing pen with a tassel, a brocade eyeglass holder, two Godiva chocolate shells, handsomely boxed, and a five-drop flacon of L'Air du Temps, all raided by Knights from their own firms or those of their clients and friends. Beside the floral centerpiece on each table there rises, like a great pennant held on high by shining chrome prongs, a brightly painted number. The top ten are up front, close to the stage where the skirted, garlanded, spotlighted table is set—places facing the audience— for honored guests, entertainers and speechmakers. Three-digit numbers are back, back toward the far wall under the gilded and festooned balconies. Tables in the two hundreds are *on* the balconies, first and second, from which leaning ladies in low-cut dresses wave programs, if not chiffon handkerchiefs, and with outlined eyes search for familiar faces.

I'm a little taken aback by all this pageantry. I hang close as Paul checks in at the ticket table and picks up our assignment to Table Number 47. Then we flow in through a curtained archway, borne by the throng into the grand arena where the champions lead their ladies, all of them caught in the sharp luster of jewels, passementerie and hair that's colored gold, copper, platinum or jet; all of them pushing their inexorable way toward the table whose shining number summons them.

"I didn't recognize him. He looks so different off camera."

". . . just bought a condo on Luquillo Beach."

"How's it going, baby?"

"Terrific. Terrific. Couldn't be better."

TABLE 47

7

Now for the jousting. Warriors at play. Show-off time. Pay-off time.

"No poor shnooks here," one man tells another as they press past me, tailored tuxedoes, strategic tonsures. These are makers and shakers, America's examples to the world, lowly born and highly risen, acting out their old dreams—success in business, high marks for charity and community service, ease among gorgeous women and other rich men, familiarity with the famous and talked about. One of these biggies, defiantly bald, shoves by me with an elbow that almost knocks me down. One of his party, hurrying along in velvet and ruffles, apologizes for him. "When you got what he's got, you don't need manners."

"What's he got?" I reply to the velvet back. "Typhoid?"

Many of the Broadway Knights are in television, advertising, public relations. "Not *into*, but *in*," Paul explains. Table 47 is up ahead, middling crowded in a side, halfway front section. I make out Oberon Morley, Bibby's mentor and benefactor, Paul's former boss. Oblivious for the moment, my husband talks on, nodding toward the down-front tables.

"Broadway Knights," he continues as if I didn't know. "They're the sponsors, packagers, vice-presidents in charge of. Dues are astronomic, to keep the riffraff out. Gastronomic, too. They have to spend over a minimum on bar and food. Plus assessments any time the kitty gets hungry . . ." He goes on about how they can take it off their taxes because of the contacts and deals they make. I'm thinking about Bibby Bosculus, such a strange fish for this sea. ". . . it's a legitimate business expense."

Not everybody's in show business. Here are doctors, lawyers, big accountants, stockbrokers, important manufacturers. They're in it for the glory. I heard that one all around me:

"Guess who was in for a checkup this morning? Sonny Cheers."

"Oh, wow! What's he like?"

"Regular guy. Just like you and me."

These non-communications members—whiskey distributors, fashion furriers, Park Avenue urologists—have got to be hungry, not just for new business, not just for warm and lasting friendships—because, for one thing, communications people are not generally the world's most reliable for either lifetime loyalty or the prompt payment of bills. What these earthbound burghers crave is association with the ever-joking, ever-laughing, up-chested, shining-armored, spear-holding, prancing and outwardly projecting Broadway Knights whose ebullience, collected in a permanently spouting font, transmits golden spirit to everyone who dips in a hand.

"There's Young and Rubicam. You're looking right at him."

"Just back from the Canaries."

"Did five hundred thousand in Las Vegas."

"Sold a station."

"She looks like his daughter."

"He must have had a face-lift."

"He's a different guy since he quit drinking."

"Stunning. It must have cost ten thousand dollars."

"They couldn't do enough for us. Steaks. Ribs. Lobster. It was coming out of our ears."

"I got a very good deal on it."

Sour grapes, maybe, and maybe I'm secretly feeling shabby —a damsel in dis-dress. No jewels on me: we give to American colleges, two kids' worth. No furs: I'm a vegetarian where luxurious outerwear is concerned. But I'm thinking that Paul —who quit the television business not so long ago, not so coincidentally, either, the year Bibby started in it—has never looked so good. Out of armor, he's easier, less vulnerable than the whole teeming cavalry of glory seekers. We're nearing Number 47 now and, to prove my point, he spots Obe Morley sitting there, the inevitable tumbler of scotch in

TABLE 47

9

hand, and greets his old enemy, his torturer, his scourge, with a graceful smile.

How the mighty have fallen! Obe Morley at our table! There he sits—sheep-haired, steel-rimmed, the eyes I remember like blue ice still but not so grim now, maybe because he's been knocked off his high horse, maybe because he's sitting beside Flossie White, the personification of black-is-beautiful, and smart, and ready to play any game you call. Obe gets up to shake hands and Flossie shines her smile on me. She's like sequinned brown velvet. The hand she extends has long, strong fingernails, frosted silver, and a blue-shining diamond on the third finger.

"Nice to see you!"

"How're you doing?"

"You're looking great."

But we're not in for smalltalk. Father Joe is there, too, in mid-paragraph as usual. He waits for us to quiet down so he can finish properly.

"If Christ returned today," says Father Joe, "he would not be crucified. He'd be packaged." Joe Farley, Bibby's old buddy from the seminary, is as seedy-looking as ever, a wind-ruffled crow with his collar turned around, gray-streaked hair licking across his forehead, prop cigarette in his mouth. Paul doesn't know him. I do.

"Packaged?" I say, trying to look arch.

"Shut up and sit down," he says. "Look at the goodies in your gift bag."

"Got a neat plastic rain bonnet in there," Flossie says, giggling. She's trying to decide whether Joe is hostile or playful. Before I can clue her in, more people arrive—a short man with a round, red, appreciative face and a push-broom mustache; a pale, gawky woman you'd take for a hick if you didn't know her. He's Yuri Marchuk, poet and floor waxer, former fellow teacher while Bibby was flubbing around at Myra Tate Community College. Father Joe jumps up at the sight of Yuri and gives him a joyous slap on the back that almost knocks the poet's mustache off.

"A medieval custom is backslapping," Yuri tells the priest, recovering his balance. "Probably a symbol of the transmission of power. Possibly a test of endurance."

I've met him a few times. When Bibby was selling books, the three of us spent a long, close night drinking. Bibby used to show me, with great pride, Yuri's poems, published in little literary journals that other poets read. Gawky Geraldine is his wife or maybe not his wife. She keeps her own name, so it's hard to tell. She's an artist—she paints with acrylics in cake-decorating tubes—and she saved Bibby's life when he was down and out in Greenwich Village.

Yuri's tuxedo is even older than Paul's and his cummerbund is stretched thin. But his mood is as expansive as his belly; he goes around the table greeting us all, introducing himself to Obe and Flossie, talking with Paul and Father Joe, easy and happy.

"I *thought* you'd be here," Geraldine says to me with a clear pleasure I share. "I was afraid to ask Bibby. I didn't want to sound gauche." She's got gingery hair frizzed around her face, two festive spots of rouge, and a slap of lipstick. Geraldine never fusses. She's in a floating lavender dress she might have picked up in one of the secondhand shops around her studio. I see Paul trying to place her.

"*You* remember Geraldine Cooper, Bibby's neighbor . . ."

"Of course," he says gratefully. "Good to see you, Geraldine."

"Can you believe this?" She sits herself down and stares without embarrassment at the dais table filling up, latecomers hurrying to their places, waiters beginning to hover. There's just enough hardness around her mouth to make you question the innocence in her round blue eyes.

"Call me Joe or Padre—whatever you like," Joe was telling Yuri.

TABLE 47

11

". . . and I can't believe he's a priest."

Joe is shaking a Camel out of his pack, littering tobacco crumbs. He's flabby and shabby and takes up a lot of room hunting for matches, lighting up, blowing out a dramatic black cloud. Flossie is tickled. "You never saw a sloppy priest before?" she asks Geraldine.

"Who says I'm a priest? It's just that my mother dresses me funny."

Joe and Yuri know each other from Bibby's weddings. "I didn't officiate, thank God," Joe says. "I'd never have forgiven myself, for that first one especially." He steals a look at Flossie in her luscious red dress, holding on for its life. "Karen and Bibby made a fine affair, but a terrible marriage."

Flossie looks straight back at him, bold and wary.

"Oh, the Church! The Church!" he goes on in an Irish singsong. "When will we accept the eternal truth of human sexuality? When will we learn to get the Cross out of the crotch and attend to *real* business?"

What a strange table we are, in the midst of all the revelry and chivalry! There are still two empty chairs, two unsat-at place settings. The bride of the first wedding is late or not coming. Either way, I'm glad. Where rat-faced Karen is concerned, the later the better and better never than late. A bell tinkles in the far distance and the waiters move in to pour white wine while eaters begin digging into their fancy goblets of frozen fruit cup. Oberon Morley—maybe to show he's not ashamed of being at Table 47—stands up to make us a toast.

He's a lot thinner than he used to be.

He holds up his wineglass.

"To Bernie Bosculus, who's come a long way." He looks downright benevolent. "And to all of us here, who have come along, one way or another."

Then, maybe embarrassed by his thoughts, he sits down fast while the rest of us add our witty comments. Obe's scotch glass is empty and it stays empty. He turns his wine-glass slowly by the stem and takes a sniff before his second sip.

"California," he says. "Very decent." He's looking straight at Paul, as if it's Paul who's very decent—a thought Obe did not entertain when he was producer of the "Evening Roundup" and froze Paul off the show.

Serves him right, Ozymandias Morley: TV powerhouse one day and Table 47 the next. I remember the "Evening Roundup" Christmas parties: wherever Obe was was the center. Everybody pressed in to get his eye, to exchange greetings with him. One word from Obe Morley added two inches of height. He was the font: spurt and steel, big mover and at the same time sanctimonious married man, holding hands with his wife, his one-woman cheering squad. Nobody notices him now, sitting with us—a testimony to the Bosculus code of loyalty—while all *his* old friends are up at Tables 2 and 3. But as he sets down his wineglass and puts his hand over Flossie's, he looks like a happy man. At least he had the grace to show up, which seems not to be true of Bibby's ex-wife and her present husband.

At this moment a busboy is clearing away their places. "Karen and Warner Pickett," Father Joe says. Provocatively. "I was looking forward to meeting the man I used to hear so much about."

"Maybe that's why they didn't show," I suggest. Pleasantly.

"I can't imagine her missing this," Yuri says. "Karen always loved a good performance."

"Maybe she didn't like the table," says Flossie. "After all, Wife Number 2 is at Table Number 3."

"All the more room for us," says Geraldine. We are seven and we all spread out, the better to see the stage and to talk to each other. Table 47 is going to be fine. Paul's on my right. Geraldine's on my left. Paul's talking to Yuri, on Joe's

TABLE 47 13

right. Joe's talking to Flossie on his left. Oberon, to the right
of Paul and left of Flossie, is looking over the menu.

It's gold, the menu, with black letters and a red tassel. On
the cover is a drawing of the Golden Cock with a scroll fan-
ning wide out of its beak. On the scroll is a deft caricature of
Bernard J. Bosculus with his long question mark of a face, a
wet washrag of a necktie drooping under it. Inside the cover,
on white parchment caught by the tasseled cord, is the order
of courses, printed in Gothic lettering.

Fruit Cup Suprême is supplemented by a central platter of
Crudités (raw veggies to us commoners of the *vieille cui-
sine*). Crusty french rolls come parted in the middle, with
fancy balls of epicurean unsalted butter. Father Joe eats
greedily. Bread crumbs join tobacco crumbs in a halo around
his plate, as Yuri watches with delicate wonder. "No parish,"
Joe is telling Paul. "I'm reached at the American Executive
Society." He's a consultant, he explains. Business ethics.
Runs seminars. "High off the hog," says Father Joe, breaking
into another roll, spewing splinters of crust.

Double Consommé au Sherry. It's a good, strong soup and
Geraldine lays into it while figure-conscious Flossie taps her
spoon and takes instead, with elegant fingers, first a radish,
then a stick of celery. Geraldine gulps the soup, to fuel her
creative fires, while she ogles the crowd. She's the first to spot
Bibby. "There's our boy!"

We're about four living-room lengths from the dais but I
can make him out coming up behind other VIPs, stopping to
shake hands, being hustled ahead by one of the stage-manag-
ing officials.

"Oh, my!" Flossie says. "To think I gave him his key to
the men's room."

"I gave him whiting," Geraldine says. "First time he ate in
my loft. Fried with the bones in. He didn't know fish had

bones. 'All's I ever had was frozen,' he told me. He almost choked."

Salade Verte comes next. Boston lettuce and chicory with a nice light coat of tangy vinaigrette. Bibby is seated now at the center of the table, Last Supper-wise. I wonder whether he's cutting the greens with the edge of his fork, as my daughter Jill instructed him some years ago when she was a snotty ten-year-old.

Filet Mignon Garni avec Champignons Glacés
Pommes Soufflées   *Haricots Verts aux Amandes*

Twelve hundred people in the ballroom and the steak is perfect. Red for Paul. Wet pink for me. Brown for Geraldine, who compounds the felony by asking for ketchup. Yuri purrs with every mouthful.

Happily eating, we strain our eyes to see Bibby. He's up there, sitting between Horace Rosemont, Grand Master of the Broadway Knights, and Daniel "Kit" Custer, the dimpled and twinkling host of America's most popular late-night talk show. Kit Custer is the evening's master of ceremonies, according to our souvenir program. Rosemont is talking, shoulders thrusting like a football tackle's. Custer is talking, with his head and hands in motion like a ballet dancer's. Bosculus sits quietly attending to his dinner plate.

Yuri washes down a mouthful and claps two hands on his cummerbund. He squints toward his old buddy, the guest of honor. "You know why Bibby chews with his mouth closed?"

"Why?"

"Because his mother used to make him count. Ten chews before he could swallow. You don't talk when you're counting."

Glaces Assorties

Three flavors of melting ice cream in chocolate sauce. Very good, believe me, and eked out by tender butter cookies on a plate on a stand in the middle of the table. The coffee comes

TABLE 47   15

with real cream and the waiter leaves the pot. Obe is smoking a filtered cigarette. "Make yourselves comfy," he directs. "Speeches start with the coffee. Prepare to be convulsed."

The shining souvenir program, bigger and brighter, sports another crowing cock on the cover. On the first page of heavy, coated paper, opposite a burnished four-color ad equating King's Ransom scotch with cushy living in Scottsdale, Arizona, is a photograph of Bibby with his small, knowing, open-mouthed smile. This is the most agreeable smile in the world, a smile that offends nobody, that offers no trace of triumph, complacency, irony or trickery; that neither invites nor rejects challenge, that never competes, never derides. It is a baby's smile, just happy to be there.

No smile has been more widely misinterpreted.

Bibby looks up out of the souvenir program, focusing just about a quarter of an inch from the viewer's eyes. Bibby's nose is long from top to bottom, short from base to tip, delicately ridged. His eyes, just a whiff too close together, are solemn and hopeful. His lips are unexpectedly soft and full. He is clearly a minor-key man, his features are not hospitable to downright feelings such as anger, defiance, pity, terror, despair or exhilaration. He is more for halftones: the shadings of rue, doubt, commiseration, resignation, amusement. The photograph is black-and-white, which is correct for a pale man with fishwater eyes. Color could only lie.

I look at his picture with some complicated emotions of my own—involving nostalgia and old affection, mixed with traces of jealousy and the fear of being left behind. For Bibby's rise to fame and fortune was not a steady climb nor a propulsive rocketing; he wafted into it like a basket under a balloon. If anybody asked me what makes Bibby run, I'd have to say: the winds, the tide, the times, the customs.

Obe is leafing through the ad-studded program; he's an old hand at Broadway rites. "It's going to be a good one," he says. "They've got Joey King and Buddy Thatcher. Those guys kill each other."

Yuri, from another world, looks bewildered.

"Stand-up comedians," Flossie explains. "They speak at each other's testimonial dinners and then they get paid off by being guest stars on each other's variety shows. But here's where they do their best work. Material, you know, that's too ethnic or too blue for the family audience."

"It's a star-studded cast, all right," says Paul. He's watching Father Joe try to brush some of the cigarette ash from his cleared place. "Bibby always said he'd pay us back for all the meals we gave him." Joe makes only a gray smudge on the tablecloth, another on the napkin.

"It's a great payback," Geraldine tells Paul. "This is a great dinner!"

"It'll do for a start," Paul says. And I wonder, not for the first time, if he knows more than I think he knows.

Flossie is on her feet, causing a lot of people to turn in admiration. Loud enough for the next table to hear, she asks Geraldine and me, "Y'all want to come to the pah-dah room?"

Naturally we detour down front, past the dais where we can grab closeup looks at the celebrities. Burt Davis, the movie star, a Knights regular who once posed in a G-string for the cover of *Pimpernel* magazine, is now wearing a pink ruffled shirt under a purple velvet tuxedo. Beside him, in pale tulle, hands folded demurely under her dimpled chin, is Zelda Blake, the elderly-ingenue columnist who eats from ten to twenty-one high-calorie meals a week on the expense accounts of network "planters"—public relations staffers who hope to see news of their programs or the names of their stars blossoming in the garden of Zelda's daily newspaper space. Walter Q. Evans, the dean of network news commentators,

TABLE 47

17

is up there on the stage, contriving to look jovial, dignified and homespun all at once.

Married to Paul, connected to the TV business for so long, I ought to know better. But the truth is I'm still dazzled.

Flossie's the city slicker, the insider. She not only knows the gossip but she has been the center of it—she and Obe. She's dazzled, too.

She tells us with discreet certainty that Sholem Aachs, the very old violinist at the end of the table, has a pacemaker and was recently advised to give up extramarital sex. He told his doctor he'd give up marital sex instead. She tells us that Adam Glantz, the Metropolitan Opera baritone seated halfway along toward center, dyes his hair and likes young boys. Lil Peters, the world's highest-paid newswoman, sitting next to Glantz, is breathtaking in a white silk gown trimmed with feathers. On her left, Jennie Swartz, the twenty-four-year-old playwright and toast of Broadway, wears a peasant dress and shawl and looks out from under her hanging hair as she speaks into the ear of the man on *her* left, Don Pleasant the disco star, dressed all in white.

"Remember when Men in White were doctors?" Geraldine says.

Her artist's eye misses nothing. Filing past Bob Ford, the comedian, she comments, "Famous men are all built like that. Big head, buffalo shoulders, deep chest. And they're always shorter than you expect." Geraldine, with her ungainly walk, follows Flossie, edging between the front tables and the stage. "Looking at these people," she whispers back to me, "you can't tell anything about them."

At Table 3 is Charlton Lyon. He shines. He emanates. I cannot resist staring at him. And who is sitting on his right? So cool, so Radcliffe, so tennis and sailing, so cover of *Mademoiselle* even in her Greek revival get-up? Chatting so easily and affably with Charlton Lyon and his wonderful wife of incredible years? Wearing something so simple and perfect that it's almost pleasant to look at her? It's Jennifer Bosculus. I met her at the wedding. So did Geraldine.

We three from Table 47 sidle by, unobtrusive as possible, but Jennifer doesn't miss a move. It's Flossie she recognizes, calls to, waves, blesses with a smile.

"How've you been, Flossie? I'm so glad you could come!"

Bibby's new wife, acting hostess. She doesn't know Geraldine and me.

"Everybody remembers me," Flossie explains. "It's because I'm black. They take special care, you know, 'cause they're so scared they'll forget and I'll think they think all niggers look alike."

Her bosom shakes, deliciously, with laughter. "They won't know another person on staff. But they'll always say Hi, Flossie!"

Now we're crossing center, parading in front of Bibby himself. I'm suddenly terribly embarrassed. I hope he'll see me and make me important. I hope he won't see me, so I can escape public scrutiny. The stage is very high and we're very low, but I steal a peep and Geraldine waves a hello and Bibby sees us. He raises his hand and waves his fingers at us, a typical shy little wave, meant to elude the teacher's eye. Flossie goes right to the edge of the stage and starts talking as if she were leaning over a backyard fence. She catches up with us in the women's room, pink marble and a show in itself.

She's put out by our pussyfooting. "Why didn't you talk to Bernie? He was hurt you ran by."

"What did he say?"

"Says he's nervous. Says he's glad you all could come but he's disappointed his first wife didn't make it. He's worried maybe somebody's sick."

"Yeah, well I'd be sick, too," Geraldine says. "Seeing Jennifer all over Charlton Lyon."

The ladies' lounge smells of dry perfume instead of air

TABLE 47   19

freshener. Geraldine is agog with the decor. She runs her hand over the marble arch between the lounge and the stalls, and she's right—it's a really splendid architectural production. The stalls are pink marble and the doors to the stalls are unblemished pink Formica with a good, heavy swing and brass locks that work. The toilet seats are heavy and oval—not the cheap hollowed-out kind that rattle—and the three of us split to be in for a while with fine plumbing and facial-quality toilet paper. Out again, we splash in lambent, wine-colored basins with brass faucets and pink cream coming out of the soap dispensers. There are brass shells for tips and nothing under a quarter in there. In the outer room, where baby-pink lights glow above the mirrors at the glossy makeup counter, other women like us perch on swivel stools, survey-ing themselves, improving themselves, making love to them-selves with pencils and brushes and gloriously packaged color from the most expensive cosmetics houses.

We Table 47 women, though, are not mirror worshippers. Not Geraldine, who hardly notices who's in there. Not Flos-sie, who gives herself a quick drill-sergeant inspection. Not I, who want to get back to the show. Not detouring by the stage, we make it to our table just in time to stand up for "The Star-Spangled Banner," led by Adam Glantz, followed by the Broadway Knights' anthem (words in the program) led by Grand Master Horace Rosemont:

> We are the Knights of Old Broadway
>   Proudly we serve
> We're at the ready night and day
>   We've got the heart! We've got the nerve!
>   (We've got the vim! We've got the verve!)
>
> We are companions of the fray
>   True to our quest
> Champions of chivalry
>   And nothing but the best.
>   (The Broadway Knights! We are the best!)

One volley of cheers and applause rolls into another as the first guest speaker is introduced. It's Bob Ford.

"I just got in from California," he opens.

"For this?"

He makes a funny face.

(Everybody laughs.)

"Do you people know how much you'd be paying if you had to pay for this dinner?

"Such as it is?"

(Everybody laughs.)

"For what this dinner is costing the government in tax deductions, they could provide free condoms for every Boy Scout troop in the country."

(Nobody laughs.)

"You think they don't need 'em? They're already talking about integration. Integrating the Boy Scouts with the Girl Scouts. Do you have any idea what that could mean?"

(Everybody waits.)

"Who is this Bosculus anyway?"

(Laughter.)

"What is it, a disease? Something you get from a Greek restaurant when they don't wash the baklava?"

(More laughter.)

"I mean every year, the guests get more and more unknown. Last year we roasted a turkey. I mean a *real* turkey. Although . . ." He casts a doubtful look toward the guest of honor.

(More laughter.)

"Now we're down to germs."

And so on . . .

Adam Glantz sings "Stout-Hearted Men."

Burt Davis, hilariously introduced, takes his place at the

TABLE 47   21

microphone and removes his purple velvet tuxedo coat and his pink ruffled shirt. There, for all to see, is his bare, hairy, definedly muscled chest. The audience, in high spirits, oohs and aahs. Burt Davis rolls his shoulders left and right, caricaturing himself. Then he comes back to the microphone and back to business.

"Okay, Bosculus," he says. "Now it's your turn."

Bibby, close by at the center of the table, looks helplessly from Horace Rosemont to Kit Custer. No help. He looks directly at the audience and says something inaudible. He ducks his long chin and smiles his secret, triangular smile.

At our table, nobody breathes.

Bibby stands up, almost jauntily, and loosens his tie as he strolls over to Burt Davis, shakes the half-naked actor's hand, and leans into the microphone.

"I want to thank you, Burt," he says in a voice I've never heard. "First I want to thank you for showing up at my party in the style to which you have made us all accustomed."

Bibby pats down some of the fur on Burt Davis's chest. "It's real," he tells the audience.

(Everybody laughs except those of us at Table 47 who are too dumbfounded to make human sounds.)

"I want to thank you secondly for all the compliments I know you're going to get around to paying me.

"And finally I want to thank you for giving me this opportunity to loosen my tie."

(Everybody laughs and applauds.)

Bibby returns to his seat, the winner.

The next speaker is president of the Foundation for Education and Research in the Broadcasting Arts. He is a tall, sharp-featured man in a plaid tuxedo. Paul says he knew him when he was a press agent. His name is Steele Carrothers II, it says in the program, and he looks like a Princeton professor. His speech, solemnly intoned, is punctuated with cheers and applause:

"Sales and earnings of the three major networks combined for the third quarter and for the nine months ending last January thirty-first were higher than the results of the same periods last year. For the first time in six years, net sales were up for that quarter. Not only were they up four-point-two percent for the quarter but they were up three-point-two percent for the nine-month period. Net income was up four-point-seven percent to ninety-eight cents per share for the quarter compared to . . ."

Carrothers, who Paul says is chiefly a lobbyist and a consultant to the Federal Communications Commission, talks on about First Amendment freedoms and the ill-advised efforts of government and consumer groups to hobble the broadcasting industry with discriminatory regulations, selective licensing, and so forth. . . .

This part of the speech is passionate but brief, and soon Carrothers turns to jollier matters, singling out the National Broadcasting System to praise its moneymaking programming and heaping individual credit on Bernard J. Bosculus.

"He's the man who turned the tide into a great wave of fortune," Carrothers emotes. "He's the quiet guy who turned up the volume. Bernard Bosculus, the sleeper who woke up the television world!" To breaking applause, he rushes across the platform and shakes Bibby's hand.

Bibby stands, smiles and nods, waves to the audience and whispers something into Carrothers' ear that makes the older man explode with laughter.

Then there's another comedian.

Another singer.

More applause. More laughter.

Bernard J. Bosculus, by way of being "roasted," is variously referred to as "the Greek King Midas," "the poor man's Gen-

TABLE 47   23

eral Sarnoff," "Aristotle for the slow reader," "the lazy man's Horatio Alger," "the tired woman's Casanova" and "the white Booker T. Washington."

He is enjoying it. His chair is pushed back from the table and he's sitting back with his legs stretched out. He's watching the speakers and his face is flushed from exertive laughing. Every few minutes he calls out a comment (unheard by the audience) or points to Jennifer at Table 3. Whenever there's a big joke on him, he turns to include Jennifer in his appreciation.

Finally one of the comedians brings her in.

"You know Bernie is a newlywed," Buddy Thatcher confides to the audience. "Let's get his newlywife to stand up and take a bow.

"God knows, she deserves it."

Jennifer, pink and smiling, stands up and looks gorgeous.

"So this is the bride," Buddy Thatcher says.

After a long beat, he produces a monumental shrug.

When the laughter subsides, Jennifer is still standing, weak from her own laughter, leaning on the back of her chair.

The comedian continues: "You know what happens to a woman who's married to a workaholic?

"You know, all work and no play makes jack.

"But money isn't everything.

"A woman also wants to be laid—

"Wait! Wait! Let me finish, at least—

"I say, a woman wants to be *lady*like. I mean, look at her, she's a lovely gal."

Jennifer shakes her patrician head.

"What do you think she saw in Bernie? Sexy he's not. Look at the ring on her hand—eight, ten carats, I bet. He thinks he's going to hold her down with a rock like that."

Ripples to eddies to waves of laughter. "Okay, honey, you can sit down," Buddy tells Jennifer. "They already cleaned under your chair."

He turns to Bernie: "You can put your foot down all you want, but you're still gonna have to get it up."

He turns to the audience and changes his tone.

"But seriously, I don't want to be mean to Bernie Bosculus. He's a man of great charity. Of great social concern. Listen. Do you know about Bernie's latest public service activity? Do you know that he put a lot of money into a half-way house for girls who won't go all the way?

"Don't laugh," the comedian says. But they do.

"Do you know why Bernie Bosculus is up here on the stage?" He looks over the assemblage. "Listen. The boy is handling a lot of money these days. They put him where they can keep an eye on him. Bosculus does so much business under the table, they decided to put his table up on the stage.

"Sex and violence, I'm telling you. That's what they used to complain about. Too much sex on TV. Too much violence.

"Now we got Bosculus. Look at him. He's too lazy for violence. He's too bashful for sex. So he's a big hero. He's saving television for when it gets married.

"But listen, Bernie. *You're* married now. *You* don't have to wait any longer. . . ."

At last Kit Custer rises to make the presentation. Kit has a shock of white hair. For twenty years America has been watching this head of hair turn from sable to salt-and-pepper to snow. In those twenty years, Kit Custer's dimples and crinkles haven't changed at all. Now he stands comfortably at the microphone, in his pale watered-silk dinner jacket with velvet collar and cuffs, the best-known smile in the western hemisphere. Everybody stands to applaud him. He accepts it with his arms outflung and his fingers spread—a medicine ball of audience adoration floating up to the great man whose greatest achievement is being dependably average. Kit Custer

TABLE 47   25

is smart enough never to outsmart the dullest reaches of his television public.

But now he's among insiders.

"I won't say that Bernie here has an eye for the ladies," Kit Custer begins. "I happen to know he's crazy for his lovely bride, Jennifer, and that nothing could induce him to look at another woman. In fact, Bernie's the only guy I know who, if Lady Godiva went by, he'd bet on the horse."

(Chuckles.)

"Actually, the only thing that would make Bernie pay attention to another woman besides Jennifer would be if that other woman was going to bring more viewers to NBS and its affiliates."

(Mild applause.)

"I don't know if this fact is familiar to all of you here. But the truth is that Bernie Bosculus is the man who discovered Anna May Magnus, our queen of the wiggle, the giggle and the jiggle."

(Enthusiastic applause.)

Custer casts his bright eye on an overdeveloped teenager at one of the low-number tables. "Take a bow, will you, Anna May?"

The spotlight finds her and lights her up—a sausage-curled, gum-chewing muscular blondie with a heart-shaped face, juicy lips, sullen eyes and a tattoo on her arm. She is dressed and made up in the purple-tinged colors of a science fiction comic book. She stands bending forward to emphasize her outsized breasts, which are further exaggerated by a laced-up bodice cinched tight around her waist. Anna May Magnus rolls her eyes, blows a bubble and recedes into her chair.

(Tumultuous applause.)

"Anna May's going to do some bouncing for us later. Right, honey?"

Anna May laughs and shakes—this time, her head. Her curls bounce.

"Who ever thought," Kit continues, "that the burned bra would lead directly to the wet T-shirt?"

(Applause and laughter.)

"Bernard Bosculus, that's who! Bernard Bosculus, the Greek Moses, who taught us all the Ten Commandments of television!"

(Expectant whispering.)

"Thou shalt not bore your viewers. Thou shalt not cheat your sponsors. Thou shalt not antagonize your critics.

"Thou shalt not corrupt your viewers' children or offend your viewers' aged parents or exclude your viewers' guests from overseas who might not know much English.

"Thou shalt not abuse your viewers. Thou shalt not confuse your viewers. Thou shalt not, above all, lose your viewers."

(Mild applause.)

"Thou shalt not lose your sponsors."

(More applause.)

"Thou shalt not lose money!"

(Growing, growing . . .)

"Thou shalt not lose!"

(A volcanic eruption of applause.)

Kit Custer waits it out. When his inner seismograph starts to settle, he turns up his big, square hands like an orchestra leader, bringing the tumult down to a burbling outflow, a thin stream, a trickle and finally attentive quiet. The spotlight turns blue and a sober Kit Custer continues:

"Now I'm going to tell you a little story that very few people know about. It's the kind of story a lot of people could tell of Bernie Bosculus, but you'll never hear it from Bernie. That's why I'm going to tell it now.

"I went in to see Bernie Bosculus one day not very many moons ago, when he was still the producer of the 'Evening Roundup.' Bernie's office door is always open, you know, and I walked in just like anybody else. Bernie was on the tele-

TABLE 47   **27**

phone and he motioned me to take a seat. I could tell he was talking to one of the many charities he supports. 'You can put me down for five hundred,' he was saying. That's Bernie. All the charities put him down. For a hundred, five hundred, a thousand. But, let me tell you, they're the only ones who put him down. . . .

"Anyway, he got off that telephone a poorer, but richer, man, and I said to him, 'Bernie,' I said, 'I want to ask you a question.' I said, 'Bernie, here I've been hosting the "Midnight Hour" for twelve years now, and we're going great guns. . . .

" 'But you, Bernie,' I said. 'You've been producer of the "Evening Roundup" for a mere couple of months, for eight or ten months at the most, and you've built up a line of sponsors that's outside the building, stretched around the corner and down the block.

" 'I'm not complaining, Bernie,' I said. 'I'm not asking you to give away any trade secrets. But tell me, Bernie, if it doesn't make any difference one way or t'other, just tell me old boy, how the hell do you do it? How do you manage to have them breaking down the doors for a show that was on the skids, losing ground—*flopping*, to be quite frank about it —before you put a hand in?'

"This I asked him.

"Bernie gave me that innocent look we're all getting to know so well. That choirboy look—"

(Chuckles.)

"—that look that says 'I don't know what you're talking about.' "

(Chuckles.)

"But I hung in there. I stood firm and waited for an answer. Finally Bernie looks up at me and he says this: 'Well, Kit,' he says—and I promise you these are his actual words— 'Well, Kit,' he says, 'we just try to keep the viewers happy. We follow the lead of Shakepeare.' "

(Quiet expectancy.)

"No fooling. Bernie Bosculus goes by the word of Willy Shakespeare. I look at him and he folds his hands together like he's saying a prayer. '*As You Like It*,' he says. 'That's Shakespeare.' He says, '*What You Will*, that's Shakespeare.' He says, '*All's Well That Ends Well*, that's Shakespeare too.'

"Did you know that?" Kit Custer challenges his audience. "Those are all Shakespeare titles."

(Laughter and applause.)

"That's the secret of Bernie Bosculus. He's got class!"

(Applause.)

"And now, without further ado, I want to introduce you to our guest of honor, a man who is personally responsible for over eleven million dollars' worth of new sponsorship on the National Broadcasting System and its affiliates . . ."

(Applause.)

". . . a man who had brought living, laughing, loving entertainment back into the American family room . . ."

(More of it.)

". . . a man who has kept that dial turned to NBS."

(Lots more.)

"The right man, right on time in the right place. I give you our champ of champions, Bernard J. Bosculus!"

(Another standing ovation.)

We all stand up, too, and clap ourselves silly with the rest of the world. Bibby seems to be elevated in his place at the center of the table, target of one thousand two hundred beams of warmth and light. He wears the expression of a sunbather hoping for a lasting tan. I wonder if he has suspended disbelief. I sneak a look at the people around my table, lost now in cheering. Have they? Interesting questions arise. Did Geraldine ever sleep with him? Does Yuri despise him for a sellout? Does Father Joe, in the privacy of closet piety, pray

TABLE 47   29

for his soul? Does Obe Morley curse him? Does Flossie thank him? Would Paul like to change places with him? Would I like that? It's a funny thing about Bibby. I'm not even sure how *I* feel. He's like a piece of architecture. Reflects his environment.

As for our absent member, the hard-bitten Karen, the wife who ran out on him because he couldn't provide, what's going on in her comfortable split-level life with her provident and protective second husband? My guess is that Karen's husband is having a bad time tonight.

Now Bosculus stands. His necktie is still loose. His smile is rueful. He has put on weight, yet he's lost his flab—either a strategic tailor or a rigorous health club or, more likely, both. Maybe he has quit drinking beer. . . .

But enough of the old Bosculus. This is, clearly, a new one. More power to him. He is behind the microphone now, man of the moment, hero of the tournament. He speaks:

"Thanks," he says. "Uh . . . needless to say, um . . . I'm extremely happy to be here tonight. I feel . . . ah . . . somewhat undeserving of the honor you're laying on me. Because I'm only doing a job, a job for which I . . . uh . . . am being . . . ah . . . extremely, I would say inordinately . . . uh . . . well paid.

"I think other people have been roasted on hotter flames. I really got off easy. In a way, I feel a little bit bad about that, a little disappointed that nobody said anything really rotten about me. It makes me realize something I already suspected and something that has always bothered me a little—that I'm kind of a straight, tame guy."

He looks genuinely sorrowful about this and the audience applauds to reassure him.

"Thanks, anyway." He waits. "One thing I ought to say before I sit down is this. The story Kit Custer just told you is basically true. Completely true, in fact, but for one thing. All the things that Kit said I said, I didn't say. *He* said them. In my office that day. I just listened. But I guess listening to Kit Custer is smarter than trying to make things up yourself."

(Applause. Laughter. Buzz of appreciation.)

"Well I'm glad that the National Broadcasting System is doing good business and that this good business is turning out to be good for all the affiliates and for all of television and for the whole economy. I hope it continues. I will surely keep trying my best as long as I hold the job."

Bibby takes a long, audible breath and makes a face as if he were changing his mind. Then he turns, about to take his seat again, when Horace Rosemont grabs him by the shoulder.

"You forgot something," the Grand Master cries. He has in his hand the Coq d'Or, the Golden Cock, the trophy, the award. "This is what it's all about!" he yells.

"Oh, God!" Bibby says into the microphone. "Did I screw up again?"

PART ONE

Who's rubbing my knee? An old puzzle for women. Is it an accident? Is it a message? Paul's on my right and he's often affectionate. But this is my left knee being rubbed. Yuri's on my left, having changed places with Geraldine to argue with Obe Morley. Yuri is pitched forward in ardent debate. He might, in the urgency of political passion, inadvertently rub his knee against mine. But this rubbing doesn't feel inadvertent. Not a knee. Not passionate, either. The rubbing by somebody's stockingfoot toe is light and tentative, yet measured. It goes around full circle, then stops and goes the other way. Too playful for Yuri.

That leaves Father Joe. He is looking particularly faraway though he has moved his chair much closer on my side of the table. I wag my knee. The unshod toe completes its circle. So I take up a countermovement, trusting myself to exert the proper ladylike yet suggestive pressure, all the time looking as demure as I can manage to look. As soon as he registers this response, Father Joe shoots a look at Paul. Oh, Father, what long legs you have! And what a lousy sense of touch! It's me! Not Paul! Can't you feel the folds of a skirt?

Paul meets the bold priestly eyes over Flossie's bent ringlets and doesn't know what to do with them. I swoop in with a quick save.

"Paul! Stop playing footsie with me! I'm your wife, dammit!"

Paul knows enough to keep quiet.

Joe's toe delicately retreats.

I'm not shocked. He's not penitent. Joe and I understand each other. There's no method to his madness, only mischief. Life offers him too few high moments and he's too lazy to go after the real ones.

"We've been friends, Bibby and I, since seminary," Joe is now telling Flossie in an ESP reply to my thoughts. "Since the Academy of the Three Saints."

Well as I know Joe, I'm sure he knows me better. I came in at a later stage of Bibby's life. I heard Joe as part of

Bibby's history. But as Bibby's drinking companion, Joe knows me from *veritas in vino*. He must know more about me than my nearest and dearest do. It's kind of exciting. Joe and I seldom meet, and then only on high occasions, as semi-strangers. We keep to our ends of the rope while Bibby jumps between us.

"We were in the choir together," Joe is saying. "I was a workaday baritone, but Bibby had a lovely tenor, so beautiful as to bring tears to your eyes.

"The boy had a promising future with the church but he had failings. He couldn't drink slivovitz, for one thing. And he never knew how to press an advantage. With one or the other talent he might have made it. But lacking both, he was hopeless."

Joe is no fraud. It's just that he's chosen an easy life and he hates himself for it. Joe needs catastrophe and instead he works from nine to five at a teak desk in the orderly offices of the American Executive Society. He's a showpiece, a mascot, vice-president in charge of doing enough good to get by with the rest. Public service, affirmative action, business ethics. That's Joe. A conductor of seminars that begin with a prayer and end with profits, plenty of Emerson in between. Bibby says that Joe spends most of his time on the perimeter of his character. That's probably why he has to play kneesie every once in a while, it doesn't matter with whom.

Now that the awards ceremony is over, people are crowding onto the stage. A loudspeaker invites us to stay as long as we like, and to show they mean it, management has refilled our coffeepot. Obe went one better and called for a bottle of champagne, which now sits in an ice bucket at his right elbow. None of us is moving. We pay attention as the waiter wraps the bottle, pops the cork and pours the wine.

But Yuri can't be diverted for long. Yuri must get to the bottom of things. "No, really, Father." He is after Joe. "How *was* it in the seminary?"

TABLE 47   35

Obe Morley is watching the champagne ritual, but he doesn't miss a line. "Is that true?" he asks sharply. "Was Bernie a Catholic priest?"

"Not a priest," Father Joe says. "Nor a Catholic. Bernie was a student and the Academy was an Orthodox institution —part seminary, part monastery, a rather exotic operation. No religion you'd be likely to be familiar with."

Bibby spent several years in some ornate, engulfing religion —Apostolic or Byzantine. Some such. He never tried to conceal those years, but he didn't offer many details. Bibby in religious robes: the idea always teased my imagination. I saw him in a high wind on a dark day, crouched on jagged rocks, kneeling on a stone floor before a crude, carved altar, appealing to implacable iron faces. I saw him in monk's cloth with his hands knotted in prayer. Young. Unquestioning. A subject for an icon. Bibby with calluses on his knees. Bibby lurching along drafty halls. He digs for strange roots. I've asked him about those days and he has always answered in his solemn and thorough way, so that I still know nothing about them. Yuri is as curious as I am. And as unsatisfied. But he has his own version. "Time out of life," Yuri says. "A sealed cave. An isolation ward. A postponement of his encounter with the world of Freud and Einstein."

Yuri the poet is not what I'd call a facts-and-figures man. And he thought *Bibby* was far out! "I met him not long after he left the place," Yuri tells us. "He didn't seem at all religious. I thought he'd been in the army."

"Out of the frying pan and into the fire." Father Joe leans back and pours himself a shallow libation. He drinks and sets down his glass. "I will tell you," Joe says, "about Bibby and the Academy of the Three Saints." He lowers his voice so we've got to lean in to hear him: an actor's trick. "How he got there was as natural as passing wind." Another one.

"Think of the Academy as a seafood restaurant and Bibby's childhood environment as a lobster pound." Joe frowns into his glass. "Dammit!" He scolds the remains of his drink. "I'm getting polluted!"

He returns to us balefully. "Bibby Bosculus—Bunny Newly then—had the kind of a childhood that leads quite naturally into one cloistered life or another.

"Like most kids, Bibby was kept in the dark. His parents did their best to avoid telling him the truth about anything. Bibby had Santa Claus until his father was killed. Santa Claus couldn't pull his father out from under the truck. I don't know the details and I don't think Bibby does either. It happened just down the road a few miles from where they were living at the time—the flat, the Quonset, the garden apartment. The war was over. Bibby was younger than five years old. Santa couldn't bring his father back.

"Bibby always pictured his father as a man without a head. The head was always out of sight as the man bent under the hood of a car or stretched out on the driveway to get under the chassis. At home he had his head in a newspaper or under a hat as he baked in the sun. Anyway, when the old man— who was actually no old man, but a man somewhat younger than Bibby is now—when he got hit by the truck, he stayed in Bibby's mind that way. Headless. That's Bibby's father image."

The call came at suppertime. They never waited for Daddy because he worked shifts or worked overtime or worked far away. They never set a family table. If Bunny was looking hungry, his mother might get up and say *Stop sniffing around and eat a regular meal*. Or she'd fix him something just because he was there, in the house, and had nothing to do.

On this night Bunny was roosted on a high stool at a chipped white enamel table, eating spaghetti with ketchup. This was his favorite dish: cut-up spaghetties or narrow egg noodles generously squirted with ketchup. Sometimes his mother added sugar and some chopped onions, a recipe from

TABLE 47 37

a supermarket magazine. Bunny was happily eating out of the red plastic soup bowl he liked. His mother was gloomily watching him. The phone rang. She was in a striped apron that was meant to protect a dress, but she had no dress under it. She wore the apron over a faded slip that drooped on her as everything else drooped on her. Her hair was getting gray and she wasn't even thirty. When the phone rang she was sitting across from Bunny, watching him eat and telling him how lucky he was to have such good spaghetti and ketchup. Bunny agreed with her. He loved to stuff his mouth with wet, heavy food. She had thrown in a chunk of margarine. The phone rang again and Mrs. Newly picked herself up to answer it. It was a stand-up phone with a round beak like a cartoon bird, and it stood on the lopsided round table from the thrift shop where she got most of the stuff they kept with them. There was a shelf under the tabletop for the telephone book, even though they had nobody to look up. Mrs. Newly took the phone call in the middle of the fourth ring. Bunny was moving a loaded spoon toward his open mouth when he heard his mother pull in her breath and saw the telephone cord sneak around the corner into the living room. He dropped the spoon. He was hollowed out with fear even before he heard her.

Where? How bad? I'll be right there.

When she came into the kitchen she told him his daddy was having trouble with the car. *I'm going to see what I can do to help.* She only had eyes and her voice came from someplace else. Bunny ran past her into the bathroom. *I want you to stay next door.* Bunny fell on his knees and vomited into the toilet. His vomit looked like pink cotton candy floating.

"That night," Father Joe continues, "Mrs. Newly took a drink to steady herself. She didn't sober up for quite some time. Her condition gave her son an early chance to prove his manhood. As soon as his mother took the bottle as her constant companion, Bunny went on his own. It was easy to be a good boy. All he had to do was keep out of the way."

Isn't he a fine little fellow? He gives his poor momma no trouble at all.

"Bunny liked praise. He cooked his own food, made his own bed. If he felt sick, he took his own temperature and kept himself warm. He learned to ride the bus. To the library. To the movies. He walked solitary pilgrimages to Five Points or across Broadway, where a grocery store and a package goods store stood side by side and would sell on credit. He would show his shopping list to the storekeeper. The storekeeper would fill a bag and give him the bill. He was no genius in school, for he was always the new boy catching up. He would have been kind to animals and other children if he'd had the chance. He would have liked to build or color, but he had neither the room nor the equipment. So he read books and watched movies. And was silent and solitary. And praised.

"Bunny must have been six or seven when his mother started him in church school. She didn't care about the church, but the school was nearer to where they lived in whatever backwater community they moved to. It was a church she'd never heard of, but the school was free and she thought it would be a good influence on a boy without a father. Maybe they took him all day instead of a half day in the public school. In any case, that's what got the boy into the hands of the Eastern Church. Bunny's momma started out freshwater American, Baptist or Methodist—one's as good as the other, you know, as long as you believe in God. Bosculus, her second husband, was a member in good standing in his Eastern version of Christianity, meaning he showed up every Sunday, kissed the icons, knelt on the floor and said the prayers. Mrs. Newly met old man Bosculus through church activities that she joined to keep up the appearance of a good

TABLE 47 39

parent, but old man Bosculus never became Bunny's father. He never adopted the kid. They were never close.

"It was another man, a man he met only once and whose name he never learned, who turned Bibby toward the faith of the church."

One day like the other days, Bunny's mother drove him to school in her battered Chevy. Bunny sat in the back seat because his mother said he was safer there. It was early in the morning and a long way to school, across the flats and out past Five Points. Bunny loved how the church rose up like a carnival, like a magic bazaar in the middle of the flat, dry country, the shining stone church with a gold-painted dome like an Arabian vizier's turban.

Mrs. Newly dumped him off, as always, where the paved road turned into the gravel road and Bunny walked, carrying books he couldn't read, along the gravel road toward the church and the little brown brick school next door. There were no other kids on the road and that was no surprise— Bunny's mother often dropped him late. But when he got to the school door, he found it locked. He tried both sides of the double door and couldn't open either one. He walked around the square brick building and tried the back door and knocked on it and pushed. He stood on his books to look in the windows. He knocked and called. Nobody there.

So Bunny picked up the books and went around to the church and up the broad, smooth, shiny-veined steps to the gates and he couldn't open the gates either. He jiggled the handles and shook and rattled the iron bars. He went all along the wide gate, hoping that one of the bars was magic and would open for him. When this did not happen, he went down the stairs again and around to the side of the church. He passed under the jeweled church windows and down some dark cement steps, where he found another door that was locked. He was not tall enough, even standing on his books, to look through the glass window, so he came up the stairs again. He walked around to the back and saw some windows low against the ground. He squatted to look through them but saw nothing, no one there—only the soot on the inside of the window.

It was autumn, early in the school year, and it was chilly. Bunny was cold under his light jacket. He shivered. The church rose out of the ground like a tomb in a cemetery. There was no one around. No one to call. No place to go. Bunny was a brave boy and did not consider crying. So he walked all around the church and the school once more and tried all the doors and gates again. And then he sat down on the church steps to wait for his mother. It was cold, sitting so still. The sky was as gray as the blackboard after he had erased his letters. There was a row of bushes across the road. There were fourteen bushes, losing their leaves. When the wind came up the leaves blew along the gravel road. After a long time Bunny decided to walk toward the paved road where his mother had left him. He walked very slowly so that she would be there. He was wearing sneakers. He kicked bits of gravel as he walked, but he kicked carefully so as not to scuff the rubber tips of the sneakers.

There were no trees on the side of the road and no cars passing. Even before he reached the paved road he could see that his mother wasn't there. So he stood, small under the slaty sky and cold under his thin jacket. And he stood for a long time, with his mouth shut tight and his eyes wide open so the tears wouldn't spill out. Then he started to walk in little, evenly paced circles for he was too cold and too scared to stand still. He was watching his feet, measuring the sneakered steps, so he did not see the man approaching him, noiselessly, up the paved road from the direction of town.

He was an old man in scuffed and swollen shoes, with a lumpy, hanging overcoat, mashed pockets, and a wool hat

TABLE 47 41

pulled down on his head. He was a man with somewhere else in his eyes, the kind of man who used his sleeve to wipe his nose or bent over the gutter to blow it with a thumb and forefinger over the bridge. He had a voice like sand and nothing better to do in the middle of the morning than to offer help to a lost boy.

Bunny knew his house and the street it was on.

But I don't know how to get there, he told the man.

The man told him not to worry. He said it wasn't too far. He said they'd be there in no time. He said he'd carry Bunny's books for him.

So Bunny put his hand into the man's hand and they walked together down the paved road toward town and the man bent over so he could hear what Bunny was telling him.

Bunny told him a lot. He told him about his school and his teacher and about the other kids in the class. About marbles he was saving and pictures he cut out. Bunny talked as if somebody had opened him up like a can of information. The man liked everything he said, so Bunny kept saying more. He listened to it all coming out of him and he liked it, too. He talked about trees and cats and what he liked to eat and what he hated to do. The man listened and nodded his head and his eyes came back from wherever they were and he smiled, showing small brown teeth.

They talked all the long way, past the empty lots, past the Five Points, the row of stores, the longer row of two-family houses, past a field and a cemetery, and garden apartments, hand in hand with the man holding tight only when they crossed a road with cars coming. When they got to where Bunny could point to his house, the man said good-bye.

Bunny was disappointed. He wanted the man to come home with him. He wanted him to eat lunch with him. He wanted to show his friend to his mother and he wanted his mother to say thank you. He wanted to keep his friend.

But the man wouldn't go past the corner of Bunny's street.

So Bunny said thank you.

Be a good boy, the man said.

Bunny walked backward, waving till the man turned and went away. Bunny started to pray at night so he could ask God's blessing for his friend.

"What it must have been," Father Joe says, "was one of our recondite Eastern holy days, so the school and church were closed. Bunny walked into his house and his mother became hysterical."

How did you get here? What happened?

"There was more accusation than concern. She hadn't finished her second cup of coffee, her crossword, her magazine confession story, her gin—whatever she did for breakfast."

Did he touch you? What did he say to you? What did he do?

"Bunny absorbed all this panic and, believe me, he was glad he hadn't brought the old guy in."

Father Joe is spread out in his chair now, sure of his audience and comfortable with his story. "I offer this anecdote," he says, "not only as a story that Bibby often tells but also as a prelude to his adventures at the Academy."

He smiles alluringly at Flossie. "Adventures," he repeats. "It's a word I use."

Father Joe's words should be salted before swallowed. He's an impact man. He likes to shake people up. His furry, low voice gyrates from depths of wrath to peaks of bliss. He has a harsh dimple under his right cheek from a smile that seldom comes all the way. His cat-slit eyes gleam malignantly, yet Flossie hangs on to his words as if he were a saint, or at least one of those saintly authorities that the dazzled young often end up having love affairs with. Geraldine, however, does not take his flashy insights as if they came off the mountain.

TABLE 47   43

"You mean to say," Geraldine says, "that this little old Good Samaritan was responsible for Bibby's going to the seminary?" She bucks her teeth incredulously. "I don't believe that. I knew Bibby at the worst time in his life and the only father he ever talked about was George Bosculus."

Yuri pounces. "Exactly!" He glows. "And George Bosculus was a creep. Imagine having to carry the name of a creep you don't like who isn't even your real father!"

"It's cheap psychology. Not everybody in religion is looking for a father."

"Oh, you intellectuals!" Obe Morley objects from above. "Can't you just let things happen?"

Yuri laughs. "That's the trouble. We can't prevent them."

Bunny became Bibby when his mother married George Bosculus and thereby changed his initials—though not officially—to B. B. That's what they called him in junior high school—B. B. "He liked it," Father Joe assures us. "It made him feel like an insider. This was the regional public school by then, the great world. When he got to high school, B. B. melted into Bibby and he liked that too. A nickname shows you've got friends."

"Oh, yes. Friends have always been important to Bibby." That's my husband talking, in a tone only I can be sure is sarcastic.

Joe breezes by it. "After high school," he continues, "was Bibby's problem. His mother was off on her own track with her second husband and he—Bosculus Senior—couldn't wait to get rid of the lad. He'd put up with his moonings and meanderings more or less gracefully for over five years. It was time for Bibby to pack up and move on. Where to? Red or black. The church must have seemed like the safer place."

"It was all the warmth and color he'd ever had," Yuri puts in.

"So that's a calling?" says Oberon Morley.

"That's *one* calling," says Flossie.

Father Joe gallops on: "You can say if you like that Bibby so loved the world that he wanted to give himself up to the priesthood. He wanted to stand between the altar and the icon screen, in white vestments threaded with gold, spired headpiece, his arms outflung and his eyes raised to the crucifix chained to the rafter above him. He wanted to float between the blood-red carpet and the sunlit, cloud-parading sky painted under the dome; under the spear-straight figures of somber, bearded saints and patriarchs with their stiff hands upraised in symbolic disapproval of the goings-on below—the sensual assault of the spiced, jewel-lit air, the swing of the censers, the tining little bells, the chanting, the wine. Bibby wanted to expand into the universe and to abase himself before the Divinities, to chant the strange-tongued liturgy, to kiss the holy pictures, to kneel before the icons and touch his forehead to the floor.

"If you are of romantic spirit, you can imagine also that he wanted to extend a helping hand to parishioners, to help them hold themselves together with the tender cords of ritual and responsibility, to lead the children, support the old and maybe even to politic among doubters and reprobates to save souls, his own especially. Bibby Bosculus even at eighteen was a practical lad, attracted to an orderly life. Even at that age he may well have seen himself as tea guest, bedside sitter, deliverer of food baskets, hope of the hopeless and scourge of the sinner. . . . Well, perhaps not scourge of the sinner. But maybe the leader of a youth group and guide to the perplexed, and all the time himself living in relative quiet comfort in a ready-made life with books on his shelves, pictures on his walls, a housekeeper in his kitchen and a warm fire on cold nights. It was a pleasant life he saw, physically bounded by a supporting church and spiritually intensified by the sweeps and depths, the spacious severities and grave splendors of the Eastern spirit.

"Souls yearn, it's true. But you can also see the priesthood

TABLE 47

45

as a practical choice for a solitary, secretly scholarly boy who distrusts physical work, does not move well in crowds and is, most poignantly, a stranger to himself. Nobody introduced him, see? Furthermore, the Orthodox priesthood was a way to beat out his stepfather, his mother's new man, the father figure who wouldn't adopt and didn't adapt, the only born believer in the family. If Bibby gets to be a priest, George Bosculus has to call *him* Father. George Bosculus has to kneel and kiss his hand. Does that make the priesthood attractive? Irresistible, I'd say.

"Of course, I can't tell you why for sure. But I know that Bibby showed up at the Academy. I was there. I still go back whenever the bishop gets mad enough or sentimental enough to want to see me."

He packed his own suitcase but his parents saw him off. They drove to the bus station in George Bosculus' Buick sedan. Bibby's mother took her hair out of rollers for the occasion. She dabbed her face with powder and rouge. She stood by the bus door and kissed him dryly, smiled, waved, looked everywhere but at him. The stepfather stood beside her, stiff and weighty, smoothing the rumples from his black church suit. He pulled his fierce features into proper Sunday solemnity, shook hands and said a few chesty words to disguise his relief at Bibby's departure. By the time Bibby was up in his seat and looking out the window, his parents were gone.

Bibby sat alone, with pale expectations. The bus hurtled forward. Bibby loved buses. The linty matter that ordinarily filled his head and blurred his images parted and fled for long, wonderful moments while he enjoyed a view of passing countryside, distant mountains, backyard clotheslines, fields, gullies, the hills of towns. When he arrived at the Academy of the Three Saints, his good-byes became real for the first time. He stepped inside the gate and the rest of the world stayed out.

Father Joe douses a cigarette in a wet coffee saucer. He fingers his squashed pack of Camels. "The Academy of the Three Saints," he tells us, "would not look to you as it did to Bibby or as it does to me." He pushes away the cigarettes, a renunciation.

"I see the main building as a country house out of Chekhov. Homely wood front. Wide, welcoming porch. Rambling rooms with old furniture, nothing matched. Worn rugs with no grip left. Chairs like old nursemaids that hug you into them and give you a hell of a fight to get up from. This was the place where the great Fathers slept and where the high-class seminars were held. So-called social gatherings took place in a grand living room with a hearth. In back was a dining room with linoleum on the floor and rows of long scrubbed wood tables.

"In Bibby's susceptible head, it probably looked like the Escorial. Bibby's favorite building was a stone dormitory out in the woods, down in the hollow. Bibby was searching for the howling bigness of your great Gothic church. He wanted to chase through arched passages and up steep stairways in the dark light of leaded windows. Old Bibby was looking for Gothic reminders that life is grim, duty foremost, suffering its own reward and pain a signpost on the road to salvation."

The Father gives up and lights another cigarette.

"What we had," he continues, squinting through smoke, "was lovely country and lots of room to be friendly with it. For acres out back there were hills and trees, quiet places with benches or little huts, and a couple of rough chapels deep in the woods where a man could disconnect himself from the worldly switchboard. Those of us who liked to pray prayed outside or alone in our rooms. The church was for corporate activities. Bibby, of course, was crazy about the church."

TABLE 47   47

Stepping in from the plain frame exterior, through the keyhole door, Bibby looked on a magic world. He knew some of its secrets. He knew it was the colored window glass that jeweled the light rising from the tiered circles of candles. He knew the smells of mildew and Lysol that shrank under the waves of incense. He knew the flat meanings of the tendriled liturgical words. He even knew what the priests wore under the brocaded vestments lovingly sewn by community women. Bibby peered through the openings in the icon screen to the altar, where the priests chanted over the preparation of the sacrament. He knew the names of the saints and patriarchs whose flat, faded, elongated figures stood along the walls and the screen, warning and blessing. Knowing it all, he was still as thrilled and heated and hushed as he was in the days when all was mystery.

Nowadays he liked to get in early and watch the community congregants arrive—stocky, white-skinned women with high-piled hair; compact, blunt-featured men, who looked like George Bosculus. So reverently they entered and knelt. Those with children brought them forward and lifted them to kiss the pictures. Taking random places—no seats in this sanctuary—all knelt and pressed their heads to the blood-red carpet. Standing again, they breathed the emanations of the priest before them, chanting.

The congregants stood in awe of the mighty impassive priest, but Bibby knew something different. He knew these priests outside the sanctuary. They were teaching priests. They loved company. Three Saints priests came big and red-faced, with heavy beards and flowing, bright-colored cassocks. Among them, Bibby found himself in the line of hurled laughter, snarled dissent, tearful sympathy. These priests pounded the table with their big fists. They crushed him with their embraces. It was Bibby's religious practice to pray before the icons. But the raging priests, reddened with wine and argument, singing above the choir, striding beyond the churchyard and into the woods, speaking the language of the liturgy—its rearing, colliding Slavic consonants skidding among the insinuating vowels—this was a force.

"Bibby was brought up on thin broth," Father Joe explains. "How could he resist this combination of thick, rich peasant soup and the heady wine of the gods? Our boy Bibby was seduced by the Church." And then Father Joe goes through one of his dramatic changes. His face darkens. His ironic smile fades into a scowl. Like movie music, the mood of Table 47 turns into a menacing minor key, two octaves down.

"Literally," Father Joe says. And then, with a long sigh, and a return to easy irony, he says:

"The fact is, I was very jealous of Bibby. He was the favorite of the best-loved teacher there. All us father-seeking boys wanted the friendship of Brother Gregory. But Bibby was the golden one and I would have given my elbow to take his place."

They met him at the gate and made him welcome, two fathers who looked like Russians playing Falstaff and vice versa. He sank under their hearty questions but his answers pleased them and that brought him up again. Bibby had his cassock, a gift from his parish priest. They gave him a bed and a prayerbook. He was an acolyte, a little brother, a ripe candidate for a life in faith.

Bibby understood why they liked him so much. He was an able-bodied prospect in a shrinking dominion. Most of the students were older, already out of college, and tame. Bibby was a bud to be nipped. He was quick and obedient, showed both qualities in his answers to artful questions. Bibby knew how to make connections between old custom and new psy-

TABLE 47

49

chology. He had a first-base kind of mind that caught a flying idea and held onto it. Sometimes he could even toss it along to somebody else. He stuttered and he was awkward but he knew that wouldn't hurt him. He was young and malleable. In fact he yearned to be molded.

So they decided to put him into their version of the work-study plan. Bibby could take secular courses at a college in the town and he would be a seminarian. And all of this favor was offered to him even before they learned he could sing.

He loved the Academy. He loved the order. The up, wash, matins, breakfast. The classes, chores, meditations, convocations. He liked his not-so-liberal arts college courses and he loved his patristics, liturgics, homilectics and Byzantine church history. He learned to read Latin, Hebrew, Aramaic, Slavonic and New Testament Greek. Music, too, of course, he loved. And even his duties: gardening, mending books. Soon he had church duties, too: in black cassock and vestment he prepared the censer, carried a candelabrum, fetched the pitcher of hot water to mix with wine for communion.

"It would have been a fine life for him," Father Joe remarks. "After money, religion is probably the favorite way for people to avoid responsibility for their lives."

He shifted in his chair and took on a more intimate tone. "I was, as I said, a few years older, and I didn't know him well. Bibby even then was someone you could easily miss in a crowd. I wouldn't have known him at all, probably, except that he turned out to have a lovely voice and even became famous for it. Did you know Bibby had a lovely singing voice? Another of the qualities that passed unnoticed in his appalling limbo of a childhood. Quite a nice voice. A teenaged alto that slipped without a break into a clear tenor. Brother Gregory, the choirmaster, saw fit to give him private lessons. That's how he came to be known as Brother Gregory's boy.

He sang solo with the choir, at services and for the occasional outside recital. Eventually he was given a room of his own in the dormitory—a cell, to be sure, but a place apart where he could hear himself sing. Those stone walls served. He could practice late in the night, disturbing no one. A great privilege, one's own room."

The edge of sarcasm is sharpening in Joe's voice. "Anyone else so honored would have been a lion," he says. "But Bibby had a world of his own. Like most people newly exposed to the rays of praise, Bibby covered his face with his hands. Praise seemed to threaten his so-called self-image, so we didn't bother him."

Meals were uproarious. The dining room was always steaming with hot cereal or hot soup. Stout women operated the open kitchen. Bibby himself had a roaring appetite after a long, cold hour of prayer and meditation. He was glad for the noise and company.

"You're crazy!"

"Dead wrong!"

"If that's what you think, go to the Catholics!"

In their zeal, they ate like pigs. Bibby, ashamed of himself for minding that he felt like a snob, looked into his plate to avoid seeing chewed food in the mouths of the contenders.

Once, early in his stay, he sat at a center table that was reserved for older students. He found himself beside a fidgety upperclassman and the least serene eyes in Bibby's memory. Neckties were required but this man's necktie was a spit at the rule, a piece of dirty rag. He talked of God and electrons with the immediacy that Bibby's parents reserved for the food on the table and the prices in newspaper ads. Nobody told Bibby he was at the wrong table, but nobody spoke to him, even to ask for the squash. Over rice pudding, the talk

TABLE 47 51

became quiet. The unkempt finger-drummer sucked in his restlessness. Bibby sat on his fear and dared to ask a question.

"Is everybody here going to be a priest?"

The answer waited long enough to punish him for being there.

"No," the restless one told him. "Some of us will be teachers, some administrators, some theologians. Some will end up in secular work. But we all love the Church, some more critically than others." He nudged the man on his other side, ungently, so the fellow spilled his pudding.

"And we all are committed to the life of the spirit as well as the spirit of life. Though not all of us have the high moral purpose essential for parish priesthood."

The man he became turns to us with the licks of old fires in his eyes, ash in his hair. "That's how I talked in the old days," Father Joe says. "I'm afraid I was a bit pretentious. I've changed my mind, if not my style, since then. High moral purpose is for revolutionaries, I find. The priesthood is for comforters."

He continues his story with a calm face and his eyes half closed. "I should have been kinder to him. But he didn't seem to need anybody. He had his music. He had Brother Gregory. You can't imagine what Brother Gregory's favor meant to us then. It was not only the perks—the room, the being excused from unpleasant duties, getting out of classes. Bibby didn't even ride on those perks. He could have cut into the chowline—*rehearsal in ten minutes*—but Bibby always went to the end and waited.

"The real privilege was the companionship with Gregory. Many of us, I for one, took up music just to be near him. I wasn't good enough to make the choir but I learned all the tones of the season and more music theory than ten priests need to know. He was a dynamic guy, the choirmaster, charming as a politician, exuberant, warm, sympathetic—

everything you'd want your father to be. And no prig was he.
He used to get his favorites excused from class to play golf
with him. With all my hardly negligible efforts, I was not
successful in catching his interest. Why Bibby did was always
something of a mystery to the rest of us. He had a nice voice,
but it wasn't—not really—*that* nice a voice.

"'Just say the word, my boy, and I'll speak to the powers.
Term papers, you know, are just to keep you students busy.
Ten pages on Abraham and Isaac aren't going to make you a
better man, Bernard.'" He put the stress on the second sylla-
ble—Ber-*nard*—the way they did back in the Bosculus household.

Brother Gregory, neither priest nor layman, neither old nor
young, was built top-heavy like a singer, with the weight of
steel in his chest and shoulders, narrowing down to small feet
in well-kept, polished shoes. He had springy, ironshot hair,
broad Slavic cheeks, eyes on the alert but as ready to laugh
as listen. When he wasn't in his cassock, he was the dressiest
of all the teachers—forget the priests in their spotted skirts
and sooty shoes. Brother Gregory liked sporty clothes, but
Bibby never felt shabby in his company. He never felt disapproved of, either.

They walked in winter cold, in heavy boots. Brother Gregory wore thick mittens. Bibby looked like a penitent with
his hands shoved into the chest pockets of a wool plaid
jacket. They walked close together, hunched against the
wind. Head down, Bibby squinted up through the rising
steam of his breath, over the skeleton trees, to see the afternoon sun like a scoop of lemon ice, no chance of melting.
Mostly he kept his eyes down, watching out for rocks and frozen roots.

"The fact is," Brother Gregory was saying, "that I hate the
cold. Some year soon I'm going to quit skiing. I only do it for

TABLE 47   53

ego. And the after-ski fire. It's the warm slippers and the hot toddy, the side dishes that lure me. Do you ice-skate, Bernard? Do you ski?"

Bibby did neither.

"Masochists and egotists. They're for winter sports. Nobody with a hair of common sense. The last time I was on skis, three weeks next Saturday, I swore never again. I had a panic. I'd gone up on one of those rope pulls, a T-bar lift. Burns your hands. Scares your pants off. One false move and over you go and everybody behind goes over you. It's a terror. I made it up to the top, a minor miracle in itself, and I found myself on this slope as steep as an icicle. All the youngsters slipped off the tow and skied blithely down. I stayed there for a while, to put myself together. Adjusting my clothing, you know. Getting up my nerve, you know? All of a sudden I saw that I was alone up there. The daredevils had all disappeared. I looked down the slope after them. What a slope! Icy. Full of ridges and sudden drops. You could fall off the edge, I thought. I swear it. I got so scared my knees began to shake. Did you ever sweat in a freeze? Terrible. The world disappears. It's just you and your fear. I thought, what the hell am I doing up here? What am I trying to prove?"

He fanned out his huge mittens. "What did you do?" Bibby asked.

"I got myself down off there. Half skiing, you know, on the horizontal, in little stretches. You dig in your poles so you don't build up speed. It took a while, but I got down."

"And you quit?"

The choirmaster cleared his throat. "Well, I had to go up again, you see. I couldn't give in to the fear. But I didn't go all the way to the top. I settled for just a bit more than halfway. It was a bargain I made with myself. There was a good place to drop off the tow. And, well, you can't live your life scared."

They pushed their way up the path, keeping their pace and breathing hard.

"Tennis," Brother Gregory said. "Now there is a worthwhile sport. Smash that ball, it's a glorious outlet. Long, low, singing shots." He exhaled a jet of steam. "Golf, on the other hand, is for the Anglo-Saxon temperament. Precise, understated, much preparation for very little action. Unbending club, compressed ball. Tennis is for Europeans. Your own game on a court that's all yours to run around on."

They climbed higher with the wind cutting at them, slicing Bibby's face. He watched the descending landscape from the sides of his eyes. He saw sleeves of ice on the branches of naked bushes. They tinkled in the gusts. Bibby's ears felt like cardboard.

"Also," Bibby said, on the side of tennis, "you d-d-don't need snow."

He didn't worry about his stammer. It was part of him, like long legs and dreaminess. People probably stopped hearing it after a while. He wished he could tell them, when they first met, that he didn't mind stammering. When he didn't try not to, it wasn't there at all. But now he was filling up with things he wanted to say. Brother Gregory acknowledged his pleasantry with a smiling nod into his scarf. They were climbing, stepping hard on frozen ruts, no give under their boots. Bibby made fists in his pockets, four cold fingersticks in the palm of each hand.

"I played baseball and b-basketball in high school." Intramural. He was a fast runner. He had good aim but bad timing. He hadn't played much, he said.

Gregory turned off the path and up a bank, cutting through tangles of frozen brambles. The tips snapped off at a touch. He held the whippier branches aside for Bibby to pass.

"I was a kick-the-can champ myself," Gregory said. "Street games. All the kids on the block."

"Country kids watch television," Bibby said. "Drink beer.

TABLE 47

55

Grow up and get m-married as soon as they can." He was shouldering his way through stiff bracken, ducking under branches. He tried something different: crossed his arms, hugged his hands under his sleeves.

"Zombies!" Brother Gregory said. "TV zombies. Pot zombies. They never learn to use themselves, poor kids. We need our heads, by God! Here, take these." He pulled off his mittens.

Bibby shook his head.

"No. Take them. I've got deep pockets."

Gregory thrust the mittens against Bibby's chest, boxing style. "Put them on, boy. I'm no masochist."

Bibby dug into the sheepskin mittens, hot inside. Warm hands dulled the chill in the rest of him. Brother Gregory, walking ahead, kicked at caught rocks, crushing the brittle brown beds of leaves like shavings. He bulled with his head and shoulders into the brake till at last he drove through to a clearing. He moved with grace, Bibby noticed, for such a weighty man. Bibby less gracefully sidled and shouldered his way behind until he stood beside the choirmaster on a broad open slope. The unmelting sun had slipped and the wind was a slap in the face. Snowy mountains billowed for awesome distances, but it was too cold to stop.

They walked across the slope to downhill woods.

"Breathe deep," Brother Gregory instructed. "We'll call this a practice session."

But the sun was sinking behind them and breath came easiest in short sips. Bibby took the lead in starting down the straightest path toward home. He looked to see if this was all right with the Brother, but Gregory was already beside him and a step ahead, easy, not minding the cold. It was a steady downhill trudge. The twists of root and stem, the grim winter growth, were black under the lowering sky, and home and hot soup were what Bibby was thinking of, much as he treasured the choirmaster's company.

They made only one stop. Brother Gregory grabbed Bibby's elbow and turned him in to see a frozen waterfall behind a low wall of piled rocks half hidden by the brake. "Here we are," he said, with satisfaction. "This is what I wanted to see today." He drew Bibby to his side and they stood, not still but rolling into themselves to keep the blood running.

The path had become a natural bridge and, beyond the stone wall, a rocky gorge cut into the hillside. The trickle of water had been caught in its fall and had frozen white. Bibby stared at beards of ice, great matted Russian beards, spiked and spoked Greek beards, ferocious and fatherly, in opaque impasto, blue-white, gray-white, a wall of beards clinging to the rocks or caught midair in their downward rush.

"It's not often you glimpse a waterfall frozen in time, Bernard." It was *his* waterfall. "It comes to life in the spring," he said. "We'll see it."

It was too cold to stay, but the moment stretched in Bibby's head. It held there, even while he did little jumps and clapped his hands like a four-year-old crazy at the circus. It was the cold, of course, but Bibby also *was* that delighted. He had missed the circuses that would have taught him what to do with delight. Joy came on him as a swelling that hurt. It kept hurting as the choirmaster moved on, and Bibby with him, almost running toward the buildings in sight below them.

"I'll tell you something just between us," Brother Gregory said. "Not only do I hate the cold but I am also not crazy about the country. I'm a city man at heart. I often ask myself what the hell I'm doing out here."

Bibby's lips were chapped. It hurt to laugh.

"I mean it, boy. Don't tell a soul."

Bibby thought he was on the pleasure dole. Days at the Academy seemed to him like candy bars, one replacing an-

TABLE 47 57

other from a free canteen. Everything he did—classes, lessons, jobs—was luminously colored and sweet. His throat opened and his voice soared. People treated him well. They called him if he overslept. They saved him a seat at the table. Only the choirmaster called him Bernard, and that was in the tone of an affectionate nickname.

"Yes, Bernard, I was almost a priest," Brother Gregory confided on a hot summer morning when it was punishment to be inside. "There's nothing a priest knows that I don't know. But I couldn't go through with it." He got up from the piano stool and restacked the sheets on the music stand. "I suffer from doubts and am too honest to deny it. Or too arrogant. That's one of the doubts."

He handed Bibby the ink-scored notebook with practice instructions. "I suffer from appetites that I am not sure are unholy . . ."

Bibby expected to be a priest. Why else would he be in the Academy, wearing a cassock, praying every day? He thought hard and often of his sacred duty to deliver God's message to the people in this world. He could understand himself as a middleman. Experience turned to sermons in his head. He was taken to an art museum. An orchestra played in the college auditorium. Bibby put the music to paintings—Breughel figures pitched their forks double-time to the tune of Beethoven's violin concerto, which Bibby thought of then as the vio*lent*, or at least very energetic, concerto. These fancies filled his mind and he tried to turn them into logical concepts to be explained to imaginary congregants. But the trails he followed usually ended up against a solid wall or in a knot of paths he couldn't get out of. He stayed comfortable by not forcing himself to conclusions and his sermons remained abstract and fragmentary, safe only with his faceless, voiceless parishioners who never put up an argument. Bibby thought, though, that he would be a good priest because of his patience and his desire to see everybody happy. He sincerely felt, in his early days at the Academy, that happy people were good people and vice versa.

Bibby prayed to the center of the universe: to a beating heart that set the electrons in motion and a ponderous mind that kept them in order. This God he prayed to looked like Brother Gregory. He studied studiously and, in the back of his head, the person who was holding the ruler, reading the report card, was also a replica of the choirmaster. Bibby had always been secretly glad to be an only child with no one to pull against him. But now he had a brother beyond sibling rivalry, a mentor, a friend. And, Bibby told himself in resonant sermon style, the confidence of his compliments.

Singing lessons took place in the music room. It was a big, square classroom with the space between blackboard and desks defined by an ornate grand piano, a bequest from a Bulgarian basso. Bibby felt small standing in the bow of that great black, claw-footed piano and struck by the light from three floor-to-ceiling windows. The choirmaster at the keyboard seemed too far away. Bibby liked better the practice sessions, sitting beside his maestro on the bench at the yellow-keyed upright in Gregory's bedroom-office. This was a wallpapered barn of a room, with bays and alcoves and shelves like a shoe store's, filled with books and boxes of sheet music. There was a gate-chambered wine rack in one corner and French art gallery posters on the walls. The sleeping part was in a curtained recess up a step. When the curtain was pulled back, Bibby could see the heavy knob of a brass bedpost and a section of patchwork quilt.

He spent a lot of time in this room. Brother Gregory took pains with him. They would rehearse a rough phrase until it became smooth, head tone to chest tone without a break, the beat deferred to a surge of expression. Gregory taught Bibby to carry a tone on a current of breath. Bibby practiced until he could float a soft, soft note that would be heard in the furthermost corner of the sacristy. He learned to sing in several

TABLE 47   59

Slavic languages as well as Greek and even a little Arabic. In time he was excused from most public devotions: he came to agree with the choirmaster that his plugging away was both work and prayer and that his performances rose to the greater glory of the Academy.

In the choir loft, Bibby stood tall and central with his feet flat on the broad floorboards. The choristers wore street clothes since nobody could see them from down below. The lead soprano, who stood beside Bibby, was a married towns-woman who wore big hats and smelled from strong de-odorant. It was a good bunch, students and townspeople, and Bibby thought he fitted in well. Brother Gregory conducted in his black cassock—over a wool sweater winters, a short-sleeved T-shirt summers, when the fan over their heads com-peted with the music. Summers, when the maestro raised his arms to lead them, the singers saw a widening arc of sweat down the side of his cassock. The loft was small. The mae-stro's back was squashed against the railing. He led with his eyes closed—because he couldn't stand the crush, he said when Bibby asked him. Only on solemn occasions, when the priests and deacons led a procession around the church and into the sanctuary, or at rare outside concerts, did Bibby wear his robe, with Brother Gregory going before him in raven splendor.

Lunch over, Bibby was sitting cross-legged on top of the table he'd just brushed clean. He might have been sewing a button. He might have been breathing yoga—in one nostril, count twenty; out the other, count thirty. He was actually sky-gazing, guessing at the weather because he'd been inside all day. Inside the building. Inside his head. He didn't know if it was rain, shine, hot or cold. Fog was in his head.

"Bosculus!" The young man had to call him twice. "Come to, Bosculus! Choirmaster wants you."

Bibby executed, deadpan, a somersault off the table and onto the floor, facing out.

"In his office," the new boy called after him.

The door was open. Bibby knocked on the wall and entered. Brother Gregory was at his desk with ledgers. The music master doubling in bookkeeping; it amused him and made him even less dispensable. Without looking up, he pointed to the armchair. There was a bowl of peaches and cherries on the little table beside it. Bibby took a hard-backed chair instead since there was only one deep one. He saw on the dresser that served as a sideboard a well-into half gallon of California Red. And a well-into goblet by Gregory's right arm. Bibby liked that: the choirmaster believed that wine oiled the voice box, one of his convenient theories.

"Help yourself," the Brother said into his books.

Bibby took a peach and ate it, waiting. It was a wait he didn't mind. It was a room he was happy in.

"So," the choirmaster said at last. "I thought you could use a little more work on the A minor. I'll steal an hour for you."

He took a long look at Bibby and Bibby wondered if Gregory saw the same odd-looking character that assessed Bibby from the small bathroom mirror each morning as he reluctantly shaved. Bibby was long—over six feet—rounded in the middle and thinned out at both ends: narrow face, narrow feet. He had nice hands—big, bony and long-fingered—but he often found them hanging stupidly at his sides. His nose was pointed as if he were sniffing for something and his eyes, fishwater blue, swam disconcertingly close to the surface. He liked the surprised arch of his eyebrows but suspected that it was only a mirror expression, seen by nobody else. On the other hand, his dull skin and the general downward flow of his features were on view at all times. He hoped that it was at least a face of contradictions.

The choirmaster put aside the papers and emptied his wineglass with a deep, satisfied swallow. Not his first glass of

TABLE 47 61

the day: Bibby noted Gregory's red face, the damp handker-chief crumpled on his desk. It was a hot day. Hot up there under the roof. Gregory was wearing a sheer checked shirt with short sleeves rolled shorter. His hair stood up in damp iron spikes.

He pushed himself up from the desk and let out a sigh of relief.

He walked, heavy on his small feet, to the piano and sat on the edge of the bench. He looked at his hands as he laid them on the keys. Bibby looked where he looked, at the sharp knuckles, the deep middle-aged ridges of the joints, the high veins. "The A minor, was it?" the choirmaster said.

Bibby, usually immune to heat, was feeling it. He kept his arms in tight as he set his music sheets on the piano stand and waited at a considerate distance while the choirmaster adjusted himself on the bench. Bibby took a stance at the maestro's right and, counting silently, came in on time and on pitch though not at full voice because it was very hot.

"Did you vocalize today?"

Bibby sang an affirmative, not breaking his line. His mouth was wide to pull air up from his chest. But the maestro broke the line. Bibby saw that his hands were shaking:

"Are you all right?"

The choirmaster gave up trying to play. "Rough day," he said. "The heat no help."

He'd been called in to settle a problem with the head cook. Drinking on the job and not the first time. "I hated to see the poor guy fired. He's a gentle fellow who can't face his problems. I talked them into one more chance. It won't work, of course." He crashed a no-key chord. "But, you see, it always falls to me. I hate problems that won't be solved."

"I'm sorry."

"Yes, well. I'll get over it. It's my punishment for spurning the priesthood. I get all the dirty work."

Bibby, very diffidently, touched his shoulder. Gregory patted Bibby's hand to thank him. "Except the choir," Gregory said. "That's clean."

He started to play. "Back to the beginning," he said, "and sing out. Sustain the rhythm."

They worked. Floating in the heat. Gregory mopped his face and neck. Bibby stood wilting, tongue thick, head heavy. He sang. Sweated more. Gregory got up to refill his wineglass and offered a glass to Bibby.

"You have a class this afternoon, Bernard. Botany, is it? Do you think they could manage to dissect a daisy without your presence?"

Bibby hesitated.

"Stay and give comfort to a troubled old man."

Bibby didn't like to miss classes. He still had an Incomplete in Old Testament, lacking a paper on Abraham and Isaac. He had mixed feelings about being known as Brother Gregory's boy, though pride was probably topmost. Pride and gratitude.

Gregory sat in the armchair. Bibby poured himself a little wine and stood by the sideboard, enjoying it. He liked their silences. It was better than the unending chess games played in the common room. Brother Gregory was better than a hundred friends his own age. Bibby would do anything for him. In any case, he missed very few classes. He tried not to be overly proud of himself for not abusing the privilege. In this case, it was already late and too hot to run. Besides, Gregory had asked him. Bibby took a long swallow of wine. Two flies had got through the window screen. He watched them explore a drop of wine making a slow trip down the shoulder of the jug.

"Did you know I was a member of the U.S. Army, World War II?"

The choirmaster was deep in his armchair. Bibby didn't.

"Did you never get a look at my old army wound?"

Bibby hadn't.

TABLE 47   63

Brother Gregory pulled himself to the edge of the chair. The unchecked sweat drops might have been tears streaming down his cheeks.

"A good thing," he said, "that I was not meant to marry a fainting maiden. I want you to take a look at this."

He was already undoing his belt buckle. He got on his feet and unzipped his pants, letting them drop. He was wearing boxer shorts with a faded blue stripe. He slipped his hand into the front.

Bibby watched from beside the sideboard. He was charmed. His head was unclear. The choirmaster drew himself out with an air of locker room fellowship. His penis was flushed and standing high. Blaring, flaring like a trumpet. Bibby was a person who never looked down when he was at a urinal in a public toilet. Often he pretended he needed to use a stall. He could not avoid looking at Brother Gregory, though, who was stepping out of his pants and slipping off his underpants, moving to face Bibby with his muscular legs apart and a fire-breathing beast between them. Bibby, staring, felt a surge of heat barreling in on him from inside the heat of the day. Heat was flowing inside him. Gregory was aimed like a cannonhead over ready red cannonballs.

"Look here," the choirmaster ordered. "Take a squat over here."

He held the cannonhead apart with one hand as he displayed his scrotum. He pulled the skin between two fingers. "See this here? Can you beat a sliver of steel finding its way in here?"

Bibby got down on one knee and in close enough to see a jagged threadline, a scratch of red ink over a ridge of white not an inch long.

"Normally," the choirmaster said . . . He had to stop to catch his breath. "Normally, you'd never notice it. You need a good light and a stretch. But it's a true scar and a deep one."

Bibby, too, was having trouble breathing. Before he could pull away, Brother Gregory said, "Feel it." He pushed himself toward Bibby's face. Bibby caught a scent that brought a rush to his groin, licks of fire.

"Come on," Brother Gregory said. "Take a feel of it. It won't bite you."

Bibby was lost as the choirmaster caught his hand and took it to him. Hand on phallus, Bibby was on fire, a fire himself, full of longing. His genitals swelled with desire, his head swam. Pressure from the choirmaster's hand sent Bibby on both knees with the choirmaster digging into his shoulders.

"Take it in your mouth."

Gregory held him back of the head and pushed. Bibby pressed his lips tight and then could not resist anymore. The flaming head, a breast, a nipple, was coming to him and his mouth went slack. But suddenly, as the penis entered between his lips, Bibby felt a shock of repulsion. Hands on Gregory's thighs, he pushed himself away, broke the hold on his neck, and got to his feet. He was doused cold, damp as clay and empty. Brother Gregory turned away and made for his bathroom, shutting the door hard.

Bibby stood still, and was still standing when Brother Gregory returned to the room. The choirmaster was pale and streaked from his sweat. He was dressed again but he looked like a ruin. He put his arms around Bibby and gently kissed him on the lips.

"I am sorry," he said. "Don't hate me for this," he said. "You know, I do love you."

This was the first time anybody had said *I love you* to Bibby Bosculus.

Bibby, regaining thought, realized his pants were wet. It was the first time he had ejaculated in company.

"This is not ugly," the choirmaster said. "This is not bad. Don't be afraid of it."

TABLE 47 65

Bibby turned up his hands. He would have liked to embrace his friend. He wanted to return the love.

"I can't," he said.

Brother Gregory looked around the room as if he hadn't been there for a long time. His spring came back as he went to splash more water on his face, picked up a hairbrush, brushed his hair back and down. Bibby saw the flies again, one lighting on the wall, the other or maybe the same one, buzzing around the mirror. Bibby turned away from the mirror. His crotch was wet and sticky. He was afraid to look down to see if it showed.

"Question yourself, Bernard," the choirmaster said. "It doesn't have to be now. Or ever. It's up to you."

He stopped in front of Bibby and his face started to fall apart again. "Don't let this hurt you," he pleaded. "This is not a sin, Bibby." His first *Bibby* caught like a fishhook on the boy's awareness. "It's another way of showing love. You can do it with women, too." He poured some more wine and held the glass out.

"Take the music with you," the choirmaster said when Bibby had drunk and was standing by the door. "Come back after lunch tomorrow and we'll give it some more practice, okay?" He laughed as Bibby went down the hall. "Cool it, boy," he called in a low voice that carried. "You're overreacting. Still friends. Everything's okay. Believe me."

Bibby turned into the first bathroom. Big old bathroom with octagon floor tiles and a tub on claws and a pull-chain toilet with a wooden seat. It was a bathroom shared by lesser faculty who didn't have their own. Bibby locked the door and lifted the toilet seat to take a confused piss that wouldn't start till he ran the water faucet. He cleaned himself with paper towels and water and then he took off his damp pants and his soaking wet jockey shorts and wiped the pants and tried to flush the shorts down the toilet, waiting and flushing again to make sure they went down. Then he washed himself very thoroughly—hands, face, between the legs, hot water and soap, hot-water rinse, and cold. Meeting his face in the medicine-chest mirror, he thought he saw holes where his eyes should have been. There was a turkish towel on the rack and he dried himself as if he were dabbing a wound. He patted neck and throat to comfort himself and flushed the toilet again to make sure it wasn't stuffed. He spread the towel on the rack, thinking what nice, thick towels the faculty got, thinking student towels were thinner, thinking it was cooler in a room with only one small, frosted window, thinking he'd been at the Academy quite a long time—could it be four years?

Downstairs and across the porch and out in the day, down the path and under the trees. Nobody there. No students. No fathers. Only the trees heavy with heat, and burnt brown grass like a long, never-ending mustache along the edge of the walk. Bibby went straight to the dormitory, straight to his room and straight to his cot, where he toppled himself flat out.

He lay with his head on the limp pillow. He lay in the hammock of his breath and when the room lost its light, nothing changed for him. Hall sounds crept across the ceiling. Somebody looked in to say it was time for vespers, time for supper. Late at night a wind came up and rushed through the high windows and rattled along the hall. Light trickled in under his door so that Bibby, turning his head, saw the thin square of carpet lift up and roll down in the wind. Out of his own high window all he saw was black sky.

He began to feel the weight of the air around him. The window was a slot. The pane was not raised high enough. The floor and ceiling pulled together and the walls were a ring of enemies. Bibby rolled out of bed and stood on his

TABLE 47 67

chair to raise the window on its metal arm. It was as high as it would go, so Bibby got down and opened the door. The corridor itself, lined with shut doors, was cramped and airless. At the end a sickly yellow bulb showed over the staircase. Bibby ran down the hall and up the stairs. The first floor was dark and the outside door was locked with an emergency alarm. So he ran up another flight. There was no window on the landing and he ran up again, around and around the narrow banister. On the top floor he found a window that was big enough and wide open. It was a casement window he could lean through with his head on his arms. He stood gratefully breathing. His heart calmed down. He saw the big night outside with many stars in the sky. He stayed there until amber streaks began to replace the stars and new morning air rose from the ground. Then he thought he might get a little sleep. He didn't want to meet any early risers in the hall.

Sometime that morning, or maybe early in the afternoon, Bibby went to tell the bishop that he had decided to leave the Academy.

Six months later the Old Testament instructor received a mailed copy of a ten-page, single-spaced paper dealing with the aborted sacrifice of Isaac by his father Abraham as precursor of the accomplished sacrifice of Jesus in the New Testament. It was an excellent paper, Bibby knew, full of primary and secondary references carefully documented. Still, he felt lucky (and relieved) when it came back with an A to his parents' house where he was staying till he could find a job.

Father Joe turns his attention to the dance floor. Down front has been cleared and music beckons. It's an old fifties dance tune that Joe is willing to listen to. None of us, though, is willing to let him.

"What was the reaction?" Yuri insists. "How was his leaving explained?"

Joe is hardly interested. Dropouts were not uncommon, he reminds us. "Word got around," he says, "that Bibby left after a bout with some piece of doctrine he couldn't swallow."

Oberon has been thinking. "It seems to me," he says thoughtfully, "that leaving the Academy, let alone leaving the Church, was something of an overreaction."

"Yeah," Flossie says. "Everybody gets hustled."

"But not by your best friend." This is Geraldine, indignant.

Paul knows Bibby from another time and another place. He's not brimming over with compassion. "I guess he was ready to leave anyway," says Paul. "Like a ball, rolling down an alley, that gets a bump and goes in another direction."

What I want to know is what happened to the choirmaster.

Joe does me the favor of telling. The maestro stayed on a few years, he says. "There were other tenors and baritones. No bassos that I recall, but a baritone for sure. Eventually he left to take another job, did Gregory. I heard he went with a big city church. Organist, in addition to choirmaster. I heard he favored the city."

I take a look at Bibby Bosculus, up on the platform of this palace of a room. Only the top of his head shows from inside a circle of admirers. For a moment I catch sight of his face with his new dashing smile and unwonted color. Paul, still competing, sees only the success. But to me it looks as if joy were forcing itself on him. Bibby has put on weight, but he carries it with the buoyancy of a high-riding steamship, smokestacks tooting to remind him that he's made it in New York City.

"When I caught up with Bibby," Joe's saying, "it was years later. He told me the story as if it had happened to somebody else."

"That's right! That's right!" Yuri's round eyes are lit with

TABLE 47   69

the triumph of discovery. "Bibby has no scars. It is you idealists . . ." and he points elaborately to Father Joe, "who get hurt. You fall from such great heights."

This stops Joe. For half a minute he seems at a loss. But then his dimple deepens and the smile almost breaks through. "Yuri, you want to put me in your character zoo." Joe won't have it. He gets up and rolls his eyes at Flossie, takes her by the hand and leads her to the dance floor. They're playing an old song:

> I'll get by
> As long as I
>   Have you.
> Tho there be rain
> And darkness too
> I'll not complain,
> I'll see it through . . .

Paul puts his hand on my knee and gives me a little squeeze that still brings pleasure to my heart.

PART
TWO

"*In vino veritas*," Yuri declares, not for the first time, as he trickles the last of the champagne into his wineglass. "I, too, have done my share of imbibing with old Bosculus. *Young* Bosculus, as he was in those days. Companion at arms through many a grim night of warding off confrontations with a pile of student papers."

"You taught with Bernie?" Oberon Morley sizes him up anew.

"Yes, indeed. We were colleagues, bringing light to benighted youth. It was a community college, not far from Cleveland. Not long ago, but still another world. That's where I met Bibby. That's where Bibby met his first wife."

Paul and I know it all. At least we think we do.

Flossie and Joe return from their dance hand in hand, swinging their arms together, looking pleased with themselves. Nice. Flossie bends to kiss Oberon's cheek before she smooths her skirt and sits. She's already picked up the conversation. "Oh, yeah. Bernie's first wife. I bet she was fat, Jewish, and intellectual."

"None of them," I say. "She was skinny, Polish, and never read a book."

"Karen," Father Joe tells Flossie with a reproachful look at me, "was very pretty and as smart as she needed to be."

Yuri concurs. "Spirited," he says with spirit. "She was an experimental version of his second wife. Only in Karen's case, Bibby didn't fall. He was tripped."

I'm beginning to like Yuri a lot. He is a collector: as long as people play their part well, Yuri loves them—villain or hero, it makes no difference. What he likes is authenticity and color. He likes bit players as much as leads. Karen he sees as a wonder of nature, a salmon going upstream, hitting against rocks, getting torn, but forcing ahead with no other thought till she reaches still waters, ragged but triumphant. For this he loves her. Okay. Yuri is a poet and that's his vision.

"In order to appreciate Karen," he is telling the rest of us, "you have to know what Bibby was like when I met him at

Myra Tate Community College. I grant that I myself was not the most practical of young men, but compared to Bosculus I was a veritable *homme du monde.*

"*Homme du monde.* Oh, boy!" Geraldine flaps her eyelids at Flossie.

"Bibby Bosculus even then looked like a prepubescent boy blown up to man size. With a mentality to match. He was incapable of putting his interests above anybody else's."

"Only because he couldn't figure out what his interests were," Paul says.

Yuri doesn't laugh. "No," he says. "It was simply that Bosculus was built without fortifications."

Yuri stands up, takes off his tuxedo jacket and arranges it carefully on the shoulders of his chairback. His white shirt has turned ecru with age but he doesn't care. He unsnaps his bow tie with a short, fat man's dignity and sits down again. He rubs his fingers across the bristles of his mustache and seems satisfied with the consistency. Clasping his hands behind his head, producing an expanse of chest and belly over his sunken cummerbund, he warms to his story:

"The campus was a polyform complex of steel and reflecting glass. A true inferiority complex, now that I think of it. The main building boasted a curved, swooping roof that glared in sunlight and collected rain. The mirrored façade reflected the absolutely nothing interesting for miles around. The inside was so open and airy that you couldn't tell if you were in or out. One freeform building was so like the next that you couldn't tell whether you were in science or humanities.

"The outside trees grew in pots just like the inside trees.

"Instead of gardens or groves, there were parking lots.

"This was where Bosculus caught up with history. This was his first encounter with contemporary American life. Everything had a number. Everyone wore an identification badge. People looked, not into your eyes, but somewhere between

TABLE 47   75

your shoulder and your belly button, where the badge revealed your name and face at the same time. No guesswork was necessary. This was Myra Tate Community College. I never found any community there. I don't think Bosculus did, either. He arrived shortly after I did and left long before."

Yuri frowns, remembering. He takes a sip of Geraldine's champagne.

"Bibby had been a teacher in a private school for girls. He had also been to Europe. He smoked a pipe. He kept losing his place. He had read everything but he still judged books by their covers. He had been everywhere but he still thought that Paris was Monet's Water Lilies and Rome the Trevi Fountain."

Yuri leans back in his chair and sets his eyes on a distant picture.

"Our friend," he continues, "had at that time the self-confidence of a sack of flour. He knew he could get where he wanted to go because he was willing to put his back into it and to plunge his arm in up to the shoulder. He was used to being alone so life didn't scare him. But he wanted to get on with it. He wanted to join the world.

"So he came to Tate Community. A characteristic choice."

❦

Bosculus walked on broad cement toward the English Department. He followed squat signs that identified his surroundings: PARKING LOT, WALKING PATH. They were a pleasant notion, like flower names in a public garden. On this fair day he felt handsome in his gray tweed jacket with black leather elbow patches. From England. In his hip pocket was a fine pipe he intended to smoke during the interview. Of

course he would ask permission first—deep voice—but he was
pretty sure the department chairman wouldn't mind. Not
when he saw what Bosculus had in the zipper case under his
arm. The résumé. Two learned papers he had written for
publication in two highly prestigious Eastern Church journals. Two letters from recognized scholars in the field of
Slavonic literature and language. With these credentials—the
degrees, the travels, the solidity of his appearance and his
worldly manner—the chairman could hardly help but see
Bosculus as a feather in the cap of this young institution.

He approached what looked like the main door but turned
out to be part of the wall. The doors were what he thought
were tubular windows, and when he finally connected with
them they revolved him into a corporate corridor made of
glass and gravel and full of students who looked the very opposite of seminarians—bland of face and brightly dressed. A
bell rang and the students disappeared. Alone, Bosculus met
his dire reflection in the black marbleized floor. The gray
gravel walls were punctuated with red doors like warning signals. Recessed lights stared down at him from the pock-
marked ceiling. He clutched his zippered case.

Because he was, as usual, very early, he stopped to read the
bulletin board by the stairway. The Young Hibernians were
having a get-together dance. Hillel was having a bagel
brunch. The Tate Gays were having a rally. The Fat People's
Club was starting a calisthenics class. There were vacation
study programs, rooms for rent, manuscript typing and career
counseling services. A representative from Revlon was coming
to reveal makeup secrets to the members of the Women's
Student Association. A soph hop was coming up on Hallow-
een. Bosculus felt good again. It was a real college after all.
He cheerfully found his way to the red door that said:

English Department
Dr. V. Chamberlain, Chairman

TABLE 47 77

Bosculus remembered to smile at the blank-faced, brightly dressed young receptionist and, as his own career counselor had counseled, made a mental note of her name. He took the seat she pointed to and sat back to assess the room he was in.

On the magazine rack were *Newsweek,* the Summer Reading supplement from a June issue of the Sunday Chicago *Tribune. Ford Times.* Some copies of the newsletter of the Modern Language Association. Recent issues of *The Tater,* the Tate Community student weekly. *Intellectual Digest. National Geographic.*

The place was neat and new-looking. A love seat, two chairs, two tables and two lamps were arranged with Scandinavian simplicity. The items on the walls were colorfully framed and hung straight and equidistant around the room. Van Gogh's sunflowers. The State University Journalism Conference award to *The Tater,* for achieving fourth place in its category. A hand-printed and illustrated quotation from Kahlil Gibran. A seascape. A citation to Dr. Chamberlain for delivering a speech before a Regional Conference of the National Secretaries' Association. A plaque commemorating Dr. Chamberlain's participation in a two-day seminar on Business English during a national sales meeting of the Singer Sewing Machine Company in Elmira, New York. A signed letter from Rod McKuen, who had given a reading in Tate Community's Frumpkin Auditorium.

Bosculus was impressed. He felt he was the right kind of person for this college: clean-cut, unpretentious, pleasant, bright. He reminded himself to face Dr. Chamberlain in an upbeat mode. Strike the Dostoyevsky style he had been considering as an alternative. Tate Community was clearly an oasis in a desert of heavy industry. His superiority would speak for itself.

Lord Chesterfield slipped into the waiting room and sat on the arm of Bosculus' chair. He leaned over and whispered into the young man's ear:

Wear your learning, like your watch, in a private pocket: and do not pull it out and strike it, merely to show that you have one.

The receptionist, ignoring the shrewd earl in wig and weskit, told Bosculus he could go in now. Lord Chesterfield gave him a parting clap on the shoulder. *"Manners must adorn knowledge,"* he advised, *"and smooth its way through the world."* Bosculus straightened up and entered the chairman's office.

A woman was sitting on the edge of the desk. High-heeled shoes and a polyester pants suit bunched at the bosom. Made-up face and blond hair forcefully waved. She introduced herself and waved him into a molded chair. Her desk like herself was neat and businesslike. As she looked through his papers, Bosculus looked at her bookcase: Bartlett's "Familiar Quotations," The Concise Oxford Dictionary, Roget's Pocket Thesaurus, Ari Kiev's *A Strategy for Success, The Elements of Style, The Art of Plain Talk, The Five-Hundred-Word Essay, The Writer's Legal Handbook, The Seventeen Guide to You and Other People.* Dr. Chamberlain kept reading. Bosculus pulled his chair closer to her desk. He loved her perfume. He decided not to smoke after all.

Dr. Chamberlain set the papers down and looked hard into Bosculus' eyes. "I have an idea," she said after scrutiny, "that our students would derive great benefit from contact with a real scholar like you."

"Yes. Well."

"Our students don't come from cultured homes on the average. Some of them never see a book in the house. We try to compensate for that. While it's vital that they should know how to communicate effectively both in speech and writing, we also feel it's important for them to learn about the great authors."

TABLE 47 79

Dr. Chamberlain continued to hold his eyes while voicing ideas that echoed his own. Literature as the road to a richer life as well as a better job. She spoke to him as a fellow educator.

"The girls here," she went on in a confidential tone, "tend to be brighter than the boys. That's because the parents of the bright boys like to send their sons to the glamour schools." Her very blue eyes sought his understanding. "State College and Poly Tech, you know. Top competition. Gold-plated diplomas." She rolled those eyes. "For the girls, it's a different story. Only the bright ones get to college at all. And they come here, near home, where it doesn't cost much. So we get smart girls and dopey boys. But you'll like it. They're very nice kids."

Bosculus sent his mind off to picture his future students, sons and daughters of the muscle of America. Inland innocents grateful for the knowledge he would bring to them, looking to him for salvation from banality and ignorance.

"I would actually, uh, prefer, ah, to teach the, uh, less privileged."

Dr. Chamberlain raised a pudgy hand with long, lacquered fingernails. Such was their understanding, she seemed to imply, that he need say no more. She stood up and snapped into action. She pulled a contract out of a drawer. The receptionist ran in with two paperback textbooks—orange-covered *Getting Your Meaning Across* by Pinetto and Enrick of Hawaii University and brown-and-black-covered *Effective Writing* by Peter Packer Swick, Ph.D. Bosculus, since the term had already begun, would start teaching on Monday. The hourly fee sounded handsome. He was away in a richer world while Dr. Chamberlain explained parking stickers, office keys, personnel forms and ID badge. Finally, she invited him to a faculty meeting that night.

Bosculus left in a haze of glory, smelling of Dr. Chamberlain's perfume. He could tell she really liked him. He spent the rest of the day bumping around the campus, looking for keys and badges and parking stickers.

"So you're a whiz at literature." This was Mr. Brindisi, the Freshman English coordinator. Friendly admiration was written across his blunt, hearty face. Bosculus was embarrassed at having so much hair, an indirect insult to Mr. Brindisi's baldness. He didn't know whether or not to admit he was a literary whiz.

"I believe that literature is the heart of the universe," is what Bosculus said but not what Mr. Brindisi heard.

"We give them as much input as they can handle," was the coordinator's reply.

Bosculus felt maybe he had pushed too hard.

"They get their Hemingway and Fitzgerald and their Kirk Vonnegut, too," Mr. Brindisi said defensively. "But first-year English, it's imperative, the chairman feels, to get them to be able to write complete sentences and then paragraphs. The chairman feels that communication is power. Once they have their communication skills, we can give them literature."

Mr. Brindisi struck a fisted hand into an open palm. "Plus," he baldly warned Bosculus, "we can't hit these kids too hard in the first year. They're not used to the college regiment."

He flung his arm around Bosculus. "I'm sure," he reassured the newcomer, "it will be very enriching for them to have you slip in your literary references from time to time. A lot of our teachers do that."

The departmental faculty meeting took place in a minitheater classroom with tiers of empty deskchairs weeping over the people assembled in the pit. Of the sixteen strangers, Bosculus wondered which one taught Chaucer? Who Shakespeare? Who the Enlightenment? On the extended arms of

TABLE 47   81

three first-row desks were a thermos jug of coffee, a pitcher of lemonade and a plate of Nabisco sandwich cookies. There were napkins, stirrers and Styrofoam cups and the teachers were helping themselves. Bosculus intercepted drifts of their talk. The Expos were losing three straight in St. Louis. The contract committee wanted to be paid for faculty meetings. A young teacher named Miss Boyle had created a scandal by failing to return from summer vacation and, worse, failing to notify the chairman of her whereabouts. A history teacher named Mr. Hart had just caused another scandal by suddenly deserting his wife and five children. A bearded foreigner by the name of Yuri Marchuk had been hired in a hurry to replace Miss Boyle and now he was to be shifted to the history department to take Mr. Hart's classes. One of the trustees was campaigning to make remedial reading a required course for students under an eighth-grade reading level.

"Nothing doing," Mr. Brindisi told the group during the open question period after the business meeting. "We're in a competitive market and Tate Community has to be very flexible. Our students don't want required courses. They want degrees and that's what they'll get—*if* they pass. On the other hand, no tickee, no shirtee. No pass, no graduate. *That's* where we get 'em on reading."

At the end of the meeting, the coordinator remembered to introduce the new adjunct, Mr. Bosculus.

Before his first class began, he tested his smile in the heart-shaped mirror that had been left on the back of his office door by his predecessor. Catherine Boyle, it said on the three-by-five card which he carefully untaped from the front of the door. Smiling into the mirror, he imagined he had Catherine Boyle caught between his teeth. He pictured her in the little below-ground office with cinder-block walls, steel desk, two molded chairs and a bare bookshelf. He himself enjoyed the ascetic decor, even to the disc of white ceiling light that showered on him as he tried out smiles in the red-framed mirror.

The tooth-trapping smile was one of many. There was a lip-biting smile that went with drooping eyelids to produce a languid, assessing, Continental expression that added years to his experience and letters to his degree. He tried a little, tight one, as if the smiler knew more than he could tell. It looked as if he were straining soup; discard. Then he practiced the smile for taking a bow after having sung the "Salut Demeure" with the high C at pianissimo streaming out to forte. This was a smile that let all his air out and told the world he had given his best. It was a fair smile, but no better than the next, the master-of-ceremonies, Jack Horner smile that announced he'd captured the plum and deserved no less. He worked for a while on a one-sided, speculatively seductive smile, but thought he'd better save that one for opportunities that might arise outside the classroom. Then he ran off some variations on the closed-mouth teacherly smile: congratulatory for the student who achieved penetration of thought and clarity of expression; sympathetic for a good try but failure to catch the proper nuance; pleased for general progress. Finally Bosculus produced the winning smile. It was forthright in its show of eight upper teeth, no fillings, no gum. It was egalitarian, the same length and angle on both sides. It was full-lipped, ingenuous and friendly. It suggested confidence, even superiority, yet was free of contempt or arrogance. It was a smile that resonated in his eyes and told his students that he liked them a lot but wasn't going to take any nonsense.

Bosculus examined this winning smile frontally and from the sides. He tried it with tilted head but decided to keep it straight. He walked around his office with it—eight feet to the far wall and back to the mirror. Then he put out the light, locked the door and wore his winning smile across the cam-

TABLE 47 83

pus to Room S24, which was a trailer behind the humanities building. He entered his classroom promptly at two-fifteen, wearing his gray tweed jacket and a colorful tie and smiling at the crescent of expectant faces. He stood behind his desk, instinctively observing the law of safe distance.

For a rough minute, as if the smile had set, he couldn't open his mouth.

So he ceremoniously set down his zipper case, which was swollen with proof of his preparedness. In addition to precise lesson plans, there was a folder already fat with clippings to illustrate incorrect and/or inefficient use of English. Bosculus was ready to expose the worst and combat it, to demonstrate the best and promote it. Still smiling, but mobile now, he opened the attendance book and drew out the class cards. Of eighteen students in Section B303 of English I (Effective Communication), two had already transferred out.

"Miss Boyle was a pushover," somebody explained. "When we found out she wasn't going to be here, some of the guys pulled out."

"But we're taking our chances with you," somebody else said. Bosculus rekindled his smile and set down the class cards.

"First things first," he said. He wrote his name on the green blackboard. He pronounced it in resonant, inspiring tones. "Mister Bosculus," he said, facing the sixteen students in a semicircle of deskchairs that was thick in the middle and thinned out at the ends. Sixteen faces were turned up to him with sixteen expressions of suspended judgment.

He shut his eyes and wrenched out the necessary words. "I'm going to expect you to work um, ah, er—*hard*." There was a crackle of appreciative laughter. "Writing is ah, uh *power*," he continued. "This will be p-p-primarily a course in writing, as I think you know." They were watching him closely, drawn by his priestly cadence. "I am g-g-going," he said, "to make you um, ah, uh p-powerful."

He noticed a pretty girl in the middle of the crescent. He
decided to call the roll.

Benedict
Busch
Dowell
Fiorello

. . .

Kassell
Kowalski
Kubelik
Kuhn

. . .

Rumako

Rumako. Her name was Karen. A freshman and very fresh,
in a flower print like a Crivelli. Bosculus noted the purity of
brow, the spiritual pallor and the spare grace in her upright
sitting posture. She was a small person who sat tall and grave
in the middle of the front row.

"Present," she said in grave response to his searching
Rumako. That's what she was, a present.

"Did I get that right? Is it Rum-*ay*-ko? Or *Rum*-a-ko?"

"Whatever you prefer."

No ragtag blue jeans for this young woman. Her small, precise flowers were neatly matched to a solid-color skirt. Her
poignant smile showed one front tooth slightly chipped and
slightly overlapping the other.

"Not as *I* prefer." Bosculus was a feminist. "It's *your*
name."

"Room-*ay*-ko," she said, gravely. Bosculus sensed deep feeling behind the modest smile.

Wadsworth
Zigabarra

On the whole, the class went well. Appraising it afterward,
Bosculus thought the students were more afraid of him than

TABLE 47 85

he was of them. One, with a beard and a plaid flannel shirt, sat low on his spine in what seemed to be a belligerent slouch. Another, with straight-parted hair and small, even features, looked like his mother's good boy. Of course, this was not Harvard: only two students were black. The boy, in a clean T-shirt, had a strong-boned, alert face. The girl was heavy and earnest-looking, with hammy shoulders and a face that kept itself cheerful. There were no discernible stars. However, Bosculus reminded himself, first impressions—his, at least—were always wrong. Busch, with his blond Buster Brown haircut, could be a sincere plodder. Fiorello, behind his wise-guy smirk, might be sensitive. Kubelik, a girl with long dark hair and irritable eyes, might not be so tart as she seemed. The other girls looked to be subdued—even Karen Rumako, who was staring up at him as if he was her hope for a better life through better English.

Bosculus sat at his desk. "In England," he read from one of his newspaper clippings, "they still sell shoes in a color called *niggerbrown*. John Bowen, bachelor, still is announced to be marrying Susan Ames, spinster. Two of these words are unacceptable in America today."

Bosculus expected to shock them into seeing and feeling the impact of the words they used. At the same time, he meant to let them know that they were not dealing with a fuddy-duddy.

Yet, the class was not galvanized. They were sitting back in their deskchairs, paying polite attention.

"Which two?"

A snub-nosed redhead named Gorman turned his head elaborately to stare at Dowell, the black boy.

" '*Nigger*,' " said Gorman.

Bosculus nodded. "Yes, that's one. And the other?"

He felt he had caught their interest.

"Maybe one of the women would venture a guess?"

The girls as one lowered their eyes. Karen Rumako was the first to look up.

" 'Bachelor' or 'spinster'?"

"Just one of them," Bosculus said. " 'Bachelor' is not, so far as I know, an unacceptable word in this country. However, is 'spinster' acceptable?"

"Nobody says that word," came from Mr. Kowalski at one end of the crescent.

"You mean like 'old maid'?" This was Busch, the Buster Brown.

"Yes," said Bosculus. " 'Old maid' is a synonym." He wrote "synonym" on the blackboard. "I believe that 'old maid,' too, would be an unacceptable, uh, phrase, ah, uh, term."

One girl saw light.

"Because like male shawvinism?" This was Ms. Kubelik, with righteousness burning. "You should say 'single woman.' 'Old maid' casts aspersions."

Bosculus was overjoyed.

"Right! Right! And 'spinster' has the same connotation."

He wrote "connotation" on the blackboard. Then he came on, with a rakish flicker of a smile: "There are also some words in reputable use here in America that would be socially unacceptable in England. Can anyone here think of one?"

"Shit," said Gorman.

It was hard to tell whether this was an answer or a comment.

"Bitch," Kowalski said casually. He was the older-looking one with the beard and the curvature.

One of the girls, encouraged, said, "Prick." Then she added primly: "In England it means to get stuck with a needle."

"Fuck," said Dowell. He gazed vindictively at Gorman. Gorman clenched his fist.

TABLE 47 87

Bosculus was delighted at his success in achieving class participation.

"Everybody's right!" he announced.

But his conscience stabbed him and he added, "Partially right." He painstakingly explained the differences between vulgar and slang usage and, in days of changing values, the variations of acceptability. "The legitimate stage," he said, "is more permissive than, say, commercial television. The college classroom is more permissive than, perhaps, a senior citizens' meeting . . ."

He paused for laughter but only Dowell, the smart one, and Kowalski, the sophisticate, seemed to understand the uses of irony. One chuckled and the other snickered.

"The acceptability," Bosculus plowed on, "of such vulgarisms as 'fuck' in both verb and noun form, meaning not only 'to copulate with' but 'to mess up,' or even, simply 'very little,' as in the phrase 'I don't give a fuck,' is more attributable to the times than to geography. Fifty years ago there was no question of acceptability in either country. Use of that word labeled a person as antisocial or of the lowest class. The term that I was considering as distinct in acceptability in the two countries is the adjective 'bloody.' In England, it is still not conventionally acceptable."

"What a bloody bore!" Kowalski interjected.

"Exactly right," Bosculus cried. The sunken Kowalski, he thought, would be a leader. The boy really caught on. Kowalski returned the teacher's approving nod with a circular wave of his index finger. Bosculus, riding on a surge of pleasure, assigned a three-paragraph essay.

The class howled.

Bosculus, undismayed, reflected that he already had them looking at words with new eyes. It would be a fine class, after all. Kowalski was a thinker. The tart-faced girl, Kubelik, would be worth his efforts to draw her out. Busch was diligent. Wadsworth *was* earnest, as evidenced by her willingness to attend remedial classes. The silent ones would soon be participating; he had seen sparks of curiosity lighting in their eyes. These students had been deprived—in joyless, repressive, regimented institutions—of truly humane learning experience. Bosculus would lay out the morsels of knowledge like a grand buffet where the hungry could dine. Dowell, he thought, would be his star pupil. And that pristine flower, Karen Rumako . . . He thought of Abelard and Héloïse and checked it.

"Don't worry," he told his class in a comradely yet paternal manner. "I'm not going to mark you on this one."

Consider each of the three topics thoroughly. If possible, prepare a rough-copy practice essay of about three hundred words on each topic. You will *not* be asked to hand in the practice essays. You *will* be asked to write an in-class essay on one of the three topics.

Choose a subject area small enough to permit informative, decisive writing. Use your own ideas; develop them fully. Be specific. Cite details and examples. Quote from readings or the statements of experts, when appropriate.

Pay attention to grammar, usage, spelling, punctuation and diction. Use paragraphs. Express yourself clearly. Remember that the topic itself is not a title.

You will be assigned one of the topics for your in-class essay. There will be no choice; you may not use notes or your practice essay. You may not use a dictionary. Write

TABLE 47   89

in ink on one side of the paper only. Leave two-inch margins on each side.

TOPICS TO CHOOSE FROM:

1. Three Big Problems
2. The Best Decision
3. The Most Significant Experience

Franklin Busch
English I Sectin B303
Tus.–Thur. 2:15
Professor Bosculus

DECIDING TO GO TO COLLEDGE

The best decision I made was to go to colledge. There was no dicesion in my house that wasnt made because we all played a part in it. My mother wants me to go to computer school My father realy stepfather wanted me to go to work. My sister said I should go to college, to learn more about the world. My brother said collage gets better jobs. I decided to go to coolidge.

To go to collage a person needs time and money. They need time to go to there classes. They need time for homework. They need money for theyre tution. They need money for the room and to buy books.

A wise man said "learning is a lifetime occupation. Colledge is the time to start.

Franklin "Frank" Busch

Bosculus confided his worst fears to Yuri Marchuk, his friend from the history department. The men were leaning over beers in the pizza place across the highway from campus.

"I think those kids are making fun of me," Bosculus confessed. "The Busch boy's was the best paper in the class."

Yuri was new, like Bosculus, but he had a philosophy of acceptance. "No. These kids are sincere," he insisted. He had a cheeky face that glowed like a polished apple. "They respect their teachers. It's just that they're really low-end."

"But they had to pass college boards." Bosculus was trying to keep his voice down. "They had to pass high school. They have to be able to read."

Yuri was so calm that Bosculus thought maybe *he* was teasing him, too. Yuri spoke so close to his beer glass that the foam took little flights on the current of his breath. His face went sad for a moment but he quickly slid into an imitation of Mr. Brindisi: "We can't kid ourselves that our students are the top layer of the cake. They're not the icing and they're not the top layer either." He added in his own voice:

"But that's why a college education means so much to them. It's their chance to change their lives."

Bosculus admired Yuri's down-to-earth dedication to his profession. Yuri had been hired, like Bosculus, to teach English I (Effective Communication). He had no teaching background in history. In fact, he had to study his own assignments in order to keep ahead of his classes. To this daunting state of affairs he responded like a member of the Light Brigade.

"Yes, but I don't know how to mark them," Bosculus groused. He was dressed like a real campus figure in chinos and windbreaker. "They don't know subject from predicate. They don't know past from present. One of them wrote a three-line composition. I guess he thought a sentence was a paragraph. They didn't use the topics I assigned. They wrote anything they felt like writing."

Bosculus paid for the beer and Yuri ordered another round. He tried to bolster Bosculus and sympathize with the students at the same time. He kept it up as they walked back

TABLE 47 91

across campus, cutting through the Student Union, where he had to shout over the din. (Bowling alleys to the right of them, pinball machines to the left.) The cafeteria was closed but the donut shop was doing big business as were the automatic canteens. The block-long lounge was filled with students sprawled on low-slung sofas and cushions to listen to the afternoon's live group, the Rockville Seniorettes, twelve sprightly old women in red tunics, white slacks and space shoes, on brass and percussion. Some of the students were reading books, but Bosculus no longer looked, as he had during his first days there, to see the titles.

Yuri was shouting, "Brindisi told me that some teachers here fail two thirds of a class. Here, it's no disgrace for the teacher. The kids take English One year after year till they pass or quit."

Bosculus shouted back, "I don't know how I could pass a kid who doesn't know grade-school grammar."

"That's what I told Brindisi."

"What did he say?"

"He said I shouldn't let it bother me. He said grammar isn't my job."

They pushed out of the Student Union and stood on the cement landing in sudden quiet. Bosculus lowered his voice and the contrast sounded like conspiracy: "So what kind of scale do you mark on?"

Yuri leaned on the iron railing. "I'm not in the English department," he said, gazing out into the early night. "It's a question of standards," he said and picked up his imitation of Mr. Brindisi. He flapped his elbows and broke out a champion's grin. "The teacher's standards have got to be flexible."

Bosculus said, "Oh."

He decided to give Busch a B-minus.

The class was over. The students shuffled and slouched their way out the door and into their late afternoon reward.

At last only Busch was left, lingering by the teacher's desk. Guilelessness was written, almost illegibly, across his pudgy face under Buster Brown bangs.

"I'm very disappointed," Busch said to Bosculus. "I was counting on getting an A."

He felt sorry for the boy. Trying to be eye-to-eye, the kid emitted a sense of brash timidity, a desperate bravura, that went straight to Bosculus' heart.

"I was up after midnight every night last week. I wrote all the practices. You could see them. I still got them home. I mean, I'm no writer. I'm not naturally verbal, so I got to work extra hard."

Bosculus understood and sympathized. "It's obvious," he started to say, "that you ah, uh . . . it's very clear that . . ."

"I memorized all three essays. Like you said. Whichever one you asked for, I was ready."

"That was expected of you, Frank. That was ah, uh, following the um, assignment. You did a g-good job."

"So how come I only got a B-minus?"

If Busch would read over Mr. Bosculus' corrections and give some thought to the comments in the margins, he would see that there was ample room for improvement. There was room and a clear path this term for progression from B-minus to A.

"Most of what's wrong," Bosculus explained, "are small matters. Carelessness. Inconsistency. They are definitely treatable and curable."

Busch did not seem to be encouraged.

"With the patient's cooperation," Bosculus persevered, "the prognosis is excellent."

He offered a Hippocratic smile, but Franklin Busch showed no taste for metaphor.

"Mr. Bosculus," he said. "What you saw is the best I can do. After a week of sweating. I'm good with machines and I

TABLE 47   93

can get along. But I'm no good with words. I failed English One last year and I dropped out the year before. I'm a senior now and this is my last chance."

"Believe me, Frank. Your, uh, problems are only superficial. You'll have no trouble raising your mark, I promise you. If you can spell college right once, you can do it all the time. And, uh, by the way—have you signed up for remedial English, where you will get individual help?"

"I'd sure like to, but I can't. I have to work after school."

Busch played in a band, he said. Tenor saxophone. He needed to do a lot of rehearsing.

"Music is my field, see? I don't need to know how to write."

Bosculus, touched, mentioned the relationship between clear writing and clear thinking. Busch, unmoved, reminded Bosculus that he had already learned, last year, to write letters of complaint and letters to order things. All he asked was to be allowed to graduate and become a self-supporting member of society. The B-minus, he said, made him very nervous.

He moved in closer and set his books down beside Bosculus' classbook. "If I could depend on a C or better," Busch said, "I wouldn't feel so insecure." He laid both his hands across his wide middle. "I wouldn't get these stomach cramps," he said significantly.

He bent over the desk, almost nose-to-nose with Bosculus. "Look," said Busch. "If I show up here every class, and I sit quiet and don't wise up. If I hand in all the assignments to my best ability. If I take all the tests. Would you guarantee me a C or better?"

"I'm sure you would get a C or better."

"But I mean *guarantee*. So I wouldn't have to be nervous."

"Frank, I can't make a deal with you."

"What kind of name is that, Bosculus? Jewish?"

"The origin is Byzantine, I understand. What makes you feel you won't be able to keep up a satisfactory level of work?"

Busch stood and sunk into himself. "I won't always have this kind of time," he said. "I mean, a whole week staying up after midnight. I'm a guy who needs my sleep. What's that Bissentine, a kind of Spanish-Jewish? Is that what it is?"

"You'd probably call it Turkish now. But the point is, you'll get the grade you deserve and I can't see why you shouldn't pass."

Busch took up his books and gave Bosculus a broad wink. "That's all I wanted to hear, Mr. Botchalus," he said. "As long as we understand each other."

He left the room with long, rolling steps. Bosculus stayed sitting at his desk for a minute in the empty classroom. *What does it profit a man?* he reflected, smiling to himself at the student's intensity.

Choose one of the following statements which you can support and can persuade others to believe. Develop it through specific evidence in a composition of approximately 350 words. Be careful to decide upon the purpose, tone and method of development before you begin to write. Limit the scope of your essay to an area you can handle adequately in the forty-five minutes allotted. Be sure to give your essay an interesting and appropriate title.

STATEMENTS

1. "Adam was but human—this explains it all. He did not want the apple for the apple's sake; he wanted it only because it was forbidden."   *Mark Twain*

TABLE 47   95

2. "Maturity consists of no longer being taken in by oneself."   *Kajetan Von Schlaagenberg*

3. "Not many sounds in life, and I include all urban and rural sounds, exceed in interest a knock on the door."   *Charles Lamb*

Kowalski, Howard Ignatius
English One
Section B303

Opportunity Knocks on the Door

I have done physical work as well as having used my brain to earn some extra money. Opportunities appear not to be a matter of finding work, but instead appear to be the opportunity to do a higher quality of work which one uses the head rather than physical labor. Concerning the manner in which a person can presently be able to get a better job, I would like to talk about how to find the opportunity to find satisfactory work that would be able to maintain a persons ability to use his head, his intelligence and to be respected by his fellow workers.

If we begin to realize that our corporations are not constructed to enable everyone to predetermine an executive position and that we need only to address what is in fact possible, then in that instance only will corporations begin to serve some viable purpose for society. We can address the problem of education, skills, training and preference, employability, and new cultural and value exposure. But do not mislead ourselves into beleiving that opportunity will knock at your door. It is a sad affair when a person awaits for the knock on the door instead of going out to confront the possibilities and embraceing the obtions that await them.

If by preparing the jobseeker to copy psychologically and economically, we may effect real and significant change in the job market including large and small corporations. Whether it be rural or urban, not many sounds in life, as said by Charles Lamb, will exceed a knock on the door of opportunity.

The End

At first it seemed to make a lot of sense. Bosculus was happy with the sophisticated vocabulary, the authoritative phrasing. Yet there seemed to be something *off* about it.

I think I know what you mean, he wrote in his gangling hand on the bottom of the last page.

But it's only a guess, he added after another reading.

Bosculus pondered over ways to help Kowalski bring more precision to his thought and language. To correct spelling and punctuation was easy. But to sweep away the mental fuzz: that was harder. He read the composition once again making notes in the margin. Sadly, he saw that he was dealing with a diaspora of meaning: not with a composition at all, but a *de-*composition.

He sat at the desk in his basement office with the cold November sun slanting in on him. It occurred to him that his students met in groups, after class, to plan their papers. Some they planned to be totally illiterate. Others they would copy from a file of A papers from Harvard and Yale, skipping one word in every four. Kowalski seemed to have been trying to meet the assignment. Yet, if written in earnest, the paper indicated brain damage. Bosculus wondered whether he should refer Kowalski to psychological services. He wrote himself a note and slipped Kowalski's paper into the folder in his leather case. Then he went upstairs, forgetting his duffel coat, and ran freezing to the classroom.

TABLE 47 97

The students were waiting for him. He was always surprised and grateful that so many of them showed up.

Mr. Bosculus wrote on the green blackboard:

> This doesn't stop me from being the kind of person who loves men, sports, activities and a distinct feeling of pleasure in learning English.

"Let's read this sentence and see if we can figure out what's wrong with it." Bosculus stood to one side and waited.

"That's my sentence!" Paula Wadsworth cried out. "What you write my sentence for?"

Bosculus assured her it was not an act of malice. "I'll be using parts of everybody's papers as examples to help all of us. We learn from our mistakes."

"Mistakes!"

"Your paper was fine, Paula. You have nothing to be ashamed of. It just happens that one of your errors is so common—I mean, typical—that it can be used as a lesson for everyone."

Wadsworth was content.

"I don't see nothing wrong with that sentence," Dowell said.

" 'Distinct' is spelled wrong," said Zigabarra. "Only I don't know the right way."

"There should be a comma after 'person.' "

Suspicion rose up again in Bosculus, a cold spread of paranoia.

But Karen Rumako saved him. "Does she mean 'sports activities' or 'sports and activities'? Because if she means 'sports activities,' she shouldn't put a comma there."

Wadsworth served her antagonist with a menacing look. "There's activities," she said meaningfully, "that aren't sports."

Bosculus moved in quickly. "How about a person who loves a distinct feeling of pleasure?" He felt now, with his own pleasure, that he had the class bending, so to speak, under the hood to examine the mechanics of language. "What does that phrase really say?"

"Ain't nothing wrong," said Dowell, "with loving pleasure." He rolled his eyes at Paula Wadsworth.

She narrowed hers at Bosculus. "You picking on me," she said.

The next sentence was Fiorello's:

> Reading "The Godfather" will help greatly in my studies as I will have to read many books and also for knowledge.

Bosculus pointed out Mr. Fiorello's sensitive, though not precisely expressed differentiation of the practical and the aesthetic value of reading. During the discussion Fiorello referred to certain family connections of his own, relating to the book he was intending to read. Fiorello, also, stood solid in the face of criticism but he stayed after class to talk it over.

"I'm not happy with that mark on that paper," Fiorello said. He took a foil-wrapped sandwich out of his knapsack, opened it and smelled it. "Tuna fish," he said and bit in.

"Very good," he said with his mouth full. He held the sandwich out to Bosculus. "Have a bite."

Bosculus politely declined, but he was glad Fiorello was friendly.

Office hours were Tuesday and Thursday from one to two o'clock. It was a peaceful, reflective time for Bosculus. Some students made appointments but they seldom showed up. The ones without appointments also stayed away. But Bosculus sat there, doggedly ready to help.

On one bleak Thursday at exactly one-thirty, a purposeful

TABLE 47 99

knock shook the mirror on the back of the door. Bosculus stuck a bookmark in *The Magic Mountain*.

"Walk right in!" He expected his voice to send the visitor scooting. But there was another knock.

He thought it was Fiorello coming to put a hit on him for a D in a reading quiz.

He thought it was Kowalski with a court summons. Kowalski had threatened to sue when Bosculus suggested testing him for possible perceptual impairment.

He thought it was Wadsworth to accuse him of racism.

Or Kubelik to accuse him of sexism.

Or Busch because he was failing.

Bosculus got up and unlocked the door.

Karen Rumako walked in.

She shut the door behind her and stood against it, framed, a Gabriel shining light into darkness. "I don't have an appointment," she said. She was dressed for winter—striped stocking cap, scarf over red sweater coat, heavy stockings, heavy boots.

"That's okay. These are open hours," Bosculus managed to reply.

Karen dropped into the chair at the side of the desk, setting bag, scarf and mittens on the floor beside her. She unbuttoned her long sweater. Ice crystals shone from her hat and sleeves.

"I wanted to ask a few things." She fished a three-by-five card out of her bag and caught her breath as she began to read from it. "First, I want to know how you mark. How much for tests, how much for homework, class participation, eck cetera."

Her face was bright from the smack of the cold. Her cheeks were smears of red; her eyes were daubs of blue.

"Then I want to know if there's a penalty for lateness.

Late homework as well as being late for class. Then, if I can do extra credit assignments to raise my grade."

She was very businesslike. Maybe, Bosculus thought, she was in a women's rights group, taking a course in assertiveness.

"Then I wondered if it would be all right if I did some extra creative writing. I mean, would you be able to correct it?"

Bosculus pursed his lips and leafed through his classbook.

"I don't recall your having any particular problems." He sat up in a professional posture. "Uh, Karen." He found her name and ran his finger along the line of her attendance and her marks. "You've missed only one class. All assignments have been in on time."

She listened, glistening.

"You've passed every test with a B-minus or better."

She clasped her hands. "Oh, I didn't know that! I guess I don't keep track very well." She giggled. "Too busy working, I guess." Her delighted smile showed small, white teeth and the delectable chip on the overlapping front tooth. "That's great!" she said.

"Of course, it never hurts to do some grammar review." He was loath to send her off empty-handed. "I'll be glad to lend you a book. And I'll let you see the answer book to check yourself."

Bosculus glanced at the empty bookshelves. He promised to bring the book to her next class.

"Where do you live?" Karen suddenly asked.

Bosculus, trained in dialectics, familiar with medieval scholasticism, was seldom unbalanced by conversational derailments. He rented a room where some other teachers lived in the home of a retired carpenter, a widower, about a mile down the road from the college.

"Oh. So he has these extra bedrooms." Karen weighed the information. "You know so much," she then said, in another of her sudden detours. "I don't talk so much in class but I lis-

TABLE 47   101

ten. You make illusions all the time to books and authors.
Like in a real college."

"This *is* a real college."

"Yes, but you know what I mean. They have jerkoffs teaching here. This is my third term and you're the best teacher
I've had yet."

Bosculus put two fingers to his lips. To ward off heresy or
to deplore the state of teaching at Tate Community. He
didn't know which.

"Would you do me a big favor?"

Of course he would.

Would he show her his room? She was having a lot of
trouble at home. Her parents lived like two rats in a sack, eating at each other. She stayed away as much as she could, but
the nights were really getting to her. She'd been having nightmares. She had to move out.

She looked up at him and he knew what she meant. She
was warm now, only the tip of her nose still red.

"So I need to find out what my options are. How much it
costs for a rented room, eck cetera."

Caught in the sharp angle of light from the ceiling and
light from the window, she shone against the dull cement
blocks—more a Vermeer gentlewoman, Bosculus discerned,
than a Renaissance saint. He told her to come by some afternoon in broad daylight so she could get a clear idea and also
when there would be people around. Bosculus, happily avun-
cular, did not want to see her compromised by anything that
could look like a clandestine visit.

He promised to ask around about available rooms.

He agreed that if it was financially feasible, living away
from home was a good idea for all college students, let alone
one with this young lady's problems.

At Table 47 Yuri Marchuk is laughing.

Tears run from his eyes. He grips the table to steady himself. "He was! He was! The sweetest of men!" Yuri turns his head toward the stage and the surrounded, laureled Bosculus up there. "He hadn't a whiff of suspicion of what he was dealing with."

None of us is laughing.

The poet composes himself and continues his story, somberly now:

"Karen was not lying," Yuri says. "I met her parents at the wedding. The father was a wounded lion. Sylvan Rumako, born of Ukrainian peasants who had learned fear and suspicion from generations of powerlessness and victimization. Exhausted by the past and fearful of the future, they brought up, beat up, wept over their scared defiant little Sylvan, who became Karen's paranoid papa. He carried a gun in those days, even at the wedding. But how he could charm his daughter with soft words, a compliment, a tender arm around her! And how she would then chide herself for her evil thoughts about him! Softened and expanding with love for Papa, she would turn to him like a little rabbit with her belly exposed. And Sylvan Rumako would skew around and rip into her, growling, clawing, sinking his teeth in. Then she would ask herself, curled up tight around her wound, 'What the hell is the matter with you, Karen? Can't you ever learn, Karen?' Her reply came in nightmares."

Here was a gentle man, the new professor. Meek and mild, like an angel child. Karen wondered, did he have a big one? Her friends said you could tell by the size of his feet. So his dick should be an artistic one, long and narrow. At rest, the color of black raspberry or maybe, on second thought, cherry (smack, smack). In action, anyway, tomato red and tomato ripe. How exciting. That professor knew just about everything under his tame, straight hair and behind his polite eyes. How exciting it would be to excite such a quiet, measured man and knock apart his pulled-together ways. Karen could send a bowling ball straight down the alley to crash into his neat

TABLE 47 103

triangle of pins. Number One, books. Number Two, art. Number Three, symphony. Number Four, history. Zingo! goes Karen's bowling ball, carrying a depth charge. It would be so much fun to break his cool and light him up.

⊛

"Bosculus," Yuri narrates, "received three visitors around the Christmas holidays. They were not Spirits of Christmas Past, Present or Future. The visits were typically *Bosculus* in that he completely misunderstood their purpose. Poor fellow! He walked down lanes of overarching question marks and thought he was carrying the answers. He was up in his twenties then but I'm pretty sure he was still a virgin. Before the Christmas holidays.

"First he planned to spend the vacation on a long bus trip. But his conscience tormented him. He had a foot-high pile of student papers on his desk, awaiting correction. I saw them. At the time I lived in a room down the hall from his. We were close enough friends for him to trust me with his doubts. Why, he demanded of me one night, should he waste his time filling up margins with *it's* for *its* and *their* for *there* as if he were working on doctoral dissertations?

"I agreed that he erred, perhaps, on the side of conscientiousness. Bosculus said the hell with it. He'd flip through the papers and give everybody B or better. He said he had nothing to lose but his students' enmity. And he went back to his room to do it, but he couldn't. He caught himself by the scruff of the neck and pinned himself against the wall. He shone the study lamp in his eyes and asked himself relentless questions. In the end, he accepted his duty to light up the semantic darkness of his classroom. Instead of taking the path of easy passings, Bosculus would struggle through the bush. (Oh, yes. Busch.) The students would sweat, but Bosculus would sweat more, and only the fit would survive.

"So he canceled his bus trip."

The first visitor, a week before the start of Christmas vacation, was Dr. Chamberlain. The chairman of the English department showed up for a Monday afternoon class, one of her famous surprise visits.

Bosculus was at the blackboard, explaining catchy leads, when Dr. Chamberlain, in a mink coat and pink satin turban, tiptoed in and took a seat in the back of the room. She slid the coat from her shoulders, engulfing the class in a tidal wave of Arpège. She crossed her legs and focused unswerving attention on Bosculus.

"Pay no attention to me," Dr. Chamberlain called out. "Just treat me like one of the students."

She offered the suggestion that a lead sentence could also be properly called the "topic sentence."

Unobtrusive as the chairman was, Bosculus felt her presence. His stutter stuck in his ears. His words blew away from his thoughts, and he had to haul them in.

The class, on the other hand, was extremely cooperative. Fiorello made a valiant attempt to distinguish between the best of times and the worst of times. Kubelik actually glimpsed, like a revelation, the dramatic quality of four score and seven as distinct from everyday numbers. Bosculus had been trying for weeks to make this breakthrough.

Furthermore, the class minded its manners. The smokers did not beg to be allowed to light up. The gumchewers refrained from popping. The sprawlers sat up. The snorers stayed awake. The hecklers listened. The gigglers, scratchers, stretchers, foot tappers, knuckle crackers, pencil droppers,

TABLE 47

105

snifflers and belchers all maintained unaccustomed decorum, for which Bosculus was profoundly grateful.

When at last the dismissal bell rang, he permitted himself to breathe freely. He felt he had demonstrated his ability. The class, having taken down the homework assignment with utmost sobriety, filed out with church faces, leaving Bosculus standing up front in a kind of glory, holding high—metaphorically—the torch of learning.

Dr. Chamberlain rose to her high heels and tiptoed across the room. She took up a perch on the edge of the teacher's desk and swung one ultra-sheer leg over the other. "Listen, Mr. Bosculus," she said. "Don't think this class is your fault. You really hit the jackpot for dummies."

Bosculus was desolate not to be praised, relieved not to be blamed, and offended for the sake of his class.

They were good kids at heart and he didn't like to see them at the bottom of the barrel.

On the other hand, if they were much higher than the bottom, he feared for the future of his country.

In fact, Bosculus was at a loss. To defend the intelligence of his students might be to make himself look like a dummy.

In the end, he made a dignified compromise. He poured out his heart into dainty teacups. He told Dr. Chamberlain how much the class had improved since its inauspicious late start. He made sure to mention his own recent offer of an after-class grammar review, to which, unfortunately, none of the students—what with jobs, science labs, and heavy reading courses—could afford the time to come.

Dr. Chamberlain swung her leg and glanced about the room. "You mustn't expect too much," she said when he had stopped talking.

"Well, I do worry," Bosculus confessed, "about bringing them up to a passing grade."

"They've *got* to come up to snuff." The chairman polished

her fingernails against her flat palms. Bosculus ventured to ask how other teachers managed it. Dr. Chamberlain started to leave and stopped at the door.

Different teachers worked differently, she said. Ms. Landers was big on true-false tests. Mrs. Finkel had them reading poetry. Dr. Janowski was very strict. Mr. Brindisi drilled grammar. "After a while," the chairman told Bosculus, "you get a feel for it."

She tucked her chin into her fur and smiled like a movie queen. "There are many roads to Rome," she said.

"Then, in the meantime, I could pass everybody?" he said.

"Oh, yes. Unless they don't come up to snuff."

After this visit, Bosculus became curious about the future lives of his students. He wanted, above all, to know how many of them expected to become schoolteachers. He asked for a show of hands. In the Monday–Wednesday section alone, there were four people who intended to educate the young. A few more were undecided.

Bosculus made up his mind. He would not be responsible for having passed any student who could not write a reasonably coherent, reasonably accurate, reasonably spelled, punctuated and presented three-paragraph composition on a reasonable subject. He announced this decision to his classes. He also printed his name, address and telephone number on the green blackboard. Any student who needed help was invited to call on him. Students who could not avail themselves of his office hours were invited to call on him at home. Bosculus would be on hand all during Christmas vacation.

The second visitor, the first day after the day of the last class before vacation, was Karen Rumako. She came to see his room.

Again she was buttoned up, tied up, wrapped up, steaming with cold, her face smudged with thanks for letting her come

TABLE 47   107

and apologies for bothering him. Her woolen arms again were loaded with books and schoolbags. Her chipped-tooth smile was wounding. Woundingly vulnerable, Bosculus thought of this tough little madonna. She seemed to like him and to trust him. He must be very careful to be warm and interested but also to keep a professorial distance. He would hate her to think he wanted to exploit her sexually.

"I really appreciate this," Karen said.

Bosculus assured her that his efforts to find her a place to live were in the line of duty. "An anxious mind, an ah-explosive atmosphere make it um-difficult to concentrate on schoolwork."

They left her stuff in the front hall and she followed him upstairs. It was a big enough, fixed-up room with a rug like Astroturf and wallpaper like striated muscles. A perforated cover had been built over the old coiled radiator, and decorative rings hung from the window shades. Old baseball pictures and a trophy were reminders of the carpenter's son, and all the built-in shelves and cornices were reminders of the carpenter himself. The professor's books spilled on every available surface—books on desk and table, on all the built-in shelves and sills, more in boxes on the carpet, under the desk and in the closet. He had a record player and a pile of albums that Karen went through—Mozart and Haydn and some names she'd never heard. There was a corkboard on the wall over his desk, with a couple of letters tacked on and some early Christmas cards. There was a maple bed with acorn posts and, of course, a chenille bedspread. Karen kept moving around and testing things. Hard chair, soft mattress, dim ceiling light.

The framed prints on the wall, stiff saints and sad angels, belonged to the professor. Karen liked them because they were dignified, yet lively. She pointed to three figures in floating blue.

"Who are those guys?"

"Three angels visiting Abraham. It's an icon."

"Oh, yeah? You pray to those icons?"

The professor was boiling water on his hot plate. He had a menagerie of teas: Peppermint, Winterberry, Red Zinger, Rose Hip. She watched his hands as he touched the boxes.

"No," he said. "I don't pray." He held up the Red Zinger and Karen nodded.

"One doesn't pray to icons in any case." He carefully transferred pinches of tea to an earthenware teapot. "One prays in front of them. They're meant to be a doorway into the world of the spirit."

Ordinarily, Karen liked a really good body. No hips. Clear skin. Strong jaw. Not too hairy. Personalitywise, she went for a cool sense of humor and even a kind of lean indifference that maybe hinted of cruelty but stayed on the right side. The professor, though, brought out a whole different set of ideas. He would take his time, she thought. He would touch all of her surfaces. But what kept sailing around her head, cutting through everything else, was the conviction that he would never hit a child.

While the tea steeped, he showed her the closet and the bathroom he shared with another roomer, a history professor. They looked at the view from the back window. Earlier snow had melted and refrozen to coat the backyard and turn the tree there into a dripping candle.

She knew she turned him on. He kept pulling his eyes off her as if they were adhesive tape.

"Forget the tea," she said. "Come on out and I'll buy you a beer."

The professor hesitated. He was engaged in a different line of action. He was straining tea. He was about to show her the room down the hall, which was smaller and a little less expensive than his. Its occupant was away for the holidays but Bosculus had thought it over and was certain that Mr. Marchuk wouldn't mind if they just looked in. Furthermore,

TABLE 47

109

the professor had gotten her some addresses and phone numbers of places with rooms to rent.

Karen was sitting cross-legged on the grassy rug. She raised herself—no hands—and strutted up to Bosculus. She took the tea strainer out of his hand and dumped the contents into the empty wastebasket. They went out for a beer.

"One time this guy made a whole romantic setup in his so-called pad. Champagne in long-stemmed glasses. Dentist-office music. Real flowers. Like he was following a recipe from *Playboy* magazine, get the picture? And he says to me, 'Do you like to be spontaneous?' And I say to him, 'Yes, I'm very spontaneous.' And, spontaneously, I walked right out on him."

College beer in a booth with high-backed benches. The noise brought their heads together. Warmed by the alcoholic content of two mugs of draft beer, Bosculus laughed at her stories of family and friends. It was soon dark and soon dinnertime. Karen slipped out to make a call. Bosculus called the waitress. He and Karen liked something in common: hamburgers medium well. (A rare order!) Something more: onions raw. But Bosculus demurred. Karen chewed what the professor *eschewed* (he explained the distinction, to her delight). He also knew the vitamin content of an onion and old monks' tales of its curative powers.

Warmed by close companionship, Karen told stories that made the professor laugh even as his mind reeled in horror. What an appalling pair of parents! Paranoid Papa packs a rod. Not so funny to live with. Mama with hair teased six inches high, like a blond loaf cake on top of her head, owns three closetfuls of matching pants suits, some with vests, all hot off the truck. Illegal, oh yes, but she knows all the politicians. This lady bailiff, with her big mouth and her big bust, spends an hour before work in front of her professional

makeup mirror. Very funny! Pleasant peasant. But not so
funny when she had to work on concealing a black-and-blue
spot, a walloping bruise on her broad Ukrainian cheekbone.
Bosculus listened, laughed and winced. He ran his fingers uncomfortably over a deep carving of a life sign on his side of
the table. "In a way," he said at last, "you're lucky to come
from a family that lets its feelings out. Yelling and fighting is
better than bottling it up."

Karen poured more ketchup on the remains of her burger
and pushed the onion back into the roll. The fake orange lan-
tern lit her face like a Fuseli. She looked up at him—glowing
amber, smudged mouth—and chastely said, "I think a little
bit of bottling up would do my family a lot of good."

In his most worshipful days, Bosculus had not adored more
ardently.

She insisted on paying half the check. He, not to be over-
bearing, consented. She also laid an extra quarter on top of
his tip. She used to be a waitress, she explained. Then he es-
corted her, two buses and a short blowy walk, to her door.

Home was in a row of two-story shingled houses, unpromis-
ing in the shadows of streetlights. Karen's house, like the
others in the row, presented a narrow, railed porch overlooked by three tall windows with shades pulled down against
the night. Bosculus followed Karen up the snow-crusted steps
and waited on an ice-ridged rubber runner while she dug for
her keys. Chilled through, he was, but she didn't ask him in.
Instead, when she found the key she pushed up on her toes
and put her hands on his shoulders.

Bosculus was shivering. Karen felt his tension and it scared
her. Karen knew only one way of reacting to fear: close your
eyes, hold your breath and drive through it. If you don't do
what scares you, Karen knew, you're lost forever. So she
kissed the professor. She had to pull him down and stretch to

TABLE 47 111

find his mouth, but she kissed him. It started out soft but all of a sudden she was pushing into his mouth. Her tongue forced its way in and attacked his. She moved it; she got around it. She caught it between her lips and sucked it into her mouth. Now the professor was fighting an uncontrollable tremor. He pulled away. He tried to compose himself. His passion was her passion. He leaned against the shingles between the door and the windows. Also breathing hard, she watched him.

"You kiss like a man," he said when he could talk.

"Oh yeah? How do you know?"

She laughed at him. "Show me how a man kisses."

When she at last put her key in the lock, she turned to him with her hand on the knob. "I fuck like a woman," she said and slipped into the house, shutting the door behind her.

He spent the next two days reasoning out his position. First off, it was necessary to stay away from Karen Rumako. She was, first off, his student. She was not yet twenty. She was wayward, forward, unfortunate, misguided. Considering the chaos of her home life, how could she be anything else? It was a miracle that she had turned out as sensitive, and sensible, as she was. Under the wildness, there was a young woman with an appetite for beauty. Appetite? (Bodily desires interrupted his lofty deliberations.)

Bosculus fastened his mind to the look on her face as she studied the Rublev Trinity on his bedroom wall. *She needs a guiding hand,* he thought. He recalled her looking hungrily at his bookshelves. A starving urchin, she. He wondered how she would look while listening to the balcony scene from Prokofiev's *Romeo and Juliet*. He knew she would blossom in a nourishing cultural environment. Bosculus was too old to turn his back on adult responsibilities. In the end, he accepted his duty not to turn his back on Karen.

(FLASH: Her tough little, soft little body pressed against the long naked back of Professor Bosculus.)

He felt all the symptoms, above and below, the lickings of libido. From the wall, the Metropolitan Alexei, miracle worker for five hundred years, interrupted his two-fingered blessing to point those fingers at Bosculus and stare him down with a patriarchal warning.

Bosculus reminded himself of the importance of keeping distance between himself as mentor and as seducer. Father Alexei notwithstanding, leaving the faith did not mean abandonment of character. On the contrary, Bosculus had always been strong on self-discipline, and was even stronger now that he accepted full responsibility for his own behavior. The relationship with Karen Rumako would be a mighty challenge. Clearly, she stood on the brink. Without sensitive direction she would run herself, fuzz-headed, into a thankless job, a joyless marriage, a pointless life repeating the errors of her parents. Given a chance to save her, Bosculus must accept the onus.

(FLASH: Anus. Karen lying on her belly with soft, peachy buttocks smiling up at him. He naked and straddling her with his banana-penis unpeeled.)

He was assaulted with the urge to prostrate himself upon his stubbly green rug but he resisted. He dared to face the Metropolitan. The Father commanded, but Bosculus refused.

He knew his example of restraint and modesty would help to calm the fires of her disposition. He would be ballast against the winds of disorder. She, her anxiety allayed, would discover herself in quiet gardens with a book in her hand and music in her ears. Her choices would abound, like flowers, before her.

(FLASH: Her pubic hair, honeysuckled, mixing with his own undergrowth. Rather aristocratic, he had always thought his was. Thick and well-defined as the beard of a Velasquez officer. Severely cropped, delicately pointed under the navel

TABLE 47   113

and curving elegantly to a mound of ah, uh, er . . . crotch,
where there appeared, like a bird in its nest, a, ah, er . . .
condor. A condor stretching its neck. Looking, no doubt, for
a condom.)

Bosculus was in a sweat. The icon was shaking its fist at
him. And well he might! What lewd games the Bosculus
mind was playing!

The girl was, he understood perfectly, in a vulnerable position. It would be easy for a young male faculty member to
exploit her. Not Bosculus. He would conduct himself as a
teacher in the finest tradition. At this very moment there
were papers to be marked. Remarked on. Remarkable compo-
sitions awaiting him, stacked high. Karen's composition was
on top of the pile.

COMPARISON ESSAY: *Long Hair vs. Short Hair*

Having recently made the transition from long hair to
short, I have become acutely aware of their differences.
Long hair is beautiful and so is short. So how should a
person decide which is the most feasible for herself. A
good way is to decide on priorities. The items that were
important to me were versatility, convenience and uniqueness.

Long hair is extremely versatile. It can be worn down,
in a bun, in curls or pulled back. It is easy to trim and
can be styled to evoke different moods such as sexy, romantic or carefree. . . .

(*And on and on.*)

Short hair eliminates a lot of versatility, to put it up in
rollers a Barbie Doll kit would have to be used. There is
no way to pull it back for a bun. Not many changes can
be made. . . .

(*And on.*)

Short hair is unique because most females have long hair.

(*And on.*)

I am happy with my short hair mostly because of the convenience. There are only two ways I wear it but that does not matter because the style fits all my moods. . . . The haircut can look very mature or very wholesome and fresh. Some of the comments I receive demonstrate that my haircut displays a lot of uniqueness! But every so often I suffer pangs of envy when I see that girl with long, flowing hair.

Karen Rumako

(FLASH: Karen Bosculus.)

The young woman was fraught with potentialities. She told him she had been a prize student in grade school. She also played the piano when she could collect enough serenity to sit still at the keyboard. Bosculus made a few marginal corrections. On the inked line two lines below her signature, he wrote:

Excellent paper, Karen. This shows the kind of writing you are capable of.

Alone in his room with his work and his thoughts, he found himself taking frequent swallows of air. Furthermore, his head was full of Debussy. The room he was alone in was not beautiful, but it had been touched by the presence of beauty. Bosculus wandered to his record rack and found the Debussy piano pieces. *The Girl with the Flaxen Hair.* Simple, soft, poignant. He needed to hear that music. Carrying the record fastidiously, horizontal between his vertical palms, he grazed it over the spindle until it slipped into place.

TABLE 47 115

(NO FLASH.)

The Metropolitan offered his blessing.

The third visitor, on the twelfth day of Christmas and the first post-vacation day of class, was Busch. He showed up during office hours looking like someone who'd gotten everything he'd asked for.

He stamped the snow off his boots, slapped his gloves on the desk, flopped into the chair, blew his bangs out of his eyes and announced to Bosculus:

"I'll never forget what you've done for me."

"Oh? What's that?"

"I mean, you're making it possible for me to become a self-supporting citizen."

"You're saying that the course has been, uh, valuable to you?"

"Passing it. That's what's valuable."

Bosculus was jolted out of his stutter. "You can't expect to pass English One?"

Busch stared at him.

"Sure, I expect to pass. That was the deal."

This was hard on Bosculus. Franklin Busch had been dilatory—a goof-off—if not from the very beginning, at least for long enough to prove himself unwilling to put forth effort. He had come to class late, left early, slept noisily while there, missed assignments, failed tests, turned in papers late and badly done and had become, if anything, *less* able to express himself effectively in written English. Embedded somewhere among the fibrous swirls of the Bosculus memory was a conversation about a deal. But Bosculus, knowing himself, knew he would never have made a promise he couldn't keep.

Busch assailed him with twin-barreled menace. "I was there every day," he said. "I done my best, just like we

agreed. I worked my tail off, Mr. Botchalus. You can't let me
down."

The little blue eyes aimed a death ray. "It don't make any
difference to you, teacher. But it's my whole life."

Bosculus was invaded by a deep sorrow. He put a hand on
Busch's shoulder and quickly withdrew it. He spoke earnestly
and honestly to the boy, sharing his convictions and explaining the terrible responsibility of upholding standards. Speaking so pensively, Bosculus was slow to notice that the face before him was growing red and puffy and that the eyes were
narrowing beneath the yellow bangs.

Bang-bang Busch. Bosculus made an analogy between Beethoven's deafness and the need for a student to rise above
difficulties.

Bang-bang-bash. Bosculus amplified his theme, explaining
how Degas had turned from oils to pastels when his eyes
began to fail him.

Busch was now inflated like a sea monster bath toy. In the
end Bosculus, having alluded to Trollope to illustrate zestful
industriousness, relented and offered Busch a chance to raise
his mark by writing an extra paper.

"I can't," Busch said. "I have no time."

In that case, he still had another term. Busch could fill his
English requirement in the second half of the year, as many
students did.

"Come on, Mr. Botchalus. Let's cut the crap."

Nothing moved.

"How do you think the administration would feel about
you screwing with Karen Rumako?"

"*Your* screwing."

"*My* screwing?"

"Grammar. Grammar." Then Bosculus sat back and shut
his eyes to watch all the icons in the world gather in an expectant circle around him. "I can't believe you said that,"
Bosculus said.

TABLE 47   117

Busch held firm.

Bosculus figured out a statement. He said, "Anything you feel you have to tell anyone about me you must tell, regardless of your grade in English One. Just as I, in conscience, must give you the grade you deserve regardless of your blackmailing attempt."

Busch was not put off. He deflated only enough to get through the door.

"Think it over," he said menacingly. "There's plenty of time."

In the end, Busch passed.

Not because Bosculus knuckled under. It was not that Bosculus feared for his job or for Karen's reputation. Nor that he hoped to spare Busch the agony of confronting himself as a coward as well as a failure.

Bosculus had considered all of these arguments. He had weighed them and studied them from many angles. He had asked himself all the pertinent questions and answered them to his satisfaction. He had concluded that Busch would never bring his accusation to Dr. Chamberlain. For if Busch failed English One, it would be too late for blackmail. There would be no reason for him to approach the chairman. If, from unreasonable spite, he did, the chairman would have no reason to believe his story. If, unreasonably, she did believe it, and then undiplomatically broached the question to Bosculus, he would have no reason to lie.

If Busch didn't know, surely Dr. Chamberlain knew what Bosculus had discovered. That great numbers of faculty went to bed with great numbers of students. Even at Tate Community. No reputation would be ruined, neither his nor Karen's. There would be no disgrace. Possibly some mild discomfort, embarrassment at the most. For these were new times. Karen was past the age of consent. Bosculus was, he had been pleased to learn, only human.

So the blackmail wouldn't work. Bosculus was outside the target zone.

In the end, Busch passed because everybody passed. Bosculus was simply unable to draw the line. For if Busch failed, then everybody who did more poorly than he would have to be failed too. That would have been over half the class. If over half the class were to fail, then Bosculus would have proved himself an incompetent teacher. But Bosculus knew he was not incompetent, so he gave only four D's—passed without credit—to the four students at the bottom, four who had not learned even to show up for attendance-taking or to turn in something, anything, when an assignment was due.

But in the end, Bosculus was fired anyway.

Dr. Chamberlain was extremely regretful. Bosculus left the scene of the painful final interview knowing she had let him go with the utmost reluctance and the deepest regret. She still liked him very much and could be counted on for excellent references. In fact, she wrote a laudatory note on the spot and had her secretary type it up while Bosculus waited. The note, on heavy bond paper with the engraved seal of Myra Tate Community College with its cap and scroll emblem, declared Bernard Bosculus to be a first-rate scholar and a topflight teacher.

However, Miss Boyle—soon to be Mrs. Hart—had at last checked in and would be returning next term. Miss Boyle, Dr. Chamberlain explained, was a very popular teacher. The students, Dr. Chamberlain said more than once, were crazy about her.

"He went to Toronto," Yuri says.

"I had no idea what went on over the Christmas holidays.

TABLE 47 119

I got back from my vacation trip and Bosculus was behaving like a zombie. I thought he had mononucleosis. He was not a person you could find anything out from. Ask him what's up and he'd give you a theory of spatial relations."

"Maybe he was on drugs," Flossie suggests.

"No," say I, Cindy Storey, with my intimate understanding of all things Bosculous. "All he was was in love."

"In any case," Yuri continues, "he made his decisions without consulting me. All I knew was that at the end of the term he was packing up and moving out. He managed to get himself a job in a private school in Toronto, where he taught the children of serious Anglophiles, Jewish refugees from Montreal and conscientious objectors from the States who had joined the Canadian establishment. Karen went with him, and went to the university there. She gave piano lessons on the side, in the homes of pupils she got by advertising in the Yonge Street Shoppers' Guide. They were married, of course, Karen and Bosculus. I stayed with them for a while after I got fed up with Tate Community."

Geraldine looks moony. "Good you quit," she tells Yuri, who may or may not be her husband.

"He makes a lot more money waxing floors," she tells us. "And he's a free man besides."

"But more important," Yuri amends. "I am making a contribution to the betterment of humankind. A clean and shining floor is a solid foundation."

"Good thing Bibby was fired," Geraldine goes on. "He'd never have quit."

This calls for a moment of silent thought. Obe Morley observes it with the rest of us, but he is a man who despises speculation. "What happened then?" he asks with an impatient gesture toward the stage.

Following the sweep of his arm, we see Bibby up there, still in the grip of his fans and sycophants. But in the foreground, whom am I amazed to see approaching Table 47 with a smile of determined graciousness, but Jennifer, the new Mrs. Bosculus, Karen's successor and the companion of Bibby's success.

Obe, deferred if not deterred—certainly detoured—makes a grimace and Flossie moves just a heartbeat closer to him.

PART THREE

Jennifer is classical tonight. Balanced and composed with fair hair piled over a Greek statue's face. Pale crepe is draped with Doric purity on her well-proportioned body.

She used to be the NBS Color Girl. Her clear skin was the tuning fork for the rightness of color tones on the home screens when Paul and color were new to TV. Paul used to tell me about the Color Girl, what a firecracker she was. But now she is seemly—processional in posture, judicial in gesture.

I lean over to Paul with unseemly envy and wisecrack, "Instant D.A.R." Near Jennifer, I remember that I forgot to shape my fingernails. I feel like a bagel on a tray of petits fours. I wish I had on a five-hundred-dollar gown, but I know it wouldn't do any good. She, with her velvet skin and enameled eyes, is walking with one of the Peters—the cartoonist or the bandleader or the fashion photographer. One Peter or another is always in the columns escorting this or that married socialite to this or that brilliant party at this or that spiffy address, including the present ballroom. I would be thrilled, but Jennifer has been Mrs. Bosculus for almost a year now and she is as unexcited as if she were asking the doorman to sign for a package from Bergdorf's.

"Oysters!" I hear her say to Peter or Marc or Burt as they break the sound barrier. "Oysters! Good heavens! The French are coming *here* for oysters. They're out of sight in Paris!"

Father Joe takes a look and continues his sentence. ". . . we're into standards at the A.E.S.," he's saying to Yuri. "More than twenty-two thousand key managers and executives have attended our training programs for building skills, developing profit strategies, streamlining systems, motivating behavior and maintaining quality."

"I know what you do," Yuri says. "You plug them in. I see your people on planes and trains, with open manuals on their lap and earplugs in their head. Your people never look out the window."

Jennifer is with us now. Her Marc has walked ahead to spare us the discomfort of introductions. This time, because we are all in place, Jennifer knows us. She goes around the table with appropriate greetings, and does it very well. Obe, of course, used to be her boss. Paul, too, she knows from the "Evening Roundup." And Flossie.

I'm sure she never noticed me, the wife of the party.

Father Joe gets up and identifies himself and Yuri stretches a hand across the table. "We have the advantage," Yuri says. "When Geraldine and I last met you, we were part of a big crowd, but you were the only bride present. And a lovely one."

Geraldine, too, shakes hands democratically. "It's a great night," she says.

"Oh, Cindy!" Jennifer turns to me with a beam of recognition. "How very nice to see you. How nice of you to come all the way from Connecticut."

It's not Connecticut but I'm warmed anyway. Jennifer's charm mechanism is near-perfect. Not cool enough to put us off. Not warm enough to draw us on. She gives us all our due and a little more for good measure before she recedes to rejoin Peter.

"Poor Karen," I say with some satisfaction. "If she'd only hung on."

Paul puts on his judge face: "It wouldn't have happened with Karen."

"Typical second wife." That's Geraldine, out loud, as soon as the coast is clear.

"Don't sell her short," Oberon says. Jennifer was his script girl while she doubled before the color cameras. "She knows what she wants and that saves a lot of grief."

Flossie translates: "He means that Jenny don't give you no helpless white girl garbage. She's all business. You can deal with her."

"She's just what Bernie needs," Obe adds.

TABLE 47 125

I must agree that Jennifer is marvelously in control of herself and her life. That's because she's single-mindedly devoted to the cause. She's her own full-time commitment.

"So what kind of a wife was Karen?" Flossie wants to know, going back to Obe's deferred question.

"The same," I say. I'm the expert on Bibby's first marriage. "Only her timing was bad. She wanted a ride on Bibby's two-seater, but he only had a scooter at the time."

Yuri is looking nostalgic. He lived with them for a while after he left the college. "Karen expected Bosculus to be famous," Yuri says. "She thought she had married a cross between the Archbishop of Canterbury and the president of Harvard. She revered him. At first."

Father Joe reminds us that he married them. As if he's reminding himself, he adds, "It isn't heaven where marriages are made. More like a cosmological laboratory. Valences. Magnetic force."

Don't listen to the celibate. Listen to me, probably the only married woman at Table 47. I'm old enough to remember movie palaces where the screen was framed with carved cupids and every story ended with a kiss. Violins played as the lovers strolled into a sunlit future with the words THE END shimmering across their forever-bound behinds. When I was a kid, that's what love meant to me.

"That's what Bibby and Karen meant to me," I explain. "They were a sweet story in a sour world. They were happy together and they cared about each other."

Yuri understands. "You had a stake in their marriage and you wanted it to win."

"One man's marriage is another man's environment," says Obe Morley, the skeptic.

By the time I met Bibby, Yuri had long ago moved out of the Bosculus apartment and was poet-in-residence at Arizona

State University, writing in the architectural style of Frank
Lloyd Wright. Whatever support he'd needed—or maybe just
the time—he'd gotten from Bibby and Karen. He was content
in his desert setting, collecting cactuses and studying the eco-
logical wisdom of the Saguaro Indians.

I heard a lot about him from Bibby and Karen, who valued
Yuri above all their highly valued friends. When I met Bibby
and Karen, they were living in suburban Long Island, close
enough to New York City to feel terrible that they couldn't
afford to live there.

This nice young couple lived in three interlocking rooms in
what was once the attic of Paul's Aunt Min's house. Paul and
I lived two towns away and so we had to visit her pretty
often. Visiting Min Crain was like taking a swim in the
Slough of Despond. She had a face like old newspaper and
she walked as if she were carrying coal. She had turned
depression into an instrument of torture and Bibby Bosculus
became her chief victim.

Obe Morley cracks a small smile at me. "Never could defend himself," Obe says.

"Bibby," I delightedly continue, "was the one who had to
sit in Aunt Min's comfortable armchair while she teetered on
a swivel stool that had lost its piano in that other Great
Depression, of the thirties."

She'd plead with him to try the chicken salad she'd just
made with her own mayonnaise.

He'd feel sorry for her: "Just a little taste."

She'd push a plateful on him. If he didn't eat it all, she'd
say, "Don't you like it?" If he ate it all, she'd look at the
empty bowl and sigh so he'd know she didn't have any left
for herself.

Karen paid no attention to Aunt Min. "She's got a son of
her own," Karen told Bibby. "Let her lay the double bind on
him."

"But he never shows up."

TABLE 47 127

"That's because he's smarter than us."

But Bibby was soft. He'd say, "It's not such a sacrifice to be nice to an old lady."

"Too bad you don't believe in heaven," Karen would say fondly. "You'd surely make it."

Paul and I heard about the people upstairs soon after they'd moved in.

"Not what you'd call a go-getter, the husband. Not very fast on the uptake, if you know what I mean. But she's very clean, the wife. Makes a neat appearance." Aunt Min rose painfully to her feet and crossed the little living room to straighten a picture. "So far they're pretty quiet," she said, transporting a dish of cherries from the table near Paul to the table near me. "Can't complain," she said regretfully. "Have some cherries."

"No thanks. I'm on a diet."

"They're very sweet. I just got them this morning." She looked so hopeful that Paul, from pity, got up and took a handful.

"You know how much cherries cost these days?" she said when he'd eaten them. "I paid ninety-nine cents a pound." She limped into the kitchen and returned with a saucer. "For the pits," she said to Paul, who'd put some pits in an ashtray.

"The wife is a little bit independent," she said. "I don't bother with her. I mind my own business. You know that."

She shuffled back to her piano stool and sat. "The baby's real cute," she admitted. "But wait till it starts running around. Then we'll see."

I met Karen in the backyard. She was having a fight with a lightweight baby buggy that was supposed to be collapsible. Paul was in the house with his aunt. I was outside on the pretext of needing to do some shopping at the German delicatessen around the corner. I took as long as I could to buy a pound of cole slaw. Then I walked back around the corner, counting to six for every step. In the backyard, when I got there, was this truculent young woman shaking the buggy and kicking at the wheels. She was small—not much over five-two—and all the head-shaking exertion made her hair shoot out like a dandelion. She was dressed in a functional, young-mother uniform and was ablaze with determination to flatten the damned buggy. I tried to give her a hand but as usual only made things worse. Between yanks and tugs, she told me she was the tenant. The baby was upstairs with his father. After I'd given up and she'd got the thing to fold flat, she took a sidelong look at me and said, "Come up when you get a chance and meet my husband. You two would get along."

I don't know how she knew that.

"My husband is a scholar," she said.

Their little red Volkswagen stood in the driveway. She flung up the hood and pushed the buggy in where the motor should have been. Then she slammed the hood down and ran into the garage, where Aunt Min's brown Dodge skulked among piles of old newspapers, obsolete appliances and boxes of old clothes waiting for Presbyterian rummage sales. Karen came out with a pair of garden shears and started to cut some roses from bushes along the back fence. She got an armful, so it had to be May or early June when I met her.

"He's writing his dissertation," Karen told me. "For his doctorate."

It was about the nineteenth-century Russian poet Afanasi Afanasievich Fet, friend of Tolstoy and Turgenev. *Chacun à son goût*, but imagine a doctoral candidate out here in the wilds of Aunt Min! I marched right up to see him, stopping only to check in downstairs where Paul and his aunt were watching her favorite TV game show. Paul was too numb to move.

TABLE 47   129

Upstairs, the roses were already in a mayonnaise jar on the kitchen table. The husband was in the living room, hammering at a low shelf. Karen introduced me as if I were a trophy: "Mrs. Crain's niece-in-law." The husband looked for a place to put his hammer. He explained, with a slight stutter, that they were expecting guests who'd have to sleep in the living room. His hammering had to do with their comfort. He finally put the hammer in his left hand and stood up and shook hands with me.

As I looked around the living room, he looked with me, for the pleasure of seeing it from a new pair of eyes. What I saw looked like an altar of books. One whole wall, floor to ceiling, window side to door side. The books were categorized, alphabetized and arrayed like an army—every spine straight, not one out of line. The shelves and brackets were polished to a high sheen.

"My wife made these," Bernard said. "She surprised me when I was away for a few days."

"For his birthday," Karen told me. "Better than all those boxes." She had a sweet smile, chipped tooth.

Otherwise there was not much to comment on. One lordly reading chair sat in front of the shelves with a ladylike lamp leaning over its shoulder. A proletarian couch, low and lumpy, crouched against the opposite wall and tried to be jaunty by wearing a Mexican blanket over its faded upholstery. In between, there were two folding chairs and a spindly card table. There were plenty of pictures on the walls, but most of them were religious—icons and such, framed reproductions. Bernard pointed out one little watercolor that was original: a small, abstract design they'd bought at a boardwalk art show during a visit to his parents at Virginia Beach. Karen showed me a painted bowl their friend Yuri, a poet, had given them.

Just inside the bedroom door was a lavish playpen, colored

plastic, with animal pictures on the padded floor and bead games set into the netted sides. Karen was very proud of it.

"My mother got it with supermarket stamps," she said. "She got us the crib, too."

They led me over to look at the baby, asleep in the crib at the foot of the bed. There was no room between crib and wall so we leaned over the long way. The baby was sleeping on his belly, a delicious lump under his foamy quilt. His fat hands were curled next to his shoulders and his face was turned toward the light. I could just make out a pointed nose, a prim little mouth, one blissfully bland eyebrow, shut eye, a bit of ear under fair hair like his mother's. Bernard leaned farther into the crib and, with his big hand spread, covered for a moment, not quite touching, the baby's face. The baby smiled in his sleep.

"We had him by natural childbirth," Bernard said as we left the room. "I was there all the time."

The guests arrived two days late. They called from Philadelphia to say they were still coming but they didn't know when. They showed up very late the next night, rattling through the kitchen and dumping their backpacks on the living room floor. Bibby gave them the low shelf for their belongings. They stood their tote bags side by side. Dody's said DODY. Kurt's said FOOD.

Bibby and Karen acquired friends as tenderly and carefully as they furnished their apartment. They polished and protected each piece of furniture: they nurtured their friends. In Toronto, before Brucie was born, Bibby's friend Yuri had stayed with them for months while they worried over him and tried to help solve his problems. In Syracuse, while Karen was pregnant, there had been a parade of roomers and boarders: his friends from the Academy of the Three Saints,

TABLE 47 131

her childhood friends from Elyria, hers from Myra Tate Community College, theirs from Toronto. Since the move to Long Island they hadn't encountered much society, so they were overjoyed to have visitors.

The present company was especially welcome. Dody had been Karen's friend since kindergarten. She was a real pianist, smart as well as talented, and weighted with delectable problems about identity and commitment. Kurt was Dody's manager, mentor, tormentor and lover. Kurt was from Vienna. He had taught music at the University of Toronto and was a man of the world who made no visible effort to be a man of the world. That was what Bibby liked most about him—no cashmere sweaters, no Sunday brunch fixations, no smelling of bottle corks and no wok in his kitchen. In fact, no kitchen.

Bibby liked Kurt's burnished look—choppy hair, gaudy mustache, a strong, younger man's jawline. And Karen was crazy about him because he treated her as an intellectual equal and flirted with her at the same time. They liked the shadows of Kurt's European past and the slight shadiness of his American present—his unsugared, undoctored consumption of life. Dody's adoration became him and, of course, nobody had to explain why Kurt adored Dody: Dody was adorable. She had an electric frizz of honey-colored hair, brown eyes forever dazzled, a body that seemed to be made without bones and a personality without edge. She wore long skirts, gypsy shawls and sandals and was the only person Karen knew who didn't shave her legs—not for political reasons, only because she didn't have to.

They sat on the floor drinking Hunter's Red from plastic cups. Karen sat close to Kurt. He wanted to know how it felt to have a baby—no, not spiritually, but where it hurt if it hurt and what kind of tension it produced. Bibby, with his knees up and his back against the reading chair, was listening to Dody.

The reason for this visit was a recital at a small Manhattan college. "I'll be so glad to play in a real auditorium," she said with a sweet sigh. "Hotel casinos are always the wrong shape. The sound gets lost. You can't bring the audience together."

Dody and Kurt had spent the winter in Las Vegas, on the bill with the comedian Buddy Thatcher. Bibby didn't watch TV and hardly ever read a newspaper, so he'd never heard of Thatcher. But he was impressed anyway. Dody could play show tunes as well as her regular repertoire, which was heavy on Mozart, Haydn and Scarlatti. In the spring she and Kurt had been trying out a piano package that included a spoken warmup and patter between numbers.

Bibby loved Dody's playing. She sounded at least as good as many of his LPs. He was glad she was finding an audience. But Kurt thought his look meant something else.

"Count your blessings, my dear Dody," he said, without removing his gaze from Karen. "Sunshine in the winter. Mountain air in the summer. Fed by motherly Catskill waiters from the best of long kosher menus."

He closed his eyes in pleasurable memory. "Who else makes love in twin double beds with vibrating mattresses and dirty movies on closed-circuit TV?"

"Kurt, you're so crazy. We only had one room like that."

"But what a room!"

Dody stood up and did an imitation of one of her club acts. People in the audience ordering drinks and yelling to their friends. Dody asking the manager how come her piano had three keys missing. It was funny. Karen and Kurt laughed so hard it was lucky they were on the floor to begin with.

"My dear Dody," Kurt said. "It's the best training in the world."

Karen was jealous. She hadn't been away since Virginia Beach, which was more of a drag than a vacation.

TABLE 47   133

"Next winter," Kurt went on, "if I negotiate *very* sharply, we'll be on two Caribbean cruises."

Karen said, "When Bibby's dissertation gets published and he becomes a recognized authority, we are going to get research fellowships to study in Moscow and Leningrad and Paris. We are going to lecture all over the world and never stay less than a week in any great city."

Kurt paid close attention. "You have it all worked out," he said. "And it will come to pass. You'll see."

Soon the baby woke up and had to be fed.

Late Saturday afternoon, Kurt and Dody still there, they drank most of a half gallon of chablis and listened to Bibby's albums of *Manon* and *Manon Lescaut*. Kurt and Dody argued for an hour about the relative merits of Massenet and Puccini. It was still light, but suppertime, and Karen ran downstairs and across the crew-cut lawn to get the teenager next door to baby-sit Brucie. Then the four grownups, very merry, trooped out to an Indian vegetarian health-food restaurant near enough to walk to.

Karen skipped ahead of the party and then skipped backward while they caught up. "I will sit in the front row of all Bibby's lectures and record them on tape." She had seen a great professor's wife do this. "For posterity," she said.

"For *prosperity*," Kurt said.

"I shall wear my hair on top of my head like a queen. I will be so classy. I can't decide whether to have fur coats or to be decent and just have elegant cloth coats of the finest cashmere."

Kurt spun her around and took her arm. "Have furs, darling. Only get them from mean animals. Mink and chinchillas. No one will miss them. You'll look gorgeous. Ermine are mean, too."

Dody was walking on her toes, rustling her tasseled shawl. "Karen, do you remember in high school how we used to window-shop? We were always in front of Oppenheimer's with our tongues hanging out. We were afraid to go in, the salesladies were so snooty."

"Yes. And you thought every style would be perfect for you."

"Yes. Because I'm so versatile."

"Me too," Karen told Kurt. "Everything looks good on me. Really. Even cheap things. It's a talent I have."

Kurt said, "I'll bet nothing looks good on you, too."

Karen laughed. "I think I look better with clothes on."

"That's something we'll have to find out," Kurt said.

"What a terrific restaurant!" Dody loved the atmosphere. Yellowed walls. Cracked ceiling. The odor of spiced grease floating in heavy drifts from the curtained-off kitchen. A couple of stained posters advertising touristic delights of India. There was no liquor license, so Bibby and Kurt went out for a six-pack while the women sat down and studied a mimeographed menu.

With the beer they ate curried vegetables and fried vegetable patties, vegetable fritters and thin soup with raisins, yogurt-soaked salad, rice with pieces of colored things in it, three varieties of greasy flat bread and a green dip that set fire to the roof of the mouth. They tasted and traded and found that the four flavors of herb tea all tasted the same though one was very red and one was very green. Dessert was cakes coiled like snakes and sweet enough to make their teeth hurt.

"It's really a neat place!" Dody raved again.

Karen credited Bibby. "He always finds interesting food. He's taught me to eat things from all over the world."

TABLE 47

135

"We always take out-of-town friends here," Bibby said. "It's not bad for the Island."

"Did you want the baby so soon?" Dody asked Karen as they hurried home to relieve the sitter.

"It wasn't *so* soon," Karen said. "We were married almost three years." Bibby had wanted to wait but Karen couldn't see it. So they left it up to fate and physiology. "We were doing really good in Toronto. Syracuse was a disaster, but we'll do better here. The university is tops for Bibby's field."

"You're so directed," Dody said wistfully.

"I like to know where I'm going. I don't mind being poor now because I know we've got a great future."

"Kurt only wants to keep moving," Dody said. "But I know I'm going to want to be connected to something someday."

Kurt and Bibby came up behind them, talking about three *pows* in a phrase from the second movement of Beethoven's Third Symphony. They all tiptoed up the back steps not to disturb Mrs. Crain, the landlady, and they got the baby sitter out fast so they could smoke pot. Kurt had some in his backpack: "A gift from one of my young friends." He dipped into the leather pouch and pulled out a big pinch, which he rubbed between thumb and fingertips. "I'm told it's the best Colombian," he said, sniffing it dubiously. "However." He had rolling papers, too. Karen couldn't stop laughing, but Bibby was serious. He pulled down the window shades. "We don't need to advertise," he said.

They passed the joint. Karen was still giggling. She said, "No fair, Dody. You and your lung capacity."

"It never works for me," Kurt said. "I'm too controlled. Can't be hypnotized either." Squiggles of smoke came out of his nose and the corners of his mouth. "My fate," he said, looking at Karen.

"Oh, yeah?" Karen said.

It made him think of a story. In Jamaica, once, he got hold of some ganja. "I was in a local bar in Montego Bay. Alone. Steel band. Women dancing. One of the dancers—an arrogant young woman with sharp shoulders and a wet mouth, very wicked, sat down with me, lit a cigarette and held it to my lips. I don't remember another thing. The next morning I was in my room at the guest house and I didn't know how I got there.

"I still had money in my pocket. My bones were in place. The concierge told me what happened. She was an Englishwoman, old, in her seventies. She told me she and her young local lover—a beautiful black man, six foot, four inches tall— they had been called to come get me out of jail.

"I took her word. I don't know how or why I got to the jail. It was apparently not such a rare occurrence with their guests." He took the joint from Dody's hand and lay back on the floor.

"That afternoon the young dancer from the night before appeared at the guest house and found her way to my room. She came in as if we were old sweethearts. She said—imagine —she could never have enough of me. I didn't know she'd had any. Alas, she had no more ganja. I don't know if I rose to her expectations or not. I had to leave eventually to make a midnight plane. But it was, I would say, a memorable evening."

He rolled over and stretched out on his side.

Karen watched him.

Dody watched Karen.

Bibby said, "If I fall asleep, I apologize in advance." He offered the double bed in the bedroom to Kurt and Dody. "And we'll move Brucie in here with us."

TABLE 47   137

Kurt wouldn't hear of it. "Let the dear child sleep in peace. Dody and I will be better than comfortable out here. The floor is a playground." He went into the bathroom and flushed his roach down the toilet. His voice came back first, saying, "In fact, I invite you to join us. One sleeping bag is better for two."

Karen got some more wine from the kitchen.

The lights were down and there wasn't a nerve in the house. Bibby was afloat in his reading chair, Dody like a pussy-cat on the floor beside him with her head against his thigh. Kurt stood in the dim light of the bedroom doorway. As Karen came by with the wine jug, he put an arm around her. She stopped and leaned back against him. He brushed her temple with his lips. She liked his mustache. "Sweet girl," he murmured.

"That's cool," she said. "Naked or nighties?" Karen never turned down a dare. She lifted her face and Kurt kissed her lightly on the mouth.

"Naked," he said.

"Not naked," Bibby said, from sleep.

Dody's arm was around his thigh. "I don't have any paja-mas."

"Karen will lend you something."

In the end they just spread out the sleeping bags and drifted down. Clothes came off and stayed where they fell. Karen, naked, curled against Bibby in jockey shorts and zipped the sleeping bag up to her chest.

Dody and Kurt couldn't get settled. They opened their bag flat out and started fooling around like a pair of acrobats. Dody squeaking and giggling, Kurt grunting, laughing. Sections of body, like cubist art, could be seen rolling, climbing —an arc of hip, a nipple, a navel passing through the thin sheet of light, a slice of back, his, hers—irresistible. Karen was circling her shoulders against Bibby, moving his hands over her breasts, lightly, so he would feel every grain of her.

They made love, each couple taking flame from the other's excitement. Some time in the night, in the shallows, Karen felt Kurt looking at her. He was lying flat on his back, close enough for her to reach out and touch. She liked an older man's thick back and shoulder. She pressed the thickness of his skin with her fingertips, liked it, stroked circles with the side of her thumb. Kurt didn't move. Dody was so soft and boneless, Karen thought he'd like to know what a tensile woman felt like, a sinewy, sinuous woman who did twenty pushups a day and jogged three times a week. She pulled down the zipper, ever so softly. Kurt reached over. His hand was thicker, harder, hairier than Bibby's. It was a forceful and demanding hand.

Bibby caught his breath, jumped, turned. Karen eased the zipper up. She was in a fever. She was all over Bibby. Bibby smelled her, felt her heat and went as wild as she. Magic happened on the other bag. Dody was up a wall—no wires, no props—a steeplejack. Another moment, she was down and Kurt was up afloat like a levitation act. Bibby went beyond himself. Karen was, for once, satisfied. She felt like the world's happiest puddle, a queen's golden pocket, turned inside out, *splat*; she felt, after the storm, pure delight.

"Three times!" She slapped Bibby on the back. "Three times in a night. Oh, wow!"

Bibby was ashamed and afraid of himself. Karen had become more wonderful to him since her womb had worked its wonders. Since then he had watched her industry increase, her tenderness deepen. To savage her in the night, he worried, was not right.

Midmorning in the kitchen, while Brucie sat in his feeding chair and Karen fed him mashed fruit from a jar, Kurt and

TABLE 47   139

Dody had a battle. Dody said Kurt took too long to come. Kurt said how could a man come while Dody was bucking like a bronco. Kurt was drinking from a glass of orange juice. He asked Dody to pour him some more. Dody said he could get it himself. "But you're standing next to the icebox, my dear."

"I'll be happy to move."

"I receive your message, but I won't play that game."

"What game?"

"I won't embarrass you by mentioning your insane jealousy."

"Go right ahead. Since you only make yourself look crazy."

"Dody, stop with the passive aggression."

"Okay," she said. "You want active aggression?" She opened the refrigerator and brought out the pitcher of orange juice. She held it over his head.

"Put that down."

She tipped the pitcher and let a thin stream of juice pour on his head.

He punched her on the hip.

She froze with the container held high. "Don't hit me. I'll hit you right back."

"I'd advise you not to."

She set the container on the table and slapped him across the mouth.

He jumped up and slammed her cheek with the back of his hand.

The baby started to cry.

"Cut it out!" Karen yelled.

Bibby came running from the bathroom.

Dody was stiff, bloodless. "I can't believe you did that." She held her face. "I'm going to be black and blue. I've got a recital."

Everybody ran for ice. The baby was interested now, watching the action, making happy sounds. Bibby spilled ice cubes on the floor. Karen picked them up in a dish towel, rapped it on the table, gave it to Dody to hold against her face. Dody told Kurt: "I'm not crying, you bastard. My eyes are tearing from pain."

Kurt held his juice glass in a trembling hand.

"Why didn't you kill me?" Dody said into her ice bag. "You've already ruined my life."

It took about an hour for them to calm down, make up, pack and get out. Bibby and Karen were only half glad to see them go.

Karen said, "I can't believe that man is almost fifty."

Two weeks later their friend Ted from Toronto showed up. He had left his wife. She, mother of three children under five, was having an affair with Ted's insurance agent. No sooner had Ted pulled himself together and found a place of his own than Liz Portland, a college friend of Karen's, called and came. Her husband was drinking, staying out all night, getting calls from women who insulted Liz and threatening to kill himself whenever Liz complained. She needed time to get some perspective. While she was there, Yuri arrived for a brief visit and shared the living room, Liz on the couch and Yuri on the floor, getting it on with her at least once after a late party. Joe Farley, the seminarian, who had happened to be in Toronto in time to marry Bibby and Karen, called from New York City one day and came out to supper. He was facing a crisis in his vocation. He wanted to quit parish work: the people were boring; he could not move them to combine faith and works; they only wanted to help their own. Joe was tempted to apply for a transfer to Mexico and work for land reform.

"Nobody's getting along," Karen remarked during a lull in visitors.

Bibby had an answer. "Nobody," he said, "is willing to move over and make room for anybody else."

He and Karen knew they weren't like that.

TABLE 47   141

They were in bed and pleased with themselves.

"Move over, will you?" Karen said.

Bibby rolled over onto his back and spread his arms out. Karen rolled into them.

These were the facts of their life:

* Bibby and Karen shared responsibilities. Bibby drove a local taxi weekday mornings and Sundays. Saturdays he worked at a discount shoe store on the highway. Afternoons and evenings he worked on his dissertation, often at the public library.

Karen prepared tasty meals from cheap meat cuts and in-season produce. She took care of Brucie and kept the house spotless. (Sometimes, scurrying about her orderly kitchen, she imagined she was in a TV commercial. She smiled with her lower lip over the edge of her upper teeth so the audience wouldn't see her chipped tooth.)

* Karen shopped in the Waldbaum's, the Safeway and the Food Fair with wads of coupons she cut from magazines and newspapers or received in the mail addressed to "Resident." She saved seven cents on a box of salt and forty cents on a family-sized jug of liquid detergent. She shopped where the sales were and also collected saving stamps, taking filled books to the trading center and redeeming them for household necessities like sheets and towels and glasses and pots.

* They loved their coffee mugs and used them every morning. These were a wedding gift from Yuri Marchuk, six flower-painted mugs, imported from Finland. The rest of their crockery was handed down or chipped. Like their furniture. Karen and Bibby felt they shouldn't buy things till they could afford what they really wanted.

* Bibby liked to wear bunchy sweaters, T-shirts, nondescript pants, torn sneakers or beat-up shoes.

Karen dressed preppy, in skirts and blazers, polished loafers and tailored coats. Most of her clothes came from her mother, who chose them to mix and match and look different with different accessories.

Karen's mother, with her superb street contacts, also provided most of the baby's things straight off the backs of trucks.

* Karen consolidated shopping and errands for a once-a-week car trip, to save gas. Bibby sometimes drove to the university and sometimes drove to the subway in Queens. Their great fear was a car breakdown and the cost of repairs.

* They owed Bibby's stepfather close to four thousand dollars for the car and moving expenses. They owed Karen's parents another thousand dollars for rent deposit, security and fixing up the apartment. They owed the obstetrician, the pediatrician, the dentist and the Easyloan of Westbury, Inc. for financing their car. (Karen tried to pay off a little every month. But she took the rent out first. Mrs. Crain was strict about getting paid on time.)

* Saturdays she'd wheel the baby to a garage sale. She'd carry only singles and change. "I only have a dollar," she would tell the man. The brass candlesticks might be tagged to sell for four-fifty. The man would be sorry for Karen and let her have them for the dollar.

* Bibby made extra money driving travelers to the airport. He put that money aside, and on a birthday or wedding anniversary used it to take Karen to a tablecloth restaurant with tasseled menus and hovering waiters who served from carts. Karen would get the wall seat so she could look out at the roomful of prosperous eaters. Bibby sat across, watching Karen enjoy herself.

* Karen saved dimes until she had enough to buy Bibby a used copy of a heavy book called *Experiencing Russian Literature*. In his rare free time—for example, on a Sunday night—Bibby would read and Karen would keep herself busy playing records, bathing the baby, washing windows, baking a cake. She kept deferentially quiet when Bibby was reading.

TABLE 47

143

* Their combined presence was pleasurable to other people as well as to themselves. They had a bodily complaisance —not that they couldn't keep their hands or their eyes off each other, but when their hands happened to touch or their eyes happened to meet, they were exalted by the contact.

Back at Table 47, I am being sentimental and regretting it. "Sorry for sounding syrupy," I tell my little audience, "but I was very fond of this young family. My own household was feeling some tremors at the time and I looked upon Bibby and Karen as a reassuring case of how married is supposed to be."

Paul forgets how edgy things were between us. Or won't remember. But he and Obe Morley pass a man's look between them. I don't know how much Obe knew in those days when Paul was riding high on the "Evening Roundup."

"I know what you mean," Father Joe says. "I thought, here was one Academy dropout who wasn't screwing up his life."

The price of belief is not to look too hard or too long.

"I saw a lot of Bibby and Karen," I continue my story.

"The dissertation on Fet went slowly and the baby grew fast. Brucie was a beautiful child. He had eyes like Pepsi-Cola and hair like buttered popcorn. He was so pleased with himself and with the world that I never heard him cry. When he started to locomote, of course, his parents had to change their ways. Fewer guests, for one thing. More outings. One or the other had to spend a good deal of every day keeping an eye on him. And he kept an eye on them, too, so they moved his crib into the living room. They didn't mind his encroachments because Brucie was a wanted baby. They saw his accomplishments as marvelous and they loved him very much.

"Karen would sometimes bring him over to visit me while

Bibby was studying. I heard all about their friends. Kurt and Dody were in Europe. Liz Portland was back with her husband and they were going to family therapy. Yuri was getting published and giving readings. And Joe Farley, if I remember it right,"—he blinks clown's eyes at me—"gave up his parish and took a public relations job with the central office of his church." No comment from Joe. "Everybody was moving up."

"Or at least moving around," Joe says.

Karen had spent the afternoon at Cindy Storey's, where Brucie had a beautiful time running free in the big backyard while Cindy told Karen about the party she was planning for the next weekend: dinner for ten, roast prime rib, hors d'oeuvres served with drinks in the living room, hired help in the kitchen.

Bibby got home later than usual from the library that night. Dinner was chicken wings and backs with spaghetti. "What page are you on?" Karen asked.

"Fifty-seven. Why?"

"Last week you were on sixty-three."

"I have to go back and make corrections."

"When will you be finished?"

"You know, Karen, this kind of work isn't once-over-lightly. It's not advertising copy."

PIANO LESSONS
IN YOUR HOME
Beginners—Intermediate
Classical—Pop
Call after 5:30   555-0302

The Shoppers' Weekly charged three dollars for the ad, but payment was required only if the ad drew responses.

TABLE 47   145

Since Karen's ad resulted in only two piano pupils, she decided not to pay for it. However, those two pupils soon referred her to two more and, at six dollars for a half-hour lesson, it worked out very well. The pupils were all children, so Karen taught in the late afternoon, after school. On Karen's teaching days Bibby stayed home with Brucie, and to compensate he stayed late at the library on the other days, usually until the ten o'clock closing time. Though it was close to midnight when Bibby got home, Karen had the table set and supper waiting. She ate with him cheerfully. Getting out made Karen livelier. But Bibby was tired. He put a lot of energy into taking care of Brucie. On the nights of his Brucie days, Bibby was too tired to work. Karen said he should cut down his taxi-driving hours and take more time for the dissertation. She said she wanted him to get it over with so they could start real life.

Bibby accepted a second after-dinner scotch from Paul Storey. It was late on a Friday night. Brucie was asleep upstairs in a blanket on top of the Storeys' double bed. Cindy and Karen were stacking dishes in the dishwasher. Bibby sipped his drink pleasurably.

"I don't have to go to work tomorrow," he said.

"Day off?" Paul asked ironically. Bibby suspected that Paul disapproved of him and his financial arrangements.

"No," Karen called from the kitchen, and continued as she returned to the living room, "Bibby doesn't sell shoes anymore." She was proud of herself. She explained that the mother of one of her pupils had begun to take piano lessons. "An hour lesson! So I'm really making money now."

Bosculus never passed a bulletin board. In the Laundromat he stopped to read about lost dogs and cats up for adoption.

In the supermarket he learned of baby sitters, dancing teachers, lawn mowers and leaf blowers for rent, K. of C. picnics, Rotary boat rides, church bazaars, rummage sales, introductory lectures on meditation, mind control, Smoke-Enders, Weight Watchers.

The public library displayed announcements of senior citizens' meetings, Great Books discussions, bridge tournaments, blood bank collections, community theater performances of *Ah, Wilderness.*

The post office kept its rate lists and Wanted offenders on a wall near the counter, and out front, on an easel provided by the Women's Club, were public notices of school concerts, Recreation Commission outings, nearby historic restorations, informational programs sponsored by the League of Women Voters. Occasionally there was a discreet card announcing a meeting of the County Committee to End Discrimination in Housing. But the real excitement was on bulletin boards in the City.

Yuri Marchuk was back in town, on a state grant to teach poetry and poetry writing to public school children in the lower grades. On days when Bosculus was utterly unable to get down to his research, he sometimes dropped in on Yuri in his subsidized studio apartment at the edge of Greenwich Village. The bulletin board in that lobby was a whole wall of cork:

Classes in yoga, jazz dance, stretch, massage, Mexican cooking, kung fu, tai chi, aikido, clowning, midwifery, Greek for beginners. Bike rentals, skis for sale, walking tours, street theater. Seminars for home birthing, career planning, personal finance, oriental medicine, dealing with death. Transactional Analysis, EST, Jungian therapy, marriage counseling, hypnosis, acupuncture, Rolfing, psychodrama. Roommates wanted, rides wanted, tenants' meetings—all with the air of urgency. Reading this bulletin board, Bosculus knew that the grass really *was* greener in the other man's field.

TABLE 47   147

On the other hand, the bulletin board at the university made him feel guilty. This one was as long as the corridor in the Administration Building. Aside from a few course offerings and vacation options, it was active politics: Maoist, Taoist, Socialist Workers, John Birch, Moral Rearmament and a Gay synagogue in the neighborhood. Posters and broadsides overlapped and outshouted each other, an unruly mob of paper agitators.

OXFAM. ACLU. SLA. NAACP. SANE. SDA. AIUSA. CORE. CARE. SNCC. ADA. ACA. IPI. PIRG.

BAN THE BOMB. BEAT HUNGER. IMPEACH THE CHIEF JUSTICE. FREE POLITICAL PRISONERS. SAVE THE BAY. SAVE THE SEAL. SAVE DAVE. CONTROL HANDGUNS. BOYCOTT GRAPES. KNOW YOUR BODY. ABOLISH THE ELECTORAL COL-LEGE. OUTLAW THE DEATH PENALTY. END MAN-DATORY RETIREMENT. RIGHT TO LIFE. RIGHT TO CHOOSE. PUERTO RICO LIBRE.

Coming up were MEETINGS, MARCHES, VIGILS, RALLIES, TEACH-INS, SIT-INS, SIGN-INS, SING-INS, BUS TRIPS TO ALBANY AND WASHINGTON, D.C., WALK-A-THONS FOR SOVIET JEWRY.

Confronted by this bulletin board, Bosculus suffered a drop in self-esteem. He felt he wasn't doing his part. Downtown was Yuri, devoting himself to the awakening of young minds. Uptown, Joe Farley was promulgating godly messages. Activists everywhere were fighting for their convictions. But Bosculus, who yearned for goodness, was cursed with the lack of commitment.

He had a devastating tendency to see both sides.

He was never so much a socialist as when a rich guy was complaining about high taxes and never so much a capitalist as when a leftist was acclaiming the merits of a planned economy.

Once Bosculus went on a march to protest the war in Viet-

nam. He felt silly straggling along the suburban sidewalks
with a Sunday school crowd of mothers and children and a
few hippies from the Teen Center. He wore a suit and tie to
show the world that the anti-war movement included respectable people. But as far as he could gauge, no good came from
this demonstration or from university rallies he attended to
show support for women's reproductive rights and for improved conditions for migrant workers.

To make conscience more complicated, Bosculus recognized one of the hated mounted police who were monitoring
the rally for farm workers. He was the same policeman who,
less than two weeks before, on a Sunday afternoon in Central
Park had lifted Brucie and allowed him to sit for a thrilling
moment in front of him, on the saddle of his horse.

How can charming people have rotten politics and vice
versa, Bosculus often asked himself. Nothing matched. Even
Fet, a writer of passionate lyrics, was personally cold and po-
litically reactionary. Bosculus was beginning to feel fed up
with Fet. He would have gladly joined a group, but picky
thinking kept him apart. It was like the Mother's Day gift
boxes he used to buy in the five-and-ten-cent store: you
couldn't get the perfume and powder without the soap.

And still he longed to fight the good fight. Especially when
he stood in front of the bulletin board in the Administration
Building.

One day he got the chance to do it.

It came on a three-by-five card:

WRITERS, RESEARCHERS WANTED
Wade Belcher's Clean Congress Project
No experience needed.   Rooms provided.
June–July.   Modest Payment.   Call, write . . .

Bibbv got a letter off to Washington that night. Wade
Belcher was a fighter for the good. His enemies were the

TABLE 47 149

foisters of poisonous food additives, unreliable car parts, unsafe children's camps and substandard nursing homes on the American public. Bibby would have worked for Wade Belcher for nothing. But the Clean Congress Project promised him fifty dollars for a finished report—which, they assured him, would take very little time; some of the researchers were putting out three and four reports a week. Bibby signed on for two weeks.

Karen was glad. She planned to paint the closets while he was gone.

Wade Belcher was the only hero left.

The beloved old pacifist-pediatrician was honeymooning with one of his former patients.

The activist-psychotherapist who had opened a treatment center for juvenile junkies had been caught having wild parties with his in-patients.

The boy genius-college president credited with breaking obsolete traditions had run off with the woman in charge of his Affirmative Action program.

The civil rights leader, now the first elected black mayor in his Mississippi county, had been caught peddling influence to blacks and whites alike.

The cancer doctor who had championed the movement for the right to die with dignity had joined a cult of spiritualists.

In and out of public office, halls of learning, bastions of faith, tanks of think, foundation offices and publishing houses—all of the likeliest places to look for a hero—none was to be found.

Except Wade Belcher.

He cared more about doing the job than getting the credit.

He lived anonymously, a middle-sized, middle-aged, plain-looking man whose personality was incidental to his efforts to make cars safe for driving, air safe for breathing, food safe for eating and summer camps safe for children.

In his work on behalf of American consumers, Wade Belcher had discovered that some legislators—including even some members of the United States Congress—did not always hold the good of the people as their primary objective.

So he initiated the Clean Congress Project.

He felt that the American public, as employer and customer of the American government, should be made aware of the private financial lives of its public servants. He wanted to make sure that the legislators weren't crooks, or that if they were, their constituents would know about it.

Bibby Bosculus, driving down the old Maryland highway to avoid expressway tolls, exulted. At last, he thought, he was engaged in his time.

In Washington he reported promptly to the Clean Congress Project in a downtown office building with two elevators so slow that most of the staff walked up six flights rather than wait them out. It was late morning on a sticky June day and Bosculus welcomed the quiet wait in the hall. He assumed that the young, jeans-clad people running up and down the stairs were to be his colleagues. They seemed very young indeed.

Waiting in the cool, Bosculus suffered his usual doubts. Could he do the job? Would he make friends? Was he too old, overeducated, dressed wrong? Would they tell him it was a mistake? With all his clouds, Bosculus lacked the silver lining of self-pity. He could not excuse himself or disarm an antagonist by saying, "I'm shy." He could only tighten up and bore in.

The elevator lurched downward. The door clanked open. Bosculus squeezed through the gate and pressed the headless button between 5 and 7. He rose so slowly that he thought he

TABLE 47   151

was going down. He got out in what looked like a clearance sale in a storage basement.

Rows of old desks were lined up and people with note-books were moving around them, taking notes. Telephones rang. Typewriters jangled. Portable blackboards stood like crossing guards:

> *foreign aid*
> *human rights*
> *worker safety*
> *education*
> *defense*

Bosculus got someone to stop:

"Is this the Clean Congress Project?"

"You bet your tushy! You here to do reports?"

"I guess so."

"Thank God herself!"

He was shoved toward the corner office of Beryl Shipley, the project coordinator with whom he had talked, collect, from home. On one wall was a sign: *Don't forget your congressperson's attendance record. Committees count!!!*

A free-floating blackboard said: *COPE, SCOPE, ROPER.*

Another sign: *Return reference books—please!!*

Bosculus suddenly remembered that he knew nothing about politics. How could he produce a ten-thousand-word report on a congressman or woman he'd most likely never heard of? Forty typewritten pages. They'd told him the facts would be at his fingertips and all he would have to do was organize material and put it on paper.

Bosculus was no fireball. He had been researching his dissertation for over two years. Also, he was a slow typist. He thought he should go home.

But Beryl Shipley was waiting for him. She was standing at her desk, straight and skinny in blue and white stripes. Everything about her was tight: hair pulled back, eyes like awls, rectangular jaw. Bosculus took confidence from her appearance.

"Bosculus," she said and pulled a card from a file drawer. "Luggage?"

It was outside in the car.

"You don't mind a dormitory room," she said. "George Washington University. Ask them for a fan if you're bothered by heat. Check in first or get right to work?"

The project operated twenty-four hours a day. Bosculus could make his own hours.

"I guess I'll start now." He didn't finish saying it.

She had already given him Tim Harrigan.

Tim Harrigan was the representative from a district in northeastern Pennsylvania. "Poconos. Tri-state area. Scranton," Shipley was saying. She handed over a map, some file cards and a folder. "Third term," she said. "Good service to constituents. Big on energy. Bad on gun control."

She told him to read the instructions and follow the outline. "Any questions, check with Izzy Johnson upstairs. When you're done, check back with me for a new assignment."

She turned away.

Bosculus found a vacant desk. People rushed in from all sides. "Where's the Congressional Weekly? You got the Chicago phone book? What happened to the Lawyers' Directory? You take the Dirty Dozen list?"

The outline alone was three pages long. It said to credit all sources in footnotes. It gave examples of journalistic style. It recommended lots of quotations and anecdotes to make the report interesting as well as informative.

Bosculus read grimly.

BIOGRAPHY, GEOGRAPHY (interviews with community leaders and opposition candidates).

ISSUES, VOTING RECORD, COMMITTEES, BILLS SPONSORED.

TABLE 47 153

Bosculus shut his eyes.

When he opened them again, he read RATINGS BY INTEREST GROUPS, CAMPAIGN CONTRIBUTORS (who and how much).

STAFF. HOLDINGS.

They wanted to know how much stock the poor guy (or gal) owned, how he or she used his or her free mailing privileges, whether there were relatives on the payroll, what the staff had to say.

Bosculus ran back to Beryl Shipley.

"Where am I going to get all this information?"

"It's all here," she said without looking up. She handed him a printed sheet:

Abel's *Politics in America*
American Voting Patterns
Congressional District Data (see file in bookcase)
Congressional Record
Contributions of National-Level Political Committees to Incumbents and Candidates for Public Office
Digest of Public General Bills and Resolutions
Dockerson's *Directory of American Lawyers and Legal Firms*

Books were on bookshelves. Pamphlets were stacked on chairs and tables. Files were clearly marked. Shipley assured him that the material was at his fingertips. A special assignment team would report on the congressman's district offices as soon as Bosculus put in a request.

To put in a request, Bosculus should check with Izzy Johnson.

"Are you sure I can do all this in a week?"

"Everybody's doing at least two a week. We've got to publish in time for the elections. We're behind already."

"And if I have trouble?"

Shipley looked up at him.

"Izzy Johnson," Bosculus said. "Upstairs."

He rushed out to find the biographies.

The H file was missing.

So he went for geography first.

Meltzer's *Profile of the United States* was gone from the bookcase. Bosculus walked up and down among the rows of desks, calling for Meltzer. Finally, he decided to look up Interest Group Ratings. He found ADA and COPE. Somebody gave him a sheet on the National Farmers' Union. Somebody let him borrow a League of Women Voters pamphlet. He found the League of Conservation Voters.

All the interest groups liked Harrigan.

Bosculus found himself another empty desk and started taking notes. A woman writing on one of the blackboards yelled to him, but he couldn't hear her. The man at the next desk shouted in his ear: "Did you make your appointment with your congressperson?"

Bosculus stared at him.

The man, in overalls and a kerchief around his neck, explained that all reports included a personal interview. Interviews should be set up well in advance. The blackboard writer was checking off congresspeople who had not yet answered their questionnaires.

Questionnaires? An interview?

Bosculus ran upstairs to look for Izzy Johnson. The seventh floor looked just like the sixth floor. Izzy Johnson's cubicle was just above Beryl Shipley's. Bosculus burst in. A man with a ragtime mustache was squatting beside a bookshelf.

"Anybody seen Izzy?" he called out the door.

"I think he was here this morning," someone answered.

"I think he's on the Hill."

"He said he'd be with Wade."

"Gee," said the man with the mustache. "I haven't seen Izzy in a couple of days."

TABLE 47   155

Bosculus decided to go out for lunch. Or dinner, now that it was after five o'clock.

Down the street he found a health-food restaurant and sat at the counter. He ordered carrot juice and a salad sandwich. He felt he needed vitamins.

The only other customer was a woman in a wrap dress and sandals, sitting two seats down, at the end of the counter. She was eating from a basket, twirling shredded vegetables on her fork like spaghetti.

"Didn't I see you upstairs?" she said.

She was a lawyer from a small town in Maryland, had kids in high school, was active in community affairs. She was "doing" a congressman from Illinois. "Good man," she said. "Very high on human rights, separation of church and state, consumer protection."

Bosculus was glad to be talking to a person who didn't seem to be on the brink of a nervous breakdown. He thought about moving to the stool beside hers but feared it might look as if he wanted to pick her up.

"I don't know how I'm going to do mine," he confessed.

She smiled comfortably. "It always seems impossible at first. I'm on my third. I've been here almost two weeks. It's really easy once you get in stride."

Bosculus moved over a seat. He hoped she wouldn't think he wanted to fuck her. She was a big woman with gray in her hair. Wholesome-looking.

"First," she said, "you have to realize you won't get much information."

He put down his sandwich.

"What you do is you use what you get. When you can't find a fact or you can't confirm it, you fudge it."

"Fudge it?"

She had never heard the term before, either.

Bosculus thought darkly. *Obfuscate. Gloss over.* He wondered if she was telling the truth.

"Listen," the woman said. Her name was Ruth. "Do you think everybody up there is a professional investigator? They're kids. You're older than most of them. Probably smarter."

Bosculus had to admit she was right.

"So you've got to be able to do at least as good a job as they're doing."

He went back to his sandwich. It was overflowing with bean sprouts, so he ate around the edges.

"Look," Ruth said. "A professional team of investigative reporters would take a year to do a workup like we're doing, right? If we do two a week, who can expect perfection?"

The carrot juice was awful, as usual, and it made him feel very healthy. In fact, he felt better about everything. Ruth had nice clean skin, no fuss, no makeup, curly hair, friendly eyes. She picked up her check and told him not to worry. She was using a typewriter on the seventh floor.

"Come by if you have a problem. I'll try to help." She said it as if most problems had solutions.

It was after midnight when Bosculus finished working on the sixth floor and checked into the Shaw Building. An unimpressed housekeeper gave him a key to Room 212, undecorated and hot but with a view: a strip of Potomac River. Bosculus set his suitcase on the cot, took off his shoes and went to close the door to the adjoining room. The light was still on in there and, sitting in the bed in a terry robe, with glasses on her nose and a book on her knees, was Ruth.

She didn't looked shocked. "Oh my!" she said, sounding

TABLE 47   157

pleased. "We're going to be roommates." She told him where the shower was.

When he came back, the lights were out and he went to sleep. He didn't see Ruth again for several days.

One morning, well before eight o'clock, Bosculus waited for the elevator with two other Clean Congress workers, one on crutches and one in a wheelchair. Everybody else was hurtling through the double doors and up the stairway, two and three steps at a time. The brass hemispheres over the elevators were broken. The arrow on one was stuck between G and B. The other had no arrow. Bosculus grew impatient, but felt he couldn't go up the stairs without rubbing salt into the wounds of his handicapped comrades.

He took a veiled looked at the resting foot of the man on crutches and thought maybe it was just a ski accident. Summer skiing in Colorado, maybe. He was a lanky young man in a Beethoven T-shirt. The wheelchair woman was sickly thin and her face as angled as a Picasso mask. Bosculus had seen her before, working upstairs as hurried and harassed as everyone else. She could streak her chair between two rows of desks, pivot, and fight for a directory as roughly as the best of them. She caught Bosculus' eye and cast a fatalistic glance at the disabled hemispheres. Bosculus made an elaborate response: eyes rolled, shoulders lifted, head dipped till ear met shoulder, palms turned up and out. Bosculus knew that all the reference material would be gone before he got upstairs. But he waited.

At last the elevator disengaged itself and opened its doors. There was a packing crate on one side and hardly standing space for two people. The wheelchair woman and the man on crutches squeezed together to make room for Bosculus.

He had no choice. He squeezed in with them. The wheelchair woman pushed the floor buttons for Bosculus and the crutches man, who worked on seven. The crutches man pushed the gate closed and they rose majestically.

Izzy Johnson wasn't in. Bosculus left a note for him. Somebody said "Good luck." Somebody else said he'd been waiting for a week to see Izzy Johnson. There were notes all over the office. *Must see! Call immediately! Urgent!* One of them was signed with the name of the President's press secretary, "OK" marked under the phone number. Workers were sitting on the floor, waiting. Somebody said Izzy was in Buffalo for a demonstration. The man with crutches swung up to Bosculus. His name was Rafael. His big shoulders stretched the Beethoven T-shirt.

"I've got to see Izzy!" an Afro-haired woman pleaded.

"Work around him," a woman with a brush cut told her.

"But who's my supervisor?"

"Fudge it."

Rafael was a graduate student from Chapel Hill. He had an austere Spanish face. "Who you got?" he asked Bosculus.

"Harrigan."

"Oh, from Pennsylvania. Good man. Good on energy. Good on conservation. You got your interview lined up?"

"I hardly know anything about him."

"Line up your interview. You can learn while you wait."

Rafael led him to a directory and watched while he called the congressman's office.

"Now, man," Rafael said, "you got to move your ass. You got two days to get your facts together and to find a report from the district office."

Bosculus couldn't thank him enough.

"No sweat, amigo," Rafael said. "Just, when you get a

TABLE 47   159

chance, put in a word for human rights in Chile." He dragged himself off between the crutches.

Two days later Bosculus sat, tight as Beryl Shipley, on a cushioned bench by the reception desk in a small, crowded mahogany office in the Longworth Building. A picture of a mountain laurel was affixed to the door over the words COMMONWEALTH OF PENNSYLVANIA and under the name TIMOTHY J. HARRIGAN. Bosculus had been there for an hour, admiring the clean-cut efficiency of the congressman's aides, who knew where everything was and where everybody could be reached.

From his frayed and weary perspective, Bosculus saw the well-run office as a work of art. One aide opened a drawer, pulled out a folder, removed a sheet of paper, replaced the folder and carried the paper to another room. This was choreography. Another aide was reading into the telephone. She finished, listened, said, "You're welcome," hung up the phone and replaced the book. There was symmetry, unity and purpose. It was like Michelangelo's Holy Family, which Bosculus had seen at the Uffizi.

Furthermore, the congressman was there. People moved into the inner office, and in a short time came out, looking satisfied. The receptionist even apologized for keeping Bosculus waiting. Tim, she explained, had been called down for a vote earlier in the morning. It had put him behind schedule.

Bosculus didn't care. He was happy in that setting of fine wood and rich carpeting, ordered bookshelves and quiet work. He studied the wall of awards from postal workers, teamsters, senior citizens, Irish-Americans, Polish-Americans, the Anti-Defamation League of B'nai B'rith, the Byelorussian Legion, the Sierra Club, Earth Watch, the National Rifle Association, the Chemotherapy Foundation and the National Camp Owners Association.

When Bosculus at last was seated beside the congressman's burnished desk, Tim Harrigan did not disappoint him. He was a small man who looked big in the context of his office, his self-confidence, his prosperity and his well-cut suit. Bosculus, slumped in a chair, saw an up-shot view that magnified the congressional chest, shoulders and jawline.

Harrigan looked into Bosculus' eyes as if he intended to remember him. When he leaned back in his leather chair, there was no one in the world but Harrigan and Bosculus.

"Wade Belcher is one of our most precious national resources," the congressman said. "I'll do everything I can to help."

"We sent out a questionnaire," Bosculus began.

Harrigan talked to his intercom and an aide brought in the questionnaire.

"I know you'll like my reasons for not returning it to you," he said, watching Bosculus. "One, I don't want anybody but myself to speak for me. Two, you didn't leave enough space on those forms. I like to explain myself, you see." He laid the questionnaire on his desk. "Ask anything you want," he said.

Bosculus had spent three post-midnight hours copying questions from the questionnaire and subtly changing the wording.

"Why don't you use this?" Harrigan said agreeably and handed him the questionnaire.

The interview was a great success. The lines on the questionnaire were filled to the edges and the continuations of the answers filled Bosculus' notebook. Only twice, to questions about mail and broadcasting privileges, did the congressman reply, "None of your business." Bosculus turned with satisfaction to the questions he had written himself.

TABLE 47 161

He refused the cold drink Harrigan offered.

"I hear," he began again, reading from his notes, "that you're almost single-handedly responsible for pushing through the recent anti-pollution bill."

"In the House," Harrigan said, "nothing is done single-handedly."

"You're, uh, known for using your subcommittee for, ah, kind of pulling bills away from other guys who might let them disappear. Almost half of the one hundred fifty bills you introduced or cosponsored this past year were, ah, related to the environment but, um, most of them were, ah, referred to the Coast Guard and Fisheries Committee."

Harrigan smiled.

Bosculus thanked the Three Saints.

Harrigan talked about improving the quality of life, first for the country at large, then for his district in particular.

"So then," Bosculus read, "how is it you advocate the building of nuclear plants in your district?"

Harrigan raised a pixieish finger and redefined the word "advocate." "I see," he said, "as does every informed citizen, that nuclear energy is imperative for our competitive strength in the world market. However, I sponsored a bill that set very tough health and safety standards for those plants."

"But you voted to give temporary permits to plants that haven't met the standards in your own bill."

Harrigan stopped smiling for a moment. He said, "Bernie, we can't outshout the utilities lobby."

Bosculus wrote. Harrigan continued:

"The environment lobby is so weak that I wouldn't want to be quoted on its effectiveness."

Bosculus wrote *Uphill battle*. On the one hand, Harrigan was working to strengthen the Environmental Protection Act. And on the other hand, he was pulling its teeth. "If plants can get permits without filing environmental impact statements, then what's the point of the Act?" Bosculus asked the congressman.

Harrigan pulled out a pack of True cigarettes, offered it to Bosculus, who refused, and lit one for himself.

"You know," he told Bosculus, "nobody wants to turn off their lights. Everybody wants to be cool in the summer and warm in the winter. You got to get the energy from some-place." He squashed the cigarette and shredded it into the wastebasket.

He spoke confidentially. "A stopgap measure like mine—a maneuver, let's say—can hold back some really dangerous movement. A-plants can get a license without judicial review, but on the other hand, at least we still have a regulatory agency."

Bosculus was glad Rafael had briefed him.

"You haven't seen anything yet," Tim Harrigan told him. "Behind the scenes, Congress is just dripping with bills and amendments to get rid of every kind of energy regulation we've been able to get going."

"But," said Bosculus, "it was you who introduced the bill to issue temporary permits—"

"I had no choice."

Back at headquarters, Bosculus climbed to the seventh floor and left another note for Izzy Johnson. Somebody said Izzy was looking for him. It was past three on a hot and sticky afternoon, but everybody seemed freshly wound up. Bosculus went to see Beryl Shipley and she was excited, too. She had a telephone in one hand and was writing with the other. Her eyeglasses were slipping down her nose.

"Talk! Talk!" she rasped to Bosculus.

"It seems to me," he said to her eyeglasses, "that Congressman Harrigan is playing both ends against the middle."

"Start writing," she said. "Verify with Izzy Johnson."

TABLE 47 163

She suddenly looked at him and smiled. "See you tonight."

Bosculus ran for a desk and miraculously found one right away. The workers, instead of rushing around and grabbing books from each other, were milling in sociable circles. The noise was different, too. The place was usually a roaring beehive. Now the bees were swarming. Bosculus drew the first sheet of paper into his typewriter:

TIMOTHY J. HARRIGAN—Saint or Sellout?

Rafael sped by, swinging between his crutches. "You'll be here tonight?"

"Every night," Bosculus said grimly.

"But tonight, amigo. It's special. Wade, you know, is coming."

Bosculus nodded and kept typing.

Rafael pulled up and maneuvered to face the typewriter.

"Get with it, man! This is elation. Everybody wants to touch the hem of his garment. Even me."

Project people were proud just to mention Wade's name. Nobody dropped it, for fear it would break. Insiders spoke it quietly, sparingly, as if overuse might wear it out.

Bosculus apologized. He agreed that only a compulsive nut would be too busy to stop and see Wade. But he had a lot of problems in front of him.

"I think I'm sitting on a pile of dynamite," Bosculus said.

"Be specific, amigo."

Bosculus showed a page of his notes:

H. consistently votes for regulations against air and water pollution but his district has some of the dirtiest water and smokiest air in U.S.A.

He turned to another page:

H. partner Scranton law firm. Name on door. One client of firm owner of 3 big summer camps—Pocono Mtns ages

6–16. H. votes against Youth Camp Health & Safety Act that wld set & enforce minimum standards.

"Everything check out?" Rafael asked.

"Everything checks out," Bosculus said. "And Specific Three is that he pushed hard for an agency to regulate nuclear power plants and now he wants to give out operating permits before the agency gets to approve."

"So what's your problem?"

"I want to be fair," Bosculus said. "This stuff could ruin a man's career."

"Don't worry, amigo. Your report will be edited and checked by a verifier and it will go back to the congressman, who will have the last chance to correct mistakes."

"But I liked him."

"Get on with it, man. I see you got a decent typewriter for once. Take advantage."

He swung off.

By six o'clock, as the climatic temperature sank and the emotional temperature rose, Bosculus was sweating over his decent typewriter, an electric Olympia with only a few broken keys. He had a desk at the end of an empty row and a box of paper all to himself. There were free phones, accessible books. Bosculus had a strong start and, though he was hot and dirty, kept pushing ahead.

"Where's he going to stand?"

Beryl Shipley and two other people talked over Bosculus' shoulder.

"Put him against the long wall so everybody can get close."

"Yes, but we need light on his face."

"Watch out you don't blind him."

They pushed the furniture back to make room for people to sit on the floor. One man climbed on a table to turn the

TABLE 47   165

ceiling lights. Someone was dragging an old microphone across the room.

Bosculus kept at it. He was getting good at four-finger typing. From notecards arranged like a ferris wheel he picked a fact here, a quotation there, feeling prowess. Through it all, in a monochrome rearview projection in his head, was the face of Wade Belcher—"a man," someone behind him was saying, practicing a speech, "who has never lost his child's-eye view of a just and reasonable world and who has dedicated his life to turning the world that exists into the one he dreams of."

Bosculus kept working till somebody pulled his typewriter cord out of the electric outlet. Then he got up and headed for the dormitory to change clothes. On the way downstairs, he heard a woman call, "Hey, Izzy!"

Bosculus wheeled around and saw a loose-limbed black man in a sweatband and a denim vest.

"I think we blew a fuse," Izzy Johnson said.

Bosculus kept going.

Ruth was climbing the stone steps of the Shaw Building. She looked as hot and tired as he was. She was wearing a sporty printed shirt over light pants, but nobody would take her for a lady of leisure.

She greeted Bosculus. "I feel like a kid." Her face was streaked with dried sweat. "Running home to get cleaned up for a big date."

She'd spent most of the afternoon in the Rayburn Building waiting for a senator who didn't show up. "I decided the hell with it. It was more important to see Wade Belcher than to wait all night for Senator Mitz."

Bosculus offered her a lift back to the office.

She accepted. "I expect to be quite human after a shower," she said.

Inside, the Shaw Building was deserted.

They separated into their adjacent rooms. Two minutes later they passed each other on the way to showers at opposite ends of the hall.

If Bosculus was fussy about anything in the world it was his shower. He leaned into the stall, reaching around the vinyl curtain, and adjusted the faucets until the water poured as hard as it would go and as hot as he could stand it. Then he slipped off his robe, hung it on a hook and stepped with dignity into the perfect shower. He spread his arms, ducked his head, arched his back, squatted low, then straightened his legs, buttocks up so the water would splash into his anal ravine and stream around the tender terrain between his spread legs. Upright again, he soaped himself lovingly, stretching and bending to receive the water on every length of his long body. Unlike Karen, a soaper of little circles, Bosculus eschewed the washcloth in favor of silky slides of hand over skin, shoulder to fingertip, hip to knee joint.

A relaxed body brought deep breath, which opened the windows and let the air in. He thought about Karen's bubble baths. A blob of bubble juice under the rushing water was enough to make a frothy mountain. She'd sit like a sundae cherry and scrub herself with the loofah that Bosculus had bought for her. Bosculus loved her wet white skin—pink in the night light, bluish in early morning. While the water drained, she'd sink into the foam till her wet curls were like hyacinths floating on the surface. She would lie back, squirming if she felt playful, to make her breasts stand above the bubbles. She would sometimes lie in the emptying tub, motionless, with her eyes on him, expressionless. She would climb out then, smeared wet with puffs of foam blooming here and there on her wonderfully whittled, dangerous little body and would come at him—dry and protesting Bosculus—and throw herself on him, leaving her wet shape on his

TABLE 47 167

clothes. Not often, though. Not lately. Brucie kept her too busy.

Bosculus looked down at his erection and soaped it. The better to wash you with, he thought, meaning for the millionth time to ask his mother how it had happened that he was circumcised. When he was clean and steamed red, he started the delicate maneuver of easing off the hot while easing on the cold. He meant to end up with an ice-cold rinse that would close his pores and lusterize his body without causing shock to his nervous system. He never quite avoided shock or reached the limits of cold, but on this occasion he was satisfied anyway as he stepped out and wrapped himself in terry cloth.

Hurrying barefoot back to his room, he again crossed paths with Ruth, her hair in a towel turban. She had light green eyes and they glistened with refreshment. Also, Bosculus could not help noticing, for an older woman she had very shapely legs.

At this moment, Bosculus' landlady and downstairs neighbor was just emerging from her own rigorous bath. Crouched in three inches of lukewarm water, she scoured herself with a long-handled brush which she rubbed into an erose cake of Ivory soap. Aunt Min lived her life in skin she was loath to touch. But she wanted it clean, so she splashed water into her private parts, closing her eyes while she did so. Other questionable areas—parts between things, like behind the ears, inside the elbows, the armpits and behind the knees—she washed wincingly with an ancient washcloth, as thoroughly as she cleaned her kitchen corners and cracks in the stove with toothpick and cotton stub to be sure no secret dirt was allowed to pile up and conspire against her.

Secure in the knowledge that she was both clean and

godly, Aunt Min pulled the plug and raised herself. "You don't want to sit in your own dirt," was what she had told her son when he was young and still frolicsome and wanted to play in the bath water. She propped herself on the sides of the tub, then straightened up rather spryly and stepped out. But as she began to smack the towel against her flaccid skin, she suddenly went light in the head. A drizzle of cold sweat came over her. Her heart beat like fingers against a glass.

Aunt Min was not aged. She felt no different at sixty-seven from the way she had felt at fifty-three, which was not so good either. But she was always careful. She quickly sat down on the toilet seat cover and dropped forward, letting her head fall between her knees. *I must be having a heart attack*, she thought.

After a while she got up and buttoned on her quilted housecoat. She walked by inches to her bedroom and lay on the bed, listening to herself breathe. She thought of calling Mrs. Bosculus, who would be upstairs at that moment, feeding her child from a can or frozen package. She thought of calling her son, who wouldn't be home. Or her nephew Paul, who might. She reached for the telephone on the table beside the bed. Upstairs was closest. *They'll be sorry I was all alone*, she thought.

"Do you have deodorant?"

Ruth stood in the connecting door, shamefaced. "I know it's awful to borrow deodorant, but it's better than being smelly."

Bosculus handed her his Arrid extra-dry.

"I'll rub it on from my finger," she promised and disappeared.

Bosculus was in just pants, deciding between a blue university T-shirt and a yellow checked sport shirt.

Ruth returned in a flowery dress and no-heel clogs on her

TABLE 47   169

feet. She put the Arrid on his dresser and dropped into the chair by the window. "Do you mind?" she said. "I didn't realize how beat I am."

"Wear the blue," she said. "Otherwise you'll look like a visiting Republican."

Bosculus was tired too. It was too hot to hurry.

"I know how that place runs," she said. "Belcher won't show up till nine, ten o'clock."

Bosculus put on the blue and stretched out on his cot.

"He won't start talking till midnight." Ruth leaned back and closed her eyes. Bosculus looked past her, out the window at leafy branches and sky, restful in the late day. Nice to know the Potomac was down there. Nice to hear no cars or people. He was glad to be with Ruth, a calm, comfortable woman who didn't need to fill the space around her. She could be still. She didn't need to explain herself.

"Are you here professionally?" Bosculus asked.

"No. Just a volunteer." She was with a Baltimore law firm and took two weeks off like any other employee. Her husband couldn't get away and her kids were grown and on their own. "I read about the Project," she said with a small smile, "and thought it would be a meaningful contribution."

"What kind of law do you specialize in?"

"Divorce."

"Lots of that around."

"You bet."

At that moment Wade Belcher was driving down Connecticut Avenue in the passenger seat of a sporty Mustang driven by Izzy Johnson. On the way out, Izzy had sped around the Beltway, skirting cars, dodging pedestrians, passing red lights, watching for cops in the rearview mirror. In Bethesda he stopped long enough to use Wade's bathroom, wash up, brush his teeth with a guest brush from the medicine chest and put on a clean shirt, one of at least eight he owed Wade. Driving back, with Wade in the car, he was a different man. Sweatband gone, his black hair was parted and combed back sleek as a water bird. Spine straight, face grave, he held his speed to a strictly legal twenty-five mph and stayed in decorous line with the other city-bound cars.

"Hey, Wade. Did you eat? Want to stop someplace?"

"Dinner? Gosh, I forgot all about it."

"Want to stop at a Hot Shoppe?"

"No. I'm not hungry."

Karen was sitting on the edge of Aunt Min's bed with Brucie on her lap. The doctor was on the way.

"Do you think you could sit up, Mrs. Crain, and have a sip of tea?" Karen shifted the baby, who was a heavy weight.

"Thanks, dear." Min Crain eyed the teacup longingly. "I think I'd better stay flat a while longer." She asked Karen to try her son again. "That boy is never around when I need him," the old lady said. "I sometimes think he goes out on purpose to avoid me."

There was no answer.

"I guess you better call Paul," she said.

They were talking about Freud. Ruth said you shouldn't throw out the baby with the bath water. Then she laughed at herself for using such a Freudian figure of speech. She said that divorce lawyers find themselves playing at marriage counseling. "It's not my job," she said. "I keep a list of accredited psychologists and family therapists and so forth. I recommend them to my clients."

Bosculus thought she was tough and he liked it.

"Usually," she said, "by the time they come to me, it's all over."

TABLE 47   171

Bosculus considered. "Sometimes divorce is best," he said. He told her about his friends the Portlands, who still lived together but got along much better since their recent divorce. He and his own wife, he said, had a good marriage because each one respected the other as an individual. After he had his doctorate and a good job, Karen would go back to college.

Ruth was interested in his dissertation. "Fet?" She had never heard of him. "How soon do you think you'll have it finished?"

Bosculus made an odd, helpless gesture and changed the subject. "What did your husband think about your coming here?" he asked Ruth, surprising himself.

"I never know what my husband thinks." Ruth made her own odd, helpless gesture. "He *said* it was fine."

"Karen was glad," Bosculus said. "She said she'd finally get the closets painted."

"Arthur," Ruth explained, "is a labor lawyer, devoted to his clients and his principles. He's always very happy if I find something to do with my time that doesn't involve him and that keeps me out of trouble.

"He never says that exactly. He's a very gallant and charming man. But I think he regards me as something like a stage setting—necessary for mood and placement in space and time, but not part of the action."

"But you have your own life," Bosculus said.

"Yes, of course. But that's in another play entirely. He knows nothing about it. He doesn't want to know."

Bosculus couldn't believe what he was thinking. Ruth was turning into a goddess figure, a piece of statuary, Roman and fleshly. He was thinking he would like to touch her. "Karen and I aren't monogamous either," he said suddenly.

Ruth started. "That isn't what I meant."

"We had the arrangement before we were married," Bosculus continued. "We're not promiscuous, but we're not possessive." He was thrilled with himself. He had never lied before. He loved it. It made him feel powerful. "We think that love is like mercury. The more tightly you squeeze it, the less it holds together."

Ruth looked at him. She was a family woman, past forty. As a lawyer, she must have heard everything. But this made her sad.

"It's just that you're so young," she said.

Bosculus said he was not that young.

"I'm forty-three," Ruth said decisively.

Bosculus got up and stood by the window. Very few cars passed. The plum of a sun was low and sinking in a lush sky streaked with the colors of a fruit compote. Ruth was watching him.

"Do you think we ought to leave now?"

"It's going to be an awful crunch."

"We probably won't get near him."

"I'll bet the sound system breaks down."

Ruth didn't move to get up.

Bosculus went to close the door.

"Leave it open," Ruth said. "We need all the air we can get."

He returned and sat beside her, on the windowsill.

"So you and your husband are possessive," Bosculus said after a while.

Ruth seemed to be dreaming. She had to think about her answer. "Not theoretically," she said at last. "But we don't put the theory to the test."

There was no call for fast talk, no hurry at all. "It's funny with us," she said. "We pay a lot of attention to details. I take out all the black spots before I cook rice. My husband checks every call on our phone bill. But we never look into the details of our marital arrangements. You kids are different. You examine every phase of your relationship with a magnifying glass."

TABLE 47 173

Bosculus ignored the "kids." "So you don't know if he's possessive or not."

"Art says I'm free to do as I want. But I think he'd be very hurt if I went to bed with someone else."

"How about you if he were unfaithful?"

"Oh, I don't think he has the time." Then she laughed. Bosculus laughed too. When one of them stopped laughing, the other started again.

"Well, you know," Ruth said. "He's very work-oriented."

The elevator was ready for Wade Belcher. For him, the door opened smoothly. The ascent, though, was slow and the hero drummed his fingers on the tarnished rail along the back wall.

"How many folks do you figure are waiting up there?" he asked Izzy Johnson.

Izzy guessed about two hundred fifty workers, some of whom would have brought friends.

"I don't want to make a cheerleader speech," Wade said. He started to feel around in his pockets for his reading glasses. "I am so grateful to these people. I am so moved by what they are doing. I want to talk to every one of them and thank them personally."

Izzy Johnson loved his boss but wished he were less sentimental. "That won't be easy," he said. "Some of these guys will want to lay a long rap on you. You'd be better with a speech and a few handshakes."

But he knew Wade Belcher. Wade had this Jesus Christ fixation. He'd be washing everybody's feet if he could. Izzy would just have to get Shipley and some other guys to run interference while Wade communed.

The elevator stopped and the door opened. Izzy parted the gates and Wade Belcher stepped out. Caruso at the Met?

Mantle at Yankee Stadium? Dylan at Woodstock? Henry the Fifth at Agincourt? The crowd parted and made way. Wade Belcher went out to his people.

It was ten o'clock. Bosculus and Ruth had been downstairs, to a Georgetown sandwich shop, for a bite of supper, unquestioningly Dutch treat. Back, tired, Ruth had prepared for bed. She was sitting in it now, in a short cotton nightgown, propped on two pillows with the sheet pulled respectably up to her chest. Bosculus sat on the end of the bed with one knee bent in front of him. He was still in his blue university T-shirt, but he had an uncharacteristically healthy glow. His usually fishwater eyes had a sunny glint and he was talking with the dash and facility that he imagined he displayed when he was drinking. He had on one or two occasions swallowed an amphetamine capsule, and the clear-sinused, bouncing-hearted, headlong euphoria of those crazy pills was what he was feeling now. He was discoursing on the need for a person to take charge of his own life. He thought he was brilliant.

"Religion," he said, repeating the words of his friend Joe Farley, "is the second most popular way to avoid taking responsibility for one's actions."

"What's the first?"

"Money, I think. I can't remember why."

"Oh, I know why," Ruth said. "Because people say they can't do a thing because they can't afford it. Really they could if they changed their priorities."

"Other things being equal," Bosculus said, brilliantly.

He said he thought he should close the door. Others would be coming back soon.

"I'm falling asleep anyway," Ruth said. She slipped down

TABLE 47   175

between the sheets and flipped her pillows flat. "Give me a kiss good-night and turn off the light, okay?"

Bosculus turned the light off first, then in the light from the hall kissed Ruth on the cheek she offered. "I really liked talking to you," he said and kissed her lightly on the mouth. She did nothing to slow up his slow march through the adjoining door to his own bedroom. In his bed, in his underpants, Bosculus thought about Ruth. He wanted to be in her arms, encircled, and to feel her breasts against him. More than that, he wanted her to be in his arms. He grew excited thinking about this. He worried about himself: was he in search of mastery? Was he no better than any macho male, wishing to smother with kisses? Was it Ruth's self-confidence and eye-to-eye comradeship that made him want to dominate her in a sexual context? These were the themes that wove in his mind a lustproof curtain behind which he hoped to fall asleep. Striking against the curtain was a mantra, like a brass gong, repeating *big tits, big tits, big tits* . . . which, with all his strength of conscience, he could not mute.

Bosculus felt himself falling. He grabbed for the mattress to steady himself. The jolt set him back in the dark, still hot, empty room. The brass gong beat again and a fire raged. Incest was the fire; Ruth, a mother, though not his. Bosculus, in heat, had never wanted anything so much as he wanted to— oh my God, he thought amid hell flames—to ram it into her.

Paul was bending over his Aunt Min, being sure, under her plaintive instructions, to pull the top sheet up from under her fifty-five-year-old quilt. He covered her to the chin, patted everything down, smoothed wisps of hair away from her forehead.

"I don't know what I'd have done without you," the old lady murmured.

"I'm glad you didn't have to," Paul said. He promised to shoot himself before he got old and helpless.

Actually, Aunt Min wasn't that way yet either. Dr. Ostrow had listened to her chest, taken her pulse, pressed here and there, and announced, "Arrhythmia," which was not nearly as serious as Aunt Min had hoped and feared.

"Your heart skipped a beat," she told Aunt Min. The doctor herself was a hearty woman, businesslike but not perfunctory. "Come to my office tomorrow and we take a cardiogram. Until then, don't worry about yourself." She spoke in the accent of her native Poland. "Maybe some smoke in her capillaries," she told Paul in the kitchen as she washed her hands in the sink.

After many good nights and reassurances to his aunt, Paul let himself out the back door. Karen was sitting on the steps waiting for him. Brucie was upstairs, sleeping.

"How's your aunt?"

"She's okay. The doctor says it's an irregular heartbeat. Nothing dangerous."

"That's good. I was really scared. She looked so white."

Paul thanked her for coming down.

Karen set out her curly smile. Paul couldn't see it but he could hear it. "Would you like to come up for a cup of coffee?"

"I'd like to, thanks, but I've got to get home."

Karen stood up. She moved as if she were oiled. "I just made a fresh pot," she said. She waited for him halfway up the steps and he knew she was not just teasing him.

Cindy was waiting at home. His good wife. Karen always looked to Paul like a sexy Shirley Temple doll. He wouldn't know what to do with her.

"Thanks, Karen," he said. "I really appreciate your offer."

He went to his car feeling old.

TABLE 47 **177**

"I'll keep an eye on Mrs. Crain," Karen called from the porch outside her door.

"Anyway," she added to herself as she went in.

Ruth opened the door noiselessly and stuck her neck out. "Sleeping?"

"No. Not at all."

"I couldn't sleep either." She came in and closed the door. Bosculus sat up.

Ruth stood away from him. He saw her bright against night light. "Look," she said. "I don't know how to say this, but look, I find myself very excited." She was speaking on no breath.

His got caught, too.

"I wondered if we might try making it together," she said.

He got out of bed and put on his robe.

"Oh, yes," he said. "Oh, yes." He went to her and put his hands on her arms. The short nightgown had no sleeves. The fabric floated in the breeze from the window. "I wanted to," he said.

She touched his face. "I'm glad."

She slipped her arms under his and drew him close to her. She was taller than Karen, bigger and solider. He laid his cheek on hers and they leaned together, as if the pressure might hold their jolting hearts in place.

She raised herself on her toes and turned her lips to him. His arms slid down her back as he supported her in a long kiss. A long and busy kiss, not over till her nightgown and his robe were heaped on the floor around their feet.

She pulled down the shade and switched on the desk lamp. She stood before him with legs apart and arms spread, stretching to contain herself.

Bosculus, still in jockey shorts, moved to embrace her.

"Aren't you going to be naked?" she said.

He hesitated.

"Oh, but I want to see!" She laughed. "Naked is beautiful." And when he slid out of his pants, she said, "See? You're beautiful."

She walked around him.

He began to go limp.

Bosculus knew from furtive comparisons in locker rooms that his dimensions were adequate, but he felt that on the whole—compared to models in centerfolds of *Playgirl* and *Gayboy*— he was a rather drab and disappointing specimen.

Ruth, however, was evidently pleased with him and the longer she looked, the stronger he became. He wanted her touch. And when at last she stood against him, he was tantalized by tip-touching, her nipples grazing his chest, his erection nosing her belly. She rubbed his tight nipples, very gently, with the heels of her hands.

She dropped to one knee and caressed his leg. With both hands she circled the calf, then the knee. She stroked him from thigh to ankle and back up. Bosculus had shapely legs.

She raised her head and let her heavy hair move against his groin and tangle with his pubic curls. His penis stood insouciant as she circled it with probing fingers but did not take it in her hand. On both knees now, she laid the side of her face against his belly, blew into his light belly hair and turned her lips to kiss his navel. "Like a little mouth," she whispered into it.

She stood up and bent to touch his breasts with dry lips and lick ever so lightly the tight tips with the tip of her tongue.

Ecstatic Bosculus caught her in trembling arms.

"I hope you've got something," Ruth said. She'd stopped taking the Pill. As things were at home, it seemed like overkill.

Bosculus had nothing. "I'll go out to a drugstore."

TABLE 47 179

"Don't go out. Maybe you could find somebody here."

Bosculus threw on his robe and ran into the hall. He ran up and down three flights of stairs and along all the hallways. He saw nobody, except, at a distance, the housekeeper, whom he avoided. Everybody was still at headquarters. It was after midnight. Bosculus had no time to wonder what Wade was talking about. He ran back to the room for his clothes, but Ruth stopped him. She undid his belt and put her arms around him inside the robe. "Did you ever hear of *coitus interruptus?*"

Ruth was tender and enveloping. Bosculus had never before felt so long and so strong. It was disconcerting that she said "be careful, be careful" as she received and absorbed him. But the magic worked anyway, and too soon; he withdrew and came in a little pool on her belly. Ruth came too, almost at the same time.

Afterward, they sat together in the wide window, she naked against him naked, with their lights out, looking into the starless night.

"Was I really good?" Bosculus wanted to know.

"You were marvelous. How can you doubt it?"

She hugged herself with his arms.

"You are a beautiful and exciting lover. Didn't you know that?"

"I wasn't sure."

"Take my word for it."

She turned to look at him. "I hope you're not going to go around feeling guilty about this."

"I don't think I could tell Karen," he said. "I mean, I might mention that I did it, but I couldn't tell her how it was."

They sat together until sheets of light began to spread through the sky. Then Ruth took her nightgown and went back to her room, shutting the door.

She was gone when Bosculus got up. That night when he returned to the Shaw Building, at last having finished his report, he found that Ruth had left for home. He never learned her last name.

Early the next morning, Tim Harrigan smashed a low backhand a bare inch over the net and just inside the line. He got the surprise of his life when Wade Belcher scooped it up and returned it, hard, to the back right corner. Tim watched it go by.

"That's deuce." Harrigan, put off, moved to serve.

They were playing on the clay court behind the house of a newspaper publisher friend of Wade Belcher, and neighbor of Tim Harrigan. Harrigan had known Belcher for some time and had watched him play tennis. Harrigan liked to know his opponents. He thought he knew Belcher, who could win by playing a consistently mediocre game while his antagonist lost points trying to beat him. Two things Harrigan hadn't figured. First, he—Harrigan—was incapable of passing up a chance to smash. Second, he—Belcher—was a better player (fiercer, abler, trickier) than a casual watcher would conclude.

Each took a set and they were long sets, hard played. Harrigan, not having won, felt he had lost. Belcher, not having lost, felt he had won. Each had to hurry to a nine o'clock meeting. Harrigan, feeling behind, wanted to talk.

"One of your Clean Congress boys was in last week. I think he thinks he made some discoveries."

"You mean about the summer camps?"

"Summer camps. Nuclear plants. Conflict of interest. Are you going to publish it?"

TABLE 47 181

"Sure. As long as it's true."

"Do you think it will hurt me?"

"I know it won't hurt you. We couldn't afford to hurt you. You're one of the best congressmen we've got."

Bosculus stayed in Washington four more days and wrote another report on another congressperson, this one a woman from the West Coast who had no conflicting interests and very little influence on the law of the land. But she was learning about power and Bosculus thought she would get some of it someday if she could keep her seat long enough. During his time in Washington, Bosculus never saw Wade Belcher and never spoke to Izzy Johnson. A week after he got home, he received in the mail a check from Clean Congress for a little over eighty dollars, his total pay with taxes and social security deducted. Bosculus wished he could return it as a contribution. Instead, he used it as down payment on a piano for Karen.

"So how'd your aunt make out?" Flossie asks Paul out of the blue.

I know better than Paul. I was the one who took her to the doctor's next day. Aunt Min was fine by then and, as the doc had predicted, her heart was back in rhythm. The doc told her not to take such hot baths.

"Aunt Min?" Paul seems to have forgotten her. She finally moved to Florida after Paul got so involved in his own problems that he couldn't worry about hers. "Aunt Min's fine," he said at last. "She's in a senior citizen's traveling glee club." This is true. When Karen and Bibby split, Aunt Min took the opportunity to snap out of her depression. I never understood the dynamics of that event, but Karen was on to Aunt Min all the time. "You ought to know," she told me one day when I was leaving Aunt Min's, "Mrs. Crain is much stronger when her relatives aren't around."

It figured.

"She was out in the garden before, weeding like crazy, fresh as a terrier."

Paul and I decided to experiment with Karen's observation. Fewer guilty calls to see how Aunt Min was managing. When she finally called us, she was good and mad but her voice was strong and she'd made some new friends at the Seniors' Center. As we crept toward the outer edges of her life, her son fell in and suddenly we were freed from worrying about Aunt Min—thanks in a way to Karen. Focus off Aunt Min, we started to look at ourselves and that's when our trouble started.

Here's what happened to Bibby: the remaining facts of his married life:

* The slam of the car door hit Karen like a punch in the chest. She was surprised. She thought she'd be glad to see her husband. She squirmed under his long kiss.

"Something wrong?" He was shining with pleasure.

"It's just I'm not used to you. You've been gone over three weeks." She wondered if he'd made it with some teenybopper.

He held Brucie close. "See, he missed his daddy."

"Brucie can walk," Karen said dryly.

Bibby stood motionless. "Oh my," he said. "You're getting to be a very noble young man," he said. Then he set Brucie down. "Let's see you walk."

But Brucie only laughed at him.

Karen had to smile. "He really can," she said.

She had no dinner. "I thought we'd go out someplace."

He had no money. "I had to buy gas."

She had almost eight dollars left from lessons.

TABLE 47 183

"Where do you want to go—pizza or McDonald's?"

"Never mind. I'll make grilled cheese."

He wanted to make love. She curled away from him.

"I feel as if I'm attacking you," he said.

"Go right ahead," she said. "I like it that way."

He came.

She didn't even pretend to, but she said it was all right.

"Did you meet any nice people in Washington?"

"I had a few friends." Bibby was always proud to have a friend. "But there was really no time for recreation."

* The Good Food Co-op was Karen's delight. Ten families belonged, including a divorcee with three kids and Berta and Bill who weren't married. Every week two members drove a station wagon to a farmers' market off the Sunrise Highway and bought produce by the case. Karen loved getting her food, first of all fresh, and second, cheaper than supermarket prices.

Also the Co-op was like a social club. At monthly meetings the couples put in their money and drew up duty rosters. Members made special requests: the Lindens always wanted scallions, for example, and others would be jumping out of their skin for grapes or corn in season. They exchanged recipes and new uses for odd products like kohlrabi and parsnips. The Opalescent apple was expounded. Berta brought in a sample of her pumpkin bread. Karen liked being in with these people. They were brainy and lively, willing to go out of their way for good stuff.

Nearly all of the men worked in the city, so the wives did most of the shopping. Wives who worked did flexible things like typing at home or selling real estate on the telephone by the hour for Dial America, demonstrating cookware at Abraham & Straus or teaching piano or a combination of these things. Warner Pickett was the only husband who shopped regularly and that was because his wife had agoraphobia and wouldn't go out. Karen was the opposite: she was the permanent fill-in, ready to go on a half day's notice. The others called her the produce junkie.

One late summer Tuesday, Karen woke to the clock-radio set for six-thirty and was ready to go before seven, waiting outside with Brucie still chewing on his breakfast bagel. Warner Pickett was right on time. He leaned over to let them into his Mercury wagon and looked as if he'd just won a big poker pot.

Karen took Brucie on her lap and sat back to enjoy the ride. Pickett was a high-spirited man in his forties with a big nose and a big mustache. He was dressed for business in a sharply cut summer suit. "The cool before the heat. The calm before the storm," he said with satisfaction. He was another who loved going to market.

The sun rose as a perfect orange circle, first over buildings, then over trees. The cramp of town gave way to the spread of country. The road glittered in the sunshine, but the fields gave off coolness from the night.

"Brucie dropped his bagel on your floor," Karen apologized.

"Young woman," said Warner Pickett, "a man like myself, who just got finished bringing up four of the world's great slobs, doesn't bother his head about spilt bagels."

He took deep gulps of country air. The gold ring on his pinky was, Karen thought, not *too* showy. She felt fresh in her light cotton dress, no makeup, hair blowing.

The market was in full swing. Trucks huddled, tails down, full of crates and sacks. Workers in high morning mood hauled the crates, called to friends, stopped to gab. Buyers roamed through the stalls, examining, judging. Karen entered the warehouse and skipped among the cribs and barrels. She handled bunches of carrots, wagging the green tops never seen in the city. She hefted full, green lettuce heads and

TABLE 47 185

effused over shining peppers, firm and blemishless, peas in their pods, fat plums, gorgeous grapes. There was a pile of watermelons; they'd be cutting into one and passing slices around. "Look at that zucchini!" Karen marveled. "Corn! We've got to get corn!" She held onto Brucie's hand, dragging him along.

Pickett was right behind them. "Who could look at a supermarket after this?" he asked the world. "Don't forget the scallions," he said. The Lindens' scallions were a running gag. Mrs. Pickett, he said, was out of her mind with the effort of dreaming up recipes for the scallions she was stuck with.

Karen gave Brucie a piggyback. Brucie wanted more. He got it; Warner took him on his shoulders. Henry the wholesaler approached Karen: "How are you, dear? What can I do for you this week?"

Warner wanted to make vichyssoise.

"I'm not going to ask you if you've got a leek," he said to Henry.

"I'd appreciate that," Henry said.

They wanted cantaloupes but how could they be sure there would be one for everybody? Henry figured eighteen in a case, but he gave them two extra—no charge for Karen. "I don't want to see all you nice people fighting over a melon," he said. Had they seen the rhubarb? And, he reminded them, this week one of the farmers had sent up a wheel of Cheddar cheese.

Karen and Warner conferred.

Henry whipped out a paper bag and a pencil stub. So much for this. That thrown in for free. Watercress cheap because he had extra this week. And tomatoes! God! They almost forgot fresh-picked local tomatoes! Henry cut one giant into four sections. He pulled out a box of kosher salt from the crate under his cash register. "You never tasted so good!" he said. Brucie's face was half tomato. Henry let him wipe it off on his apron.

They filled the back of the wagon and Warner Pickett's only regret was that he had to go to work and could not stay to help Karen and Ethel Linden divide and box the food in the Lindens' garage.

* "I had a crazy dream." Karen was cleaning up after breakfast.

Bibby was drinking coffee.

"You want to hear it?"

Bibby was reading.

Karen made a fierce face and held up her hands like claws.

She put the milk in the refrigerator. She wiped the table around Bibby's cup and book. She scrubbed the sink with cleanser and washed the floor with a sponge mop. Then she went out on the porch to watch cars go by. Then she came into the living room, where Bibby had moved to continue his reading.

"Fuck you," she said.

He jumped out of the chair.

"What's wrong? What did I do?"

"Nothing."

* Karen was offered a morning job in a nursery school, playing piano and helping out in the office. She had it all figured out. Brucie was good and could entertain himself for long periods of time. Bibby could work at home and supervise him. If a taxi job came up, one of the Co-op women or even Cindy Storey could take Brucie for a few hours. Bibby hated to impose on people but Karen explained that people *like* to help—you do them a favor by giving them a chance.

"I'll need some new clothes," Karen said.

"Sure. You need shoes, too."

TABLE 47   187

She caved in a little. "It'll probably cost more than I'll make."

"Yes, but it's important for you," Bibby said. He said he'd refinance the car.

Warner Pickett was a man who made his own hours and who liked to help his friends. He got the helpful idea to pick up Karen after school and drive her home so that Bibby could drop her off in the mornings and keep the car for himself. Sometimes Warner and Karen stopped for a late lunch in a businessmen's restaurant. This example of neighborliness illustrated Karen's theory.

Soon Pickett was combing his hair over his bald spot and across his forehead. Soon he was wearing brighter neckties and suits more dashingly cut than ever. He was remembering to do his morning sit-ups and airplane twists. He jogged five miles three times a week. There was spring in his step on the dreariest winter days. The increasingly dysfunctional Mrs. Pickett spent *her* winter at a spa in Clearwater, Florida.

* Even before the piano arrived, Karen felt guilty. She knew she should value a husband who was kind and considerate and who put her needs on line with his if not ahead of them. She knew she should show her appreciation. The piano, arriving for her birthday, overwhelmed her. "You are such a good person!" She wept. She embraced him. "I love you!" she said with laughter and tears. She played Chopin all evening while Bibby read and listened.

Cindy Storey was in her customized kitchen when Bibby showed up, alone. He knocked, then opened the unlocked front door and stood in the hall looking about him as if he'd never been there before. He seemed incomplete without his busy little wife: the air hung heavily in the space around him. Cindy's daughter Jill was home for once. She peered at him from the dining room, where she was setting the dinner table. Jill lived in a late junior high limbo and she didn't like Bibby and Bibby didn't like her.

"Your friend the brisket is here," is what Bibby overheard her tell her mother. Cindy called him into the kitchen where she was performing her octopus stunt with pots and plates. It was five-minutes-to-Paul. Bibby apologized for the hour and suspended himself in the doorway.

Offered a drink, he filled a water glass with Dewar's from the cabinet. He opened the freezer door and sipped enough out of the glass to make room for an ice cube.

"Having dinner with us?"

"That's all right. I've already eaten."

Paul came in from a rotten day. Cindy ran through her geisha steps to cheer him up. Bibby accepted his fatalistic greeting and they all sat down at the table. Nobody said much. When Bibby went into the kitchen for a refill, he thought he heard Paul say *Oh, my God.*

After dinner, while Jill disconsolately loaded the dishwasher, Cindy and the two men arranged themselves in the family room, where Bibby at last started to weave toward the point of his visit.

He did not want to be melodramatic.

He took a swallow of scotch and smiled into the glass.

Then he looked at the ceiling.

Then he smiled a shrewd, one-sided smile and raised and lowered his eyebrows.

Then he readjusted his shoulders.

Then he said, "Karen is sleeping with some old guy."

"How old?" Cindy asked.

"Paul's age at least."

Cindy turned to Paul. Paul looked at Bibby. "Cindy is the

TABLE 47   189

same age as I am," he said. He got up and moved to a chair closer to Bibby. Cindy moved to the chair Paul had left.

"Who is this old guy?" Paul asked.

It was Warner Pickett.

"He's the schlockmeister," Cindy reminded Paul. His name had come up, the great friend and benefactor of the Bosculus family. Schlockmeister was, in fact, Paul's word to describe Pickett's business operations as a subcontractor, packager, middleman, agent. Anybody with goods or services for sale could come to Pickett and Pickett would find a customer. He worked on fifty percent from one end or another, or twenty-five percent from each. Bibby respected this operation and considered Pickett an admirable man, still did. He didn't blame Pickett for wanting to enjoy life while his adrenaline still flowed.

Drinking made Bibby, if anything, more judicious. He explained that Karen also could not be blamed for her infidelity. Life was no picnic for her, coming home from work only to start work again. Brucie had become a handful. His rubber legs had turned to steel. Taking proper care of him was more, Bibby said self-righteously, than sitting him in front of the boob tube. But Karen and he agreed it was worth the trouble.

"If you agree on Brucie, that's the most important thing," Paul said.

Cindy got up to look at the row of plants on the floor by the picture window.

Paul kept talking. "Isn't there enough in Karen's life to burn up all that amazing energy of hers?" He stared accusingly at Bibby. Cindy went into the kitchen. Bibby continued his defense.

Even the piano, he said, had failed to improve her life. Playing brought out her romantic longings. Bibby could only imagine the depth of her sadness. Warner Pickett, on the other hand, showed her a good time. One night when Bibby was working, Pickett took Karen and Brucie to a Chinese smorgasbord where they had as much lobster Cantonese as they wanted. Flaming appetizers and steak on skewers. Pickett had a wallet full of credit cards. Pickett was always at Karen's service. Pickett bought a giant stuffed koala bear for Brucie.

Cindy returned with a pitcher and watered the plants. "I suppose," she said, "that nobody ever heard of for richer or poorer . . ."

Paul was actually more sympathetic. "You don't *know*, Bibby. He's probably just a lonely guy who likes young company."

"That's right," Cindy said on her way out again. "You may be jumping to the wrong conclusion."

Bibby shook his head. "Karen told me they're fucking."

Cindy turned in the doorway.

"She'd like to stay married," Bibby said. "She wants to keep seeing him but also to be straight with me."

Cindy sat down again, still holding the pitcher. Paul leaned forward with his elbows on his knees. "And what if you say no?"

From upstairs came a shock of sound: *soft* rock, from Jill's room.

"Of course," Paul was saying, "a woman isn't a piece of property. But the question is do you want exclusive rights?"

"That isn't the question at all," Cindy said.

Bibby stood up. Of the three of them, he was the least disturbed. "It's so good of you to take this time . . ."

"Just how do you define your problem?" Paul asked.

Bibby went through his tic again. "I don't know if I have a problem," he finally said.

Cindy assured him that he did. "What are her feelings about Mr. Pickett? Is she in love with him?"

Bibby didn't know. "I thought things were getting better,"

TABLE 47   191

he said. Karen's nightmares had almost disappeared. Bibby liked taking care of Brucie.

Cindy shook her head. "I've seen so many lonely people."

"Yes," said Paul. "And most of them married."

Bibby took an anxious swallow of air, digested it and took another. "So what do you think?"

"I think it's terrible, that's what I think." Cindy reached for Bibby's hand but drew back. "I think you're hurt and I can't understand what's happening to her. I think that when two people can get along and make a home and bring up a beautiful child like Brucie, it's a pretty precious thing and maybe worth a little bit of self-denial, if such an old-fashioned term is allowed."

Paul seemed surprised at his wife's passion. His own reply was cool.

"If she wants to play around," he said, "she shouldn't expect to do it wearing your stamp of approval. On the other hand, if she likes to screw this guy Peckeridge and it keeps her happy, why interfere? Modern couples are supposed to be liberated from archaic ideas about monogamy and so forth. Besides, Peckeridge is an 'old guy,' as you say. She'll soon get tired of him."

"Assuming, of course," Cindy said, "that you want to stay with her. Assuming that it's your choice."

"Come on, Bibby," Paul said, changing keys again. "You mean to say you'd never pick another rose off the bush?"

"Of course he wouldn't," Cindy said.

Bibby walked around the room for a while. Then he stood still for another while. He said, "You guys are real friends. I don't know how to thank you." He shook Paul's hand long and solemnly. He shook Cindy's hand, too, and then backed out of the room, still thanking his friends. He called from home later that night to thank them again. He said he had thought it over and had decided to follow their advice.

"What advice?" Cindy asked.

"You know. To cool it."

"Oh, right," Cindy said.

Early morning on a Saturday two weeks later, Bibby
punched Karen in the shoulder and she punched him back,
blackening his right eye. A chair was overturned. A glass
pitcher was smashed against the side of the refrigerator. Mrs.
Crain was awakened from the best part of her sleep by their
yelling and jumping and by the crying of the poor little boy,
also shocked out of sleep. Mrs. Crain called the police. The
next day she asked the Bosculuses to find another place to
live. She had been wanting to get rid of them anyway, ever
since that little wife started staying out till all hours.

Bibby went to New York City and stayed temporarily in
the studio apartment of his friend Yuri, who was away for a
month at an artists' colony in New Hampshire. Warner
Pickett decided to divorce his wife who had, in a way,
deserted him by removing herself to Clearwater, Florida. In
any case, the coast was clear and Karen and Brucie moved
into Pickett's roomy ranch house.

PART
FOUR

Bosculus stayed angry for three months. He learned to gnash his teeth. He learned to sit in one position—upright in a mangy armchair with his arms on its arms, his knees pressed together and his feet flat on the floor straight and centered. He sat like this for hours at a time while murderous acts took place in his head.

Flossie's big jeweled earrings are lying on the table in front of her. Geraldine has pulled up a chair from another table, slipped off her shoes and put her feet up. Only Oberon is still in his tuxedo jacket. Brandies are scattered anonymously around the table, one or two untouched. Bosculus has left the platform and joined his wife at her table. A crowd has gathered there, chairs clustered around him two and three deep.

"Ask who got him a lawyer," Paul says in one of his nastier voices. "Ask who offered him her son's room."

"Why shouldn't I? Tony was at camp."

"You made it easy for them to split."

"Bullshit! They saw a marriage counselor."

Flossie looks at Father Joe: "Couldn't a clergyman help?"

"We don't save marriages anymore," Joe says. "We save people."

"Sounds very religious," Paul says.

"In a way, it is."

Bibby's life came down like a rockslide. You had to drive around the chunks and splinters and you couldn't see ahead for the dust he raised.

I found him a lawyer named Spritzer who said he could wait to get paid.

Joe made up the daybed in the front room of his two-room apartment in Morningside Heights.

Yuri got a call one midnight and grabbed a taxi to meet drunken Bibby at the Corner Bistro at the north end of the West Village.

Karen asked for nothing, not even child support. She had no hard feelings. Bibby had no feelings at all. He came to our house sometimes on Saturdays, with Brucie. Jill would take Brucie to the playground while Bibby lingered at the lunch table. In a deliberate voice, he talked about his moves. But, to speak metaphorically, he never took his hand off the chesspiece.

He put off his dissertation to look for a job. Found one, lost it, found another, forgot to show up. He moved out of Joe's, to Yuri's, then to a place of his own without a telephone. We lost touch for a time.

Bosculus wandered, detached from himself, thinking weighty thoughts that cracked in the middle and slipped out from under him. He was certain that these intricately philosophical, cosmically relevant thoughts would lead to understanding if only he could keep on top of them. So he walked the streets of Washington Heights up to Fort Tryon Park and down along Riverside Drive. In March the wind from across the Hudson cut cruelly under the sleeves of his windbreaker. He walked in Soho and the East Village and on the Bowery as newspapers blew in the wind and empty cans rattled along the gutters. On the coldest days he wore boots. After the freeze, his pants legs were splattered with slush splashed up by passing cars. Wherever he walked in whatever weather, people looked at him as if he weren't there, a dying

TABLE 47   197

*person too fearful to contemplate, a drunk too shameful, a
potential mugger, a junkie.*

*He had the car but he used it only to get Brucie. He kept
the stereo set, too, which he thought he would pawn, but the
time didn't come for that. His mother sent money. Cindy
made him a small, unreported loan. He sold a ring he never
wore. Joe paid him extravagantly for typing a speech to be de-
livered at an executive conference in Tarrytown. Bibby kept
to beer, telling himself that beer was nourishing. His belly
swelled and his chin dropped.*

". . . and he lived in this hovel," I explain to Flossie.

"Oh, *hovel*," Joe protests. "You suburbanites don't know
what a real hovel is."

Geraldine protests too. "Don't forget, I still live there."

Yes, but her place is downstairs, and up front where there's
daylight.

"We, at least, have hot water and a bathroom," Yuri adds
generously.

Flossie is putting two and two together. "Hey!" she says to
Geraldine. "Did Yuri introduce you to Bernie?"

"Not quite. I met Bibby on my own. In the hall. He
dropped a bag of groceries and his oranges rolled downstairs.
I helped pick them up."

She goes off into a small dream that makes her smile.
"Bibby's apartment wasn't so bad," she says. "*He* seemed to
like it."

"That's exactly the point," says Yuri.

Believe me, it was awful. He telephoned one morning to
give me his new phone number. I had a pair of tickets to a
dance show in Soho, bought from my local dry cleaner whose
son was living with the choreographer. Paul would never go.
Nor would I, except I saw a chance to get Bibby out. He said

I should come up for dinner with him first and I was smart enough to say no, I'd just come up.

On Daniell, off Bleecker, you had to pay attention to broken sidewalks, dogshit, spilled garbage and legs jutting out from doorways. Late afternoon, late spring, the old-timers on folding chairs leaned against the buildings talking Sicilian and watching their neighborhood recede under an oncoming slick of aging hippies, artists, homosexuals, blacks, Latins and even Asiatics from across Canal Street. The yellow brick front of Number 72 stood flush between a Chinese laundry and an Italian grocery. The plate-glass entrance looked respectable compared to the scarred wooden doors of the grimy buildings on either side. There was a small, tiled vestibule with doorbells and mailboxes, though there were no names in the slots beside the doorbells and all the mailboxes had been bashed in.

I let myself in by the broken door lock and climbed three flights of dark and fetid stairs. And rested before the remaining two.

It was not a cheerful apartment. It was one room with a bisecting wall like a prop to hold up the sagging ceiling. Two squinting windows overlooked a sunless shaft out back. The view across the shaft was other depressing buildings.

One section was a living room/dining room/kitchen. I recognized the picnic table from Aunt Min's backyard. The square, sunken armchair originally came from my own basement but it looked worse than I remembered it. The light came from an ugly brass floor lamp with a cracked dome. My poor old chair was full of wounds with tongues of shredded foam hanging out. In the corner was a closet wall with half a stove, half a refrigerator, half a sink and half a cupboard, all stained with rust. Even in the bad light, the walls were bruised.

In the bedroom part, the bed and dresser were so close that

TABLE 47   199

you couldn't open the dresser drawers all the way. The toilet was out in the hall next to the broom closet and a tinny shower stall. I didn't sit down when I went to the toilet. Bibby said there weren't many cockroaches but I didn't sit down in the armchair either.

He'd found this jewel of an apartment in a New York *Times* ad. "It's really a bargain," he said. He didn't mind heating the water on the stove. He said it was probably safer that way.

I sat uptight on the picnic bench and tried to think of something complimentary to say. I thought how glad I was I hadn't accepted his invitation to dinner. He opened the refrigerator door and pointed to a half gallon of Gallo chablis lying all alone on its side.

"Thanks a lot," I said, "but I think we ought to get going."

It was an hour before show time and the theater was only a few blocks away.

"I wanted someplace where Brucie could stay with me on weekends." He pointed to the double bed. "Most places I saw were only one room." On the dresser was a fire truck, also a couple of picture books.

Suddenly I knew what to say and it would be true:

"I bet Brucie loves it here."

"Yes, he does. He thinks it's real neat. He thinks we're a couple of explorers."

Bibby double-locked the door when we left; I couldn't imagine why. Walking by Washington Square Park he told me that Warner Pickett was being very good to Brucie. Brucie wanted Karen and Bibby back together again, but he wanted to keep Warner too. In front of the theater I handed the tickets to Bibby. It wasn't the feminist thing to do, but Bibby's pride was more important.

The abstract dance concert stank, but I was glad at least that I'd gotten the poor guy out of that hovel.

Nights at home alone were filled with visions. He sat, night after night, in the caved-in armchair in the pinched, airless room, a companion to bugs, with his feet on the floor and his arms flat out, palms down, as currents of hatred ran through him.

Sometimes he thought about violating Karen. Karen had breasts like miniature twin haystacks with a tiny bird's nest on the tip of each. Once Bosculus had been a happy farmer cavorting about them, but his pastoral dance was over. Now he wanted a pitchfork to jab and stab and break them up and scatter them. He wanted to set Karen on fire and watch her burn. He wanted to mow her down with heavy farm machinery.

In the dead of night, he saw Karen's face as silky smooth as lemon pie. He wanted to smash it against a fence. Other times he saw her as a sharp little fox to chase and spear. He saw the virgin of a Botticelli Annunciation grow old, lose hair and teeth, sour and wrinkle into a coarse Breughel peasant. He wanted to ram a broom up between her legs. Into her snatch. Her bush. Her twat, cunt, pussy. He could not remember her misdeeds. He could not recall the details of their fights. It was pure rage that flew up in him, beating at him with electric wings.

Once he closed his eyes and his mother stood in front of him, clear as a calendar picture with her arms folded across her stomach, her clean-featured face staring straight at him. Clean teeth. Eyes you could sail on. Fluffy yellow hair. She looked altogether wholesome, like enriched bread in a catchy package. Bibby clapped the package and exploded her.

Fire entered through the soles of his feet and the palms of

TABLE 47 201

his hands. It burned to his mouth and he spewed it at her. Brimstone, too, fiercely yellow. Thirty-two years of volcanic buildup, colonic detritus. He couldn't stop heaving it out. How he hated this woman! Where was her love? Where was her care? Where was the place in her that yielded to his hunger? She had betrayed him with false and hollow niceties, hid blind selfishness under her polite face, hid greed and mean spirit behind gentle gestures. O vile woman: Spare thyself and maim thy child! His wrath erupted for hours, molten, surging. Her image was scalded. Her smile charred. Her eyes pitted. She sank before him into a seething pool only to rise up again when he thought he was all fired out. This was no dream.

This was a terror. Those hallucinations had the power to scare the viscera right out of him, into a long kite string with his heart floating out on top, sailing redly in the high night sky, shooting pulses of fear into spheres of space along with the rest of the fallout. The corners of his room curved around his specters. The dreams glowed in the dark. They played themselves out. When it was over, he wrapped them in a square package, tied it with double string, and slid it into the deep bottom drawer of his scuffed dresser, squeezed it in as he squeezed everything else because there wasn't enough room to open the drawer all the way.

Mornings after nights like that, he went warily barefoot into the hall toilet to take a piss and brush his teeth. One thing he had learned from his mother was to give himself a thorough tooth brushing. He had a jar of instant coffee in his half cupboard. There was often a can of frozen orange juice in his half fridge. Okay. So he spent several hours a night hallucinating.

He still had his days.

He had rent to pay. He had a body to maintain. He had Brucie.

Up on the West Side one day a burly, stubble-faced man started to shout at him. "Cocksucker!" the man shouted. "Fucking cocksucker!" It was mid-autumn, late afternoon, and the sky was gloomy.

Bosculus could just make out the fellow's face—a smear of beard and bulging eyes. Looking harder, he saw that the face was well formed under the bruises and bafflement. It could have been a noble face. Bosculus discerned with terror that the man, so old and unhuman, was probably younger than he.

A bottle pointed out from a brown paper bag and he shook it at Bosculus. He jerked it and spurted the stuff all around him, a sprinkling on Bosculus, who backed off fast. People looked away. They stepped into the street.

"Somebody call a policeman," a jogger said quietly as she passed along the curb.

A man with two colorful shopping bags slowed up: "Nah. He's harmless. It's payday for the SRO's. Poor guy probably spent his whole check." He moved on into a store.

The bottle wielder turned his bag over and was spilling booze onto the sidewalk. He seemed to be emptying himself at the same time. He moved into the doorway of an empty shop and twin streams made puddles around his feet.

Bosculus stood between two parked cars and watched the man try to drink from the bottle. Finding it empty, the man started yelling louder than ever. He hurled the bottle to the ground with such force that shattered glass leaped across the sidewalk and against the parked cars and in the road between them. A sliver shot into Bosculus' sneaker, but he left it there till he was far enough away to feel safe stopping. Leaning on

TABLE 47 203

a fender halfway down the next block, he took off the sneaker and shook it out, felt for the splinter and found it stuck to his sock. He could still hear the guy singing, some menacing and mournful amalgam of "Show Me the Way to Go Home" and "When the Moon Comes Over the Mountain."

Bosculus continued down on the Broadway diagonal and turned east on Seventy-second Street to avoid the prosperity of Lincoln Center. He was mentally transposing the two songs into a contrapuntal study, as an academic exercise, of course, not as an authentic composition. Bosculus thought, between Columbus Circle and Times Square, that there were an inordinate number of antisocial, erratic people in New York City. It was something one had to get used to. Passing Macy's and moving down Seventh Avenue, he noticed that dusk had become night. People seemed to be hurrying, buttoning up their coats. Bosculus thought it must be getting cold out. On Fourteenth Street, the last of the stalls were being locked up by sagging vendors. There were crowds on Sixth Avenue, for Village night life, he supposed. Tourists, he supposed. They were looking at him with curiosity.

Father Joe made it a point to call once a week. One Sunday he found that Bibby's phone had been cut off. He rushed into his clothes and drove downtown.

Bibby was a neat sleeper so Father Joe didn't know he had slept in his clothes. He was relieved to see him alive. "I've come to take you to brunch," he said when Bibby answered the door.

"What day is it?"

"Sunday."

"No service?"

"I went early."

Inside, Bibby explained that he'd forgotten to pay the bill, an oversight. But it was the weekend and he couldn't pay till Monday. Father Joe strained to see his friend's face. It was a clear winter day but you couldn't prove it through the windows.

"Yes, I guess you wouldn't want to miss any calls from Brucie."

"No. Well, Brucie doesn't call. I call him. I don't want to put any calls on Pickett's phone bill, you know. Not that they would object. Pickett is, you know, very good about things, very generous . . ."

"Yes, but I suppose you need the phone. Calls about jobs and interviews and so forth."

Bibby opened the refrigerator door and looked inside, shrugged and shut it.

"Do you hear much from Cindy? And Yuri? How are they doing?" Joe's tone was flat and casual.

"Fine," Bibby said. "Everybody's fine."

They walked to Christy's, where they got a table almost immediately. They stepped around platoons of potted flowers and sat behind place mats with a floral centerpiece between them, holding their heads very still to avoid the greenery hanging from the ceiling. The first of "unlimited" screwdrivers were brought while they waited for their eggs Benedict.

"So, what's up, Bibby?"

"Nothing much."

"Do you have any plans?"

"How do you mean, plans? You mean short-term plans like going to the movies next Tuesday? Or do you mean a blueprint for life?"

"I'm sorry, Bibby. I don't mean to crowd you. But if there's anything at all I can do."

"I'm fine," Bibby said. "Really."

TABLE 47   205

Then they talked about the cook at the Three Saints who really understood how to make a poppy-seed roll.

Bosculus was on the Bowery, but he didn't want to stay there. It was January thaw and the winos were out wiping windshields for quarters. Bosculus walked past store windows crammed with lighting fixtures—floor lamps, sconces, chandeliers, track lights—none of them lit. Restaurant supply stores, wholesale only, showed steam tables and coffee makers, giant mixers, all empty. On the other side of the street were the two-bucks-a-night hotels. Through the second-floor windows he could see beds in a row, beat-up guys sitting on some of the beds.

Drunks in the doorways were laid out like sled packs or propped up like terrible life-sized dolls. Bosculus understood them as abstract works and, crossing the street, smiled benignly on all. Up close they became children of the storm, he a Pater Noster walking by. He saw the value of downing a pint of something that would excavate the alimentary canal and bulldoze the imps that danced in his head. Glancing down at the hands that hung gloveless from his sleeves, he noticed they were shaking. He cut down East Seventh Street and stood in front of a Ukrainian store with colored eggs and peasant dresses in the jumbled window. The imps in his head leapt viciously. He peered into the store—they sold honey, phonograph records, fabric, books in Cyrillic—and when his anxiety attack was over, moved down the long block to Second Avenue, and remembered he hadn't eaten yet.

In a single clap of the eye, he registered a geographical kaleidoscope of restaurants: Chinese, Indian, Jewish dairy, Jewish kosher, macrobiotic, cafeteria-style Russian and pizza parlor. Bosculus knew his way around. He slipped into a corner luncheonette where excellent soup was available at forty cents a cup or sixty-five cents a bowl. It was either early or late for lunch because the place was nearly empty, just a couple of people at the counter. His soles were so thin he could feel the ridges of the octagonal floor tiles as he walked past the curved counter to a table in back. He picked up the soiled menu and read it like a newspaper.

The waitress had clear blue eyes and could not have been older than Karen was when he first met her. Her cheeks had a healthy red tint. She brought him a saucer with two slices of rye bread smeared with circles of margarine. She had tiny breasts and her arms filled her sweater sleeves. Bosculus ate a piece of bread, crust first, till she returned and set the cup of soup in front of him. She smiled when he thanked her. She, too, had slightly overlapping front teeth.

The soup was tasty with chunks of meat and cabbage. He pressed his spoon down and ate the liquid first, to make it last. The luncheonette was warm. The other tables were unoccupied. No need to hurry.

Then someone was shouting, a little whip of a man in a light suit too big for him. Something about the coffee. He turned his head and Bosculus saw a face knotted with anger, a white, tight Czech or Polish face, a head of thin white hair. The man was shaking his arm, shouting:

"I don't want the bitching woman to bring me coffee!"

The waitress stood against the dessert case, turned away, eyes blank.

The customers at the counter studied their plates.

"Fucking woman! Filthy hands!" the crazy man cried. He had little gray eyes like spitting snakes. The proprietor went over to talk to him. The short-order cook leaned over the counter. "You had your coffee," the proprietor said in a placating tone. "Take it easy," the cook said.

But the man couldn't be calmed. He got down from his stool and leaned across the counter. The waitress backed off

TABLE 47

207

along the steam table. "You shit!" the man spewed at her. She looked scared.

Suddenly Bosculus could stand by no longer. He yelled at the proprietor, "Get that guy out! He's disturbing your customers!" The lunatic spun around. "Get him out of here!" Bosculus yelled. "We have rights, too!"

The little man lunged at Bosculus. Bosculus jumped up and grabbed his chair. The man caught a leg of the chair and wrenched it from Bosculus' hands. He was a strong old man, tensed like an animal. The proprietor and the cook rushed up and seized him by the shoulders, lifting him off the floor. One of the customers got the chair away from him. The man pulled loose and shot Bosculus a punch in the jaw that made him reel. He fell to the floor, nicking his arm on the edge of the table. By the time he sat up, they were hustling the old man out the door. He was still shouting at Bosculus, wrenching his head around trying to see him. "I'll be out here waiting, son-of-a-bitch bastard!" He straightened himself up. "I'll get you, don't worry! I'll kill you when you come out!"

Back in his chair, Bosculus dipped a paper napkin into his water glass and held the wet against his jaw. He thought the other customers would rally around him and express their pleasure that someone had dared to speak up. In any case, *he* was glad he'd done it. His only regret: he was too shaken to finish his soup.

The waitress brought his check. She looked at Bosculus just as she had looked at the old guy, away from his eyes, as if she wished she weren't there.

But Bosculus insisted on contact. "That's intolerable," he told her in a calm voice to show he wasn't crazy. "You shouldn't have to take abuse like that."

Her shoulders sank. She seemed to be on the edge of acknowledging his concern, but she held back. She kept her eyes down. "It happens all the time," she said.

Bosculus paid at the register. He left the change from his dollar on the table. He knew he had two dollars put away in his top dresser drawer. That was to go to Long Island next Saturday and pick up Brucie. If he went the long way, by the Queensboro Bridge, he could avoid paying a toll.

He stopped again at the cash register. "Do you—ah—think that man is—ah—waiting outside?" he asked the proprietor.

The proprietor shook his head. "Nah. He don't remember one minute to the next. He's a harmless old guy."

But Bosculus didn't believe it. On the street he looked carefully around him, behind parked cars, in store entrances. All the way across town he kept turning to see if anyone was behind him. At every corner, he stopped and looked in all directions.

"He was a mess in those days," Geraldine says at Table 47. She sips a very expensive brandy and thinks about the patterns life takes on—when you look back.

Bibby ran into Geraldine one night on his way home. She had a bagful of groceries in one arm and a stretched canvas in the other. He held the door open. She recognized him from the oranges.

"I get wrapped up in my work," Geraldine explains, "and forget what's happening on the street. I hadn't given him a second thought. But on this night I got an impulse. I felt sorry for him, I guess, because he looked so down and out."

Geraldine asked him in. "I'm just going to throw a few things on the stove. I've got enough for two."

Bibby felt his face. He hadn't shaved.

"Thanks a lot," he said. "I've been gone all day. I have some things I need to take care of." There was mail under Geraldine's door. She was sure there would be none under his.

TABLE 47   209

"Listen," she said. "You could just come down for a little while. You could go right back after dinner." She was amazed at herself. "I'd be glad to have the company," she said, which was untrue. Geraldine had trouble enough fighting off life so she could get to work.

Finally Bibby agreed. He went upstairs first and changed to a cardigan without holes. He brought down the remains of a jug of Almadén white. The front of Geraldine's apartment was all studio—he could just make out the easels and the boards leaning against the walls—but Geraldine called him to the back. He set the wine on the counter that separated the cooking corner from the little round eating table and sat himself on one of the rush chairs.

Behind the counter Geraldine picked up two flour-dredged fish and waggled them. "I hope you like whiting." She dropped a lump of butter into a frying pan. From her half-refrigerator—shining clean—she took out some greens and tore them into a salad bowl. She poured some dressing on the salad and flipped it around with a fork. There was half a loaf of Italian bread and a leftover potato to slice and fry. Bibby watched her jiggle the fish in the pan. "I never cook till company comes," she said. "It's too boring."

They ate from pottery plates on straw place mats. Bibby, afraid he'd act like a starved animal, turned out to be less hungry than his hostess. He ate limply.

She apologized. "I shouldn't have made fish. You don't like bones."

"Oh, no. I'm really good at fish. I'm a surgeon at heart."

They both looked at his plate. "This was an exploratory operation," Bibby said. He tore off a piece of bread and when Geraldine went to the stove, he forked some lettuce out of the salad bowl and let the wet drip off. She returned with potatoes. Theoretically, he had no objection to potatoes fried in fish drippings. But put to the test, his theory failed.

"I'm kind of a closet eater," he explained.

"No sweat," she said. "I don't get my kicks from feeding people."

There was instant coffee and no dessert. Bibby stayed with the wine. In the warmth and light, he relaxed enough to take a good look around. Rag rug, posters on the doors, dried flowers in a fancy mustard bottle, some books of California philosophy, washing machine and dryer, a male nudie calendar. The owner of the establishment sat on a bentwood chair, embracing her coffee mug. He could not imagine what she wanted from him, if anything. He wondered whether she'd be offended if he washed the dishes or if he didn't offer.

He tentatively carried the plates to the sink.

"Put the bones in the garbage," Geraldine said. "Save the skin for the cat." It was a stray she fed, or somebody else's cat eating for two.

He washed the dishes and put them in the drainer. She sat staring out the shaft window. He dried his hands on a paper towel and said, "Well, I'd better get back."

And she said, "Thanks for coming."

And he said, "Thanks for having me. It was delicious."

She moved to give him the wine jug, but there was none left.

"Thanks for the wine," she said.

And he said, "You're welcome. I'm sorry there wasn't more."

And she said, "Come again."

And he said, "Thanks. Good-bye now."

He backed out the door. "Sorry to rush off," he said, "but I've got to pick up my son tomorrow."

Karen was in a woolly green housecoat, hugging herself against the cold. She looked out past Bosculus. The long

TABLE 47

211

slope of lawn was deep in snow. "Where did you park?" The road had been plowed but all the cars in sight were hidden under drifts, blocked by ridges.

"I—uh—came on the bus. My car has a—ah—flat."

"Take my car."

She had her own now. *Good for her*, Bosculus thought. He refused the offer, though. He said Brucie liked to ride buses. Brucie, all set in boots and snowsuit, wool hat under the hood, fat mittens, was tugging on his arm. Brucie had a bedroom and another room to play in. He wanted his dad to come in and see the train set Warner had given him for Christmas. Every week Brucie tried to get him to go in and look. This week Bosculus had a good excuse not to. They had to hurry to catch the bus.

In the Museum of Natural History, they stood together in front of the bones of a brontosaurus. Bosculus had an armload of boots and mittens and hooded jacket that he hadn't checked because he didn't have tip money. He had sloshed through twenty blocks of city snow, many of them with Brucie on his back, to avoid the extra bus fare. Brucie was full of pep. He hung over the railing in front of the steep glass case.

"That animal was a vegetarian," Bosculus told his son.

"I'm a carnivore," said Brucie.

"Not today, you aren't. I've got peanut butter-and-jelly sandwiches." They were in his pocket, wrapped in aluminum foil. Bosculus had enough change for a hot chocolate for Brucie in the downstairs cafeteria. Monday he'd pick up a check for some free-lance dishwashing. Then he could get his car started.

"I would like to be a carnivore and get a hot dog," Brucie said.

Bosculus promised him a hot dog next week.

Information about the brontosaurus and its Jurassic fellows

was etched in a silver column on the glass. Bosculus strained to read it closely in order to explain it—not for the first time —to his son. Brucie waited. He was a gentle child with straight yellow hair, sharp cheeks and light eyes that usually expressed approval of what he saw. He touched his face, enjoying the warmth of his hand against the cold of his cheeks. A man and a woman standing nearby smiled down at him. Brucie, with his fingers against the side of his face, smiled back. He pointed to Bosculus.

"That's my dad," he said.

"Didn't he work steady?" Flossie is practical. "What did he live on?"

"Well, he worked *often*," Geraldine says. "His friends kept getting jobs for him."

Joe wasn't so high up then with the American Executives, but he came up with occasional by-the-hour jobs. Yuri, being a poet, never had much clout but he once got Bibby into an after-school recreation program.

"He had unexpected skills," I tell Flossie. "He could pick up a buck any number of ways."

"And did," Paul puts in. "He was less incompetent than he looked."

The best job, the one he kept longest, came from Warner Pickett. "It was funny," Geraldine says, "because it was at *my* place."

This is news to me.

"At that time," she continues, "I thought Bibby was a permanent bum or an alcoholic, so I was really surprised to see him at the Decorator Arts Atelier." (Geraldine pronounces it

TABLE 47 213

a-tell'-yer.) She dips a toe in the stream of consciousness and before you know it she's swimming like a champ.

"That first night Bibby came for dinner," Geraldine begins, "he didn't even look at my work. I was glad because I hate explaining. I thought he just didn't care about art."

"Or just didn't notice," Paul says.

"Or was afraid he'd appear snoopy," Yuri says.

I'm a snoop. And not afraid to show it. "Where did Pickett come in?" I unhesitatingly ask.

"Warner Pickett was an amazing man," Geraldine says, plunging in. "I'd seen him around and I'd heard about him. He could come up with cheap copies of anything. They'd sometimes look better and work better than the original. He knew everybody—department-store buyers, fancy decorators, real estate big shots, entertainment people. He could get an oil painting put on as a prize in a TV show, with a closeup shot, you know, and Decorator Arts in the credits. It was worth thousands of dollars in advertising and he could do it with a phone call. He got my boss's name into the gossip columns and he got our pictures hung at big society parties. He could get your company's brand of whiskey served there or your dress design worn by some stunning show girl.

"So after I found out that Warner was kind of related to Bibby by marriage, it didn't seem too out-of-the-way to bump into Bibby at the Atelier. But Bibby was really knocked out to see me."

Selling art was a thing Bosculus had never done, but he knew he could do it. Bosculus was sensitive to works of art. He had always hung fine reproductions on the walls of his life. People had admired his choices.

Bosculus sat in his depleted armchair and reflected on his proven ability to do what was expected of him. If Pickett owned a piece of this art business, Pickett would be the beneficiary. Pickett was casting bread on the waters. Bosculus might well prove to be a pearl. A good man, Bosculus reminded himself, is hard to find.

It was a Sunday evening, summer because it was both late and light. The houseflies were lazy in the heat and Bosculus, immobile, felt for cool from the airshaft. There was no cool and, while he was not a man who sweated, he could feel the wells of moisture mobilizing under his skin. A glass of red wine was balanced on the flat of his chair arm. He raised it and took a thoughtful swallow. He would be an asset to this art association, he thought. For did he not respond to line and color? Could he not discern Dutch genre from French impressionism? Had he not, only that afternoon, spotted the Van der Weyden Annunciation from all the way across the room? Pickett knew what he was doing, all right. Art was a métier that Bosculus could enter with confidence.

It had rained most of Saturday and he and Brucie had played Parcheesi on the picnic table. Sunday they had met Cindy and Jill at the Cloisters. Cindy had driven Brucie back to the Picketts' house. Bosculus thought it was rather a case of poetic justice for Pickett to set him up like this.

Brucie, while gazing up at a glorious altarpiece—a Birth of the Virgin by the Master of Flémalle—had announced that he was expecting a little brother. It was cool at the Cloisters, the best place to be on a hot Sunday afternoon. Jill was unusually well-behaved probably because her brother Tony wasn't around. She took Brucie off while Cindy and Bosculus squinted at miniatures, cloisonné, filigree, illuminations. Of course, it might not be true. Brucie could have been overexcited by all those golden madonnas. Bosculus thought again of his qualifications as a seller of works of art.

It was a business building in a block of warehouses in the West Twenties. Bibby was there at 9 A.M. but the elevator

TABLE 47 215

made him late. The elevator was as big as a phone booth, though somewhat faster. All the way up he could see through the gate the names of ambiguous businesses. General Public Loan. A. Anthony, Immigration Attorney. Obdurate Enterprises. The Mah Jongg Society of America. Amazing Imports. Bosculus smelled a rat. He thought of CIA covers, gangster fronts, tax shelters, vice rings. He himself was fragrant as a flower, combed, shaven, jacketed, necktie and all. He got out on the top floor, saw the sign on the frosted glass of the door, turned the knob and walked in.

The square expanse was lit by a row of floor-to-ceiling windows and a broad pool of light from the roof. Rows of fluorescent light tubes seemed to patrol the inside walls, and all over the room, like three-legged prisoners, stood the easels on a gray-painted floor splotched with spilled color. The props were all appropriate: rags, newspapers, pails, cans and, of course, palettes and paintbrushes. Smocks and aprons hung around on pegs. A discreet arc of toilet seat showed inside one of the open doors. Another door led to an office that Bosculus entered, where Vernon Alda was waiting for him.

The head of the Decorator Arts Atelier—a short, bald, hypertense man a little younger than Bosculus—hustled him into a backless chair and came right to the point. "You don't need to lay on a hard sell," Vernon Alda said from behind his warped Victorian desk. "These pictures speak for themselves. We're so on target it's not even funny."

Vernon Alda jumped up and ran around the desk. "You got good friends," he said, with a mingling of curiosity and respect. "Just follow what I tell you and you'll be in big bucks every week."

He led Bosculus to a back room where paintings of many different sizes were standing on the floor and stacked on shelves. At 9:50 Bosculus was squeezed in the elevator with six canvases, all thirty-six inches long by twenty-eight inches high—exactly perfect, Alda said, for over a couch in a small reception room. There were three fruit and three desert

scenes, all wrapped in brown paper and tied with heavy
string. The fruits were in bold colors with no wrinkles. The
deserts were muted, smooth and in long perspective. Bosculus
was to show them one at a time in the order Alda had arranged. "That way," as Alda had said, "they might buy the
first one and you won't have to open up the others."

Bosculus walked east and took an uptown Madison Avenue bus. He stood in the aisle and held the paintings straight
between the seats. The places he had to visit were all on the
upper East Side between Fifth and Park, mostly interior decorators, but also a bank and a clinical psychologist's office.
No credit. No consignments. No checks. Cash only. Two
hundred fifty dollars a painting. Two for four seventy-five.
Half for the studio. Ten percent for Bosculus. The rest for
the artist.

Spring had come. It was a beautiful day. The sun was playing hide-and-seek behind wispy clouds. Vernon Alda was so
right that Bosculus ended up feeling more like a delivery boy
than a salesman. The last customer on his list was a real estate agent who met him in the empty manager's office of an
empty bank. He took two of the last three paintings. "Fruit?"
the real estate agent said. "That's very nice. Giant fruit is
good." There were twin couches in the office, with a square
table between them and a bare wall behind. "I'll take the ap-
ples and pears," the real estate agent said. "I don't want the
peaches." He said the peaches were too sexy. They looked,
he said, like bare behinds.

At three fifty-five, Bosculus got on the Fifth Avenue bus at
Eighty-fifth Street and sat on an empty pair of seats with the
painting on his lap and twelve hundred and twenty-five dollars in his pants pocket.

"I wouldn't want to mislead you," Vernon Alda said as he
took the money. "Today you had one of the most popular
sizes. The bigger ones cost more. We got whole-wall-size ones

TABLE 47 217

that go for fifteen hundred dollars. Those ones the customers don't buy so fast."

Only the smell of oil and turpentine, the disarray of easels and drying fruits and deserts, and the rubble of cigarette butts and soda cans indicated that the place had seen life during the day.

But Vernon Alda was lively as he advised his new employee.

On Vernon Alda, everything moved. His feet tapped. His fingers drummed. His head swiveled. His eyes darted. "They like to hang them up and look at them. They want to sit with them for a few days. Sometimes they want you to bring something different. They can get pretty fussy with the big ones."

But Bosculus managed. Some of the big ones were so big that they had to go in a truck, Bosculus and picture. Some went to nearby locations on a roller that looked like a stretched-out skateboard. Often the delivery took more effort and ingenuity than the sales pitch. Bosculus quickly became a character in a play that took place in his head:

> BERNARD J. BOSCULUS: *Protagonist. An up-and-coming young man, dealer in works of art. Knowledgeable, worldly, nobody's fool.*

He never forgot that he was selling not prints, not reproductions, but signed originals albeit not with the painter's real name. He played his scenes in settings of the highest style. He was welcomed into fashionable town houses which served as office-showrooms for some of the city's most elegant decorators. He was received at exclusive medical offices. Central Park South, Gramercy Park, Sutton Place were his new milieux and he even sold to the art buyer at Bergdorf Goodman. He made his entrances, placed himself advantageously and spoke his lines. He wore suits with vests and on at least two occasions, men made passes at him.

He returned to the Atelier late one afternoon, rolling a thousand-dollar canvas ("Picnic on the Grass") into the freight elevator in the back of the building. Vernon Alda was waiting to close up. Bosculus was a trifle wilted. He had an idea to improve the system.

"Maybe we should let the clients come here and pick what they want."

The boss stopped pacing and gave him a searching look, as if he had known all along that Bosculus was going to be trouble.

"Lookit," Alda said. "Don't think you can run the place just because you came in on pull. I'm still the boss here."

Bosculus was taken aback.

Edgy Alda loosened his collar. "They can't come in here," he said, trying to cool down, "because we got a mass operation. They think they're buying one-of-a-kind."

Bosculus still felt classy and debonair. But he reminded himself to stay humble.

During his second week of work he came back early one day, while the painters were still there, and saw somebody who looked like Geraldine. She was painting at one of the easels. She saw him and waved her brush. It *was* Geraldine.

She came over and poked him in the ribs. "Hey," she said. "I hardly knew you in your fancy suit."

Bosculus was unamazed. The suave salesman did not relate to the artists. They worked in the glare and blare of hot lights and loud music. They started late, most of them after Bosculus had already taken off with his daily consignment, and they were usually gone by the time he returned. Even when their presence coincided, Bosculus saw them only at the edge of his mind. They, like their paintings, all looked alike. Long-

TABLE 47   219

haired men, short-haired women, everybody in overalls or cut-offs, foreigners who didn't speak English, hippies who didn't speak English, all vaguely menacing as they stood around talking, smoking, drinking from cans, spreading purple on their mountains and brown on their desert sand.

The paintings were sleek, streamlined and unblemished—like the offices they were to decorate and the people who frequented those offices. The painters were from another world. Even Geraldine only looked like someone who looked like Geraldine. She wore a terry-cloth sweatband across her forehead, spotted jeans and a man's shirt with the tails tied under her chest. On her easel was a mountain exactly the same color as the eggplant on an easel a few steps away.

"You walked right past me one day," she told Bosculus. "I was washing brushes." She pointed to the toilet. "When I looked up to make sure, you were gone."

Bosculus explained himself.

"That's great!" Geraldine had to shout against a battle of Latin music against rock. "So, you doing okay?"

Bosculus automatically touched his wallet pocket. He said, yes, but how about Geraldine? What about her studio downtown?

"That's my real work," she said cheerfully. "Up here is schlock art. We do pretty good here. Vernon is, like, my patron."

That night Bosculus and Geraldine had dinner together for the second time. They took the subway downtown and bought a pound of homemade linguini and a pint of white clam sauce at the homemade pasta store on Houston Street. Bosculus had grated cheese upstairs and enough wine for the two of them. Geraldine had greens for salad. They stopped at a bakery and got two butterfly pastries, sopping with custard and rum. They went to Geraldine's apartment and he set the table while she boiled the water.

This time they talked. Bosculus felt almost comfortable,

which meant he had to watch himself not to blurt out anything that might damn or humiliate him. Geraldine also was not the world's most outgoing person, but she was sociable enough. She ate zestfully and seemed not to mind the company. They were both careful not to infringe on each other's privacy, but they managed to enjoy themselves.

She knew a good cheese place on Sullivan Street. Smoked mozzarella.

He'd try it. The packaged kind was always too salty.

He'd seen the Women's Collective art show on Wooster Street.

She was there last Saturday. There were a few things she'd liked a lot.

"Remember those uh-oversize watercolors of parts of flowers?"

"Oh, yeah. They were great. Very scary."

"Scary?" He examined the coarse brown grains in the sugar bowl.

"Well, you know. Threatening," she said. "I also liked the interiors. Remember the beach house? With the table and chairs on the planked floor?"

Bosculus remembered.

There was also a new dry-cleaning place around the corner, but neither of them wanted to pay the high prices there.

The basement playhouse in the next block had shut down. Geraldine had always wanted to catch one of their shows; somebody in her stretch class had been in the company. But that's how it was when you lived in New York.

Yes, Bosculus agreed. The best things were so close that you never got around to going.

After dinner Geraldine wanted Bosculus to see her studio. He was really glad because last time he'd been afraid to ask her. He hadn't wanted to impose. But now she led him up

TABLE 47   221

front and turned on the battery of lights. "I need for you to see these after uptown," she said.

They were different.

No deserts. No fruits.

Bosculus did not pay a polite visit. He moved all over the studio, around and behind things. He peered, pointed and asked a lot of questions. He intruded—looked into portfolios, carried canvases into better light. He asked the painter to hold up paintings that were standing on the floor, to turn those that faced the wall. He went to the other end of the studio to get a long look.

The painting she was working on was still wet and strapped to the wallboards. It made him take a breath. It wasn't a landscape or still life and it surely wasn't pretty. There were only a few slashings of harsh, straight lines against a shadowy background. But this painting had muscles and nerves.

Bosculus kept looking.

Geraldine stood back, out of the way.

The place smelled, like the uptown place, of paint, turpentine and oily rags, only no pot. Bosculus sneezed and grabbed his handkerchief. Geraldine said *Gesundheit*. She scratched the end of her nose with the back of her wrist. She was not a person who was embarrassed by silence.

"Okay," Bosculus said at last. "Well, listen. This is a neat painting. Why don't I take it when I go uptown someday?"

Geraldine didn't understand.

"You know. It's a five-hundred-dollar size. Why can't we show it to the customers? There's no rule, is there, that I have to show only what you do in the uptown studio? Vernon wouldn't mind as long as he made his money."

Geraldine looked like a little girl invited to play a naughty game. Then she giggled. She said okay, just to see what would happen.

In fact, Geraldine's downtown work was neither unsold

nor unsung. She showed Bosculus a few photographs of a painting in a museum in Minneapolis, another in Hartford, Connecticut, others in colleges here and there. But, in truth, she was more sung than sold, and the prospect of making some money did not rub her wrong. So one day that week Bosculus wrapped up the painting and took it uptown. He got a big old taxi and stood the painting on the floor between him and the partition. It was just high enough to obstruct the driver's rear view, so Bosculus called out instructions for changing lanes and turning corners.

The Gramercy Park decorator was a moist, baggy man with a mustache like sardine tails. He took the painting from Bosculus and unwrapped it as if he were pulling aside the robe of a prospective bed partner. The painting was as long as his arm spread and as high as his belly button. Unframed canvas stretched on wood. The elemental vitality of chalk and coal. Bosculus felt joy at seeing it again, alive and strong. Now it was his turn to stand back and watch the customer's reaction.

The decorator cleared a table and set the painting on it to lean against a wall. Then he backed away through french doors into the next room. He returned and closed the curtains. He put on lights and looked at the painting. He opened the curtains and studied it from one side, then the other. He came up close and squinted at it. He backed away again and cocked his head. He licked the tips of his mustache. He put his hands on his hips. He squatted and he straightened up. He took a long last look and turned to Bosculus, shaking his head.

"If I want art," the decorator said, "I'll go to a museum."

"Show me beige," he said.

Bosculus was making good money. So he bought Geraldine's painting himself.

TABLE 47 223

✿

Sometimes, though, even with a steady job Bibby felt low. In the slow time between day and darkness, the imps of possibility danced nastily beneath the surface of his skull. Sometimes the possibilities danced right out of his head and up in front of him like a line of toy balloons. At such times he might walk over to West Fourth Street, where the prosperous and festive gathered to saunter and shop and see one another. He'd look through the glass enclosures at the sidewalk tables of dashing little restaurants, dressed-up people rapt in eating and drinking at congenial tables, protected from the cold. Dusk after dusk he'd walk past place after place, never seeing anybody he knew. Nobody he saw ever knew him. He returned late to Daniell Street. Under the streetlight in front of his building, rows of imps sat leering at him from gutters strewn with limp balloon skins.

He thought of friends he might call on the telephone, but he didn't call them. What would he say? *I'm low. I'm lonely.* What could they do? Try to cheer him with accounts of their own problems. Feel embarrassed for his difficulties. Ask him to dinner. Sit at a bar with him. That wasn't what he needed. His friends would go home and he'd be alone again, worse than before. So he didn't call his friends and when they called him, he said he was doing fine.

He had his job and he had his son, but his nights were empty and his bed was empty. Sitting in his only, lonely chair, Bibby acknowledged his failure to be self-sufficient. What he needed, he divined, was a loose form of permanent companionship, an adult connection that could fuse without burning up the wires, an incorporation of elements of sympathy, respect and concern with provision for privacy, individ-

ual development and free movement. Bibby was after an at-
tachment rather than a commitment, something more
political than romantic, yet not devoid of feeling. It was hard
to frame in his mind exactly what it was he needed so badly.
The idea kept jumping out of his grasp.

Then one day, unexpectedly, he caught it.

It was in the IRT subway on his way back from a sale in
Riverdale.

He had sold a painting to a redoubtable private school that
was trying to change its image delicately enough to retain its
traditional high-class enrollment while pulling in necessary,
more prevalent kids who would have been filling the class-
rooms of public schools in the suburbs but that their newly
single parents had moved back to the city. The come-lately
parents, accustomed to the gentler rigors of upper-middle-
class educational collusions, were loath to submit their children to the rougher collisions of life in schools with police in
the halls and bars on the windows, with shell-shocked
teachers and not enough textbooks to go around. So against
their egalitarian principles they chose private education; but
to retain their self-esteem, they chose schools with a liberal
look.

The trustee who bought the picture from Bibby was an
old-family woman who, though repelled by graffiti, was able
to read the handwriting on the wall. The picture she bought
was already hung in the reception room, replacing a Venetian
canal-and-gondola scene with an incorrigibly eighteenth-cen-
tury look. The new picture was chic schlock. It was one of
the picnics, but it was the kind of picnic that city slickers
make before summer Shakespeare. Crystal stemware, Irish
linen, cold lobster and Montrachet. It set exactly the right
mood for the reception room: nostalgia for the old families,
anticipation for the new.

The old-family trustee had the handshake of a metal com-

TABLE 47 225

pressor and she liked the picture so much that Bibby gave her twenty-five dollars off the price—an institutional discount, he told her. He was full of bonhomie and noblesse oblige as he climbed the steps to the IRT's last stop at 242nd Street and Van Cortlandt Park. He felt the pleasure of two hundred and seventy-five dollars crumpled in his pocket. It wasn't until the train went underground at Dyckman Street that he started to be scared.

This seemed to be a dead spot in the public transportation day. Neither morning nor evening rush. Not lunch hour nor school dismissal time. Neither theater opening nor theater closing. So Bibby sat in an eerily empty subway car and began to think he'd be killed there. At each deserted station he imagined a single gunperson rushing in as the doors were closing, or a group of teenagers bursting through from the next car. He'd give them his money, of course, without a murmur. But should he try to get away with giving just the wallet? If they searched him and found the rest, they'd surely kill him. But maybe they'd kill him anyway so he wouldn't be able to identify them for the police. He thought what he'd do would be to be very slow about getting at his money and maybe by then somebody else would have come into the car. Given a choice, he thought he'd like it to be a uniformed policeman.

At 137th Street a short stocky man in a sweat suit got on and slid into a corner seat. Bibby hoped he was an off-duty cop.

Bibby ostentatiously read the car cards. A school for cosmeticians. A school for data programmers. A warning about rip-off schools. Give to Cystic Fibrosis. Join Vista. Drink Brim instant coffee. Borrow from Household Finance. Bibby wondered if he was safer in the car or on the platform. He was sure the man in the corner was looking at him but he was afraid to check it out. Two more people came on at 116th

Street and another at 103rd but Bibby felt more and more like a marked man. He was the only one in a business suit. At Ninety-sixth Street the car began to fill: everybody was black, Latin, Asian or Chassidic.

"This is only what I wear to work." Bibby mentally stood up and apologized. "I vote Democrat," he mentally announced. At Seventy-second Street, a fat, strong-smelling man sat beside him and almost pushed him through the window. The man got off at Forty-second Street and left a magazine on the seat.

The magazine that changed Bibby's life.

He picked it up and leafed through. He was stopped by a center page with an inch-high headline:

HOW TO FIND SOMEONE TO LOVE

Bosculus smiled an ironic smile.

START RIGHT NOW TO MEET AND DATE DOZENS OF EXCITING, FUN-LOVING WOMEN!

He read on. START RIGHT NOW *a cordial, close relationship to last as long as you want to keep it.*

Bibby flipped to the cover, where an overdeveloped young man crouched under the weight of the red-lettered name *Muscle.* Under the cover boy's high-arched feet was printed the slogan A *healthy mind in a healthy body.* Bibby pondered over the larger meaning of that equation. . . .

In all his life he had never read a physical fitness magazine. As a child he had loved *TipTop Comics.* In his prepubescent years he discovered that photography magazines featured pages of female nudes. Older, he made occasional stealthy stops at back-of-the-store racks to peruse *Playboy* or *Cavalier* or to gape at jacket copy on the back of paperbacks he wouldn't dream of buying. Such current publications as *Clean-Shaven Muff* he ignored and disapproved of. Pop magazines were just not part of his life. *Muscle* was one he would

TABLE 47   227

pass with the same unseeing eye that overlooked *Popular Mechanics,* *Vogue* and *Better Homes and Gardens.*

He turned back to the center-page advertisement.

UNLOCKED AT LAST!
THE SECRETS OF GETTING WOMEN
TO FALL IN LOVE WITH YOU!

There was a photograph of a man and a woman kissing. It was an upshot profile of an everyday kiss. The woman's eye was closed. The man's eye was open. At the bottom of the ad, Bibby read that the keys to this kingdom were to be found in a book called *Meeting and Mating.* There was a mail-order coupon saying RUSH ME MY COPY!

He missed his stop. An ample brown woman sitting beside him was looking at the magazine on his lap as if it might be covering an entertaining secret. She caught his eye and smiled with an indulgent heave of her big chest in a wide-striped T-shirt. Bibby put on his severest Orthodox face. He rolled up his magazine and got off at the next stop.

The Canal Street station looked like a plaster cast with the arm pulled out. The walls were bathroom tile which, from the smell of the place, was appropriate. People moved quickly toward the exits and Bibby moved with them, glad he was going someplace even though it was back to where he should have been. *Muscle* magazine was in his pocket, cover side in. Bibby intended to read it for insight into other people's lifestyles.

He went up the Downtown stairs and down the Uptown stairs and waited on the Uptown platform, pressed against the wall so that nobody would push him onto the tracks. School had let out: four teenagers with book bags were huddled in an alcove, doubtless trading pills or glassine envelopes. Even as he registered and reacted to these surroundings, Bibby was rapt in subterranean thought about how far he had gone toward losing touch with the masses. He was no man of the people, he thought. Privacy and privilege had turned him into an outsider. He was not, as he had once imagined, above it all; he was simply apart. He had used his high IQ and his academic achievements as an escape from real life.

The train came on like a fast punch. Bibby got a seat and pulled out his magazine:

> *Don't let the fears, the inhibitions, the coldness of modern life keep you in harness. Break the rigid, self-destructive habits of shyness and insecurity.*

He was sitting beside a Chassid, who leaned away from him.

Bibby saw that this ad was addressed to him as well as to less privileged human beings. He was no better than anyone else who needed to know "*a simple, upfront way to let a person know you're attracted to them without appearing weak or desperate.*" He, too, wanted to "*quickly master the art of being outgoing, looser and friendlier at parties.*" Elitist though he suspected he was, he had to admit that he would welcome "*a sure-fire method of bringing out the witty, charming side of your personality when you feel yourself starting to clam up and get formal and stiff.*"

A man must lose himself to find himself, Bibby recalled as his train muscled into the Thirty-fourth Street station. When he got up to get off, the Chassid beside him brushed off his black coat where Bibby had sat against it.

"*This is not some philosophy book about love,*" Bibby read as he climbed the stairs to the street. "*To the contrary, it's a practical guidebook that will tell you exactly how to meet someone you can truly share your life with.*"

He went directly to the main post office on Ninth Avenue, two blocks away. He bought a stamped envelope and a money order for six dollars and ninety-five cents plus another dollar to cover postage and handling. He filled out the cou-

TABLE 47   229

pon, tore it off the page and folded it into the envelope, which he then addressed to the Harmony Press in Sterling, Illinois. There is no growth without change and no change without discomfort, he told himself as he walked purposefully to the mailing wall and slipped his letter through the slot.

Geraldine was still working when Bibby got back to the Atelier. She was standing away from the easel, staring critically at a poreless southwestern landscape of beige sand and pink rocks with two beige donkeys with mahogany shadows. Bibby stood by the door for a moment and watched her. She was wearing a faded blue work shirt with the sleeves torn out. She had strong, skinny arms and Bibby thought she must be a really anxious, high-metabolism person. She moved in on the painting with a brush as determined as a Leonard Bernstein baton.

A couple of the other painters were still there, cleaning up, getting dressed. Arturo was an illegal alien from Colombia, a bearded ex-soccer player who sold hand-made jewelry on weekends at a stand in Washington Square. Maisie was a rope sculptor from Arkansas. She was scraping her palette while her sky dried. Her red hair was chopped short and her sumptuous behind stretched her jeans tight. She was shaking the behind in time to a reggae beat from Arturo's transistor. Bibby had seen slides of her rope pieces: heavy hangings, huge knots piled on the floor.

Vernon Alda had a corner to himself. He always worked two or three easels at once, in addition to his office duties. He was the only one who didn't have *real* work outside the Atelier. Bibby watched how Vernon looked over at Maisie and dropped his eyes when she caught him looking. Jumpy and money-crazed as Vernon was, Bibby suspected that he had a way with women. Here was this hyper, early-balding guy with his shirt open so low that you could see not only the hair on his chest like a welcome mat but also the shelf of belly he was putting on. It was a feeling Bibby had, that Vernon went to bed with a lot of women.

Geraldine saw Bibby. "How're you doing?"

Bibby joined her at the easel. "How's it going?"

"Great."

"Great."

"You going home from here?" Geraldine asked him.

Yes. Just as soon as he straightened up with Vernon.

"Okay. I'll wait for you." She frowned at the painting. She touched up a wave of sand. Vernon Alda stopped in mid-stroke when Bibby came over. "How'd you make out?" he asked as he led Bibby to the office. Bibby decided not to mention the twenty-five-dollar discount.

Downtown bound, he thought he might tell Geraldine about *Meeting and Mating.* He could make it an amusing anecdote, told in a dry, satiric tone: "Today I broke a lifelong pattern . . ." But the subway was crowded and noisy, and anyway he was afraid she'd miss the humor. They got out at Houston Street, which Bibby now pronounced "house-ton" like a true New Yorker. They walked east for a few short blocks. Bibby turned north on Daniell Street. Geraldine turned south.

"See you later," she said. She was going to her karate class.

Meeting and Mating arrived in less than a week. In a brown paper wrapper. Bibby sat up that night, reading.

What you do with your eyes, how you open and close them, speaks volumes. It's almost automatic to close your eyes when you kiss. Try giving into an impulse to close them before the kiss (in anticipation) or after the kiss (to let the effect linger longer). . .

TABLE 47   231

What kiss? Kissing whom? When? Bibby had never thought about the opening and shutting of eyes. He had a long way to go before he'd even get to kissing.

Seated on his ascetic throne, Bibby fled to a critical distance. The book had a flexible cardboard cover. Big print. Fair paper.

Then he thought about prostitutes. Whores. Professional fuckers. He thought of women on the street in all sizes and colors. Spaced out. Chewing gum. Wearing white boots. Wearing hot pants. Reeking perfume. Breasts bulging out of tank shirts. He could not remember having thought of them before. These women had been there all along, not only in New York but on all the street corners of his life. A past of waiting, beckoning, available women strolled, strutted, sidled, sashayed, slithered and strode across the runway of his mind. And his mother? That faded lady waited in the wings with her arms folded across her stomach and her eyes looking right past him. He stared her down and she receded out to the fire escape. Bibby shut the window on her. The prostitutes returned for curtain calls. They were all in red satin tights and gold lamé tops, bare midriff. They formed a chorus line like a frieze across the back of his mind. He pushed down the urge to jerk off. He didn't have time.

He turned to the chapter on Good Looks.

Gloria Mundy, the pseudonymous author of *Meeting and Mating* said that a good attitude was more important than good looks. She said that men worry unproductively about the size of their noses and the angle of their ears. Statistics showed that women didn't really care about noses and ears. On the other hand, over twenty percent of all American women, according to a national poll, were primarily interested in "a small, tight ass."

Bibby supposed that his behind was pretty flabby. All he'd been doing was sitting on it. But Gloria Mundy told him not to concern himself about his ass, either.

A man can't feel very horny, can he, when he's sitting around obsessing about not being attractive enough. Concentrate instead on the inner you, who is lusty and physical, an exciting sexual partner . . .

Gloria told him to go to parties and open up.

Bibby set the book down and tried to remember how he felt at parties.

He felt okay.

Thanksgiving dinner at Cindy and Paul's had been comfortable. It was mostly family and there was a lot of warmth and affection. Everybody was nice to him, even Jill. Tony was very friendly. And the food was great.

Social evenings at Father Joe's involved small groups of renegade priests who worked as psychotherapists or ran homes for runaway kids. Food wasn't much but the talk was terrific. Late in the night, as the jug level went down the hilarity increased and everybody did imitations of bishops and metropolitans.

Yuri invited him to an occasional poetry reading. Nothing happened there but total absorption. People who arrived together went home together and Bibby never caught any wild vibes of horniness or erotic derring-do.

Bibby picked up the magazine. Clearly, he was way off course. He was a man who had been content to sit in a daddy-corner and let the excitement pass him by. Bibby had never hustled. He must have been, he concluded, repressed out of his skull. It was time, he decided, to come out of the closet and start acting like a heterosexual.

Brucie and Bibby were cuddled like spoons together in the hollow of Bibby's bed. Saturday was rainy and they had played a lot of Parcheesi. Bibby had run downstairs for a pizza for supper. Now Brucie and Bibby talked about Sunday.

TABLE 47 233

The Egyptian tombs at the Metropolitan Museum or the three brown bears at the Central Park Zoo. Brucie had touched all there was to touch at the Touch Me exhibit in the Museum of the City of New York. He had also touched things at the Frick Collection, where he was no longer welcome. Brucie had eaten Sunday brunch at more than a dozen restaurants with Tiffany lampshades, chopping-block tables and hanging plants. He had brunched on eggs Benedict, eggs Florentine and eggs Sardou with croissants and brioche while his father had drunk pitcherfuls of screwdrivers, bloody marys and weak champagne cocktails. Not yet in kindergarten, Brucie had already seen *The Nutcracker* at the ballet and *Hansel and Gretel* at the opera.

"And so, Buddy, what are we going to do tomorrow?"

"I don't know, Buddy. What do you want to do?"

Bibby proposed the bears if it was sunny and the tombs if it continued to rain.

Brucie was satisfied.

"But listen," Bibby said. "Next week I want you to come only on Saturday."

"Not sleep over? How come?"

Bibby thought maybe he should have just collected him next week and brought him home that night without discussing it first. But there would be Brucie with his little pajama bag unopened. Bibby couldn't bear to think of it.

"We'll still have Saturdays," he said, pitching his voice low to keep it manly.

"Why can't I sleep in your bed anymore?"

"You can. You will. But just not for a while."

Brucie's back was curled into Bibby's front, and the lights were off. But Bibby could see the disappointment on Brucie's face.

He had a glib excuse in mind: he was going to say how much nicer the Picketts' house was than Bibby's cruddy apartment.

"The fact is," he heard himself saying, "that it's time for me to meet some more grown-up people. I've got to find some new friends. So I thought I'd spend Sundays with people my own age."

Brucie was quiet. The boy who knew more knock-knocks than any other child in his nursery school class was speechless. Bibby turned on a light and turned Brucie around to look at him.

"You're my best friend, you know. I really mean that. But I have to be with people my own age sometimes."

Brucie, with serious eyes and a plaintive little mouth, was still sweet as a peach. Bibby had to squint to look at him, so painful was his beauty.

"We could make friends together." Brucie reached up and stroked his father's hair.

"It wouldn't work out, Brucie. But listen. It won't take very long. After I meet them, we can all be friends together."

Bibby described future friends who might be excellent cooks, who might have nice apartments with color TV that Brucie could watch when he got tired of playing three-person Parcheesi, who might know—as Bibby never quite did—when it was too cold to go out without a sweater and whether a movie would cause bad dreams, and who would, in the end, make life pleasanter for both of them.

Brucie looked doubtful.

"I mean it. My friends will love you. If they didn't love you, they wouldn't be my friends. We'll have a lot of good times together."

Bibby sighed. "It's only Sundays," he said. "Saturdays will be the same as ever. Saturdays we'll still be friends by ourselves."

At last Brucie took a breath. Bibby hugged him hard. Brucie hugged back and Bibby mentally awarded himself the Father of the Year medal. He felt so good all week that he kept Brucie overnight the next Saturday and brought him

TABLE 47 235

back to the Island early Sunday morning. In the early afternoon—a crisp, clear, nippy example of autumn at its best—Bibby went, alone, to the Museum of Modern Art.

Daring, innovative color combinations will begin to change the way you think about yourself.

He wore a new green corduroy jacket over a royal blue knit shirt. There was no line, so he circumnavigated the chestnut man and the two o'clock rendezvousers and entered confidently through the revolving doors. As he reached for his wallet to pay admission, he nearly bumped into a woman crossing in front of him on her determined way to the bookshop. She was thirtyish and handsome in a blazer and jeans, straight black hair to the waist.

Let your emotions "float free" in your eyes. Almost everybody, except the pathologically shy, loves to be looked at, especially in a way that says, "You turn me on."

He stared at the woman, who kept going till she reached the edge of the bookshop. Then she wheeled around. She had wonderful light blue eyes. He continued to stare

approvingly, lingeringly

until she made a terrible face at him and, he thought for a hysterical moment, looked for a guard. But all she did was spit out one word. "Pig!" she said. Loudly enough to be heard at the admission booths. Bosculus looked innocently over his shoulder and moved on.

In a discreet corner of the second floor was temporarily housed a traveling exhibit of works by Amedeo Modigliani, a painter Bosculus admired as much for his recklessly bohemian life as for his seminally modern oeuvre. Bosculus walked past impressionists, expressionists, cubists, futurists and surrealists to arrive at the Special Exhibition galleries and encounter this volatile Italian Jew who, Bosculus reminded himself, was no *ist* at all, only an *I*.

The first room was nothing but portraits. Bosculus was alone with eight ruddy-skinned, elongated, body-conscious, painfully alive people who looked down at him, languidly or curiously, as if he were the one who was on display. He fended off paranoia by confronting the portraits one-on-one, starting with the most benign. He was approaching a lovely, warm-skinned nude with big, melting thighs, sloping shoulders and a most receptive tilt of the head when a young girl wandered into the room. "Why is a 'young girl' older than a 'girl'?" was a question Bosculus had often asked himself and repeated in the present instance. He watched her with keen peripheral vision.

She was a coltish thing, long and slim with a gauzy knit scarf doubled loosely around her long neck. She was a dear-looking, wistful thing with pink glowing skin, a twist of nose, a flower-bud mouth and pale blue blurs for eyes. Bosculus pulled his attention back to the wall display. He acted out the authoritative manner of a schlock art customer about to put down big cash. Bosculus was already on intimate terms with these portraits but, to impress the young girl, he treated them like strangers. He scrutinized from near and far. Appraised. Communed. The young thing looked around her with placid interest. She didn't notice him.

Do it even if it frightens you. ESPECIALLY *if it frightens you.*

Gloria Mundy's example was a woman reading a book on a park bench. The man was to go up to her and steal a look at the cover of the book. Then he was to lean over her shoulder and say, "You'll love it! Should I tell you what happens at

TABLE 47   237

the end?" Gloria had provided openers also for a woman on the beach and a woman in the supermarket. But what about a woman in the Museum of Modern Art?

Whether you succeed or fail is not important. Taking a risk is itself a mind-opening, life-expanding step . . .

According to Gloria Mundy, the "surefire line you can always fall back on" was blunt, awful honesty. "Excuse me," the man was supposed to say in a pinch, "but I just had to tell you. You really turn me on."

Bosculus was turning this over in his mind when the young girl drifted past him and out of the gallery.

He followed her. There were more Modiglianis in the next one. The dear young girl stood raptly before a famous seated nude.

Bosculus stood beside her. He examined the flatly laid-on patches of color. The young woman, too, had laid-on color. Her pink skin tone dwindled away just above the jawline. The paint on her glowing cheeks was caked. The sweet blur of blue eyes was a blur of blue eye shadow. Bosculus compared the art of Modigliani to the art of the makeup artist and found that the former turned him on more that the latter. He stood back to get a longer look at the live woman.

Clearly outlined against the white wall, her cherry-colored hair sprang away from the nape just above the surface of the scarf. He was following the flow of her dress from shoulder to waist when she opened her mouth and spoke.

Bosculus jumped.

Sweetly unfocused, she flung up a limp hand toward the portrait.

"I don't like this artist," the young girl told Bosculus. She repeated the artist's name, pronouncing it Moe Dig Leone. "He doesn't do noses well," she said with a fragile sniff. "Or eyes either." She blinked.

Bosculus looked down at the young girl's long, narrow feet, very nice, in tapered pumps. He thought, as he left the museum, still alone, that there was a place in the world for discrimination. He thought, on his long walk home, how glad he was that he was still a man with standards. Turning into Daniell Street, he thought he saw Vernon Alda slipping out of his apartment building. At first he thought Vernon might have been looking for him.

But Vernon waved nervously. "How ya doin'?"

"Just great. How's it goin'?"

"Everything's cool," Vernon said.

They both slowed down but didn't come quite to a standstill.

"You live here, too," Vernon said. "I forgot."

Bosculus had an inspiration from *Meeting and Mating.*

"Yeah," he said. "Give me a ring next time you're around."

It sounded okay. He hoped Vernon wouldn't think he was pushy. He scowled as he moved away, to show that he wasn't pleading for friendship. On the way upstairs, he started to wonder if Vernon and Geraldine were lovers. By the time he got his key in the lock, all he could think about was Vernon with Geraldine.

Next time you're with a desirable woman, don't sit wondering. Imagine making love with her. Undress her mentally. Imagine kissing, caressing. How would it feel to lie naked with her, fusing your body with hers?

Bosculus thought about Geraldine but every time he tried to mentally undress her, she pulled her clothes together. He'd unbutton her blouse and she'd grab the ends. He'd put his hand on her thigh and she'd leap out of the chair. He'd try to touch her hair and she'd snap her sweatband on his fingers.

He tried wondering about her breasts. What color her nipples were, whether they were flattened out or nubby. But he

TABLE 47   239

felt underhanded when he did this and couldn't get his mind to hold still enough for a clear picture. Geraldine was a failure as fantasy. Fucking was out of the question. He'd get a glimpse of her pubic area and she'd dart behind a canvas.

By certain physical and subliminal sexual signs, the woman will get your message.

He'd be ashamed for Geraldine to get that message. He was better off screwing strangers.

Bosculus thought if he ever got enough money together, and got all his debts paid off, he might go and see a shrink. Not necessarily for a whole exhaustive, exhausting analysis. But a little spot therapy might help him a lot, smooth out some of the rough places in his head. It was bad enough, for example, that he still occasionally erupted with hatred for his mother. But he was also becoming obsessive about Vernon Alda.

Bibby had begun to imagine that Vernon Alda was screwing all the women at the Atelier. Once or twice, sitting in his armchair, he got crazy and telephoned his jumpy phantom, hanging up as soon as Alda answered. He only wanted to see if Alda was home. If there was no answer, Bibby would make a pretext of needing something suddenly and go down to Geraldine's to borrow it. One night he went down after midnight to deliver some smoked mozzarella he decided was too good not to share. Geraldine worked late in her studio and thought nothing of it. Bibby, once sure she was at home and alone, calmed himself and went to bed.

Bibby was not insane. He knew that people were making love all over the city. All over the world, in fact. He simply didn't want anything happening under his nose. Not while he was deprived and desolate. He moved restlessly about his apartment. His lust rose like a geyser, faithfully, exploding in the air around him. It fizzled, dwindled and disappeared, but he knew it would be on him again.

The point was that Bibby liked clean sex. He liked honest erotica—or at least knew he would have liked it if he'd had the nerve to pursue it. Bibby hated what was cheap and gross. He masturbated seldom and reluctantly, feeling almost always that it was a shame to be doing this alone, turning nature's great communal act into a solo performance. Much as he enjoyed, even went crazy over, the needed release, he felt that masturbation missed the point. Yet when he did it, he did it in style.

Bibby could masturbate cold turkey: it was a special talent of his. No pictures, no magazines, no fantasies. Nothing on his mind but the mechanics of the deed itself. He liked to do it with panache. He like to show respect, if not reverence, for an excellent instrument that could rise from limpness into pulsing life. He watched his penis intensely as it thickened and swelled until its skin stretched pearl-like and translucent, silken and responsive to the most breathlike stroke of his fingertip. Exquisite touchstone: he could intoxicate it with a feather. The tip of a sable brush barely touching it's quivering head. Bibby could masturbate, if he chose, with his eye on a Veronese Venus. But with a calendar cutie, never. Most of the time he tried to catch his desire and fling it off in some nonerotic direction. When he succeeded he felt victorious. Yet, he could not remember having been told that sexual behavior was degrading or dangerous. His mother had never talked about sex. Something, though, he thought, must have hobbled him. He was unable to go at things in a direct manner.

He and Geraldine took a walk one night and stopped at John's for pizza. They talked about everything. Geraldine said she had never lived with a man. They had the corner table near the counter. The pizza crust was really thin and

TABLE 47 241

tasty. Geraldine shook red pepper on her slice. Her hair hung limp around her round, pale, freckled face.

"I mean," she said. "I've been with my share of guys. But I just never *lived* with them. I didn't want to get that involved."

They had a small pizza with sausage slices. Geraldine bit in and stretched the cheese like taffy.

Bibby understood. "I liked being married," he said. "But there was a big price tag on it. I liked having somebody." He folded a slice and took a horizontal bite. "The fact is, I don't seem to function very well on a general social level. I find that I'm very conflicted about casual sex."

Geraldine sprinkled grated Parmesan on her second slice. "I know what you mean." She laughed. "I like a lot of variety."

Bibby didn't know whether she meant pizza or men. He thought of asking, but couldn't bring the question out. "I function well in almost every other area," he said.

"Me too."

They were both very hungry, so they got another pizza before going home and splitting.

Cindy got Bibby invited to a big city party on the Upper West Side. Bibby showered in the hall and got dressed in festive clothes.

Any occasion may be THE occasion.

He took the IND subway to Columbus Circle and walked up Central Park West. He entered a gilded building where a resplendent doorman met him with the word "Banks?" Bibby checked his written instructions and said "Yes" and the doorman pointed to an elevator and said "Sixteen." The elevator opened onto a vestibule that was seething with overflow from the party. Bibby could hardly get in.

Watch the reactions of the opposite sex. They'll look
at you with approval, once you really believe you are
worth looking at.

Bibby was too busy looking at *them*. A sea of souls he
could drown in. As his eyes became accustomed to the
brightness, he saw that he was in a frothy mix of people who
did not fit into familiar categories. One tweedy old man was
wearing a jeweled dog collar. A younger man had a baby
strapped to his back. Another wore a ruby in one ear and a
gold *chai* on a chain around his neck. One woman was in a
sequinned sweat suit. Another had green hair and a ghostly
leer. Bibby didn't worry about his nose or his ass. He worried
that he would never find Paul and Cindy. Or the bar.

Put yourself into a positive frame of mind. Be aware
of your feelings and the kind of signals you're sending
out. . . .

Bibby, up against the wall, felt that his signal was an SOS,
but nobody heard it. So he rose above the crowd and an-
alyzed them. All these animated, multicolored, socially
oriented people were:

a) daytime office workers acting out nighttime fantasies.
b) a group of post-Freudians who had reached consensus
   that civilization was not, after all, worth its discontents.
c) a biological experiment on human responses to confine-
   ment in tight places with a glass in one hand and a
   cigarette and/or canape in the other.
d) all of the above.

He thought he should undress the guests but couldn't because he wasn't sure, in some cases, which of them were
women. Besides, they were packed so close that he couldn't
see them apart. Was this, Bibby moralized, Walpurgis Night
or a step in the right direction? Sodom and Gomorrah or the
road to higher rationality through individual freedom? Bour-
geois decadence or healthy catharsis? Bibby didn't know.

TABLE 47 243

"My mastectomy? It's marvelous, though actually if I'd been given the choice, there were a lot of other parts I'd rather have gotten rid of."

"I pay eight dollars a pound for my special blend, whole-sale. I mean, I go out to Smithtown for it. For me, coffee is serious business."

"My daughter goes with this Portuguese socialist. He's very nice, but he carries a picture of Lenin in his wallet and I'm afraid he's going to shoot us."

"Marcel Marceau? Come on, now. Give me Harpo Marx."

"My mother said I couldn't go unless I got a diaphragm. She made me see her gynecologist, or else she said she'd have Bal-Krishna up on charges of statutory rape. So I got the diaphragm and Bal-Krishna and I went to Boston to the sem-inar on holistic medicine. We didn't even sleep together."

"They have these Korean masseuses in short red pants and a row of cubicles like beach lockers . . ."

"And I said, look, you're promoting this guy who has only been here five months. I've been here over a year, I said, and I know the work better than he does. I think this is sex dis-crimination, I said, and he said, Let's talk about it over din-ner tonight. I couldn't believe it. I thought he was gay."

Have another drink. Get up and move over to a group. Begin to talk about something that interests you. You can do it in a nice way by saying, "Excuse me for chang-ing the subject, but there's something I'd really like to talk about."

Bibby worked himself along the wall into the next room. Using the advantage of empty hands, he elbowed his way around and between the thick of the crowd and inched along until he reached the bar. He got himself a scotch on ice and felt good about it. He thought he might eventually edge over to the sideboard for some cheese and crackers. A young woman who looked like Alice in Wonderland walked by as if

her legs were tied together. She wore, on a shoulder strap, a
box like a tourist-attraction audio tour but it wasn't wired to
her ear. In fact, the box was clipped to the top of her dirndl
skirt and the wire seemed to disappear inside. The woman, a
Victorian Alice, made it to the bar and returned with a glass
of something red. She said, passing Bibby, "I'm afraid to
drink anything strong with this wire up my ass."

So then, Bibby thought, the box must be a kind of inter-
nally attached pacemaker for some lower organ. He nodded
sympathetically.

"You see," Alice stopped to say, "I'm in this study at
N.Y.U. to find out how body temperature affects moods. I
have to write eight reports a day about how I feel."

"How *do* you feel?" Bibby asked.

"Very irritable, with this probe up my ass."

She shuffled off carefully and Bibby backed into a neutral
corner. A broad-shouldered woman standing nearby was sending out companionable signals. She had heavy brown hair
and a gentle, somewhat strained face. Bibby liked her shoulders, like Joan Crawford's in old movies. He pulled in beside
her and she stepped out of her high-heeled shoes.

"Do they ever hurt!" she said, looking up at him. She had
big teeth and heavy lipstick and a really friendly smile. Bibby
turned to see if she wasn't talking to somebody behind him
but everybody else was turned away. The woman was looking
into his eyes.

Her name was Lissa.

> *Do you sometimes feel that you'll never ever be able to
> change the way you act even though you know perfectly
> well that your behavior is self-destructive?*

Gloria Mundy insisted that Bibby could change his ways.
So he tried very hard to be vivacious, aggressive, reckless, insinuating.

TABLE 47   245

"Would you like me to freshen up your drink?" he said sensuously.

He came back with two drinks and she was waiting for him. He was astounded. He felt the muscles in his face tuning up. A couple of people smiled toward him. His jacket felt tight, as if his chest had swelled a size or two. He squared his shoulders to give himself chest room. Lissa smiled a rich red thank you as she took her glass. It was too noisy to hear what she said as she put it to her lips. He leaned close to her ear:

"You know," he said. "When you were looking at me before I wasn't sure if it was me or the rubber plant."

"I don't know one plant from another," she shouted.

"I, uh, find you very attractive," Bibby said.

"Oh, I'm so glad!" Lissa cried. "I'm transsexual, you know. I just got back from Yonkers last week and I'm still feeling really insecure."

"I didn't know," Bibby said. "I mean, it's really a good job. I couldn't tell the difference."

Lissa was gratified. "This is only my second time out in public." She released her pelvic contraction and straightened up. "I'm seeing a speech therapist to get my pitch raised. Weren't you even suspicious from my voice?"

Bibby shook his head. "If you hadn't mentioned it, I'd never have guessed."

Lissa's name used to be Arthur. She was the father of a six-year-old boy named Bennett. She and her ex-wife Helen were still good friends. Lissa had always wanted to be a woman and her psychotherapist—Arthur's psychotherapist, more accurately—had helped her bring this wish into her conscious mind. Once she knew what she wanted, she went for it. "You don't have to make do these days," Lissa shouted.

Lissa wanted to talk about her operations, her therapy, her support group, her voice lessons, her body movement classes. Bosculus was interested for quite a while but when at last he saw his friend Cindy—looking very straight, very down-to-earth, very ordinary as she came toward him—he was very glad to see her.

"Where's Paul?" Bibby said.

Cindy had let her hair loose and was wearing a pretty, low-necked dress. "Paul's tired," she said shortly. "So I came alone."

Bibby made introductions and Lissa excused herself after shaking hands with Cindy and putting her shoes back on.

Bibby would have sworn she looked down Cindy's neckline.

"Do you want a drink?"

"I'll get my own, thank you. You want to come with me?"

Cindy moved easily through the crowd and ordered a vodka martini from a bartender who smiled at her. She looked the room over and found a quiet place to stand. She greeted people she knew: pleasantness personified. But her face changed as soon as she got Bibby alone. She was furious with Paul.

"Do you know how many basketball games I have sat through? Do you know how many office parties I have been charming at?"

Bibby wouldn't commit himself. He felt for Paul. He knew how it was to come home from work all tired out and find your wife ready and eager to kick up her heels.

"Come on, Bibby. Work isn't that hard. You think if somebody called up with a basketball ticket, he wouldn't be ready to dash out?"

She took a swallow of martini. "It's not just tonight. Whatever I want is too much for him. It's a power game he plays. I'm demanding. He's deserving."

They were in a space between a fireplace and a glass cabinet full of geodes.

TABLE 47 247

"Listen," Cindy said. "If you want to meet women, you better circulate."

"In a marriage," Bibby heard himself say, "somebody has to make a living and somebody has to make a life."

"Very pretty," Cindy replied. "And who gets to have fun?"

She looked around the room impatiently. "Have you met Marianne?"

Bibby looked blank.

"Marianne Banks. Our hostess."

Bibby hadn't.

"She's in the back room, smoking pot. I can't go in because it gives me a headache. Do you want to go back and meet her? Or into the dining room? They've set up the buffet."

"I don't see why you're so mad," Bibby said. "Paul let you come to the party."

"Let me! Let me! What does that mean, let me? What is he, my shepherd?"

Bosculus, drunk on scotch, was offering his dazzling smile. His fishwater eyes were glazed.

"Come back," Cindy said. "We'll look for Marianne. Maybe she'll introduce you to some nice young ladies."

She was togged out to spite Paul. Normally she didn't bother. Tonight, Bibby noticed, she was attracting attention. She moved with a dangerous swing, taking up a lot of space, spreading herself around. He thought, not for the first time, how different she was when Paul wasn't with her. Maybe Cindy was right. Maybe marriage was limiting.

Then he thought he must be very drunk. Marriage was meant to be limiting.

The back room, as Cindy had promised, reeked from grass. So they went around to the kitchen where guests were leaning against cabinets, eating with plastic forks out of paper plates. The spread on the dining room table had been reduced to half-empty platters of salami and parsley-flecked doilies with crumbs of pastrami and corned beef. All that food, Bibby thought. Marianne must be Jewish. He filled a plate with cole slaw and pickles. Cindy took some coffee from the sideboard. She was too mad to eat. Besides, she had decided, she said, to lose twenty pounds and make a new life for herself.

In the living room people were sitting around, on couches, on the floor, listening to Simon and Garfunkel records. Cindy made Bibby nervous. She introduced him to everybody she knew and then everybody else. She started conversations with strangers and told them intimate things with the kind of abandoned familiarity Bibby was familiar with only in bar-rooms. She revealed personal secrets Bibby had never heard and had not suspected. She expressed firm opinions she would never have uttered in her natural habitat. And she kept throwing out lines to draw Bibby into the colloquy. She presented him as "my friend." Nobody asked where Paul was.

Simon and Garfunkel elided into Pearl Bailey, and after a while it was the Beatles again.

Bibby was sitting on a carpet cushion leaning against Cindy's chair. The Alice minced by on her way out. With a coat on, she looked pregnant. People were leaving, many of them in twos, Bibby noted, who had arrived singly. Lissa waved good-bye from the side of a woman in a felt fedora. The coffee urn was low and the ashtrays were full. Marianne was stretched out on a sofa, hostess gown flowing to the floor, a cordial glass in one hand, the other arm dangling. Marianne's man was flat on his back on the carpet, smiling. Somebody asked Bibby if Cindy was his lover.

"What did you say?" They were alone in the elevator.
"I smiled mysteriously."
"What a rat you are."
"If I'd said *No*, they wouldn't have believed me."

TABLE 47   249

Bibby felt wonderful. Light and effervescent. Liquor alone could not have produced this effect.

Cindy, in contrast, seemed spaced out. She had discarded her strong sense of direction. Her air of competence had misted over. The elevator made a smooth four-point landing but Cindy stood with her back against the door. "Give me a kiss," she said.

Bibby almost died.

She was challenging him.

She was smiling. She was playful. But she meant it.

He wanted to run away. She was Cindy. Of Cindy and Paul.

But she moved in and flattened him against the back of the elevator. She lifted her heels and gave him a sweet kiss. She was solid. She felt soft and solid against him and her lips were warm. "That's very sweet," she said. "You smell good."

The elevator started going up again. She carefully kissed the soft of his neck, where jaw met ear. "Very sweet," she said. The elevator stopped and she sprang away from him.

It was Marianne's party. Four sleepy people rolled in. Everybody smiled knowingly. Cindy made kindergarten faces at Bibby. Bibby felt heat under his skin and liked it. Then he felt terrible. He felt guilty. He was a man of imagination. Comets of intimacies with Cindy had occasionally shot across his mind. But he was a man of conscience and he had dutifully blacked them out.

But he couldn't black out a living Cindy, teasing him.

It occurred to Bibby that she was drunk.

They stood on the sidewalk under the scalloped canopy. The park was across the street, scene of fun and crimes. Lights betokened safety but nobody was on the benches. Cindy's Pontiac was up the block. Bibby's subway station was two corners down. He walked her toward the car.

"Maybe I'd better drive you home," Bibby said.

"Don't be silly. I'll drive *you* home."

She got into the driver's seat and opened the door for him.

She turned on the light and started the motor. Bibby quietly thought that he was turned on, too. She pulled out and drove downtown, forward in her seat, close to the windshield, a little bit night-blind.

She didn't seem drunk.

Bibby sat back. Nothing in *Meeting and Mating* had prepared him for Cindy. One word from *Meeting and Mating* and she would laugh herself into sanity.

"What's funny?" she said.

"I'm thinking about this book I've got, that tells you how to make out with women."

"You? Really? Where'd you get it?"

She didn't think it was so funny. "So what did you learn?"

"Well, you know, I don't *use* it. It's all about eye contact and projecting self-confident sexiness."

"Ummh?"

"And getting rid of your inhibitions and imagining yourself in bed with people."

"Sounds like fun. Does it work?"

"Not so far. But I've had some pretty good fantasies."

She stopped for a light and kept looking ahead. "Was I ever in them?"

"I never let you."

He was afraid to ask if he'd been in hers. He thought she probably didn't have any. She was always so busy. Paul was always so present. One afternoon, when Jill had taken Brucie to the park, Cindy had been folding laundry. She and Bosculus were standing, facing each other, talking, as she folded, and Cindy laid a brassiere, satin and lace, very delicate, separately on the arm of a sofa. Bosculus had noticed this action but discounted it as an accident.

Freud says, Bibby reminded himself, that there *are* no accidents. It came to Bibby that he really didn't know Cindy as well as he thought he did.

TABLE 47 251

On second thought, he thought he'd like to keep it that way.

"I mean, uh," he said, "that I do have fantasies but I value our friendship a lot. So I, ah, don't include you in the category of possibilities."

They were cutting over to Broadway at Lincoln Center and Cindy pulled into an illegal parking space.

"I don't think I like that," she said.

She slid along the seat and pressed against him. What started as a closed-mouth, Viennese kiss from, say, *The Merry Widow* turned into a ripe Italian *Traviata* and then something unstoppably Germanic like *Tristan*. Cindy got scared and tried to pull away. But Bibby, suddenly superstrong, swung her around against the seatback and kissed her until she gave up fighting.

Then he released her.

"Come on," he said. "We'll go to my apartment."

He put his hand on the door handle. "You want me to drive?" he said.

He turned down Broadway and around Columbus Circle. Cindy stared out the window. It had begun to rain. She thought about Bibby's apartment.

"You know, Bibby," she said. "I think we'd better not do this. It will spoil our friendship."

"The hell with our friendship!"

Cindy was a Sunday-school girl, married young, in white, in a gray stone church, by a minister in robes. She had never made love in an automobile. She thought it was time to try it. The car, she thought, was a better locale than Bibby's apartment. Bibby, she thought, would be a better partner than some stranger she couldn't depend on. She was very fond of Bibby. He always talked to her as if she were a real person and not just Paul's wife. Also he was young and not bad-looking.

"I can't wait," she said to Bibby. "Let's park the car."

Passing Times Square and Herald Square, Bibby tried to address himself in the voice of reason. Where to park without bringing on the police with flashlights? He pulled up in front of a row of gated stores. Traffic was thin. No one was walking.

"Not here!" Cindy cried. "The street's too narrow. All the cars can look in on us."

He drove past Madison Park to where the road widens at Union Square. Cars passed at a distance. Sidewalks were empty. He pulled into a diagonal space by the park and shut off the motor, shut off the lights, locked his door. He put his hand on Cindy's pantyhose. Karen wore panties under her pantyhose. Cindy didn't.

Cindy put her hands under Bibby's jacket to feel the shape of his ribs. She started to pull his shirt out of his trousers. His shirt had a very long tail. Meanwhile, Bibby was stroking her thigh with one hand and her back with the other. She wasn't sure what to do next.

Suddenly lights shone in on them. It wasn't the police. Two hoods, teenagers, were peering in on Cindy's side. One had an iron poker and the other a pocket flash. They were well dressed and so respectable that it looked as if they were trying to break into their own car after having locked themselves out. Bibby couldn't see their faces clearly, but he thought they looked embarrassed. The light went off and the boys ran. Bibby turned on the motor and drove away.

He addressed himself in the voice of reason. Where, he asked himself, could he park in order not to waste this moment of rare unconscionability? Where would police not shine in and passersby not get an eyeful? MacDougal Street was still active even though it was raining and way past midnight. Cindy's hand was moving around inside his trousers.

"Be careful," he said. "You'd better stop." The words titillated him like a delicious remembrance of things past. But present was Cindy—caring, solid Cindy whom he truly loved,

TABLE 47 253

now turned soft, hot and fluorescent, eager and accessible. Praised be the inventor of automatic automobiles. Bibby's was the only clutch going. It reached between Cindy's legs, from which the pantyhose had slipped and vanished. O *wet and swollen crotch*, his mind sang as his hand danced and his middle finger won the right of passage.

They were up West Fourth, past wrong-way Sullivan Street and traffic was slow. Right hand under Cindy's skirt, left hand on the wheel, he drove looking straight ahead. She sat close, also eyes ahead, with her left hand busy in his pants. Bibby turned into Daniell Street, where it was darker and almost empty. Cindy, two-handed, undid his belt and unzipped him. His cock jumped out and all but crowed. Barely missing a parked bakery truck, he pulled up by a hydrant and grabbed for his handkerchief.

They sat still for a while before they started to put themselves together. Rain on the windshield. Bulging garbage bags leaning against the hydrant. One or two late walkers. The Pontiac was pointed at the curb with its tail out in the street. Passing cars steered clear.

Bibby zippered his fly.

Cindy fixed her dress.

It was late.

Cindy was peaceful. "I liked that," she said.

She leaned over and kissed him on the side of the mouth.

"Let's still be friends," she said.

Bibby was elsewhere. Or nowhere.

"You want to come upstairs?" he asked.

"No thanks. I've got to get home." She looked at Bibby. "Are you all right?"

He said he felt terrible. He said he could never face Paul again.

He got out and Cindy slid behind the wheel. He bent and kissed her on the forehead before he shut the door.

Having money made a big difference. Bosculus could afford to go to the movies. Soon after Spritzer the lawyer told him he was a divorced man, Bosculus went to a reading at Yuri's place and got talking with a spirited young poet who said she would kill herself before she joined the Establishment. She was wearing an evening gown and sneakers, her hair was done in dozens of tiny braids and her poetry was all about chairs. Bosculus thought she wouldn't have much trouble staying out of the Establishment. He asked her if she would like to go to a movie with him. He mentioned a Joan Crawford double feature at the Elgin. The poet had never heard of Joan Crawford, but she went anyway.

A few weeks later, shopping at Macy's for a gift for Karen's new baby, Bosculus struck up a conversation with an energetic accessories buyer, who told him the difference between silver plate and sterling. She also told him the difference between a frying pan and a skillet and blue cheese and Roquefort. She explained that the accessories she bought were fashions for women, not accessories for cars. Bosculus invited her to an Alec Guinness double feature. She said she'd love it.

Taking women to the movies hit the spot. He didn't have to talk much until after the movie and then he had the movie to talk about.

He asked Geraldine and she accepted, too, though she insisted on paying for herself. They went out for soup afterward and divided the check in half.

Sometimes he took Brucie to the movies but never to a G-rated family film. Bosculus considered G-rated family films obscene, a poisonous source of shallow and selfish values. It was bad enough, Bosculus told his friends, that Brucie had to

TABLE 47 255

spend most of his time in the Land of Smiles, where his mother was trying to achieve a wrinkle-free and dirt-repellent existence. It was bad enough that Brucie had to spend five days a week in a Disney-decorated schoolroom with a teacher who looked like Snow White. Bosculus had attended a Parents' Night and nearly puked. So he took Brucie to French and Polish and Swedish movies for slices of life that were not enriched or prepackaged.

Sometimes he took a woman friend and Brucie to the good old places—the museums, the zoo, the Planetarium, and the Botanical Gardens in the Bronx. Brucie was unfailingly polite to each new woman friend, but he stayed close to his father. At the Atelier, beige gave way to burnt umber and that, after a while, to ecru. But the pictures still sold and Bosculus continued to make enough money to pay off his debts to Bosculus Senior and Spritzer the lawyer and to pay child support so he could hold up his head when he went to the Picketts' house to get Brucie. Brucie's little brother was named Winthrop and Bosculus did his best to ignore him.

"He's not my whole brother," Brucie told his father, "but Warner loves us both the same."

Still, Bosculus thought he caught Pickett staring adoringly at that baby, though that baby was a washrag compared to Brucie at his age.

Bosculus gave a little party of his own. He bought some cheeses—a creamy *chèvre*, a buttery Swiss, and real Roquefort. He picked up a pâté at the Charcuterie, fruit from Balducci's and, of course, Zito's whole wheat Italian bread. He got freshly ground Colombian coffee and some very nice California wines. He scrubbed the walls of his apartment and bought a new, brighter lamp. He borrowed rock records from Geraldine and dusted off his classical albums. He invited just a few good friends—some priests and poets and one or two schlock artists. That was the night Geraldine met Yuri. Those two got along very well. In fact, the party was a success and Bosculus was very happy.

Having money, being single, dating, watching Brucie grow: at last Bibby was able to think about his life without wincing. He was, he felt, pulled together. On the other hand, when he thought about his life he also thought he should be thinking about his future. Bibby was over thirty, soon to be over thirty-five. He was pulled together all right, but he was not going anyplace. He sat in his chair and wondered why.

He was proud of the fact that he had not, like so many of his contemporaries, detoured and/or derailed into the emotional chaos of drugs and psychopolitics. At the same time, he was mystified by the fact that he had never been on a track to begin with. Bibby noticed that his thoughts did not follow a logical progression. They came on like puffs of a Fourth of July rocket, brilliant illuminations here and there, one turning on as another fizzled out.

People on tracks had goals to attain, ambitions to realize, principles to practice. Bibby, in a short, purple puff, saw himself as a wayside wanderer, a strange duck out of the mainstream. Why was this? he charged himself. Childhood shock suggested itself to him in a little sky trail of silver stars. His father's death. His mother's indifference. Didn't all achievers require pushy mothers?

But Bibby was there to think about his future, not his past. How. Not why. All Bibby was sure about was what he did not want:

    a) to finish his dissertation
    b) to be a teacher or a scholar
    c) to be a schlock art salesman
    d) to live in these glum rooms

His waking nightmares were over. Dream scenes no longer starred his mother as murder victim. He still enjoyed a bit of

TABLE 47   257

erotica but even these dreams had diminished as he began to live them. These days his chief fantasy was occupational:

It took place at a party.

PARTY WOMAN: What do you do?

BOSCULUS: I sell art.

PARTY WOMAN: Oh, really? How interesting! What kind of art—contemporary? Old Masters? I adore the French Impressionists.

BOSCULUS: I sell schlock art. Like that picture over there.

(*Response* A. The woman takes a look at the picture and hastily excuses herself.)

(*Response* B. The woman says, "That desert scene? Why, I think it's lovely." And Bosculus excuses himself.)

The next woman comes along and says, "What do you do?"

BOSCULUS: Do? Do? I'm a rich man. I don't do anything!

This was what he was telling Geraldine one gray velvet night in early June. They were sitting on the doorstep, a break in the long, thin line of seated Italians. Now that Geraldine was seeing Yuri—they were talking about spending a weekend together in the country—Bibby and she had become close friends. Summer vacation was going to be his time of reckoning. He was going to make a move. Or at least conceive a plan. Or, in any case, think about it.

Geraldine was in work clothes, overalls and espadrilles. There were a couple of Dutch blue spots on her moony face. She'd been working in her studio. She smelled pleasantly of oil and turpentine.

"You must have a real big hangup," she told Bibby. She was looking at him the way she looked at her canvases but rarely at people.

"I guess so. Something must be bugging me. I seem to be living in circles."

"Yep."

"The circles have got a lot bigger," Bibby said defensively.

"I know, but you'd like to get on a straight line for once."

Bibby nodded. He wondered, as relatively clean night air came down to sweep away the waste of the city day, why he and Geraldine had never gotten together.

She told him she'd been to a shrink for a while. The shrink had been good for her. "Helped me get some of the cobwebs out of my head."

Bibby said he might go someday if he ever got himself together.

Geraldine said he should join a chorus or maybe a church choir. "Singing can be really therapeutic," she told him.

Geraldine was a solid person herself. Bibby suddenly warmed to the thought that she was really concerned for him. He could talk to her.

"When I first moved in here," he told her, "I was very horny. I used to think about you all the time. Every night, I kept wanting to come downstairs and knock on your door."

"I would have welcomed you," she said. "I was lonely, too."

It was a good thing the light was fading. Tears swam up behind his eyes. A fishwater curtain opened on a spaced-out *pas de deux*.

Bosculus—lean and meaty in skin shirt, black tights, ballet slippers, bulging thighs and high-mounted cup—stretches as the orchestra leans into the longing strains of Gustav Mahler. He lifts on vertical feet into a torsion of hip, waist, chest, bending away from himself, reaching out. . . . For what? To whom?

To the ballerina. Her faded peach-colored costume hangs without a ripple as she moves fluidly across the stage, on

TABLE 47
259

point, step by tiny step, on her turned-out legs of steel, her straight line passing just outside his circle.

This is the Bosculus ballet.

He, in an upstage corner, turns toward her, taking an extended fourth position, a slowly wrought lunge, his back leg and long back forming a low diagonal line that is lengthened by the reach of open arms and craned neck. He holds the stretch, turned toward where she no longer is, then lifts himself by straightening his front leg. She returns to her starting place with another *bourrée*, this time even slower. Left foot, right foot, high on point, each tiny step articulate, straight from the hip, the body pulled high, back and shoulders melting.

He, center stage in a deep *plié*, extends one leg and, in a slow *rond de jambe en l'air*, winds into an arabesque as he straightens the standing leg. He reaches out in a lovely, lonely *port de bras*, but she, the elusive partner, in her cool longitudes, continues to fail to intersect his circle. At last she comes to her own stopping point—*passé, développé, arabesque, balancé*—but he by this time has turned inward. Folding into a contraction, he slowly sinks to the floor on crossed, bending legs. Now she approaches him with long extensions, inquisitive waist bends and half turns in the air. He arches his back and she spins away with crisp pirouettes.

Come on, you guys! Get together! It's after midnight!

They do get together. He rises and walks across the stage to lift her from the waist, carrying her five steps, then setting her down to do a couple of small turns and two forlorn ankle kicks. She ends the phrase with one foot over the other while he chain-turns into the far corner. It's all quite remote: he's occupied with his private fears; she is wary and confused. They try a few more gingerly lifts and balances—a beautiful adagio—but they never connect.

The dance ends. She, looking past him, backs off the stage.

Slow turn into arabesque, *posé, tendu, passé, développé,* slow turn into arabesque . . . repeated until she slowly disappears into the wings.

He, center stage, is winding down. The *rond de jambe* closes in and stretches out again, and again in slow circle he turns on his bent leg around and around, lower and lower as the curtain falls.

An old question came up as they sat talking and not talking:

"Geraldine, would you tell me something? Just to—ah—satisfy my—uh—curiosity?"

"Sure. What?"

"Something I've been wondering about for a long time."

"Sure. What?"

"It's not important, but—uh—you know Vernon?"

"Vernon from the Atelier?"

"You don't have to answer this if you don't want to. But I used to be kind of curious about—uh—did you and Vernon ever—ah—go around together?"

"Vernon from the Atelier? Vernon our boss?"

"Yes."

"You thought I and Vernon had something going?"

"I wasn't sure. But I saw him around here a couple of times. I thought he was coming out of your place maybe."

He could at least see her goofy smile in the streetlight.

"He did used to stop by but he never came in." She dropped her voice. "Vernon gets kind of crazy sometimes. He gets a little paranoid, you know? He starts thinking that everybody in the city is making it with everybody else except him. He thinks all New York is in bed together."

Two aged Italians made a lot of noise folding up their chairs and scraping them along the street.

"So he sits around getting upset about this one sleeping

TABLE 47 261

with that one. Manic jealousy. It comes and goes when he hasn't got anybody."

Two well-dressed couples walked past them toward an expensive restaurant on the next corner. Casual but gingerly, they looked like an ad for Caribbean travel.

"So he used to call me up at odd hours and then call you— to make sure we weren't together."

Bosculus could hardly believe it.

"It's true. He laughs about it when he's sane. A couple of times when you didn't answer, he came down here just to check it out."

"That's really crazy, poor guy." Bosculus brooded for a while on the vagaries of human behavior. Then he looked at his amiable companion: "So why didn't he ask you out?"

"I don't know. I guess it didn't occur to him."

In July the schlock art business was slow and Bibby took Brucie for a long overdue visit to Mr. and Mrs. Bosculus, Senior, who were then living in Virginia in the backlands between Norfolk and Richmond. Bibby hadn't seen his mother for more than two years. It was even longer since she had seen Brucie.

Bibby and Brucie drove on a long stretch of empty road between cut cornfields. They parked out front and walked up a long path. The old frame house was different from the shined-up, picture-windowed bungalows that Bibby's mother had always occupied before. This house had a sprawling front porch and Bibby's mother was standing on it with her arms folded across her stomach. She came down the stairs when she saw Brucie and opened up her arms. Bibby saw with a wring of pain that her hair had turned white, but he had never seen her eyes so lit, not even when she was high on gin. Her eyes were on Brucie as he ran into her arms. Bibby watched grandmother hugging grandson and remembered himself as a little kid who needed a hug. His fears of Brucie's shyness and his mother's distance drifted into the heavy air along with his wonder and regret. After she released Brucie, Mrs. Bosculus straightened up and kissed her son on the cheek. She patted his arm. "Real nice to see you," she said.

Bosculus Senior was glad to see them, too, when he got home. He washed his hands and took off his shoes and asked Brucie if he'd like to take a walk later and see some cows down the road. He said he lived far from the plant he managed because he wanted a house with space around it. He told Brucie there was an old swing out back.

Bibby looked at his former adversary and saw that the old man's weight was sinking into cushions under his face and ribs. He saw siftings of white in the old man's hair. He saw a face that was harmless and simple and wondered if the old man had sprung all his traps or, maybe, if there hadn't been any traps in the first place.

They didn't have a lot to say to each other. Bibby didn't understand plant management. Bosculus Senior didn't like New York. But Brucie kept everyone occupied. The old folks sat on the carpet and played with him. Mrs. Bosculus had stocked up on Hawaiian Punch and had gone into town to buy a set of alphabet letters that could stand on top of each other like acrobats. Bosculus Senior brought home comic books. Brucie loved everything, he was that kind of a kid. He and his dad shared an upstairs bedroom with dormer windows and twin beds with chenille spreads embossed with daisy designs.

The biggest change, though, was that Bibby's mother didn't drink anymore. She was a member of Alcoholics Anonymous. She went to meetings every Wednesday night. She had taken up knitting, drank a lot of tea and club soda and bowled with a group from her church, where she also worked with senior citizens three mornings a week in the winter. She hadn't told Bibby because she wanted to surprise him.

TABLE 47 263

"Besides," she said, "I didn't know if I'd be not-drinking by the time you got here. We can never be sure about the next day, you know."

Bibby's mother encouraged her husband and son to drink beer. "It don't bother me," she said. "Long as I got my club soda and my candy mints." But Bibby noticed her hands were never still. He didn't like his mother calling herself an "alcoholic." He knew she used to drink a lot, but an alcoholic was something different.

"Don't believe it," she told him. "I didn't used to fall asleep at night. I passed out."

Old Man Bosculus sat opposite her in the cool of the back room. The TV sound was turned down, only the picture of closeup crime scenes occasionally drawing his attention. He had a can of beer on the arm of his chair and in his hands a puzzle he was trying to work out for Brucie, two pieces of twisted steel to separate and align. "She's a different woman," the old man said warily, as if not looking at his wife would make her not hear him. "She made up her mind one day and she hasn't been the same since. Thank the Lord for that."

But Bibby didn't like it. He didn't like the drinking but he didn't like the quitting. Why couldn't she quit without making a club of it? Why did she need to fill her life as she had filled her drinking glass? Why must she be on the telephone three or four hours a day talking about not drinking with other people who couldn't do it on their own? Bibby took Brucie to Virginia Beach, but Brucie's grandmother had to stay home and see an AA buddy. He took Brucie to Charlottesville to see Thomas Jefferson's house and the college he designed. But Brucie's grandmother was too tied up—hung up, Bibby thought: she's not hung over anymore, she's just hung up. The best the poor thing could do was tiptoe through the day and make a sparse, underseasoned supper for them to eat when Old Man Bosculus got home. The old man, at least, took an active interest in Brucie. The old lady only stared at her grandson, like a lover.

One day Old Man Bosculus took Brucie to the plant with him and Bibby, restless, took a long drive to Richmond. Returning late that night, he hurried up the path and took the porch steps two at a time. The TV was on in the back room but the only light came from the kitchen. Bibby walked through the house unheard. He stood in the kitchen doorway watching the three of them—his mother, Bosculus Senior and Brucie—sitting like a little family around the kitchen table. Bibby had never, in his whole childhood, had a supper like that. Brucie sitting there happily eating, secure in the company of a pair of loving parents. Bibby saw himself in that white, rib-backed chair, saw himself holding that fork, dipping into that stew, and as he saw himself he saw Bosculus disappear and Mrs. Bosculus float upward and through the ceiling. Anger beat at him from inside. He was full of turbines.

"Why don't you have a drink, Mom?" he said. They all looked up.

"Hi, Dad!"

"Did you have a nice day?"

"Pull up a chair, Son." Bosculus Senior had taken to calling him "Son."

"Hey, Mom. Why don't you have a drink? A nice, cool gin and tonic would sure hit the spot tonight, wouldn't it? Table looks so bare in here. Everybody looks so serious and church-like. *I'd* like a gin and tonic. You got some gin around? If not I'll run right out and get some."

"We got a nice stew, Bibby. Do you want to wash up first?"

"It was real neat at the plant. Grandpa took me all around."

"Come on. We need a party tonight. Where's the liquor

TABLE 47   265

cabinet? What kind of goddamn house is this without a liquor cabinet?"

Bibby's mother got out of her chair. Her face was gray. She stood still and looked across the room at him. "What's the matter, Bibby? What are you saying?"

Bosculus Senior put down his fork, still stuck in a wet potato.

Bibby started opening closets and cupboards, slamming the doors. "Your son doesn't come home very often. When he's here, you ought to celebrate." He was squatting on the floor, opening pot shelves, the cabinet under the sink. "Where the hell's the booze around here?"

Bosculus Senior came over to him, pulled him up by the elbow. "Son," he pleaded. "If you want a drink, come on. We'll go have a drink. But why don't you have a beer for now and some good supper? We can go out after." He pulled on Bibby's arm. "I know a club, a nice place to drink."

Bibby shrugged him off. "I want to drink right here," he said. "I want to drink with my mother. What kind of mother is she anyway, won't sit down and have a drink with her son?"

Mrs. Bosculus' hands began to tremble. Brucie stopped eating and stared at his father. Bibby looked at nobody. He ran out of the room. "I'm going out," he called. "I'm going to bring back a whole barroom. One of everything and we're going to drink it all!" Bosculus Senior followed him but Bibby was in the car before the old man reached the steps.

Hours later, after Bibby's mother had lulled Brucie to sleep, after she'd talked on the phone and calmed herself with camomile tea and honey, Bibby came back, drunk, and said to her:

"You had a kid of your own. How come you didn't love that one?"

Bibby's mother listened with a stricken face. Tears came

into her eyes, but she did not reply. The next day she got up early, put breakfast out and left the house before Bibby arose. He started packing that day and by the time his mother came home, just before noon, Bibby was ready to go.

"Don't you want me to put your clothes through the washer?" Mrs. Bosculus asked him.

"No," he said. "No." He'd take care of that when he got back. He had already said his good-byes to Bosculus Senior. Brucie was all set, too. Bibby said Brucie had had a wonderful time.

She wanted to make sandwiches since they wouldn't stay for lunch, but Bibby resisted. "Look," he said. "I hope you'll forgive me for last night. I can't explain it. I can only apologize." He wanted to take her hand but couldn't. "And deeply," he said.

Mrs. Bosculus shook her head. "I did the best I could," she said and almost imperceptibly opened her hands.

Driving home, Brucie kneeling on the seat beside him, looking out the back window, Bibby wondered what his mother could have said or done that would have satisfied him. Weeping, begging his forgiveness, scolding, justifying herself—there was nothing, only his anger. She was simply not the woman he wanted her to be and that was all. It was a long, quiet ride and they did not reach Daniell Street until midnight. By that time Bibby had decided to quit the schlock art business. He had to think about Brucie. Brucie's father needed a real job—with benefits, with a future, with a name Brucie could pronounce with pride.

Even if it meant—as it surely would—taking a big pay cut, Bibby had to start a career.

PART
FIVE

Table 47. We've got our distinctions. We've known Bosculus the best and the longest. But here it is late, with the crowd starting to thin out, and not one of us has been up to see the man.

I'm Cindy Storey, thinking this but not doing anything about it.

Yuri Marchuk is thinking about it too. But he has the gumption to get up out of his chair and grab Geraldine:

"Let's go say hello to Bibby."

The last revelers are hanging in. The tables down front are still occupied with late-night drinkers and smokers and talkers and starers. Somehow, late at night and tired, people are more likable. Or maybe, when I'm wound down myself, I'm more tolerant. Anyway, as I watch streams of exiting celebrants meet in a slow surge out the doors—the women with their plastic gift bags, some carrying floral centerpieces, and the men pushing from behind like street sweepers—I feel rather philosophical. No skin off my nose, the playfolks. I've got what I want. Let them play.

I get up with Geraldine and Yuri. And Paul, amiably, gets up with me. Father Joe grabs a last swallow of brandy, pours some more and carries the glass with him. Obe and Flossie exchange signals. She smiles a dare; he braces himself. He rises; she takes his arm. Obe had major surgery last year—people said cancer—but he looks to be in good shape. Flossie walks beside him with just a suggestion of swagger.

All we need is fife and drums.

Strike that.

We don't need a thing. Bibby sees us coming and jumps up to greet us. He shines. He looks big, like all successful men. He looks born to his tuxedo.

Except. I recognize, as I move in close, the edge of doubt in the corner of his eye. Bibby still suspects himself a little. He hopes and prays he'll be as good as his word. Or at least that nobody will find out if he isn't.

But he's so glad to see us. He opens his arms for a second.

"So good of you to come!" he says, meaning it. "Did you see everything? Could you hear? Was the t-t-table okay?"

He addresses us corporately.

We respond the same way.

"Cindy! Paul!" He kisses me on the mouth. He takes Paul's hand. "It's been ages, hasn't it! How are Tony and J-Jill? They must be through with college by now. God! Joe!"

He seizes Joe's free arm with both of his. Joe assails him with congratulations. "A great night for us all! A truly beautiful occasion! I wouldn't have missed it for the world. Much joy to you—and your lovely wife." Joe bows toward the stately Jennifer.

Geraldine spills her arms around Bibby's neck and kisses him cheek to cheek. Yuri claps him on the back, embraces him. I hear Bibby say, "I guess you guys aren't married yet."

Obe and Flossie come on with aplomb, Flossie queening it to rival Jennifer. She does it for Obe, I figure. She sets the scene so he can walk on like a king. And he does.

On cue, Jennifer steps to her husband's side. If anybody frees Bibby Bosculus from the habit of asking himself uncomfortable questions, it will be Jennifer. Jennifer has all the answers.

Stuck with us Forty-seveners, she automatically adjusts her thermostat. Watch out, Jennifer. We know Karen. We'll make comparisons.

Jennifer takes hold of her husband's arm. She produces a smile more lustrous than Karen's and with teeth that have been straightened to perfect occlusion.

"It's been madness," she confides to us all. "We've been in the duplex almost a year and it's still not completely furnished. Just finding the decorator was a major project. Then we were put on a waiting list . . ."

This, it is understood, is all by way of explaining charmingly why we old pals have not yet been asked up—we disadvantaged who own neither yachts nor Hamptons beach

TABLE 47   271

houses, who do not hobnob with senators or vacation on the Mediterranean, and are not in the habit of telling our dreams to writers who put them in plays. Jennifer lifts her Greek drapery ever so lightly from where its undulating hemline comes into contact with my spreading taffeta.

"You really must see the apartment," she says unconvincingly.

I feel suddenly exhilarated about Paul's new photo business that makes him nobody's boy.

The Peter person, Jennifer's old buddy, has reappeared. "Steven, love," she says. "I'd like you to meet some very dear, very old friends of Bernard's."

She pronounces it the fancy English way, like the poetic "burn-*ed*."

"These are the . . ." She looks, stricken, from Paul and me to Yuri and Geraldine. Then she pulls up even higher. "I'm so sorry," she says, holding her Greek hairdo very straight. "I'm having a block," she says. "It's so late—all this excitement—I can't remember anyone's name."

She used to work for Paul. When she was the Color Girl, he was the Company Manager. He was the one who saw she got paid. And treated well. I knew her only slightly in the days before she became a Greek goddess, but in those days she knew my name. Now she stands beside Bibby, and doesn't need to know anyone but him. He is looking fondly, almost longingly, at Yuri.

"We've really got to get together," Bibby is saying with fervor. Yuri's eyes are cast just enough below Bibby's to avoid a meeting.

"I'm going to call you next week," Bibby says. "You and Geraldine will come for dinner. We've got to spend more time together." Bibby's unusual color spreads like oxblood shoe polish across his cheeks. "I owe you a dinner, Geraldine."

She doesn't need it. Geraldine's work is moving. I went to

a recent show on Fifty-seventh Street. Her painting, without losing a grain of muscle, has changed its mood to a kind of modest joy. She's got authority and sophistication: the New York *Times* reviewer said so. One of these days dear Jennifer is going to let Bibby take his Geraldine original out of the closet I bet she keeps it in. She'll hang it as the main feature in that showplace living room.

"At least we can have drinks after work," Bibby says to Yuri.

Me, I hate long good-byes, so I'm part of the effort to disengage and minimize the discomfort. We march back in full array, but before we sit down Obe Morley comes up with a great idea: Let's go back to his place.

Nobody hesitates.

Not even Paul.

We grab our paraphernalia, including the gift bags, of course, and Flossie takes the flowers off the table. We run for our coats and the tournament is behind us, Table 47 a deserted wheel in an emptying fairground. Far up front—it looks like miles from the doors we flee through—Bibby and Jennifer still stand, like Menelaus and Helen, like wind-up dolls with their keys hidden under fancy clothes, bidding royal farewells to the last of their illustrious guests.

They're still there, I imagine as our two taxicabs streak up Third Avenue in the purple slick of a post-midnight rain shower.

Streetlight rays skid off the wet of moving cars. Tires splash through oil puddles shining lurid with reflections from the night signs of bars and all-hours donut shops. The evening's snow has been sloshed away but the warmer weather is still cold. I huddle against Paul for his body heat. Geraldine is beside me and Yuri in the jump seat. The others are up ahead in a little cab. Passing cars shine yellow, purple, blue and

TABLE 47 273

green in our faces. Stopped at stoplights, we change color and listen to the wet while New York night people—dog walkers, late daters, homebound workers—cross in front. The green light sends us skidding into speed and the midtown colors fade into uptown neutrals—the grays, tans and beiges of upper East Side residence.

The taxis turn into an Eighties street and into the oval driveway of a narrow, wide-windowed building. Obe pays his driver. Paul pays ours. What spiff! The doorman a monument of uniformed decorum. The lobby a poem in calculated understatement, all texture and monochrome. Yuri nudges Geraldine: "I'd never get past that door in the daytime."

"We live rich," Obe says as we shoot upward in the elevator, so fast Father Joe can't get a crack in. The door slides noiselessly open on a carpeted hall with soft recessed lights. "Flossie is still working," Obe says.

"Obe ain't destitute. Or prostitute," Flossie says. "*And* the building is rent-controlled." Obe wields his key like a scepter and Flossie leads the way past the door he holds open. Inside, they are more relaxed. Inside, I am more surprised: no hint of decline here, no whiff of the austerity you'd expect from a man with a high-alimony wife, kids in graduate school, no steady job and who knows what weight of serious illness on him?

Two broad steps of what looks like llama wool bring us down into a corner living room that's big enough for a grand piano and a conference-sized inlaid lacquered-wood table desk. Flossie pulls cords and silk curtains open to show us the wet night sky and the luminous tops of skyscrapers. Oberon goes to the wall-colored built-in bar for old cognac and crystal snifters. We guests drop our coats on a French bench in the foyer and spread out in an urban sprawl of wallowing chairs and love seats, buff in color like the hairy rug, arranged around a brassbound, glass-topped table on which Flossie sets two enameled ashtrays and a china bowl of nutmeats. Books, the best and brightest, line half a wall, the other half given to an impressive audio system with enough records and tape decks for ten years of uninterrupted music. I'm tempted to request a little jazz but Paul is talking now, answering a question. About Bibby, of course.

Paul is refusing credit for putting Bibby on the road to the Golden Cock.

"I helped him out," Paul is saying defensively. "But not because I believed in him. Just the opposite. I didn't think he could do a job. He had no gas pedal, no steering wheel. No style, either, that I could make out. I'd have given him a ten as a loser."

"But you were wrong," says Flossie with half a question mark.

"Not completely. I was right about Bibby. I was wrong about what it takes to get ahead."

"Nevertheless—" I say.

"Nevertheless," he says, "I did get him a job."

"Literally, starting at the bottom."

"Right. In the basement bookstore in my office building."

"*Former* office building," Obe says helpfully.

"*Our* former office building."

"Right." Obe and Paul have one of their rare meetings of the eyes. Obe breaks first this time. He finds a fleck in his brandy.

"I knew the manager of Tripler's bookstore. I didn't want to stick my neck out but I was pretty sure of Bibby's reliability. He'd show up regularly and he wouldn't steal. You'd put him into a job and he'd do it. And he spoke good English. That's what I told the manager and it was enough to make him hot to see Bibby."

Geraldine doesn't believe it.

I explain. Bibby wasn't on dope. He didn't run out every two hours to make a chorus call. He didn't use the place for a

TABLE 47

275

numbers drop. He came back after lunch not reeking from alcohol.

"He came back after lunch," Yuri tells her. "Do I have such luck with my help?"

"The point is," says Paul, "that the manager was grateful.

"We sat Bibby down and told him what to say. Mention graduate school. Skip schlock art. Nobody would believe he'd voluntarily leave a job with such a big income. Mention teaching. Unemployed teachers are believable. The manager hired him on the spot, starting as a stockboy."

Yuri is picking out cashews, eating them one at a time. "Good thing he'd held on to the Daniell Street apartment. He could hardly afford *that*. But Bibby was happy in the bookstore and I was happy to have him there. I got books at a forty percent discount."

"I," says Paul, "took my browsing to a different store. Too hard to think of things to say. Bibby's up on a ladder or behind a counter. After the fourth time, *How're you doing?* sounds pretty dumb."

He stretches out like a leaning board and pushes his shoes off. Resting his head on the cushioned back of his chair, he squints up at the soft lighting. "I don't mind telling you," Paul says, "that it was quite a surprise when he showed up at the 'Evening Roundup' office. That was an idea that never crossed my mind, getting him a job on my show."

Oberon Morley is wide awake. His jacket is off and the top shirt button opened under a loosened tie. "All this is revelation to me," he says. His silver hair, the steel frames of his eyeglasses, his bony face and cold gray eyes look downright spartan in this sybaritic setting. "When I came across Bernie in Tripler's, he impressed me as very earnest and not incorrigibly dopey. He looked like a throwback to 'Gasoline Alley.' Anyone remember that comic strip? Do I give away my age? I was impressed with his good will and earnestness. Unlike so many others of his generation, he did not center his concern upon *life* in italics. He was earnest about doing a job."

Oberon sits upright. I can see how he was once a power in the so-called communications industry. He has a fierce, purposeful energy when he turns it on.

"I pegged Bernie as a sober, methodically bright young man with a promising deficiency in leavening. Lack of irony makes good workers and loyal friends. Better still, he had no need to assert himself. My reading taste was not his. He appreciated my desire for hard facts and strong overview without ever trying to advance his own preferences, whatever they were."

Oberon pauses for impact.

He says he's worked with the world's most ambitious people. Bibby he recognized as a man of almost divine disinterest. "I didn't have to buy books," Obe says. "Publishers would send me anything I wanted, by messenger, on the spot. But I bought from Bernie because I liked dealing with him."

"Besides, it was on your expense account," Paul reminds him.

"You'd be the one to know," Obe says without rancor.

Flossie is also in good spirits: "I got books from Bernie." She reaches over to pinch Paul's arm. "Remember when we went on the remote? Down the Amazon on a houseboat?"

Obe leaps to his feet, digs his thumbs into his cummerbund and walks while he talks.

"Methodical? Bernie typed up a bibliography. He made me an authority on Brazil. When we got back, I stopped in to thank him. He asked intelligent questions."

Obe stares us down like a lion tamer. "Not showoff questions to tell me what *he* knew. But questions out of honest interest. Very refreshing.

"I had some questions for him. And he had the answers. What was going on in the book world while I was away? Bernie knew. Not only that, but the next day he handed me five

TABLE 47 277

books that I ought to read in order to be *au courant*. That was class. I appreciated that.

"Bernie's bosses appreciated him, too. Bernie was made assistant manager shortly after I got back. In a month or two, he was manager. I congratulated him but he wasn't too happy about the promotion. He was afraid he'd be upped again and sent to the main office. He said he'd probably take it because of the prestige and the pay, but he'd miss working directly with customers. He said he liked getting to know them and, in a way, prescribing their books."

Discovering Bernie Bosculus was clearly a high point in Obe Morley's life. Gradually I see him as the kingmaker, legs apart, suspenders hanging around his flat hips, shirt open to the waist. Under the lights, the fine hair on his chest glows like frost.

"One day I seized the idea that Bernie belonged upstairs with us. Wasn't that what we did—prescribe entertainment and information for the general public? I could count a half dozen jobs that Bernie could do better than the yolds who were doing them."

He looks at Paul. "Present company excepted."

Paul laughs. "Damn right."

"The next day I stopped in and told him to come up and see me. I said I might be able to do something for him."

What a story! Direct from the boss's mouth. I'd heard that story before. From Paul. From Bibby.

"I don't know what to do. . . ." Bibby was on the telephone.

"Go up and see him. Why shouldn't you?" Cindy was surprised at the snap in her voice.

"Oh, I want to. I've been breaking my back being nice to him."

"So?"

"Well, Paul."

"What about Paul?"

"D-Don't you think if Paul wanted me to work there, he'd have asked me to?"

"Sure. And if God wanted people to fly, he'd have given them wings.

"So he didn't ask you. So Oberon asked you. So what?"

"I don't want Paul to think I'm encroaching on his ah-um-uh-territory."

Cindy kept herself from hooting. "Bibby," she said severely, "This is your life. This is business. Your career has nothing to do with Paul."

"Do you think I should tell him?"

"No. This is between you and Oberon. You don't need anyone to put in a good word for you."

"That isn't what I meant."

"You don't need anyone to put in a bad word, either."

Bibby was silent for a while. Just when Cindy thought he'd hung up, he said, "I guess you're right." Then he thanked her repeatedly and at last he did hang up.

Paul had been in such a rotten mood lately that Cindy decided to forget the conversation.

Paul Storey still had the window desk. That put him a notch above his office mate, Gene Dooley, the talent coordinator, who had been brought over from the other network in a wrap of rumors that Obe Morley intended to groom him for the associate producer's post. In the late morning, just before Bibby's first appearance, Paul was looking down from his window at pinhead people and matchbox vehicles moving along the tic-tac-toe of Manhattan streets. Gene Dooley, at the inside desk, was bent over charts, pencil in hand, telephone clamped between shoulder and ear. Dooley always whispered monosyllables into the phone. Gene Dooley, Paul

TABLE 47 279

thought morosely, was a sly trombone, brassy tinhorn, standing tall over secretaries and script assistants, compressing himself in the company of peers and superiors.

Paul never used to object. In fact, he used to admire people who knew where to expand, when to contract, whom to warm up to, whom to turn from. But lately he had changed his mind about flexible manners, political efficiency, and some other business practices. *Getting old,* Paul reckoned. He turned to look up at the slanting heights of nearby buildings, across the sun-shot angles into the sky. But the open sky made him wince. He used his increasing free time to telephone his stockbroker, work algebraic puzzles, do isometric exercises and work out "Evening Roundup" budgets that he knew would be shot down by Obe Morley at the next staff meeting.

It was no fun to be on the cold end of a freeze-out, but Paul kept at his job with the same diligence that had got him the window desk in the first place and the thirty-percent-bracket salary on which his dependents were so dependent that he couldn't consider quitting no matter how low the temperature dropped.

Gene Dooley hung up his phone and left the office. As the trombone tootled down the hall, Paul heard an accompaniment of greetings, "Hi, Gene!" "How's it going, luv?" in the key of high favor. Shortly after, the script girl Flossie White looked brightly in at the door. She dimmed when she found no Dooley. "Tell him I'm looking for him," she told Paul without interest. Bracelets jingled as she moved away.

Paul's self-esteem had been dropping with the temperature. He didn't know whether his skeptical attitude had incurred the loss of favor or vice versa. He'd been unquestioningly on top in the days of the old producer. He was on the wrong side when Morley came on: loyalty to the old regime was political suicide. Not that he refused to embrace Morley, but that he continued to talk to Morley's predecessor, Ed Parker.

To go out for drinks with him. To shut up when the staff started trading stories about Parker's women, his gambling, his indelicacy with sponsors. Paul wasn't sure whether sticking by the old producer had been a matter of principle or plain midwestern mulishness. But he couldn't do otherwise. Obe Morley took it personally and Paul was getting the freeze.

He figured he could stand the cold. He'd have to. He was a man over forty in a young man's business. So he did his window watching, his isometrics and his diligent job, knowing he could be frozen but not fired. His paycheck was safe as long as Lil Peters was the star of the show.

Lil and Paul were good friends. That's all. But in the television business, a fellow needs a friend. While Lil Peters stayed up there as America's favorite co-host, the apple of dinnertime America's eye, the million-dollar darling of the National Broadcasting System, Paul would have a job. So far, he still had the window desk. Which was a lucky thing because when Gene Dooley was out, very little happened in that office.

On this particular morning, nothing happened until Paul heard unusual footsteps in the hall and turned to see Bibby Bosculus walk past his door. Bibby had entered through the back door from the back elevator. Paul was sure Bibby was looking for him. He got up and went after him. Bibby was walking straight down the hall, looking neither left into the offices of the higher-ups on the window side nor right into those of the lower-downs on the windowless side.

"Hey! I'm back here, Bibby," Paul called.

Bibby turned around and stopped to wave. He looked confused.

"Hi, Paul," he said and started to walk toward him.

Then he stopped and waved again.

"Good to see you," he said. He turned again and continued down the hall.

TABLE 47   281

Paul watched Bibby proceed to the front office. He figured the poor guy had come up to get a book order.

Bibby approached the great, glistening apse. Blood-red carpeting and chrome-framed glass panels were lorded over by the hanging chrome statue of the Big Bear, the NBS symbol, which slowly turned, sending strobe beams toward the executive offices. Behind the bank of reception desks, ten-foot blow-ups of Lil Peters, cohost Wade Somerset, news commentator Fred Shea, sports commentator Joe Addison and movie reviewer Sydelle Gorenstein smiled foot-long smiles from a separating wall. Reverently, Bibby reached the row of receptionists.

"Do you have an appointment?"

"I do."

Oberon Morley's was the corner office, more like a living room with couches and bar. It was a sanctuary cut off from the outer clangor by an anteroom with business props and two secretaries to work them. Bibby, nodded through by the two secretaries, felt a good-boy euphoria. Oberon Morley was standing at one of his window walls. He was a different man in his office. He turned to Bibby with a sudden smile.

"You feel like washing up? You want to take a shower?"

Bibby was impressed with Morley's dressing room—brown tile, beige fixtures. He didn't have time to bathe but he said he liked the bathroom.

Morley unbuttoned his cashmere sport coat.

"See this shirt? Pima cotton. Like silk, only cooler. Feel it."

Bibby touched the front.

"I get them made, a dozen, two dozen at a time. Assorted colors. Monogram on the arm." He took off the jacket and showed Bibby a very small, embroidered OEM in an oval border just above the elbow. "On the pocket is out," Morley said. "On the arm is in."

On the onyx bar shelf along the inside wall, a bottle of Johnny Walker Red had already seen action. Outside the sun was shining at near-vertical pre-noon pitch. Bibby thought how pleasant weather was, any weather that you could look out at. Tripler's was underground. He never knew what kind of day it was.

"I got a house in Sands Point," Morley was saying. "On the shore. And an apartment in the city overlooking the East River. I travel first-class. The world is my oyster."

Morley put his jacket on and buttoned it. "But that's not the best of it," he said. "Best of all is the power to do good."

There was a healthy tan on everything in the office including Morley himself. "Twenty million Americans," he elaborated, "watch my show five nights a week before, during or after dinner.

"What I tell them, they know.

"What I show them, they believe."

Bibby hoped the office lighting made his skin look healthier. There were rows of plaques and parchments on the two inside walls—awards, letters to thank and congratulate. A poem from Cassius Clay. A photo of Liza Minnelli and her mom, of Jane Fonda and her dad, of Albert Schweitzer, Gloria Steinem, Pope John, Bob Dylan, Eldridge Cleaver, all signed with personal messages, most with Morley in the picture. There were more photos of Morley on a camel at an elephant hunt, on a raft shooting rapids, in a parka cutting through the Northwest Passage.

"Can you grasp the range of influence of a major television force?"

Bibby said no.

"Do you have an inkling of the workings of this operation —the step-by-step accretion of minuscule details, the tiny pieces that add up to the total concept?"

TABLE 47 283

Bibby shook his head.

"Good!" Morley roared. He sat behind his long, inlaid, lacquered wood table desk. "A clean slate," he said with satisfaction. "No preconceived ideas." He stood up and clapped Bibby across the shoulder blades. "I want you to come up here and learn the business. From the bottom up. How does that grab you?"

Bibby was silent.

"I'll put you in training. You'll work on the set. See how the stage crew works. Get the feel of the show. Meet the talent.

"I want you to stand behind the cameras and sit in the control room.

"You'll learn how we make the schedule. See what the writers do. Sit in on pre-show interviews, makeup sessions, staff meetings, budget meetings. Get the whole picture.

"I want you at meetings with the network news execs and out with salespeople to call on the sponsors."

Bibby searched for something to say.

"The whole shmeer," Oberon Morley said. He stuck a finger between Bibby's chest and belly button. "So that's okay, is it? You'll start Monday morning eight o'clock? You'll work a ten, twelve-hour day, weekends when necessary. Bag packed at all times, ready to travel. Passport in order. Shots and visas for everyplace."

On Morley's beautiful desk, Bibby noticed a muscular brass monkey about four inches high, holding a tray in outstretched paws. Bibby wondered what the tray was for—ashes? paper clips?

"We'll start you at twelve thousand a year. For the training period. Oh, hell. Make it fifteen thousand. You've got to earn more than the secretaries or they won't respect you." Morley, deed done, went back to his leather chair, but Bibby was not dismissed. He felt too tall, so he sat in a low sling chair.

His words came out like bubbles. "That's wonderful, Mr. Morley. I know you won't be sorry because I'll do my very best for you. I'll lay down my life. But I can't start Monday. I have to give notice at Tripler's."

Morley's face became red as a tomato aspic with eyes like hard-boiled eggs stuck in. He was heavier in those days, altogether less ascetic, with crew-cut hair starting to go gray and a pair of black horn-rimmed eyeglasses on his desk.

"You want us to wait till you give two weeks' notice?"

"I think they'd understand if I gave just a week."

Morley got up again and came around to the front of the desk. He rested his behind on the sculptured corner curve. He seemed to teeter between rage and delight. "That isn't the kind of spirit I'm looking for," he told Bibby. "I need loyalty. When I say *shit*, I want you to shit. This is a big future we're talking about."

Bibby looked far out of the window. "I'll be that way when I get here. But now I have to be loyal to my present employer."

Morley decided to laugh it off. "What do you make there —a hundred a week?" He laughed till he coughed and then he coughed and laughed.

"Bernie," he said, choking out the words, "you'll start Monday. I'll call Manny Axe, the president of Tripler's. He's a poker pal of mine. You won't lose your reference." Still laughing, he handed Bibby a cigar. Bibby took it and put it in his pocket for Father Joe. He could hear Morley, still laughing, as he fled through the reception room.

Paul Storey checked his wristwatch against the clock at the mailroom counter. The consensus was one-thirty. Bibby couldn't still be up front. He must have left by the main door. Paul slipped his jacket on and eased out by the back door. He thought he might stop down at Tripler's and see if Bibby wanted to have lunch with him. He'd have to treat the kid, but what the hell. Turning into the elevator bank, though, he remembered it was probably too late for a lunch

TABLE 47   285

invitation. Besides, it was always tough trying to make conversation with Bibby. Also, Paul admitted to himself as the bell chimed and the DOWN light lit red and the doors opened to him, it was unseemly to go sniffing around for information.

Everyone was warm to Bosculus. Not since the early days at the Academy of the Three Saints had he felt so accepted, protected and loved. He was given a desk of his own in an inside office with two production people, his own telephone and an ID card that entitled him to go anywhere in the building. Oberon was like a father to him. The rest of the crew were like brothers and sisters. No—not even at the Three Saints had he found such a supportive group, comrades so eager to help.

And how attractive they all were! To a woman, to a man, they shone with good health and healthily directed energy. There was not a lisp, a pimple, a crouch, a patch of unsightly facial hair among them. Not a crossed eye or a crippled leg or a serious obesity problem. They were ballplayers and roller skaters, cheerful in the morning and cheerful at night.

At one time, Bosculus might have felt like a shadow against this brilliant circle of the most-likely-to-succeed from every region of the country. But his vagueness of perception and his slowness of response were taken as positive traits, indicating that the man was judicious, not prejudiced, and thoughtful, not glib. Bosculus, indeed, began to see his way clear. He began to value the very qualities that had seemed to trip him up in earlier environments. On the "Evening Roundup" he flourished like a tended petunia in the best of soil and sunlight. He soon began to feel as beautiful as the others.

Oberon Morley took his new boy to lunch at the Private Eye, a theme pub in the East Fifties. The maître d' had a corner table for them. The friendly waiter looked like a spy from an Italian movie. He suggested the special appetizer called Undercover Salmon—salmon cold, in dill sauce.

"Mr. Morley," the waiter said while the men were deciding. "I watch your show every Monday. That's my night off. My wife watches every night. If she left me, I'd sue Wade Somerset."

Morley ordered a dry martini. Bernie, off hard liquor, had vermouth, half sweet, half dry. Morley made a face when the half-assed drink arrived, but Bernie knew what he was doing and wanted to keep it that way. The waiter waited reverently while the men examined the horizontal menu printed on slick paper to look like a business card:

PRIVATE EYE

discreet dining

That's all it said on the outside. Inside the print was sharp and black. Appetizers were listed as Accessories Before the Fact. Salads were Accessories After the Fact. Desserts were Just Desserts.

Bernie thought the menu was clever. He also liked the decor —framed reproductions of tabloid spreads with banner headlines about murder, abduction, sex scandals and bomb threats. He was glad this place had crime posters instead of plants that tripped you up and obstructed your vision. Unshaded light bulbs glared down from the rafters. Unpolished chairs and tables suggested the cheap office furniture of a Sam Spade. Some of the waiters wore eye patches. Others wore shoulder holsters. Bosculus hoped the guns were fake.

"You're right," Morley said. "Our set designer could learn a lot from this place. I'm going to send him around."

TABLE 47 287

Bernie ordered lamb chops from the Third Degree Grill. Morley had another martini. Bernie said the set designer should notice the coordination of details. Salt and pepper shakers were shaped like miniature revolvers. The napkins had printed bullet holes. The wallpaper was striped like prison bars.

"That's a great idea, Bernie," Morley repeated. "Our sets need more pizazz." A third martini arrived. "Damned creative," he said. But he wondered aloud if the Electri-Fried Chicken-in-the-Casket wasn't carrying things a bit too far.

Bernie nodded thoughtfully.

Picking at his own small KillerDiller steak, Morley began to talk about himself. "I used to be the best documentary maker in the business," he said, "before success spoiled me." He told Bernie how it had been to make tough, fearless films. He had, as a very young man, interviewed survivors of Hiroshima. He had taken his camera into flattened streets, shacks of refuge, desperate hospitals. He had shown what he saw, told unspeakable truth on campuses, in meeting rooms of churches, in congressional committee rooms—wherever he could catch an audience or make a dent in the surface of complacency or raise some cash to help the victims. In his old lean, ardent days, Oberon Morley had lived in his gut. He'd been in the civil rights movement when the action was there. He had photographed what some people didn't want seen and what other people didn't want to know about. He had been attacked by police dogs, whipped with water from fire hoses, beaten with lengths of rubber hose. His cameras had been snatched and bashed. He had spent nights in country jails, expecting to be killed before morning.

"After you've faced the worst," Morley told Bernie, "there isn't a hell of a lot that can scare you."

"I know," said Bernie, thinking how scared he was most of the time.

Morley had another martini while Bernie had Strawberry

Tort with no coffee. He told how his films had beaten their way to the mass audience. In the turbulent sixties Oberon Morley's hard-hitting docu-papers were fed into the main channels, the often bitter dose forced on the American public. They swallowed it for their own good, Morley asserted.

"Nothing," he told Bernie, not for the first time, "is as hard as facing the truth, except one thing." His eyes were like hard-boiled eggs again, under fierce eyebrows. "And that," he shouted, pounding his fist on the table, half rising from his chair, "is *not* facing the truth!"

Bernard J. Bosculus, friend and confidant of this great man, a little drunk on the great man's martini breath, felt, as usual, two ways. First, he was profoundly moved by the heroism of Oberon Morley and wanted to be his loyal adherent. Second, he was aware that he was a guest on an ego trip—a very well-treated guest who wanted the hospitality to continue.

He suggested to the producer that the "Evening Roundup" devote part of a future program to a visit to an overcrowded prison. "We could show the physical setup and interview some of the prisoners about how they pass their time. We could interview some guards. People ought to know what it's really like in jail."

Morley lit a thoughtful cigar. "You're right," he said. "But we've got to find an angle. This is an evergreen," he said, "a story you can do anytime, so you have to find some new hook."

He went on to explain that when all the network news departments went liberal, it was no longer bold and daring to defend the underdog. Leaving his battles to tamer hands, Morley pursued wild adventure. An elephant hunt in East Africa. A bullfight in Portugal. Scaling Dalmatian mountains. From silken tents in Syrian deserts to ice huts in Antarctica, he had seen all, shot all, shown all to entranced viewers in family rooms and finished basements.

TABLE 47 289

And when the network needed a producer to replace easygoing Ed Parker whose "Evening Roundup" was no longer highest in the early evening ratings, somebody upstairs thought that maybe Obe Morley, past forty by then, might be getting tired of running around the world and might be tempted by a steady and large paycheck plus a big corner office, prestige, power. . . .

Morley blew smoke like a blessing over Bernie's head.

"Ed Parker," he said, "moved aside with grace and good humor. I say that for him. I say, too, that he moved into his proper line—quiz shows, game shows, that kind of thing. The network took care of him and a few of his people went along. The associate producer, who would have been out of his depth in my kind of operation. A writer who'd been sleeping with him, woman writer, couldn't write anyway. The rest of the staff stayed on. As long as they could do their job my way, what the hell—I didn't want any purges."

Morley declared the changeover a success. "A couple of staff meetings and we were in business. We sharpened the show. News pegs. On-the-spot reporting. Guests from the inner circles. Right away the ratings went up.

"And the staff made it clear they were glad to be aboard my ship."

Bernie sneaked a look at his new self-winding watch. It was almost two-thirty. He thought he should be getting back to work but his boss made no move.

Morley had brought in Gene Dooley, a sinewy journalist, a buddy from newspaper days, to work alongside the "Roundup" staff and let the new producer know whom he could trust with what assignments. "I'm a fair judge of people myself," Morley admitted, "but this was not exactly a hand-picked staff and I couldn't afford to make mistakes."

Bernie nodded intelligently.

Things had worked out well. Gradually the Parkerites— writers, directors, editors—began to show up at Curley's, the corner bar where Obe and his cronies hung out after the show. Soon they pulled over a second table. Before long there were three tables pushed together. The Parkerites relaxed their manners and their guard.

Bernie understood. He had studied history. A large-minded, surefooted man like Oberon Morley didn't need to eradicate the Old Order. A bloodless revolution had taken place.

With only one burr still stinging Morley's sure foot: Paul Storey. Bernie heard the name without showing a flicker of recognition.

"You've met him of course. The company manager."

Bernie as a child had learned the uses of an immobile face.

"He's a rare bird, Storey. Both compulsive and creative. He can add and he can also dope out a way to shoot several blocks of Fifth Avenue without showing people or cars. And I'm sure he's quite honest." Morley stared glumly over the brim of his glass. "You know what I mean, Bernie?"

Bernie hummed a neutral tone.

"What I mean is, he's not one hundred percent my man. He never sits down and has a drink with me. I don't feel I can depend on him, you know?"

Bernie took a pensive breath. "Maybe he doesn't drink," he offered.

Morley ignored it. "Anyway I'm stuck with him. But I don't have to be his best friend, you see. Gene Dooley is already doing part of what used to be Paul's work. I want you to take over on some of it, too."

He signaled for the check.

Bernie thought about what to say. The waiter came over and told Morley how much he'd enjoyed the interview with the ballerina who'd just defected from Russia. Of all the things Bernie might say, there were none that could do Paul any good. Morley told the waiter that they'd had trouble with the translator, a violently anti-Red woman who kept injecting her politics into the ballerina's statements. A perfect com-

TABLE 47   291

ment entered Bernie's mind: words to promote his friend's interests while keeping his benefactor's favor. But when the waiter finally took Morley's credit card, Bernie had forgotten the comment. In any case, he reasoned, he'd be better able to help Paul if he were really in solid with the producer. What was important right now was for Morley to know that Bernie Bosculus was trustworthy.

So he concluded, sipping on a second vermouth, long nursed, that he must after all reveal his connection with Paul. Sooner or later Morley would find out anyway. Bernie thought he ought to try smoking a cigar sometime. He could pull in a lot of smoke and let it out slowly while he figured out what to say next.

Watching himself thinking this way, Bernie began to suspect—and not without enjoyment—that he was, maybe, a rather complicated person. He thought that would be nice.

"You know," he said to Morley at last, "Cindy Storey, Paul's wife, is a, an—uh—old friend of mine."

Morley looked at him. They held each other's gaze for a relatively long moment. Morley began to look dreamy and pleased. Bernie could hear himself apologizing to Cindy: *He wouldn't have believed me anyway.*

"Nice," Morley said. He added, "Paul has a friend, too. Paul is very cozy with Lil Peters. Or so I gather."

Bernie remembered something. His retrieval system screened a picture of Paul with a perky young secretary. It was not Paul's infidelity. It was Cindy's suspicion. An adjustment was made: the little secretary took stronger shape and deeper color as the formidable Lil Peters moved into the frame, giving new depths to Paul himself.

Morley stood up, suddenly gruff. "Got to get our asses back to work." The restaurant was empty except for a few stragglers at the bar. The waiter came with Morley's receipt. The maître d' shook Morley's hand. A guy at the bar waved as they made their way out.

"Work," Morley said as they hit the sidewalk. "Getting

across is what counts." They stood a moment till their eyes got used to the daylight. "Who's the boss, the producer or the talent—that's my problem. Keep clear of confrontations—that's my answer." He walked close to Bernie, bent into the wind, down Fifty-second Street. "Wade and Lil, they sometimes get the idea they own the show."

He took Bernie's arm. "They make more money than the executives, so they think they have the right to call the plays."

Bernie listened. "They can't call the plays," Morley told him. "They're only the talent. They don't have the judgment." He glared into the cold sunlight. "They don't have the brains."

The common people crowded the side street on the chilly spring afternoon. Occupied faces approached and passed. Pressing backs loomed till they were overtaken. Bernie Bosculus, walking hard to keep up with his boss, tried to organize the strands of their conversation. He had all the parts but he couldn't consolidate the theme. Oberon Morley at a drinking lunch only *seemed* to be a random talker.

"The point is to play along," Morley said as they turned the corner at Sixth Avenue, cutting through a clump of people waiting for the green light. "Keep up the morale. Era of good feeling. Never confront. That's all you have to remember. Do your job. Stick with me. You'll make out, believe me."

Bernie didn't understand, but he believed. He was starting to fell like an insider. He called it *Sixth Avenue* in his head. Never even thought *Avenue of the Americas.*

One leafy suburban morning, Paul Storey stepped on the guaranteed-accurate, blue-to-match-the-tiles, designer-styled Detecta scale in the master bathroom and saw, unbelievably, that he weighed almost one hundred and ninety pounds.

TABLE 47

293

He had always thought of himself as a lean guy.

He wrapped his hips in a thick and thirsty blue Fieldcrest towel and stood in front of the long mirror on his closet door.

He saw a roll of flesh along the upper edge of toweling.

He went back to the bathroom and put his face under the lights of the medicine chest mirror.

He decided to shave off his beard. And did.

When he went down for breakfast, Cindy was waiting with freshly squeezed orange juice and crisp protein-bread toast. "What's new?" she said as he sat down at the table.

Paul looked at her.

She looked back at him.

"I shaved off my beard," he said.

"Oh, my!" she said.

Then she said, "Why? I liked it."

"I got tired of it."

She saw with dismay that the beard had covered a double chin that wasn't there the last time she'd seen his face shaven. "Well, you look very handsome," she said. She refilled her coffee cup.

He spread out the morning newspaper.

"How's Bibby?" she said.

He read the paper. "Rotten," he said. "Disgusting." She didn't know if he meant the news or Bibby.

"Always there. Always kissing ass."

He meant Bibby.

"I talked to him," Cindy said. "He says he tries to be close to you. He says you keep putting him off."

Paul slapped down the paper. Just what he needed—a human report card. But he said evenly: "What does he expect me to do? Fall all over him like the rest of the flunkies? I don't even do that for Obe Morley."

"It's hard for Bibby," Cindy said. "He's your friend and you hate his boss. Bibby says Oberon Morley is very good to him."

"That goes to show how smart Obe is."

Cindy shut her eyes to hold back a killing comeback. Instead she said quietly, "That isn't very generous of you."

"I don't feel very generous." Paul picked up the paper and set it down again. "Where the hell is the butter?" he yelled. "This toast is like a piece of shoe!"

"No longer can we be content to take the judgments of the few on decisions that affect the lives of the many. We cannot allow the rich to speak for the poor."

The guest was Mitchell Robb, the new U.S. ambassador to the United Nations. He was a small, well-made man who, though he was black looked distinctly Hungarian.

"People will no longer allow themselves to be controlled by forces they don't understand."

It was his first television interview in office, but he was clearly accustomed to being in the public eye and ear. He answered Lil Peters:

"Yes. I got a first from Oxford University. A first means top honors like *summa cum laude* here. My mom came over for the ceremonies. Her first airplane flight, I might add. She said to me, 'Son, what you doing here with all these fair-haired folk with Shakespeare accents?' I said, 'Mom, I got my b.a. here in England but I'm going back to the States to learn the rest of the alphabet.'"

"Marvelous!" Lil Peters marveled. She glanced down to her lap for the next question.

Lil and Dr. Robb sat in a fragment of a living room. Their chairs were angled so that they could face each other and still be in the eye of three cameras—one stationary in the back of the studio, the other two close in and moving on dollies like aggressive giraffes in search of the good leaves. Monitor screens posted high on the walls showed the scene, excluding the banks of lights that beat down on the faces of interviewer

TABLE 47   295

and interviewee, and excluding the wires that were coiled and knotted at their feet. A strategically placed coffee table hid the sight of Lil's lap on which was lying a triple-spaced script with numbered questions for this ad lib interview.

"Tell me, Dr. Robb," Lil murmured confidentially, "I've always wondered what happens when a person like you—a cultured, highly educated and, I must say, a very attractive man of the world—has to do business, I mean negotiate and mingle socially, with a person from a really racist country, like someone from South Africa, where the government doesn't grant full citizenship rights to blacks?"

Mitchell Robb understood the question. In fact, he and Ms. Peters had talked about it before the show, along with all the other questions that the writer had written after an interview in Dr. Robb's office a few days earlier. Dr. Robb turned his head toward the camera with the red light because that was the one whose picture was being broadcast at the moment.

"No government believes that blacks are not entitled to human rights," he said with a knowing smile. "Recognition is a matter of public policy, not private conviction. Racism is politics. There is nothing personal. So I am not personally slighted. Individual diplomats tend to be rather sophisticated people with excellent manners and sharp intelligence. We get along well when we are not making official statements."

His eyes narrowed and seemed to send out sparks as the camera panned in on him. "You might say, if you cared to make light of the matter, that some of my best friends are Apartheidists."

Off the set on the floor of the studio, crew members scurried about with plugs in their ears and clipboards on their arms. It was not an audience show, so the tiers of seats were occupied only here and there, with friends of a guest, an agent or a public relations representative, with network personnel and official observers from sponsors' ad agencies. On the walls and over the sealed doors were red-lit signs, ON THE AIR and SILENCE.

Tension was high, for everybody there knew that a scuff or sneeze would be carried out to forty million listening ears and a move in the wrong place would show up before twenty million pairs of viewing eyes. There was a floating fear that a nervous guest might pick his nose or scratch his crotch on camera. Any faux pas was irrevocable, undeniable, *done*. Such were the high risks of live television.

Up in the control booth, overhanging the studio, the director sat among engineers and technicians in front of complicated panels glowering with dials and switches. The director was the man with his hand on the switch that determined which camera view would appear on the nation's TV screens. Oberon Morley sat beside the director.

Bernie Bosculus stood behind Oberon Morley.

There was a cut to a commercial and Lil took advantage of the off-camera sixty seconds to smooth her skirt and tuck her blouse in. She glanced at the magnified clock on the back wall and as the second hand hit eleven she poised herself and took a deep breath. When it reached twelve and the camera light lit red, she began to talk, adjusting her speed to fill the seconds until the end of the segment.

First she expressed appreciation for Dr. Robb's visit. Then she wished him well in his new assignment and invited him to return to the "Evening Roundup" real soon. Dr. Robb had just enough time to mention his pleasure in having been there. As the second hand returned to eleven, the camera caught the two smiling together and held them until twelve when all the red lights went off and everybody in the studio relaxed in relief. Lil Peters and Dr. Robb hurried off the set and the prop people moved in. On the monitors a large dog and a small cat shared a bowl of pet food.

Bernie watched them rerun the segment in the control room. He was impressed by the professionalism of those

TABLE 47 297

around him. He was impressed even more by the concentration of the professionals. They were watching the screen with the intensity of a laser beam. Bernie felt wonder and envy at their single-minded engagement in their work. In all his experience—the spiritual life at the Academy of the Three Saints, the intellectual life at Myra Tate Community College, married life with Karen, single life in Greenwich Village —he had never felt a comparable connection to the project at hand.

The rerun ran out and everybody cheered.

Oberon then turned to Bernie and pointed a finger at him. Bernie clasped his hands and shook them over his head. He *was* a winner. This was his suggestion, at a staff meeting less than a week ago, to try to bring Mitchell Robb on the show.

"Get him," Obe had said.

And Bernie—working with talent coordinator, researcher and writer—had got him.

Karen telephoned one Tuesday night while Bibby was examining the floor molding in his new apartment on the good side of West Eighty-first Street. NBS had a Saturday morning kid show called "The Kid Show." Karen wanted tickets for Brucie and a few of his first-grade friends.

"I can never reach you at your office," she said. "You're always out."

Bibby explained that he did a lot of legwork. However, he said, he was sometimes only upstairs in the library. "Tell them to find out if I'm in the building and to transfer the call."

Karen said there was a year's wait if you wrote in for tickets to "The Kid Show."

Bibby said he'd see what he could do.

"I saw your name on the credits," Karen said. "Production supervisor. It sounds important."

Bibby said it wasn't really. He said he did a little bit of everything. He called her back Wednesday night after he had stained the molding in his living-dining room. He would be mailing her six tickets for two weeks from Saturday.

"It was no trouble," he said.

"It's great for Brucie!" Karen said. "I don't want him to feel that Winthrop is getting all the attention."

Just as things were looking good on the show and Bibby's heart was settling down, he began to suffer from pangs of guilt about Brucie.

Brucie was a big part of the reason for his dad's move uptown. Bibby looked at the complete little kitchen and pictured Brucie on the counter watching him fry bacon and eggs. Bibby saw the tiled stall shower in the tiled bathroom and pictured himself and Brucie taking turns soaping each other's back. The small spare room was what finally decided him on the apartment. *There* was Brucie's bedroom. Bibby pictured a double-decker bed so Brucie could bring a friend sometime. Bibby and Brucie would go together and pick out unpainted furniture and they'd bring it home and assemble it and sand it down and paint it up. They'd hang posters of planes, trains and rockets. There would be a stack of family games and a reading table.

Brucie was excited to get started on the room but Bibby hadn't had the time yet. Now, when Karen talked about Winthrop, Bibby felt a glacier of sadness sliding in on him and melting into anxiety around the edges.

Bibby arrived at the studio theater just in time for the end of "The Kid Show." Brucie caught sight of his dad and completely blew his first-grade cool. As prearranged, Bibby took the six boys on a backstage tour where, besides touching the controls, they got to talk to the Chief and the Zooman and Lotty Appleby. Each boy was given a prize and a set of

TABLE 47

299

autographed photographs. Brucie was so happy that he seemed to float. When Karen returned from her two hours of shopping the sales at Saks Fifth Avenue, Bibby gave her six beatific boys to go back to Long Island for their lunch party. He walked with them to the parking garage and helped the boys climb into the Mercury station wagon.

What he needed, he thought, was a good woman to be like a mother to Brucie.

Bibby leaned on the open back door of the wagon. "I'll see you next weekend," he told his son. "Or, at the latest, the week after."

Brucie looked out from the back-facing seat. "That's all right, Dad." He was smiling and waving as the car pulled away.

"Next weekend," Bibby called after him. "It's a promise and a date."

It felt funny to come from uptown to downtown as a visitor to his old building. Geraldine's apartment looked unchanged with Yuri living there, but Yuri was not a man who required a setting. Bernie, on the other hand, had been to so many fancy places lately that Geraldine's now looked a little bit seedy and off the beaten trail. He felt he should have brought them something they needed, like a dozen wineglasses, instead of a routine present like the bottle of Zinfandel. But they were so happy to see him—both of them—that he knew it didn't matter what he brought.

Yuri talked the whole time as he fixed a dinner of chicken with olives and eggplant that turned out surprisingly edible. Geraldine had made a chocolate silk pie. The other guest was Beverly, a sculptor who worked with pebbles and shells. After dinner they listened to records and Beverly took out a loose joint from her art deco cigarette case.

She was a shortish, solid-looking woman with curly black

hair and a Mediterranean face. She had on a crocheted dress and wooden earrings as big as jelly jar tops. Bernie took a puff when she passed the joint, just to be a good sport. Actually, he didn't trust marijuana. It was scotch he liked and he was down to almost none of that. He passed the toke to Yuri.

They listened to Vivaldi and talked about their parents. Geraldine's weren't smart, she said. "It took all their energy to get through the day. They had nothing left to think about making improvements." She had no malice in her recollections, but far more distance than Beverly, whose parents had met as teenagers in a Hitler concentration camp. "They still live afraid," Beverly said. "They wrap themselves up in their house. And me."

Yuri knew only his mother, who had worked in a bar to put him through school. Bernie talked about Bosculus Senior and how much less of a creep he had become. Meanwhile they played Telemann, then Corelli. They were all over thirty, no longer angry at the old guys.

Late in the evening Yuri asked Bernie about his work.

"I'd do it for nothing," Bernie said.

This made Yuri very happy. His face grew rounder and redder. "The best kind of work!"

Geraldine explained to Beverly that Bibby was paid a small fortune for talking to interesting people, staying at luxurious hotels and dining at expensive restaurants. "Such a paradox!" she said. She was very proud of her friend and former neighbor.

Yuri had made a total of fifteen dollars on his last three published poems.

"In addition," Yuri interposed, "to six free copies of the quarterly they appeared in."

"A very highly respected quarterly," Geraldine said.

Beverly said that one of her shell sculptures was going to be installed in the garden of a state psychiatric hospital and convalescent home complex in the Bronx. "It's called

TABLE 47 301

'Charmed Pharmacy' and it's in ten connected parts. It won second prize in the Lehman College competition." Nobody would buy the sculpture because it was too big, Beverly said, but she hoped the opening would be reviewed and that her work would get some notice.

Bernie said he might drive up to the Bronx to see it.

"That would be so good!" Beverly said. "I always think my shells must be so lonely up there."

"Maybe they'd put the garden show on the 'Evening Roundup,' " Geraldine suggested.

Bernie didn't like hearing her say that. It made her sound like almost everybody he'd been meeting these days. "It's a possibility," he said as he almost always said. "But not probable."

When he looked up, he saw that Beverly was studying him. Her expression changed and she moved closer.

EVENING ROUNDUP TO LONDON . . . TV's top-rated newsmag will originate in Merrie England Sept. 21–25 . . . superproducer Oberon Morley promises closeup coverage of the Anglo-sexin' scene from rock-stars and style-setters to MPs and an unprecedented, un-interrupted half-hour interview with Sir Laurence Olivier. . . . Live siteseeing will include Guardchange at Buckingham Palace, Crown Jewels at the Tower, shops of Portobello Road and a boatride on the Thames River to Kew Gardens, botanical showplace of the world. . . .

Oogie Watts in "Watt's New?"
New York *Daily News*,
September 10

Dear Brucie,

You would love this place. We have three floors of a hotel that used to be part of a king's palace. There are crowns and crossed swords over the doors. Every room has a marble fireplace. We can look out in the morning and see the gargoyles on the Cathedral of Notre Dame. We can imagine horses clomping on the cobblestone streets.

Plane trip was super. First class, natch. I watched a pretty good Peter Sellers movie that maybe I'll take you to when I get back. Someday I'll take you to Paris. In the Luxembourg Gardens there is a big pond where kids rent toy sailboats and push them into the water with canes. I thought about you when I was there and when I saw the puppet show in the park. Tomorrow's show will come from the foot of the Eiffel Tower. I'll bring you some pictures of all the places I see. I wish I could bring you some of the pastries. When you come here, I promise to stop at every bakery we pass for a *croissant,* a *pain au chocolat* or a *tarte aux fraises,* none better.

Tonight your Dad is to have dinner with Catherine Deneuve. Later I'll meet the Minister of Culture—who is not a clergyman like Father Joe, but a statesman. But before I go out, I have to make sure that there is a roll of facial quality toilet paper in Wade Somerset's bathroom. I also must get a permit to keep traffic off the Place de la Concorde for a few hours on Thursday. The permit has been granted, but I've got to have it in my hand.

Lil Peters asked me to send you a special hello. I hope you had a great Thanksgiving and remembered to feel thankful. Hello to your Mom and Warner and Winthrop. I hope Winthrop is over his chicken pox and that you don't catch it. I hope you're doing better with script or else you'll have to learn Hebrew, where *everybody* writes from right to left!

> Much love, many kisses,
> Dad

TABLE 47   303

*Excerpt from the personal secret journal of Flossie White,
production assistant on the "Evening Roundup":*

I have to stay in the office with the secretaries, but it's
more like a Hospitality Room. They took the Suite with
the biggest bar. I have to help Mr. Bosculus with the
room arrangements because Mr. Storey didn't come and
Mr. Bosculus has to work with the camera crew.

It's plenty complicated. Men with wives are on a
different floor, away from the singles. Guess why? Miss
Peters needs a suite on a floor all by herself. She needs a
supersize dressing room because she has her own
hairdresser, makeup artist, dress pinner and so forth.
Maybe a makeout artist, too. Everybody is very discreet.

Mr. Bosculus keeps an eye on things. He makes sure
there's booze in all the rooms. He gets passes to shows
and sports events. Everybody calls him for everything. I
think he goes in every morning to wipe Mr. Somerset's
ass. He has to listen to Mr. Somerset talking about his
house and his recipes and his flowers and his pressure
points. He has to pay attention to Mrs. Somerset, who
talks baby talk half the time. Mr. Bosculus acts like he
loves it, but I guess that's his job. I'll learn to love it,
too.

Mr. Morley is the great white father. He likes to have
all the people around him. Everybody makes wisecracks.
I used to think I was pretty sharp but I keep my mouth
shut among these dudes. Mr. Bosculus does, too. He's
smart like me. He listens and he don't drink. I think he's
the hatchet man. If somebody does wrong, Mr. Bosculus
talks to them. Mr. Morley stays the good guy.

He has surely been good to me. Last night he came by
himself to make sure I'd be down with the people for
dinner. He always asks do I have everything I need. I

don't know for sure if he's after my ass or if he's trying to atone for slavery. He's in good shape for a man that age, almost my Daddy's age, I guess. His wife doesn't travel with the show. Isn't anyone here I feel close enough to talk to, so things will have to stay mysterious for a while. We're in Rome now. I almost thought Vienna. Hard to tell because all they do is stay in the hotel and drink. . . .

"Don't ask me for gossip," Bernie told Karen. He was behind the wheel of his new white Cutlass. "You know me. I just do my job and mind my own business. I don't know what goes on in that shop. I read about it in the columns. Even then I don't believe it."

But the Color Girl, Karen insisted.

Yes, that story was true. She had indeed been Bernie's brainchild. People on the show respected Bernie's ideas. He functioned as their link to the outside world of people who actually watched the "Evening Roundup." Unlike the veterans who lived television, Bernie was fresh from real life. When he learned that TV color cameras needed to be warmed up before each show, tuned like pianos to reproduce true color tones, he thought about Gloria Mundy and how she'd do it.

"Why not use the real thing?" Bernie Bosculus suggested one morning at a late breakfast with Obe Morley. "Why not use a sexy girl as a pitch pipe of color? Get a healthy, all-American college girl face and use it for all the publicity it's worth? We could call her the NBS Color Girl."

Obe was hung over. "Colored girl? You want to use that little Flossie White from Research? She's the best-looking colored girl I ever saw."

Bernie was patient. "We can't use a black person," he said. "It's not discrimination, only that we need a pink-and-white

TABLE 47 305

complexion. With subtle pastel color tones because they're the hardest to catch."

"Oh, yeah," Obe said. He was drinking tomato juice with pepper.

"Basically, if we get this girl, we can run her through the press department. We'd use her for all the live color shows. She'd have to show up a half hour before every show and just stand there for the cameras."

The idea was called brilliant. Bernie got the go-ahead.

"It was easy," he told Karen while Brucie went inside for his overnight bag. "I called a couple of model agencies. The women were crazy for the job. They wanted the exposure." Bernie offered their regular agency fees. He interviewed half a dozen and chose Jennifer Wheatley because she had the best coloring.

She was a sportswear model with hair like corn silk, skin like peaches and cream, eyes like Iowa sky on a clear day, and strong white teeth. She was full of wholesome enthusiasm. Everybody had always been nice to her.

The choice was called brilliant. Bernie got the credit.

About the casting couch insinuations? "No truth at all," Bernie told Karen. There was no couch in his office.

❦

Obe Morley had to be tactful with the talent. He couldn't send Bernie Bosculus to negotiate with Lil Peters and Wade Somerset. Obe had to talk to them personally. He gave them ear. He gave them leverage. There was no question of keeping Lil and Wade in line. They were not in a line to begin with. What Obe had to do, at all emotional costs, was avoid confrontation. For if Wade or Lil decided to test his or her power, where would Obe come out? He didn't know. That was the point. He didn't want to learn. Therefore he hedged and hondled. Wade wants two extra weeks off. Lil wants one of her college chums, who just published a book about women's fantasies during marital lovemaking, to be interviewed on the show. Lil wants to accept an invitation to be guest star on a dirty sitcom called "The Raunchhouse." Wade wants to campaign for a radical senatorial candidate in his home state of Wyoming. One of them wants to fire a director or change the theme music or get rid of a sponsor whose subsidiary company exploits the poor in the Philippines.

Obe Morley knew how to handle these problems. He would arrange a conference, listen attentively, offer positive feedback and promise to give the matter his first consideration.

Then he would clear out his office and sit down at his desk and look out his corner window and think about how much he could get away with not giving away.

He would concede all the unimportant requests, making them look like big concessions. When it was important not to concede, he would be firm but never inflexible, serious but always smiling.

Of course Lil's friend could come on the show. (Memo to Bernie Bosculus.) Of course Wade could take two weeks off. (Buzz to secretary to call Paul Storey and tell him.) Impossible to fire director; she's a union member. Impossible to dump sponsor; they've got a long-term contract.

The negotiable questions took more thought. Standing in the corner of his corner office, Obe would look out of one window, past crests and crevices of skyscape, all the way across the city and across the river to the mountains, which ranged like a dark and lumbering herd of prehistoric animals. He would look out the other window at pressing battalions of long necks of shorter buildings and one sudden open area where the spires of a Gothic church shot up like a pair of

TABLE 47   307

fangs to menace him. His predatory fancies helped him think. It was never a matter of holding to the letter of Lil's or Wade's contract. It was a matter of retaining good will. Obe had to know on what ground he could appeal most effectively: Lil's determination to be a classy lady; Wade's earnest picture of himself as a man of honor.

Just let Lil know that a Radcliffe graduate headed the Women Against Pornography group that was boycotting sponsors of "The Raunchhouse." Mention to Wade that none of the heavyweight news commentators would so much as endorse a political candidate, let alone actively campaign. Once he had figured out the approach, Obe could usually win without a contest.

However, when requests became imperative and demands became excessive, he did not negotiate. He could not afford to hammer out an agreement. He did not give in gracefully or explain why he couldn't give in. He did not offer an attractive alternative. Instead, he would have a deceptively casual talk with a network vice-president, followed perhaps by another talk with a vice-president of the parent corporation. Soon after, one of the vice-presidents or perhaps the president himself would descend from executive quarters down to the "Evening Roundup" offices and would have a somewhat less deceptive and less casual talk with the manager of Lil Peters or Wade Somerset. The manager would then remind the talent, with pointed tact, of certain stipulations in the talent's contract. There would be a good deal of coming and going up and down the elevators. Obe Morley stayed in his office and drank more than usual during these times. He was never sure until he won that he wasn't going to lose.

Bernie Bosculus was a comfort to him. It was Bernie who knew that women's rights groups fought pornography. It was Bernie who pointed out the fairness code by which newspeople refrained from taking sides on public issues.

Bernie drank less than ever. He was pleased at how well he

was managing to get along with everybody. He was in Obe's office as much as his own and he sat at Obe's right during staff meetings. He had to stay on his toes, of course. But things were going very well. Obe's style had gone over. The sponsors were lining up for more time on the show. As Wade Somerset told a reporter from *Time* magazine, "We never had it so good!"

"Hi, Paul. Where've you been keeping yourself?"

"Well, if it isn't Bibby B! I have been keeping myself out of harm's way. Stateside, alas, but safe and sound."

They faced each other in the long hall.

"I haven't seen you around much."

"I've been around. You've been away."

The walls of the hall were hung with posters. Trevi Fountain: *EVENING ROUNDUP in Rome.* Arc de Triomphe: *EVENING ROUNDUP in Paris.* Cable car: *EVENING ROUNDUP in San Francisco.* Dome of the Rock. Taj Mahal.

Bernie knew that Paul was getting the freeze. It was Paul's own fault. All he'd have to do, even now, was show a little warmth toward Obe Morley. Reach out. Join the drinking crowd once in a while. Bernie wanted to tell this to Paul, but he couldn't get the words out.

"How's Cindy?" he said instead.

"Blooming." Paul smiled for a change. "She got mad at me and went back to college. Public administration or something like that. She intends to be a community planner."

"She'd be good at it," Bernie said. "She's always been a first-class organizer."

"That's what they tell her. She's going to run for town council."

TABLE 47 309

"Well, give her my best," Bernie said. "We'll have to get together real soon."

"Sure thing."

The next day Paul took up jogging. He started in his old sneakers but by the end of the summer he was up to two miles a day and bought himself a pair of running shoes. In the fall he bought a light blue warmup suit with a navy stripe down the side. He thought he looked pretty good even though he hadn't lost any weight.

Paul liked jogging because it reminded him that he was still a free man. Relatively free. He jogged along quiet streets where pleasant-faced houses rose from collars of flowered lawn. He liked his car but he was growing to like even more to go on foot or to borrow one of the kids' ten-speed Paris Sports. In the quiet rhythm of jogging, he could think about what he liked: walking in the woods, swimming in cold water, cooking, eating, making love, watching ball games.

As the sun rose over the hedges, he turned into open road where grassy shoulders were shot with little colored flowers. He was careful not to let his pace pick up. Regularity was the ticket. Jogging regularly, he remembered that he was a justice buff, no bleeding heart or collector of the wretched, but simply a man who knew right from wrong and preferred right. He hadn't thought about it for a long time. Jogging, he thought that people who spent their lives perpetrating wrongs, accepting wrongs, ignoring wrongs or pretending that wrongs weren't wrong were people who, in the long run, lost more than they gained. Paul grasped such ideas quite firmly when he was jogging.

He turned downhill toward the high school thinking he had never been a man who would be king. He had left Indiana not after fame or fortune but just for a chance to be in

on the action. Sweat streamed under his T-shirt and his heart
hit his ribs. He had achieved his ambition. In the news business, he was there. On the "Evening Roundup" he'd come
into more action than he'd asked for. He'd been offered siz-
able bribes to see that certain products appeared, label in
view, on the "Evening Roundup" set. Musical guests or their
managers wanted to give him joy with the latest in pills and
powders. One kinky movie star had invited him to a private
party—group sex for six—in her Plaza suite. One thing he had
learned in televisionland was to cherish his inhibitions. His
reserve had won him a good name and weighty responsibilities under Ed Parker. It had made him unpopular and
suspect with Obe Morley.

Paul jogged along the path at the side of the ivied school
building and onto the running track. He felt nothing now
but a clear head and the motion of movement, no exertion.
He had seen action, held almost every job in the so-called
communications field. He was a damn good company manager and, if he played his cards right, he could be a producer.
There were still places for him to go.

But the action had shifted.

He was tired of loud laughter coming from faces with dead
eyes. He didn't want to drink with the gang and pretend that
Obe Morley hadn't screwed Ed Parker. He rounded the track
and headed for the road, only his thoughts working. He
thought he'd like to go down to Florida and see his aunt
Min, who wrote how much she was enjoying her upholstery
class and the chorus she sang in. Aunt Min had become a
fighting member of her community recreation board. She'd
sent clippings about her recent speech against extra pay for
meeting attendance. "None of us have got anything better to
do," she was quoted as having controversially declared. Paul,
himself, following her example, had been speaking up. A few
weeks earlier he had addressed a town council meeting about
the illegality, let alone immorality, of certain restrictive zon-

TABLE 47   311

ing laws. One of his neighbors had taken a punch at him. That was action.

He was glad when his house came into sight. He didn't fool himself. If it weren't for Lil Peters, he'd be collecting unemployment insurance. If it weren't for her sense of humor and street-kid stubbornness, he'd be more depressed than he already was. He stopped in front of his driveway and pulled a damp handkerchief out of his waistband. He wiped his face and neck. Then he sauntered up the driveway feeling pretty good.

"Mr. Bosculus, Mr. Morley would like you to join him for lunch on Friday with the baseball commissioner."

"Oh, sure. Where's it going to be?"

"Downstairs at Twenty-one. Reservation is for twelve-thirty."

"Hi, Joe. I wonder could we change our lunch to middle of next week? I got called to a Friday meeting."

"Sure. Tuesday and Wednesday I can't make. I'm running a seminar in Tarrytown. How about Thursday?"

"Thursday looks good. No, hold it. I've got an eleven o'clock with Maria Monte, the opera singer. It'll probably run into lunch."

"Hey, will you get me an autographed picture?"

"Sure. I'll say it's for my kid. How's Friday for lunch?"

"No good. I've got a weekend workshop in the Hamptons. How about the week after? Tuesday?"

"Tuesday for sure. I'll call you in the morning."

"Bernie? It's me, Obe. Come on in a minute. We've got a little problem."

Burt Davis was scheduled for the next night and his manager had just called to say Burt would not talk about his marriage breakup.

"What the hell does he think we put him on for?" Obe
demanded.

Bernie had the two-week schedule. If push came to shove,
they could scrap Davis and slip in next week's heartthrob.

"We'll figure something out," he said.

"Hey, Bernie? Mr. Pickett called while you were out.
Warner, he said to say. Something about coming out for dinner this weekend? I said I didn't know when you'd be back."

"Thanks, Flossie. I'll catch him later."

"Mr. Bosculus, is it all right if I wait in your office? I've
got to be on the eight o'clock and nine o'clock shows."

"Sure, Jennifer. Make yourself comfortable. Don't they
give you a room to stay in?"

"Oh yes. With a couch and a dressing table and my own
color TV. But it gets very lonely there."

"You're always welcome here, of course. By the way, you
should call me Bernie. We're all on first-name terms."

"Oh, that's great! Thank you, Bernie."

She was wearing a blue blazer and a lighter blue blouse.
Bernie couldn't get it straight in his mind how someone
could look like the wholesomest college cheerleader and a
Playboy centerfold both at the same time. He'd been on his
way out to join the "Roundup" gang at Curley's, but he
thought it would be unthinkable to leave the poor kid after
she'd specifically said she was lonely. She was not much older
than Paul and Cindy's Jill, maybe twenty-two at the most.
Bernie took her out for a sandwich after she'd stood up for

TABLE 47 313

the nine o'clock cameras. Walking in the halls, on the street, into the Brasserie with her, he noticed that everybody looked at him with admiration.

Most nights after work, Bernie showed up in Curley's, the bar on the corner where the insiders met to drink away their jangles and rehash the day's events. He was glad he was popular but he wasn't surprised. Why should he have enemies? He wasn't a class-conscious person nor was he sexist. He was friendly to secretaries and not just because a secretary could get him an appointment, put in a good word, push through a phone call, pass on inside information. He was friendly also to the man who emptied the wastebaskets and the man who sold homemade candy on Tuesday afternoons. Bernie was unpolitically friendly. That was one of the reasons he was so good for the show. He had his finger on the pulse of the people. He knew the views of the people on the street and in the supermarket. The big shots were too busy for long raps with nobodies. They were too busy, at first, even to talk to Bernie Bosculus. By the time they saw the neat, Slavonic handwriting on the wall and realized how tight Bosculus was with their boss, it was too late for those big shots to start cozying up with him.

Among themselves, at Curley's, before Bernie got there, they made jokes about the male *yenta*, who gossiped with script girls and secretaries and who sometimes at staff meetings asked uncomfortably personal questions. But when Bernie arrived, they quickly made room for him and pitched their wisecracks at safer targets. The big shots soon came to understand that nothing happened on their show that didn't pass Bernie Bosculus' inspection, one way or another.

Paul Storey, watching from a distance, thought it was quite a comedy. He could imagine the scene at Curley's. "Now that we no longer supply his booze," Paul told Cindy, "he's gone over to ginger ale."

"I got a little present for you," Lil Peters said.

It was Affirmative Action time. Naturally, the women brought their demands to Bernie Bosculus. He was the only man they trusted. The signatures covered two sheets. Every women in the shop had signed. And a few of the men who weren't trying to climb the corporate ladder.

Lil leaned over his shoulder as he read the petition listing the women's demands:

- more promotions based on seniority and merit
- more responsibility through a more equitable division of labor
- more visibility on camera and in studio
- more input at staff meetings
- an end of "women's interest" programming that funneled female staff into 4F segregation—fashions, furnishings, food and family.

Bernie thought the demands were reasonable. "Obe would be glad," he said, "to see that there are so many ambitious women around." He looked up at Lil, not focusing on her famous face. "We *need* people to take responsibility," he told her. He promised to talk it up.

And, in fact, Oberon Morley turned out to be so sympathetic to the cause of feminism that he immediately appointed Flossie White his special assistant for women's rights. He brought her to the executive section and gave her the office next to his. He took her out to dinner several times in order to hear her views and to explore ways to incorporate them into the philosophy of the program. True to his reputation as a humanitarian, he declared himself an enemy of male chauvinism and made Flossie ombudsperson for female workers in an effort to stamp out sexism both on and off cam-

TABLE 47 315

era. Bernie was to help her out when she needed him. One of their first projects was a stylebook of on-the-air terminology:

DON'T SAY	DO SAY
man and wife	man and woman; wife and husband
mankind	people; human beings
salesman	salesperson, salesclerk
forefathers	ancestors

Lil Peters was looking over her script.

"Oh, brother!" she exclaimed.

"Try, *oh, sibling,*" said Bernie Bosculus, who was beginning to be known as a bit of a wit.

He got a poke in the arm from Lil.

Obe explained his position to Bernie over another martini lunch at the Private Eye. Obe was deeply interested in the women's rights project though, he said, he had not until recently understood that women were underdogs.

His own mother, he said, had always scared the shit out of him. His wife was no shrinking violet either. However, he was willing to admit it wasn't their fault that society had turned women's strong arms into tentacles of manipulation. He was willing to take the long view and even, if necessary, to bend over backward.

In order to raise his consciousness, Obe said, he was spending a great deal of time with Flossie White. If anyone could get it up, it was Flossie. He was thinking, in fact, of putting her in to replace Gene Dooley as talent coordinator. There was a spot in sponsor relations for Gene if he wanted it. It would help the show to have a talent coordinator who was black as well as female. Obe would have to work very closely with her for a while, but he was willing to do that.

Sourpuss Paul was watching Flossie clean out Gene Dooley's desk. She decided to fix him up with a big smile. She had been brought up to be friendly.

"Mr. Storey," she said in her smiliest voice, "don't you want to take home some of these books? I'm only going to give them away." Books were like toothpicks on the "Evening Roundup." The show was on every publisher's giveaway list: a plug on "Evening Roundup" was reputed to be worth more than the front page of the New York *Times Book Review*. Gene Dooley's shelf was piled high with ghost-written autobiography, how-to psychology, and get-rich-quick economics.

Paul shook his head but he had to smile back. Flossie friendly was impossible to resist.

"Here's one on quilt-making," she said. "Maybe your wife would like it."

"Not *my* wife," said Paul.

How many times had Bosculus telephoned Yuri or Joe or Cindy or even Karen just to say hello so they'd know he hadn't gone high-hat? Of course, he liked his old friends, but a man had to move ahead too. Brucie, of course, he loved more than anything in the world, but Jennifer was probably right when she said that he (Bosculus) was overcompensating for having left his (Brucie's) mother. Bosculus would have to reconsider his relationship with Brucie. After all, he was not going to live forever. The Middle Ages were upon him: past thirty-five was time to stop being a kid. Time to stop kidding himself. Time to step into the future. He wanted to be loved, of course, but not at the expense of living his life to the fullest.

Here's how he looked entering the office at ten after ten on a clear, mild morning. He wore a burnished black trench coat from Burberry's. His shoulders were high. His arms swung loosely. His Bally shoes were new and buffed not to look too shiny. His face was confident, compelling, keen, bony. The

TABLE 47   317

lines of his mouth expressed determination, sensuality, hope. In his fishwater-blue eyes was the suggestion of a distant storm. The close set of those eyes was counteracted by widely separated brows, the work of a judicious electrolysist, a motherly Russian émigrée named Olga, who removed the mustaches of afflicted female stars. The Bosculus hairline had ebbed, but masterful cutting and shaping—at Lloyd's, where all the top executives went—gave his coiffure a fluffed, full look over a high, intelligent forehead.

On the morning of this description, Bosculus was thinking about joining a health club. He thought he would like to play racquetball. He wanted the use of swimming pool and sauna. He also thought it would be good to get away from turned-on women. Bosculus was not cut out for casual relationships and he was afraid of passionate ones. He was often embarrassed to look up during conversation and see the woman he was talking to staring at him with out-of-context intensity. He was glad to have Jennifer around as a protection from other women. She was so fresh and innocent, Bosculus thought, that she was like a living health club herself.

Lil Peters was a different story.

People at parties always asked Bernie what Lil Peters was really like. The question was asked in about a four-to-one ratio of Lil over Wade Somerset. People were more curious about women at the top.

Bernie always answered in a pondering manner, as if it were the first time he'd been asked.

"Lil Peters?" Bernie would repeat, seeming to be taken aback by the novelty of the question.

"You've seen her on the show? That's what she's really like," Bernie would tell the crowd around the sour cream-and-crabmeat dip. "She's a real grown-up, down-to-earth woman, hard-working and honest."

This was true. Lil Peters was plugged in to her job. She had put her whole life into getting where she was and she meant to stay there.

"Lil Peters is one of the smartest people in the business, but she doesn't make a show of it," Bernie would tell the woman on his right as they sipped hot consommé Madrilène. "She has a very strong background in politics, literature, the arts, you name it."

This was partly true. If Lil wasn't exactly a high-honors intellect, she surely knew how to get top mileage out of her IQ.

"Lil takes her responsibilities very seriously," Bernie would tell the woman on his left as they spooned their raspberries *au Kirschwasser.* "When you get past the mystique, she's a very self-contained person with no need to play relationship games."

This was pushing things a little. True, Lil regarded herself as a clean-living, clear-thinking example for all American women. True, she was one of the few sexually functional persons on the "Evening Roundup" who didn't sleep around. She was not moved by a defeating need to make all men love her. But Bernie knew there was more to Lil than met the naked eye.

He also knew that party talk got around.

Bernie was full of praise.

In truth, his dealings with Lil Peters usually were negotiated through one of her two secretaries, private and personal. Better than Bernie knew Lil, he knew her expense sheets, handed to him each week by Jo Greer, the private secretary. Lil's expenses were reasonable—much more modest than Wade's. Lil took cabs while Wade hired limousines. Lil went to expensive restaurants while Wade called in chefs to cook for him at home. Lil didn't drink. As the jobs on the show were clearly outlined, there was seldom a reason for Bernie to talk to Lil, and Bernie was not the kind of weasel who would go out of his way to manufacture one. Weeks might pass without a face-to-face meeting between cohost and assistant

TABLE 47   319

to the producer, as Bernie's title now read on the credits and the floor directory.

It was different on remotes. Everybody was closer when the show was out of town. Staff doubled up and improvised. Once in London, for example, Bernie had to fill in for a missing chauffeur and drive Lil (on the left side of the road) to a private interview at Windsor Castle. In Paris, once, she had come rather shyly into the office suite to ask if Bernie could get her invited to an exclusive customer showing at Givenchy. It took some dogged telephoning but Bernie did it and sent the word through Alice Aberasturi, Lil's personal secretary.

The next afternoon, Lil stopped to thank him. Bernie was having tea in a little alcove off the lobby of the George V Hotel, sitting by himself at a sparkling table by a marble fireplace. Lil spotted him and went right over. Bernie grabbed the napkin off his lap and stood up. Lil looked with approval at the uneaten Napoleon waiting on his plate. Bernie thought of asking her to join him, but he couldn't. Napoleons were sloppy eating; he would die of awkwardness, custard dribbling, flakes on his chin, the fork refusing to cut through.

So he thanked her for thanking him and was grateful when she left.

In Lisbon they got to know each other better.

She caught up with him in the lobby of the Estoril-Sol. By "Evening Roundup" standards it was a fair stop—a big, modern beachside hotel with employees who spoke Portuguese. The weather was hot. The air conditioning was cold. The carpet was red. There was a good fish restaurant across the street. Lil, in a beige bouclé shirt over skinny white pants and flat sandals, crossed in front of Bernie, stopped and turned around.

"Just the man I'm looking for."

Bernie waited.

"I want to hear *fado* tonight. I'm afraid they'll send me to some tourist joint. Can you find out where's a good local spot?"

Bernie already knew about Emilia's.

"Dinner? Early show?" He also knew she'd have to be on camera in the morning.

"I guess early," Lil said uncertainly. Then she took a more confidential tone. "I was going to go with that man from the government. That count we met yesterday in the mayor's office. But he didn't call." She looked as if it really bothered her.

"Maybe he's standing me up," she said. "But I don't want to miss *fado*. I don't want to pull the usual 'Roundup' stunt."

Bernie laughed. He knew what she meant. "Yes. London without going to the theater."

"Right. Vienna without the Staats Oper. Paris without the Follies."

"I had snails in Paris," Bernie told her. "I sneaked out to the Pied du Couchon at six in the morning and had snails and onion soup."

"Wish I'd known."

"Next time," Bernie said.

"Yes, but this time is here."

Bernie promised to reserve a table at Emilia's for her. Lil thanked him, formal again, and walked off.

"What if the count doesn't show?" he called after her.

Lil looked back over her square shoulder. "I'll take Alice," she said. "That's what secretaries are for. Didn't you know?"

Bernie thought he should say something flattering, but then he thought how silly it was for him to feel sorry for Lil Peters. Bernie was getting to be a grownup, too, past poor-little-rich-girl fancies. Lil was a woman whose contract called for first-class air travel and a hotel suite. If the hotel didn't have a suite, she got the biggest room.

Not much later, when Bernie called her suite, Lil herself picked up.

TABLE 47   321

He had a corner table for her, near the stage. Nine-thirty, which was early dinner in Lisbon.

"No count," Lil said dryly. Then she said, "Listen, Bernie. Are you sure they'll give me the good table if I show up just with Alice? Will they let us in?"

Bernie didn't laugh at her. "I'm sure you'll be treated very well. I told them who you are."

Everybody on the show, including Lil herself when she was in a good mood, joked about her horror of not being recognized by headwaiters. "I must be full of feelings of inadequacy," she told Bernie. Her voice scratched its back along the phone wire. "If I ever get psychoanalyzed, I'll learn what it's all about."

Bernie sympathized with her. He himself was content to be anonymous, but he knew a lot of people whose idea of heaven was when Saint Peter knew they were coming and was holding a good table. Bernie himself liked a back seat from which he could watch the action.

In the end, it was he who went with Lil. Alice couldn't make it, Lil said. Bernie thought it extraordinary for the devoted Alice not to drop everything. But, on the other hand, he could think of no good reason for Lil to make up a story.

Unless she was the kind of woman who would rather go out with a man—any man—than be seen publicly in the company of another woman.

Unless she and Alice Aberasturi were lesbian lovers and dared not appear together in places of public entertainment.

Dressing, Bernie calmed himself with even wilder variations on the theme of Lil Peters's private life. Peering into the wall mirror in the painted tile bathroom, he rejoiced that he had made time to spend on the beach. It was really amazing what a suntan could do. Four caps and the critical attention of an East Side dentist that Obe recommended had made Bernie's smile quite princely. He slipped into his linen jacket, Paul Stuart's smartest; the buff-colored slacks were pressed to Portuguese perfection. There was time to report to

the poolside bar to drink (Perrier for him, martinis for them)
with Obe and Flossie White.

Obe's hand was resting on the table with his lazy fingers
tangent to Flossie's braceleted wrist. Bernie's glance passed
twice to make sure they were touching. He noticed, while
looking, that Flossie's hands—all of her, actually—were unusually well attended to. Nails handsomely manicured. Nice
rings. She had always been a pretty woman in a pert and
bouncing way. Now she had turned elegant. A wonderful
new haircut. Classy clothes. Bernie thought maybe it was just
that he was more alert lately, noticing more. Less worried
about himself, he grew more curious about others. It was hot
out there on the patio and the three talked in floating frag-
ments. Over Flossie's high-held curled black head and Obe's
sinking gray one, Bernie watched the last of a fire-and-blood
sunset.

Obe was too far gone to insist on an answer when he asked
where Bernie was going. Flossie, too discreet to repeat the
question, only winked with wicked joy as Bernie rose and excused himself.

One of the hired drivers took them into Lisbon, along the
highway beside the Tagus River and into the flat center of
the city that had been plowed by an earthquake a couple of
hundred years before and retained the shape of the catastrophe. They turned up toward the rocky heights of the Old
Town, the bohemian quarter, the Alfama, where cobblestone
streets and thick-walled houses had endured the riving of the
city. Shooting up the hills, swerving around sharp corners of
streets that ended in staircases, nosing into alleys and magi-
cally coming out the other end, tooling around tiny plazas
and behind sudden churches, upward always toward the Castle of Saint George, along the wall under the battlements and
precipitately down again toward the river, they spun into an
unlit cul-de-sac and pulled up at an anonymous doorway in
one of the old stone houses.

TABLE 47 323

Francisco, the driver, opened Lil Peters's door. "Emilia's," the driver said. "Wait or return?"

Bernie climbed out.

The door was carved wood with a small nameplate too faded to read. Bernie tried the latch and the door opened. Beyond the haze of smoke and red lighting, he heard a swarm of talk and saw moving silhouettes.

He told Francisco to come back in two hours and wait outside. Lil was already in and down three steps, a pastel fluff in the sifting darkness. The maître d', a black man in a black suit, couldn't possibly make out her features, let alone recognize America's favorite TV hostess. But he heard the authority in Bernie's voice and felt the higher authority of a bill pressed into his hand.

It was an excellent table: small as a tambourine, candle-lit, flush with a sunken platform on which a man sat in a thin ray of light, plucking a guitar. The desultory chords cut into the flow of foreign murmurings and arranged it in neat bales afloat on the red haze. There was no cloth. No wine card. An ashtray as a candlestick.

Bernie recognized the sound of the voices, even when he didn't know the words. The sound was prosperous, cared-for, expectant of accustomed pleasure. Expensive places were the same all over. Bernie, with a walletful of escudos, was as good as any man at any of those tables. Lil Peters, he was pleased to see when he *could* see, was really excited to be there.

Lil surprised him. It turned out that they had enough to talk about. He had thought that she moved too fast to catch the shop gossip. He had thought she was above idle chatter. He was wrong both ways and glad of it.

"I like a little malice," she told him. "It's no fun being Goody Two Shoes all the time."

Bernie had picked up a habit of moving slowly and looking all around him. He had collected many details of behavior to put before Lil's consideration. He was delighted to find her so interested. He ordered a bottle of the local wine, which turned out to be old Dão, very pungent.

Lil really trusted him, he could see. In the first place, it was rare for her to drink. In the second place, she swore him to secrecy and then told him her theory about Wade and Betty Somerset: that Betty knew all about Wade's paramour but pretended she didn't. . . .

"Oh, right!" Bernie caught on. "Because if Wade knew she knew, he'd feel guilty, and knowing Wade, I guess he'd have to tell her everything."

"Right!" Lil crowed. "And then Betty would have to deal with it and make some kind of decision."

"Which is the last thing she would want to do!"

"Oh, right!"

Lil adored the phrase *éminence grise*. She'd never heard it before but she understood when Bernie explained that he sometimes played that role. People around them were eating from bowls of spaghetti that hissed. Bernie pointed to order the same but the platter turned out to be tiny, spaghetti-thin fish fried in oil and garlic, served sizzling, and swallowed whole, eyes and all. The New Yorkers ate bravely, washing it down with Dão and laughing at themselves. Bernie was glad to see Lil having such a good time. He suspected that this was for her a rare carefree night in a life that was usually tense and watchful.

Lil could speak freely because she had nothing to fear from Bernie and no need to impress him. She told him about her childhood as Lola Picone with a Jewish mother and an Italian father, the family fights, the constant relocations in the forties when she was tiny and her parents worked in war plants. She felt far enough beyond boundaries to help Bernie finish the wine before the show started. . . .

When Lil began to ask idle questions about Obe Morley and Flossie White, it was like family talk. Bernie was happy to share his observations. He liked Flossie. He liked the way

TABLE 47   325

she cared about Obe. Watched out for his drinking. Made sure he was in good shape when he went home at night.

The guitar man stopped playing and pushed his chair into the shadows. The platform was small and bare, starkly lit. From out back a woman wandered in and stepped down to the stage as if she were lost. She was all in black, black shabby pumps and a black shawl over her head. She was a most forlorn woman. Bernie was about to offer her a guiding hand when she centered herself on the platform, nodded to the guitarist and started to sing. She sang, in Portuguese, a song as despairing and forlorn as she was. As the song went on, she took the shawl from her head and let her hair fall over her shoulders.

She used the shawl for a prop. A skirt to flirt in. A shield to defend herself. A blanket for love. A baby's wrap. A tearful handkerchief to wring. All this in one long lament of a song sung in a voice that careened from a thin wail to hollow moans. At the last note of the song, the singer dropped into an exhausted bow and the place exploded with applause stamped, clapped and yelled.

Another bow for singer, for guitarist, for singer again. Another song, as desperate, as stirring. When this singer finished her set, another came on dressed the same, singing the same songs.

Bernie was more excited by being there than he was by the performance itself. He felt sure, though, that if he came often enough to *fado*, he would learn to tell the singers apart.

Between sets Lil returned to the subject of Flossie.

"Do you think she's really bright?"

Bernie was sure. "She's a graduate of the University of Wisconsin," he said. "That's no playground." He thought further. "I think people put her down because she's so pretty."

Lil agreed.

"Some of the women think they were passed over for her.

But the fact is, she's very good at her job. She doesn't just put on an act to make it look like she's under pressure. You know that act."

"*Do* I!" Lil exclaimed. "But the other girls think Obe favors her." She hung a wispy question mark on the end of the sentence.

"You know our shop. Rumors proliferate."

"But of course he's seeing Flossie."

"But of course." Bernie wasn't giving any secrets away. Obe and Flossie were out in the open. He'd met them himself one Sunday afternoon. They were strolling beside the East River, hand in hand, swinging their arms like a couple of teenagers. Bernie was driving by with Brucie. He honked his horn at them. They heard him and waved. Bernie assumed that everybody knew.

He and Lil were drinking port now. The fourth singer was on. They were still waiting for Emilia herself.

"That doesn't mean favoritism," Bernie said. "As you know, we are a meritocracy. Flossie earned every increment she's had." He was carefully sober. "She has earned her promotions. She's an excellent talent coordinator. Obe says there's nothing she can't do."

Lil played with her glass.

"We had to promote women. The fact that she's a woman and black was basically helpful but not decisive. I think she's sincerely in love with Obe. If she were using him, she'd be looking to go on the air. Don't you agree?"

"Oh, I don't know. Not everybody would want to take that kind of pressure," Lil Peters said.

"But she *is* damn good."

"Yes. I imagine she is."

"At her work, I mean."

"Of course," Lil Peters said.

It was time for Emilia to sing. The whole room was calling for her. Lil and Bernie had small cups of muddy coffee in front of them. Lil put two fingers on Bernie's wrist.

TABLE 47 327

"Look, Bernie," she said, leaning toward him so that he could smell her classy, dry perfume. "I wouldn't mention any of this outside. You know—Obe and Flossie. I don't know what's going on with Obe's wife, but he wouldn't want the story to get around. It would be really bad for the show. Our great family image."

"I know. I know." Bernie heard himself sounding more sober than he felt. "One thing about me you can count on, it's discretion. I learned it early in life. My seminary training."

After Emilia finished her set, Lil wanted to hear all about the Academy of the Three Saints.

"I had the feeling she wanted me to come back to her room." Bernie was confiding in his friend Yuri at breakfast in a West Fourth Street bakery. They had a sidewalk table against the glass partition. It was raining in the light of a sun that seemed surprised at the weather. Bernie and Yuri were eating croissants with salted butter and strawberry jam.

"So why didn't you?"

"I thought it was my imagination. I couldn't believe she meant it."

"You are really a madman." Yuri was in high spirits. He'd just bought a quarterly called *PigIron* with three of his poems on two of its pages.

"I know," Bernie said. "I went up in the elevator with her, to her door. I took her hand, you know, to shake. You know, to shake hands good night. And she gave me this long look, you know, this eye contact thing. I didn't know if it was intended or unconscious. So I looked away at a picture in the hall. She kept hold of my hand. I didn't know what was going on."

"Very masterful," Yuri said, clearly feeling very masterful himself. He had just begun his floor-waxing business. He was amazed at how much money it brought in. He thought of poems while he worked and he worked only mornings so he could write in the afternoon.

"I just couldn't believe it," Bernie said again. "She could have anybody. Why would she want me?" They were drinking orange juice, waiting for eggs.

Yuri shook his hands over his head. "You were there," he shouted. "Marcello Mastroianni was someplace else. Get it?"

Bernie had never seen him like this. "I thought you were building up self-esteem," Yuri scolded. "You're a big man in a big job and you're still afraid to be seduced? And by Lil Peters, Lord help you!"

"It's my prick," Bernie said with dignity. "Why are you getting so upset?" Living with Geraldine had changed Yuri. He was a different kind of poet, extroverted. "I don't tell you what to do with Geraldine."

"Geraldine is an artist," Yuri said. "Nobody does anything with her unless she damn well wants to do it. Then you'd better be on your mark."

The eggs arrived, poached hard on burned English muffins. "I don't like to mix business with private life," Bernie said defensively but enjoying the phrase. "Besides, as you just implied, it's not much fun when you're expected to give a performance. The question is, do I want to be compared with a bunch of diplomats and movie stars?"

"You think she sleeps with everybody?"

"How should I know? If she wanted me, she can't be too fussy."

Actually, they had talked for a long time at the door of Lil's hotel room, the door open, the suite beckoning. Lil wanted to know about Bernie's connection with Paul Storey and his wife. She especially wanted to know what Bernie thought of Cindy.

Bernie answered carefully. He couldn't ask but he saw that

TABLE 47   329

Lil cared a lot about Paul. Bernie cared a lot about Cindy. Just good friends, of course, he and Cindy, Lil and Paul. He thought, somehow, with port-induced sentimentality, that it would be appropriate for himself and Lil to get together. But he also thought, with port-induced illogic, that if Lil Peters really wanted to make love with him, she would know how to ask.

"Furthermore," he told Yuri as the waiter set down two mugs of coffee, "I didn't think I could handle being rejected. I'm supposed to function as a liaison between Lil and her producer. My effectiveness would be impaired if I were also her spurned suitor." Bernie watched Yuri pour half a pitcherful of milk into his coffee.

"Got you," Yuri said. His eyes shone with fondness for his friend. After a long, fond look, he recited in deep poetic tones:

> *How often I recall*
> *Those words with a dying fall*
> *"It was not what I meant at all."*

He dunked eggy muffin into his coffee. "Still," he sighed, "I'd like to have heard how it was."

Actually, they had stood in the doorway a while longer. "I know you're having a hard time," Bernie said. There was hush-hush warfare between her and Wade about the division of news reports. Same old story; Wade took the meat and left her the fat. Lil had complained indirectly. Obe had been avoiding the issue. Paul Storey, who used to be Lil's champion, was no help now with Ed Parker gone.

"I want you to know," Bernie said, in all port-induced sincerity, "that beyond the admiration I have for your talent and ability, I find you a very attractive, desirable woman." He felt a bit self-conscious but saw her need as greater than his vulnerability. "I'm tempted to try to take advantage of your low mood and move in on your emotions."

Bernie had worked hard on building up his confidence. He was a man who didn't sweat much but now he felt sweat dripping from under his collar. He felt like inept, spaced-out Bibby all over again. The *but* hung over him like an overloaded waterbed. Lil waited, dry as her perfume.

"But it wouldn't be fair." The line of sweat trailed down his back.

Lil leaned coolly against the wall inside the door. Bernie could see around the corner into the Portuguese version of a swanky sitting room—the long, low sofa, a glass table with flowers and a cocktail tray.

"Are you currently involved with anyone?" she asked him.

"No one special." He couldn't mention Jennifer. They had a crazy, undefined relationship. She was like his incestuous daughter. "I see, ah, different women." He forbade himself to reach for a handkerchief.

Lil dropped the capelet she'd been wearing to cover her shoulders. She was blue now in the light from the beach windows. The capelet fell on her message stand.

"Right," she said. "Well, I'm glad you're not a male Cee Tee." Her voice became hard, like her news delivery. "Lots of male Cee Tees around. Cunt teasers? They make a play to see how far they can get. Then they're scared to pull their pants down." She seemed angry. She pulled pins out of her hair and shook it loose.

"It's not easy to be a famous woman," she said. "A lot of guys are turned off by fame and fortune when it isn't theirs."

Bernie remained on the doorsill.

"But I knew you were different," Lil said. "As soon as you joined the staff, all the girls knew you weren't going to be a member."

"A member?"

TABLE 47 331

"Of the Broadcasters' Swordsmen's Society." She did not smile.

He tried to be nice before leaving. He began a glorious statement about Lil's being different from other women, but she gave him a light push and waved him off. He walked down the two flights of stairs to his room wondering if she would hate him forever.

MANHATTAN IS WHISPERING ABOUT *the knock-'em-dead diamond ring on the third finger, left hand, of Flossie White, new talent coordinator of the "Evening Round-up." Produced by Oberon Morley?*
                                Oogie Watts in "Watt's New?"
                                New York *Daily News,*
                                March 30

. . . the week was also notable as the first in which ABC's "World News Tonight" inched past the NBS "Evening Roundup" in the ratings, by one tenth of a point. The shift, which will take some weeks to confirm because spring viewing patterns are not typical, could foreshadow a crisis at NBS News.

                                Wes Gray
                                New York *Times,*
                                April 25

The highlight of the executive session was the announcement by John C. Dilworth, vice-president of Dilworth & Dobbs, that that agency will not renew its contract for 3-times-a-week participation on NBS' "Evening Roundup." Dilworth, who is also D & D Media Director, will accept presentation proposals starting next Monday.

                                ADNEWS
                                New York *Post,*
                                May 18

Les Steele, president of NBS News, told the affiliates that Miss Peters and Mr. Somerset would continue in the fall as co-anchors of the NBS "Evening Roundup," a program that has been strengthened, he said, by the recent appointment of Bernard J. Bosculus as associate producer.

Mr. Bosculus, a former university professor, has been for three years assistant to producer Oberon Morley. Mr. Steele indicated that the changes made by Mr. Bosculus were already in evidence. The newsmagazine format, he said, now has a "faster, smoother pace," contains more features than before and puts "a greater emphasis on real people."

> Wes Gray
> New York *Times*,
> May 25

"It's a funny thing," Bernie told Jennifer. They were going to a movie that night. She'd come to call for him. "The more Obe's job is threatened, the better he looks."

The conflict seemed to dignify the producer. He seemed not merrier, but happier. His inner dogs had quieted. The red had gone out of his face and he was losing his belly. There were rumors that he was ill but Bernie discounted them. Obe could afford to be serene: Bernie was holding the fort.

"What about his wife? How does *she* feel?"

Bernie didn't know about his wife. "She drinks a lot, too, is all I know. She has her own life. I don't think she cares about him as long as she's provided for."

"But about Flossie? About Obe's leaving home after all those years? And the children?" Jennifer was indignant. She was ever a defender of family values.

"The kids are grown. And look, if a marriage is dead, there's no use kicking it."

TABLE 47   333

"It just seems inappropriate is all. Flossie is so much younger."

"She's older than you. Obe is not very much older than I."

"We're different," said Jennifer. "And you're much younger."

She was no longer the Color Girl. She had been replaced by a printed card and a computer system. But that was okay. She had plenty of modeling jobs now. She was on a floor wax commercial and in a Jell-O magazine ad. She had fashion calls all the time.

They ran to make the late show. Jennifer was like the childhood companion he'd never had. She had a lot to learn and he was glad to teach her. Even when they made love, they were like gleeful buddies.

"And, you know, she *is* black." Jennifer ran beside him, looking almost prim in a white middy blouse over knickers. "*I'm* not prejudiced, but everybody else is. Everybody says he's going to lose the show or else he'll have to lose her."

Bernie shook his head. "This isn't the fifties," he said. Still, he thought it was a shame that word had gotten out. He wondered who could have been mean enough to leak it to the press.

Bernard J. Bosculus has been named Executive Producer of the NBS-TV "EVENING ROUNDUP." Mr. Bosculus, a former publishing executive as well as a seasoned broadcast specialist, succeeds Oberon Morley, who will take on new duties in the NBS documentary division.

Mr. Bosculus served for three years as assistant producer of the "Evening Roundup" and for several months as associate producer. His most recent assignment was a series of special features from Rome and the Vatican. In the past year he has produced originations from the political and cultural capitals of the world.

The new executive producer brings a varied background to his assignment. A former English literature professor, art dealer as well as publishing executive, he is a graduate of the Three Saints Academy at . . .

NBS Press Release
August 22

"Nobody can replace Obe Morley," Bernie told reporters. The news conference had been set up in the corner office by Gene Dooley, now in the NBS Press Department and assigned to the "Evening Roundup." Bernie had had more bookcases put in. He was thinking about buying some art. Meanwhile, he sat resplendent in Italian tailoring and faced the dozen or so reporters standing around his desk. He had seen Obe act like a king without losing the common touch. He had observed different styles in other executives. He was trying for a composite of the best.

"Obe is simply not a replaceable guy," Bernie said compositely. "However, I'm sure he knows, as the rest of the staff knows, that I intend to give this job everything I have."

Lil Peters sat at the side of Bernie's desk looking radiant in newly auburn hair and a modestly cut, cement-colored dress. "We'll all miss Obe terribly," she said when it was her turn. "But I couldn't have chosen a better replacement if the choice had been mine to make.

"Bernie Bosculus is a rare bird," she said. "He knows television inside out and he is also a man of the world."

Wade Somerset sat beside her in flannel pants and an Irish linen jacket. He was less radiant than Lil but his smile was still broad enough to travel. "I want to take this opportunity," he told the reporters, "to publicly congratulate Bernie Bosculus, to praise the job he's been doing ever since he came on

TABLE 47   335

our show, and to wish him well as our producer." Wade took the opportunity also to announce that he, Wade, and his adorable wife Betty were about to embark on a second honeymoon, a tour during which they planned to visit most of the Third World.

After the formal statements, including one from the president of NBS, who sat on the other side of Bernie's desk, the press was free to mingle informally with stars and executives. Paul Storey, the company manager, was on hand to see that plenty of coffee and Danish was passed around.

"I can't make it," Bernie apologized to Joe Farley. "I have to clear off my calendar this week. Sales meetings. You wouldn't believe the pressure. If it weren't for Jennifer, I swear to you, I'd be up in Payne Whitney."

Joe understood. He'd had weeks like that himself. The weight of office was staggering.

"But I want to talk business with you," Bernie continued. "I want to initiate a program for news personnel. Effective team building. Situational management. Performance measurement. First I'm going to need one for myself in Time-Planning Skills. I tell you, Jennifer has been a lifesaver."

Joe said he'd call next week.

"The kid has some head on her shoulders," Bernie said. "She understands the problem. She does what's needed. No fuss. No questions. She got me a housekeeper, can you believe it? She picks up my cleaning. Last Saturday I was stuck at the office, she showed up with a shopping bag full of food from Zabar's."

"I'm glad you've got someone to look after you," Joe said sincerely.

"I tell her she should be out having fun, but she insists on hanging around. Last night she helped me move furniture. She says nothing is a sacrifice if you really want to do it."

"Bless her," said Father Joe, not so sincerely.

Bernie and Joe made a tentative date for the following Thursday.

Attentive as Jennifer was when Brucie was around, the boy refused to take to her. He was becoming fretful, teasing, hard to please.

He seemed to play for attention. When his father called, he tried to provoke him with disturbing, obviously untrue reports about feeding marbles to Winthrop and setting fire to a neighbor's cat.

Thanks to Jennifer, Bernie was wise to these ploys. "The best thing you can do for Brucie," Jennifer said, "is to fulfill yourself. Treat yourself well and let him see you happy. That will help him grow up guilt-free and independent."

So Bernie ignored the teasing and the disgruntled expression that had moved in on his son's face. "Be sure to listen to Warner," he told Brucie on the phone. "And help your mother when the new baby comes."

Brucie wanted to know when he could come and stay with his father.

"Pretty soon," Bernie promised. "As soon as we get the apartment fixed up. Jennifer's making it really spiffy."

In fact, Jennifer had turned the spare bedroom into a study, so that the living room could be terraced and used as an open party space.

Bernie filled the doorway to Paul's office.

Paul looked up from his desk and marveled at how big the man had grown.

"You ought to move out of here," Bernie said. The room was as cluttered as when Dooley was in there. "I'd like you to take the office next to mine, Flossie's old place.

TABLE 47

337

"Lil has been telling me about the kind of job you used to do for Ed Parker. That's what I need. I'm going to require a lot of close help with logistics."

Paul had expected something like this. Bernie and Lil were thick. Lil was ever Paul's advocate. So strong was the wind change that in the past week, two people—neither of whom had spoken to him for a year—had asked him out to lunch.

"I want you up front, Paul," Bernie said. "I want you to take a more active part in the show. I plan to make company manager a bigger job, including more personnel management, for instance. The job will be on a par with associate producer. I'll need your input."

It might have gone the other way. Bernie might have used this chance to get back for the old days, when Paul didn't bother to pretend that he thought very much of Bibby Bosculus. But Bernie wasn't like that. Putting first things first, he remembered his old admiration for Paul as a pier of respectability and the kind of man who holds the world together.

"The fact is," Bernie said, "I'm depending on you."

Paul was listening.

The prospect was tempting.

And that was all he needed to clear his head so he could see the future he really wanted.

He wanted to be on his own. With Cindy working and college paid for, he was ready to become independently poor. He had a few skills to market with pleasure as well as for profit.

It was easy for Paul to quit. The agony was over as soon as he made up his mind.

"He supported me long enough," Cindy told Bernie when the producer called her. Bernie wanted to assure her he'd done his best to keep Paul on the job.

Cindy didn't blame Bernie *or* Paul.

"I supported *him* long enough," she added. She tried to explain her position. "Do you have any idea of the energy it takes for a woman to live with a man who's unhappy at his job? When both of them feel it's her fault that he has to stay there?"

The day Paul quit was the day Cindy began to feel like a powerhouse. The next day Paul started to build a darkroom in the basement. "Only for twenty years he's been talking about it," Cindy said. "He'll make it a business. I know Paul."

Bernie was too busy to stop and try to figure out the dynamics of the Storey family. He succeeded in persuading Flossie White to stay with the show. He needed all the good people he could get. Keeping her on, furthermore, was a way to maintain friendly relations with Obe Morley, whose benefactions he would never forget.

During his first year as producer of the "Evening Roundup," Bernie Bosculus won awards from both the National Organization for Women and the National Association for the Advancement of Colored People. He and Lil Peters continued to be the best of friends.

Why not?

It's morning already. Dawn is shooting through the sky like popcorn. Obe Morley is watching from the window. He's a thin man now. His hair is almost white and he wears it combed back severely. At the moment he's nostalgic. I'm Cindy Storey, watching him, and feeling glad that he's got Flossie and this awesome view of the city.

TABLE 47 339

Obe had some tricky surgery not very long ago. Flossie saw him through it. It was the kind of operation that people don't like to ask about. My belief, unverified, is that he and Flossie came into the open only after Obe learned he had cancer and was not going to live forever. That's how long some people have to wait.

Paul, my lazy husband, lets out a long yawn. It isn't a hint. It's a condition. "If you get up, I'll get up," is what he's saying to me.

In fact, I'm the one who needs to get home. I'm the one who has to get dressed and go to work.

Geraldine is a free lance like Paul, meaning she too can sleep late. She leans out of her chair to look at Yuri's watch, and then collapses back into the cushions.

"This woman wants to have a baby," Yuri announces. "But she never wants to go to bed at night. She believes that babies are made like paintings are made. By inspiration and effort."

"It would be a very beautiful baby," Geraldine says, half asleep.

It's Joe who finally stands up and means business. He bows toward Flossie. "It has been a truly fascinating evening," he says, "but I must be off."

Paul hears something that I miss. "Going someplace?" he asks Joe.

"The night was a proper farewell." Joe is being dramatic as usual.

"A farewell to whom?"

"Or to what?" Yuri asks.

Though I have grown up a lot in the last couple of years, I have retained a number of my old prejudices. For example, I still find it hard to take Father Joe altogether seriously. Maybe because he finds it hard to take himself seriously.

"Farewell to all this," he says with one of his grand gestures.

He says he's going to Mexico.

That sounds serious. He has mentioned this idea before, but this time he has a plan. After all the seminars he has run in Human Needs, Motivation Techniques, Formulating Policy and Resource Management, he says, he finally got the point.

"Quitting the American Executive Society?"

"A sabbatical," he corrects me. "Hedging my bet."

First stop is to be a small communal farm in Virginia, run by an Orthodox priest who doubles as a social worker. There Joe plans to train in preparation for a rugged existence. He says he'll have to modify his lupine eating behavior as well as his overfed arrogance of mind.

I'll believe all this when I see it.

"Meanwhile," he says, "I'll be briefed from some real priests about political action as the highest form of charity."

Yuri the poet is ardent as a schoolboy. He thinks Joe has had a call.

"Call it a call, if you will. I mean to throw some stones. I don't want to break down the church, mind you. I only want to wake up the janitor and get the furnace cooking and get the water running."

Obe is listening from his stand beside the window. "Joe," he says. And when he has drawn the requisite attention: "Aren't you activist enough? Saving the souls of all those corporations? That must be very heavy work."

"Oh, yes." Father Joe concedes. "But all I can save are the executives. And they are all saved by now. All the drinkers have switched to light wine. Everyone who still smokes is on low-tar cigarettes. Gluttony is in the hands of diet doctors. Pride belongs to the advertising industry and envy is a grace that fuels the fire of ambition."

What a performance! He could have been a Jesuit.

"The only sin left is greed," says Joe. "And greed is not a rewarding sin. If virtue is its own reward, then greed is its own punishment. I am simply not needed here."

TABLE 47   341

"Oh, boy!" Geraldine stirs herself. "You're going to be a revolutionary!"

"Evolutionary," says Joe. He puts on his beatific look.

Yuri is truly moved. He eyes his old friend tenderly. "Have you told Bibby?"

"No," says Joe. "I only made up my mind last night."

Bibby will wish him well. And when Joe has worked out his first solution to his first problem, Bibby will go down with his camera crew and show how it works.

If it pays.

Meanwhile, the night is over and Bosculus is far behind. With the glorious Jennifer. I hope they'll make a good life for themselves. And Brucie. I really hope for Brucie.

"Too bad they weren't at Table 47," Flossie says. She's standing beside Obe. The day is breaking fast. The city is going into action. "That was the good one."

"We'll get them yet," says Father Joe. "The show isn't over."

"You're right," says Paul. He's burrowing in the coat pile and comes up with ours. We're going now. "This is just the start."

ROLAINE HOCHSTEIN is a graduate of the Syracuse University School of Journalism and attended the graduate writing program at Columbia University, where she studied with V. S. Pritchett and Anthony Burgess. She has worked in advertising and publishing and has written five books and more than 200 articles, essays, and short stories. She was New York cultural correspondent for the Toronto *Star* and has been a regular contributor of humor, profiles, and public affairs articles to *Good Housekeeping*, *Woman's Day*, and *Ms.* magazines. Her nonfiction books include three volumes written in collaboration with psychologist Daniel A. Sugarman. Her stories have appeared in *The Atlantic Monthly*, *Redbook*, *McCall's*, *The Massachusetts Review* and other quarterlies, collections, and anthologies. She has won fellowships to the MacDowell Colony and Yaddo, and has been represented in the O. Henry Prize Stories. Her first novel, *Stepping Out*, was published in 1977.

Ms. Hochstein was born in Yonkers, New York, and now lives in New Jersey with her husband Morton Hochstein, a newswriter for the National Broadcasting Company who also writes frequently on wine and food. They have three children—Eric, Kate, and Bess.